Greig Beck grew up across the road from Bondi Beach in Sydney, Australia. His early days were spent surfing, sunbaking and reading science fiction on the sand. He then went on to study computer science, immerse himself in the financial software industry and later received an MBA. Greig is the director of a software company but still finds time to write and surf. He lives in Sydney, with his wife, son and an enormous black German shepherd.

GREIG BECK

THE FIRST BIRD

momentum

First published by Momentum in 2013
This edition published in 2013 by Momentum
Pan Macmillan Australia Pty Ltd
1 Market Street, Sydney 2000

A CIP record for this book is available at the National Library of Australia

The First Bird: Omnibus Edition

EPUB format: 9781743342718
Mobi format: 9781743342725
Print on Demand format: 9781743342732

Cover design by XOU Creative
Edited by Vanessa Lanaway

Macmillan Digital Australia: www.macmillandigital.com.au

To report a typographical error, please visit momentumbooks.com.au/contact/

Visit www.momentumbooks.com.au to read more about all our books and to buy
books online. You will also find features, author interviews and news of any author
events.

For my little sister Cory – may life always float you on
a Sammy the Seal.

PROLOGUE

1932 – GRAN CHACO BOREAL, BRAZIL

Esubio slammed into a tree and crouched there, sucking in wet ragged breaths and hugging his prize. His head pounded and his skin itched, but still he grinned. Esubio Salamanca Urey had enlisted with the Bolivian army to fight against Paraguay in the war over their disputed border, but his real goals were vastly different. He needed transport to the most impenetrable and secretive jungle in the world. Legend had it there were riches there ... and he had a map.

More missiles flew – the natives had found him, letting loose another flock of their four-foot long poison-tipped arrows. The only thing that blunted their aim was the tangled vines and creepers, so tightly woven in some areas that they formed a single knotted mass.

He clutched the idol to his chest and darted off again, zig-zagging along an animal track that was little more than a parting of fern fronds, young trees and fungus. The ground squelched under his feet as he bullocked through the mad green hell. He stumbled again; the golden object was heavy, and slippery, but he would die before he released it.

Esubio sucked in more humid breaths, coughed wetly and spat. His head hammered, and his lips, ears and eyelids tingled strangely. He increased his pace, knowing that if he could make it to the river there was a good chance he could find his squad. Next time he'd come back with his own army of trusted friends … after all, he'd found enough gold to make a hundred men rich for a thousand lifetimes. Together, they'd clear these strange gorilla-people out. He'd bring dynamite to reopen the now-collapsed hole he had found in the mighty cliff walls, and then they could fill boxes with the stuff.

More arrows flew. He tripped as he tried to avoid the deadly projectiles, cursing at the natives' aim, speed and ugliness. *More like apes*, he thought. Getting to his feet, Esubio wiped his face. His sleeve came away wet with blood. Had he cut himself? Probably. He staggered on, grimacing as a weird sensation came over him. The constant itch had changed to a mad crawling sensation, as if a million ants had taken up residence beneath his skin. He knew that in the Gran Chaco everything that could crawl, slither or fly wanted to suck your blood or feed on you – or in you – but this felt strange, like his entire skin was … shifting.

Esubio dove into the hollow of a tree and tried to calm his breathing, letting his gaze move over the thick jungle. He rested the golden idol on his leg. It was getting harder to hold as his hand became even more slippery – unnaturally so. He raised his arm to examine it.

"*Madre de Dios.*" His lips pulled back in horror. The skin seemed to sag like an oversized glove. He touched it with his other hand, and his fingers went through the skin as though it was nothing more than tissue. Esubio's eyes widened in terror. As he watched, more of the skin sloughed off his arm. He leaned forward in horror and clumps of hair, some still with scalp attached, came away from his head and plopped wetly into the mud.

"*Por favor Dios, por favor Dios.*" He put a hand to his face and felt looseness. "No, no, no." He got to his feet, letting the idol fall into the soaking earth, instantly forgotten. He looked again at his hands, praying the horrifying vision had just been a trick of the light, or a touch of jungle madness.

It hadn't. Both hands were now were red and glistening. The outer layer of skin had entirely slid away, leaving muscle, tendon and bluish veins exposed to the air. Esubio wailed, and spun helplessly, just as a long arrow took him in the chest. He sank to his knees as the natives caught up and surrounded him. As his vision began to fade, he saw them halt suddenly, recoiling as if he was some sort of poisonous reptile.

Infectado, he thought, and could have laughed at fate's mockery. He had hacked through miles of strength-sapping jungle, found the hidden place and crawled on his belly though a tiny rift in the cliff wall. He had seen things in that strange secret world that shouldn't have existed and then found the mountains of lost gold. And now he was being brought down, not by the arrow, but by something so tiny as to be near invisible? Some ancient god's joke, surely?

He wailed. This is not how it should end!

Another arrow pierced Esubio's neck and he fell forward. The small golden idol sat upright in the mud, its leering face staring back at his disintegrating frame.

As his fading vision swam red and life left him, Esubio felt the gentle touch of the soft earth as the natives threw its dark dampness over his corrupted body.

Padre Celestial, por favor perdóname. With wet earth in his eyes and mouth, darkness and silence took him.

EPISODE 1: A WONDROUS DISCOVERY

CHAPTER 1

TODAY – GRAN CHACO BOREAL, BRAZIL

Pieter Jorghanson nodded and smiled, nodded and smiled. The small group of indigenous people he sat amongst were in the "lost tribe" category, found either by satellite photography or accidentally, during mining surveys.

This part of the jungle was unique and mysterious. Its informal moniker amongst academia was "the green boneyard". For every ten scientists or enthusiastic professors who entered, only five returned, and of those who did, few had penetrated its dark heart.

The Gran Chaco Boreal, on the border of Paraguay, Bolivia and Brazil, is one of the last truly unexplored places on earth. Modern man knows more about the moon and the fathomless dark ocean trenches than they do about the deep green lands in this jungle. Two hundred and fifty thousand square miles of cover, so thick that from the sky the tops of trees looked like lumpy green hills.

To add to its impenetrability, armies of poisonous reptiles, insects and sickness-bearing parasites, as well as thorn forests with spikes long and sharp enough to penetrate the toughest leather or canvas, surrounded its core. Hacking through this dense biological barrier was slow; it could take a day to progress little more than twenty feet. Luck, a local guide, or a helicopter drop were the only ways in.

Pieter nodded and smiled again. A small woman smiled broadly in return. Gho-ka had taken a shine to him, and seemed to assume responsibility for teaching him their ways. Her first husband had been killed in the jungle, and now, as was her right, she was free to choose another mate. Pieter wondered exactly what she had in mind for him.

He looked at her closely – receding chin, thick brow ridge, squat torso and heavily muscled arms and legs. *Very primitive-looking*, he thought, as she touched his arm lightly and then pulled back, giggling and covering her mouth full of shovel-like teeth.

Overall, the tribe was friendly but extremely secretive. Pieter found that his rudimentary inquiries about the jungle were mostly met with patience or good humor. Very few questions elicited a more vigorous or aggressive response.

The Ndege Watu, as they referred to themselves, were like brightly colored birds, with their orange ochre body paint and red and yellow feathers hanging from their hair and groins. It had taken him months to find them, and then several more weeks to get close enough to share a smile and avoid being pierced by one of their poison-tipped arrows. Eventually, after weeks of swapping food and gifts, he had finally been invited to join them.

As a scientist specializing in social anthropology, Jorghanson was a barely competent linguist, so although he had first thought the Ndege Watu's dialect might be associated with the Panobo group of languages, he had soon found it more song-like, punctuated with glottal stops, before moving back to a high-pitched whistling. Jorghanson had only managed to pick up the odd word and inference here and there.

What excited him most was the strange and amazing script the Ndege used. It far surpassed the simple nature of their language. Raised glyphs, more like artwork than anything he had ever come across, adorned totems and the walls of their largest huts. He needed an expert appraisal, but already he was thinking the language was a root dialect merged with some sort of Amerindian influence. But the writing ... he looked at his notes and penciled some sketches of their character sets – Incan influence with a hint of Oceania, and more – definitely logographic and certainly unique.

He shaded in the characters for what might have been the Incan images for valley, or walled place. Most of the early tribes that encountered the Incans or Mayans were absorbed, used as slaves, or exterminated. Somehow, these little guys had managed to survive as a distinct and unique tribal group. Either some quirk of fate had caused them to be left alone, or the major races had wanted it that way. The Ndege had been lucky ... and now so was he, he thought, smiling and nodding to his new friends.

He felt he had more than enough information to have the tribe given do-not-approach status under the Funei collective of South American lost tribes. That alone would gain him scientific kudos.

Jorghanson nudged Gho-ka, eliciting significant mirth from the other squat brown women, little bigger than children, but with brightly painted sagging breasts on their barrel chests. She covered her mouth again, hiding the long canines, but he could see her smile. *I guess flirting is universal,* he thought as he watched her join in the cooking of meats and tubers.

He made some more notes and smacked his lips; the smell from the fires was making his mouth water. He craved more food but was too polite to ask for it, nor did he know how. Besides, he didn't feel he deserved it as he had never attended a hunt. He would probably scare the game, anyway. The only time he had tried to indicate his desire to come with them, he had been forcefully rebuffed. It seemed some parts of the jungle were strictly off-limits.

Jorghanson was financing this trip with his own money. He could have sought funding from his university, but doing so would have meant that any discoveries would be jointly credited. Though not mercenary, he knew that a solid discovery meant recognition, significant future funding, publication, and perhaps even approaches for nature documentaries – hello, David Attenborough. *That'd be more like it*, he thought.

He looked again at the picture writing – would it be enough? He needed an angle, a hook … he needed there to be a link to the great Incans or Mayans, or at least a perceived link. Hmm. Keepers of the Incan secrets – nah. Last of the Mayans? No, too much like *Last of the Mohicans*. Hmm, ancient Incans found – wait: ancient Incans found by intrepid explorer! Not bad. He'd need to think on it, but it was definitely coming together.

Jorghanson coughed and slapped at his neck in a vain attempt to catch an annoying insect. Too late; he felt the lumpy itch of multiple bites already at his collar. He didn't care, it was a small price to pay. This was going to pay off a lot quicker than sitting at a desk, or delivering yet another lecture to bored students who'd rather be doing something, anything, else.

His stomach rumbled again. Through much excited gesticulating and a great deal of guesswork on his part, he'd deduced that the evening's dinner was to include an animal that was a delicacy of the tribe. He watched hungrily as a layer of clay was cut away, followed by the steaming leaves, and the creature was broken up into smaller pieces. Everything would be eaten, and nothing wasted.

The animal looked to be the size of a good turkey. Handfuls of meat, skin and bone were piled onto pieces of bark and handed along the lines, firstly to the tribal elders, then to the warriors. Eventually Gho-ka brought him a mound of blackened flesh and bone, and he tried to make the difficult glottal-guttural sounds for "thank you".

The small woman just smiled and nodded, grabbing a piece of meat and pushing it into his mouth. Delicious! It could have been rat for all he cared. High-protein food was hard to come by. Besides, the food wasn't always cooked, and some things in the jungle, when eaten raw, were hard for a middle-aged westerner to keep down, no matter how adventurous he thought he was.

He coughed again as he savored another small piece of warm meat. Strange, he'd assumed it was a bird, but it didn't really taste like one at all. He'd tried alligator, snake and even goanna in Australia. Like this, they were a solid type of meat, more like white beef than soft poultry. He'd love to know what he was eating.

He turned to the male next to him, pointed to his food, and made the sound for "good", following it with the opening hand gesture that indicated a question. He raised his eyebrows and shrugged, hopefully indicating curiosity about what he was eating.

Jorghanson concentrated as a torrent of impenetrable words and sounds tumbled toward him. The small man pointed to the jungle and made flapping motions with his arms. Okay, a bird from the jungle. Jorghanson nodded and raised his eyebrows. The man snapped his jaws together, pointing at his own teeth. Yes, we're eating it, got that too.

The man shrugged and went back to his food, and the scientist frowned, none the wiser. It had been months, and he still only understood a fraction of their language. He was a better karaoke singer than he was a linguist.

He picked up a chunk of meat attached to a flat piece of bone about three inches long, nibbled the clinging flesh off and then examined the shard. Odd. It was solid, not the lighter, hollow bone he expected from a bird. He picked up another piece, also flat, and fitted them together – it was the side of a skull, containing some upper jaw, and ... teeth. Teeth? He held the fragment close to his face, then rummaged for his glasses to examine it more closely.

I'll be damned, he thought – acrodont teeth on a bird. He swung to Gho-ka next to him and uttered a string of glottal stops and short vocalic sets, hoping upon hope that for once in his life he had got the translation right. *Where?*

The woman at first shook her head, her eyes going wide, but after some stroking and smiling, she smiled shyly in return. Pieter knew she'd tell him. He also knew he had just found his angle.

CHAPTER 2

*LOS ANGELES INTERNATIONAL AIRPORT,
INTERNATIONAL ARRIVALS TERMINAL*

Pieter was hot, damp and itched from his scalp down to the soles of his feet. The flight from Brazil to LA had taken nearly ten hours. This was after spending a week hacking out of the damned jungle.

And now this grotesque indignation. Though he was glad to be home, the stifling heat and humidity of the jungle was actually more pleasant than standing in an early morning queue at arrivals, waiting to have his retina scanned as part of the disembarking procedure.

At last the officer glanced up at Pieter's face, then flipped through his passport, looking at the stamps, and pointed with his pen to the scanner. Pieter guessed that a small smile and a "welcome back" would only be delivered if he successfully passed the screening process.

Pieter leaned forward and widened one bloodshot eye. Even his eyeball felt gritty and itchy, and he longed to rub it. The small scanner flashed, and then … nothing.

The officer continued to look at his screen for a second, and then frowned. "Once more please, Professor Jorghanson."

Pieter tried again, and the officer, sounding bored, simply said, "One moment please," then leaned back to call another of the immigration officials standing behind the row of desks. The official sauntered over, giving Pieter's disheveled frame and face a quick, seemingly disinterested glance that in reality took in everything about him. Pieter's interviewer pointed at the screen, and the man leaned forward and frowned.

"Oh, for fuck's sake," Pieter muttered, not caring if anyone heard. He stepped back a pace from the desk, stretched, and glanced around at the waiting crowd, a hundred different nationalities all glaring at him, united in their frustration at the sweat-rumpled desk-hog he'd suddenly become. This time he did rub his eye, and annoyance welled up inside him, threatening to boil over into anger.

Normally a patient man, his crawling skin beneath and sweat-damp clothes magnified the delay to the point of insufferable torment. This is what hell will be like, he thought, grinding his teeth as the two men whispered urgently at the computer screen just out of his sight.

Pieter knew that an individual's retina was unique, and that scanning it was one of the most precise and reliable biometric tests that could be brought to bear. Its error rate was around one in a million – *when it fucking works*, he thought, as his skin tingled like a living thing beneath his damp, stinking clothes. Even he could smell them – ammonia. *Smells like I pissed myself*, he thought.

At last, the official called him closer. He held out a small vial of eye drops. "Professor Jorghanson, have you ever suffered from a degenerative retinal disorder?"

Pieter thought about refusing the drops, but guessed that would probably just lengthen the delay, so he shook his head, mouthed "nope", and snatched at the tiny bottle. He squeezed a drop into each eye. Both immediately felt better – still itchy, but less grainy.

"Once again, sir." The man motioned to the scanner.

Pieter sighed theatrically and did as requested. He stood back and waited as both officers peered at the screen, then looked at each other and shrugged. His original interviewer looked up at him and smiled. "Welcome home, Professor."

Pieter snatched his passport with a grunt and headed toward the luggage carousel, mentally checking off his next steps: collect the suitcases, duffel bags, and crates, then navigate customs. That wasn't going to be pleasant – *Round 2*, he thought morosely.

* * * * *

Nearly an hour later, Pieter was waiting in the taxi rank. The people either side of him gave him a few extra feet, possibly due to the aura of prickliness and anger coming off him in waves, or more likely due to his unsettling odor, a mix of ammonia and cloying sweetness.

In the taxi, Pieter calmed himself by planning his evening's presentation. Though physically fatigued, he was emotionally and intellectually charged. An early night could wait. It was only late morning, and not too late to invite a small but influential group of anthropologists, biologists, and – what the hell – paleontologists, just to make things interesting. He knew exactly which buttons to press to entice them, and an appeal for secrecy would guarantee that word would get out. Academics leaked like the *Bismarck*.

Once he had knocked their socks off, he'd graduate to a larger audience. Pieter knew he was on the border of Nobel Prize territory – how could he not be? He had his research, an exotic location, the secretive tribe and their fantastic language, and he had his specimen. That alone would crown his work, and lift him above all other academics, adventurers and poseurs in the country – no, the world! He snorted softly at his own hubris.

The specimen would be quarantined in a secret location for the next eight weeks, but that wouldn't stop him from taking to the road long beforehand, or from securing a form of scientific copyright over the discovery. The respect of his peers was one thing, but that didn't put food on the table ... or rather, champagne in the bucket. He could sell it, and make a fortune. Hmm, he did have a contact, he mused, and sunk back in the vinyl seat, feeling the prickling on his skin again.

"Please turn the air conditioning up."

The driver's gaze flicked back at him, and he leaned forward, toward the dashboard. Jorghanson wasn't sure the man had made any change, as he was still stewing in his own secretions. He pulled a handkerchief from his pocket and wiped his brow, excitement outweighing his discomfort.

He could almost see the look on his peers' faces when he presented the images of the primitive-looking tribe. He'd discuss samples of their ancient and unique language. The audience would start to become restive, having expected more, given the expectations he had set. There'd be muttering, glances at wristwatches.

He'd play it cool, take some questions, then show the Ndege Watu's glyph writing style – itself a wonder. Then he'd stop at what he knew to be a crude representation of the specimen and begin to discuss what it could mean. Perhaps he'd even allow some of his more esteemed peers to suggest an answer. They'd all be completely wrong, of course.

Almost as an afterthought, he'd answer the original question he proposed. Colombo-like, he'd reveal pictures of the live specimen – they'd be dumbfounded. His body juddered as he contained his laughter, delight making his eyes water.

If only he wasn't still suffering from some type of jungle itch that was driving him crazy. He scratched at his chest and stomach, and wiped at his brow and his neck with the rumpled handkerchief, still in his hand.

He'd shower and grab an hour or two of naptime, then he'd jump straight into his delivery at the Santa Barbara University's Lecture Hall. He couldn't get the smile off his face as he gave the taxi driver directions. Stuffing the damp square of cloth back into his pocket, he didn't notice the brownish stain on its soiled surface.

Pieter Jorghanson hummed to himself and leaned his head out of the car window, allowing the warm mid-morning air to dry the red sweat on his forehead.

Yep, things were going to turn out just fine.

* * * * *

"Shut the fuck up!" Mitch kicked the cage, then knelt down to read the tag. "I can't even pronounce this – some sort of rare fucking parrot or sumthin ... from ... Brazil." He lifted the cloth and peered into the shrouded enclosure. "Je-zuz." He recoiled as the creature hissed at him, and the cage rattled and clanged as the animal backed its ungainly body against the bars.

"It stinks. No wonder it's in quarantine – looks sick already to me."

His colleague, Barbara Hernandez, snorted. "Yup, sure ain't a looker. Just make sure it's kept warm. It just came in from the jungle."

"Well. It'll love LA in the summer then – freaking jungle out there, baby."

Mitch Merkhal got down lower and pulled out his flash-light, flicking it on and shining into the cage depths. The creature turned its head and fixed him with a small, ruby red eye. "Yecch." Mitch reached between the bars, picked up a small piece of meat and flicked it at the bird. The food bounced off its wing, the bird casting only a momentary glance toward it before glaring once again at Mitch. It hissed and clanged once again, small taloned fingers on the apex of its wings clutching at the bars.

Mitch snorted in disgust. "Yeah, I wouldn't eat that shit either, fugly." He got to his feet, dropping the shroud back over the cage and wiping his fingers on his pants. Inside, the bird looked down at the morsel of food. A scattering of iridescent feathers fell to the cage floor, where they stuck, their quills coated in brownish blood.

* * * * *

Pieter Jorghanson woke at four, and sat up slowly. He'd taken painkillers for his headache, and after a shower and a nap he felt marginally more refreshed, but his body still tingled all over, and when he rubbed his forehead, his hand came away greasy and brown. He snorted – *still exuding Amazon mud.* He remembered falling face-first into the mud. They had to run for it – the Ndege Watu had been a lovable bunch until he went to leave with the specimen. Then they'd turned from friendly little doves to angry hawks in a flash.

Gho-ka had trapped one of the creatures in a plastic bag he'd given her, as she refused to touch it. Apparently the men always brought them back dead, drowned. He remembered when she had returned to him, sopping wet after an apparent swim. His breath caught in his throat and his eyes widened when he first saw it, its serrated beak bound closed with a small length of vine. Gho-ka had flatly refused to take him to the wall of flowers, where the creature had been living – at least, he thought so. That was as close to a translation as he could get. It didn't matter, his prize was enough, and he could always come back with enough gifts to buy another dozen ... or maybe not. Gho-ka had tripped as they ran. She'd cried out for him, but he had sped on. He could still hear the wails that had continued for many minutes before being abruptly cut off. He was sure she'd be fine. It was better for her to be with her own people anyway.

They had chased him for miles. Even now, he still didn't get it; what did they care? It was just another plate of food to them, but it was his ticket to greatness. *Greatness.* He smiled and swung his legs off the bed.

Dressing quickly, he contemplated a quick bite but decided against it, hoping that the university room would provide a tray of sandwiches, or at least a plate of cookies. He chuckled when he thought of the facial expressions of his small audience as he talked through his presentation, seeing their polite boredom gradually turn to interest, then on to incredulity and wonder.

They'd be falling over each other to learn more about his work, to get access to it, to study it, then to try and hitch their own academic wagons to his speeding train of discovery. *My turn*, he thought, and chuckled again as he walked into the small bathroom and picked up his comb.

He smiled into the mirror. Learn more about it? Sure. Get access to it? Maybe. Study it? Not a chance. He'd already negotiated rights with an interested corporation – they got exclusive information and the location, and he got the academic recognition, and personal remuneration in the seven-figure range. Who said academia didn't pay?

He looked harder at his reflection. Jesus, he looked terrible. His skin was gray and sagging – corpse-like best described it. *Must be more tired than I thought. Maybe a week off before any more presentations.*

He snorted; who was he kidding? A week off now? It was his time in the sun. Right here, right now.

Jorghanson ran the comb through his hair; his scalp tingled, and he was alarmed to see the teeth of the comb come away tangled with strands of hair and sticky with a brownish substance. He stared at it in confusion for a few seconds, then brought it to his nose. Phew – sickly sweet and ammonia-like. It reminded him of something that he couldn't quite place.

Shit. Why now, goddammit? He dropped the comb into the sink and instead splashed water on his face and ran his wet hands up over his sparse hair, slicking it into place. The cool water felt somehow distant, like he had stretched cellophane over his skin. Straightening, he saw that the pallor of his skin hadn't changed. He hoped it was just the lighting. Blue-white energy saving coils – always bad for complexions.

Jorghanson gathered his laptop, his presentation loaded, as well as some loose notes. He sucked in a deep breath. Tonight was the night – he'd never forget it. He hoped no one else would either.

* * * * *

Mitch Merkhal's fingers itched constantly now, but not to a degree that worried him. Nearly time to knock off. He was looking forward to his first brewski. He whistled as he sauntered along the cool and dry aisles of the private quarantine station – long rows of mostly wooden and mineral items that only needed a short stay – and then sniffed back some snot. The dry atmosphere always made his nose run. He wiped it with his hand then ran his fingers up through his hair, pushing it back off his forehead and leaving a small red streak of brown.

The itch wasn't enough to worry him … yet.

* * * * *

The lights were killing him.

Jorghanson had managed to struggle through his presentation and, as he had hoped, his small group was on the edge of their seats. Suspicion and skepticism had changed to enthusiasm.

Now to take it up to the next level – *awe*, he thought with satisfaction.

There were no more questions as he came to the final image. He stood back for a moment and drew in a breath. He tried to smile, but his lips felt funny – rubbery and numb. His skin was still itching, and also felt weird to the touch. Looking down at his hands, he had the weird impression that the skin was sagging, like a pair of ill-fitting gloves.

Jorghanson blinked a couple of times and wished he had worn a hat. Wearing one indoors was a bit pretentious, but given his recent trip and the images on his presentation, a little Indiana Jones flair would probably have been forgiven. He gathered himself, ignoring his torments, and smiled down from the small stage, which was little more than a single step a few inches high. He cleared his throat.

'Ladies and gentlemen, the Ndege Watu is an ancient race, perhaps one of the first races to have existed in their secluded part of the Gran Chaco Boreal. Based on my fieldwork, it seems likely that they have resided there for untold generations … perhaps even millennia. They know their land – a dark and hidden land. But they also know the secrets it contains." He paused for effect, and placed one hand on his chest. "They shared those secrets with me, and now, tonight, I wish to share them … with you." He smiled benignly, then reached toward his computer and pressed a single key, moving the slide show to the last image.

The detail was exquisite, the lighting perfect, the specimen revealed in all its glory and phenomenal strangeness.

Pieter Jorghanson raised his head and closed his eyes. His voice was strong and sonorous, and sounding more like a

Sunday preacher than a university professor. It had to be; already their voices were welling up in an academic fervor. He went on, even louder.

"Friends and colleagues, I give you an anachronism, a living fossil, and a biological time machine. I give you the mother of feathered flight, the first bird ... the archaeopteryx!"

Chairs were knocked backward and pushed aside as the crowd got to its feet. They surged forward like some many-mouthed creature, yelling questions and jostling with each other, trying to get to the screen, to Pieter.

Then came the most beautiful sound Pieter had ever heard in his entire, unremarkable academic life – applause. He had done it, he was famous. His name would live forever with this find. A Nobel Prize for science and worldwide recognition would be his. It would happen.

He was dizzy. Perhaps the lighting and the euphoria were getting to him; making the blood pump from to his head too quickly. He leaned over his computer to steady himself, just as a small dark clump of something plopped onto the keyboard.

He frowned as he tried to work out what it was, and reached out to flip it over, thinking that perhaps someone had thrown something at him. But his fingers refused to grasp it; their tips felt squashy and somehow disconnected.

"What's going on here?" He looked up at the crowd, and immediately there came a yell from the front row.

"He's having a stroke!"

"Who, me? I'm having a stroke?" His vision grew more in-distinct as something slipped down over his eyes. He moved a hand up to the side of his face – it sagged. No wonder they'd assumed he was having a stroke. His features were hanging limply, more like a hound's dewlap than a human cheek.

Someone else screamed, a woman's voice this time, he thought. The high-pitched cry went on and on, and was like a dagger into the center of his brain. Those damned lights. He looked up toward them, cursing their tormenting brightness for intervening at the moment of his triumph, but the thick veil had now slipped completely over his eyes.

The room spun and he fell to the floor.

CHAPTER 3

TWO WEEKS LATER

Matt Kearns stretched out on the float in the center of the small swimming pool. A hat concealed his face, and he could feel the sun's warmth like a blanket on his belly and thighs. He might just roll into the water again soon, or maybe he'd have another drink. *Decisions, decisions,* he thought, and sighed.

He was in Orange County for a week to attend a conference on sub-Sumerian languages and their dialects. It might have been a dry subject for anyone but a handful of archeologists, anthropologists, and paleolinguists, but for Matt, one of the youngest and brightest in the business, it was a little slice of academic heaven. And that was before you factored in the extra benefits.

"Honey?" He used the tips of his fingers to paddle his float backward to the edge of the pool. "Meg, honey, can you get me another drink?"

He breathed in the smells of coconut suntan lotion, chlorine, and a thousand more scents of summer that emanated from plants overhanging the tropical-style swimming pool. On days like this, nothing could go wrong … and only one thing could make it better. "Megan, can you …"

The pool erupted around him in an explosion of water as a human cannonball hit its surface, blowing him off his float. Matt came to the surface spluttering, his hat floating like a lilypad beside him. His girlfriend surfaced face-first, her long hair cascading down over her slim, tanned back and shoulders.

That's what you get for dating younger women, he thought, spitting water. The fun never stopped.

At twenty-five, Megan Hannaford was one of his best students, and that wasn't just because she happened to be sleeping with him. She was a tomboy at heart, and as athletic as they came. Smart as a whip, she would make a terrific scientist in whatever field she chose. He'd probably end up working for her one day.

He looked into her beaming Nordic features and smiled. Matt was nearly ten years older than Meg. He'd been the youngest professor of archeological studies at Harvard University until he decided to jump the rat race. He was now at Asheville UNC, where he met Meg. His longish hair, youthful features, and sharp mind made him a favorite with the faculty and students.

She said he had wise eyes, ancient eyes, the eyes of a man who had seen things. She didn't know how right she was.

Megan threw her head back and laughed, hugging him. She pressed one sharp fingertip into his shoulder. "Look at you – you're going to end up lobstering, and then you won't want me to touch you."

Matt ducked underwater and came up to spit a stream of pool water onto her chest. "The important areas were covered. You can still touch those." He raised his eyebrows comically.

She reached under the water and squeezed his groin. Her eyes widened in shock. "Where's it gone?"

He laughed. "The water's cold." He waded to the side of the pool and lifted himself out. Megan followed and sat next to him, and then leaned over and kissed him, softly at first, and then a little harder and deeper. She reached down again. "Oh, there he is. Welcome back, big fella." She continued kneading his groin.

Matt pulled her closer and Megan drew back from the kiss. "What about a drink first, handsome?"

"Mmm, yes please. I think I must be in heaven." Matt went to lie down on the warm pool deck.

"Good idea ... make it two." Megan smiled and fluttered her eyes.

"But, I thought ... oh, I get it – cute *and* pushy." He jumped to his feet and walked across the warm flagstones to grab his towel from the back of a banana lounge. He saw that his footprints had already started to evaporate in the hot afternoon sun.

They'd head back to Asheville tomorrow. He was actually looking forward to getting back to work – cushy trips for lectures were fine, but he loved his job, and he could never complain about being paid to do something he would have done for free if given the chance.

The phone rang as he stepped inside, and he danced lightly across the rug to pick it up, wiping his hands on the towel around his waist.

"Professor Kearns? Matthew Kearns?"

It was a woman's voice, and not one he recognized. He responded warily. "Yes?"

"Professor Kearns, my name is Carla Nero from the CDC. Do you have a moment to talk?"

"The CDC?" Ignoring the wet towel around his waist, Matt sat down. The Center for Disease Control was like a giant coiled spring, ready to be launched at any serious domestic disease incursion. With enormous funding, human resources, and scientific firepower at their disposal, these guys didn't exactly make house calls to see if you had an upset stomach from last night's shrimp.

His mind worked furiously over the recent trips he had taken in and outside the country. Nothing disquieting came to mind.

"Talk ... about what?"

"Something you're very familiar with, Mr. Kearns – old languages."

Matt frowned. "I don't get it. When you said CDC, you meant the Center for Disease Control, right?"

There was light laughter. Matt quite liked it. "Yes, we're that CDC. We have a small outbreak we're running down, and need some clues as to its provenance. We're hoping you can assist us with that."

"Look, Ms. Nero ..."

"Carla."

"... Carla, I'm heading back to Asheville tomorrow, and I should be in the office the day after that—"

She cut him off. "I just need a few minutes. In fact, I'm just down the road."

"I see. I take it a no is probably not an option then?"

There was that disarming laugh again. "Of course you can say no. Don't be so distrustful, Professor. We were just in the area and your name popped up. Coffee okay?"

He grinned crookedly. Too many spy movies. "Sorry, suspicious nature. Comes from working in faculty – everyone's always looking over your shoulder. So, sure, where?"

"Café Glace Noire, just around the corner from you. I'm at a table out front right now. I could only save one extra seat, so please come alone."

"Glace Noire it is. I'll see you in ten." He hung up and glanced across at Megan. Her hair sparkled in the sun, and she leaned back, giving him a clear view of her flat belly and full breasts. He should have asked for twenty minutes at least. He dropped his towel and was about to cross to her when he had a sinister thought – how did Carla know he wasn't alone? He looked up at the trees surrounding the secluded pool area as his suspicious nature returned in a rush.

* * * * *

Carla watched the young man saunter down the street. He had excellent academic credentials, was physically fit, spoke every major language and could read or interpret hundreds more. At just thirty-two Matt Kearns was one of the most respected paleolinguists in the world today. He also had a history of working with government departments and came personally recommended by an old friend, Colonel Jack Hammerson. *Perfect*, she thought.

She looked him up and down: hands in the back pockets of his jeans, hair hanging down to his shoulders and stubble on a healthy jawline that spoke of forgetfulness rather than fashion consciousness. *What's not to like?* she wondered.

This man could help, and he was right here, right now. She didn't intend to let him off the hook – too much depended on it.

Carla turned to a large man in a dark blue Ford Taurus down the street and nodded imperceptibly. The car pulled out and drove slowly away.

Kearns slowed as he neared the café's numerous outdoor tables and she watched, slightly amused, as he glanced at a few of the patrons, unsure whether to approach her or the older woman with the severely pulled back hair. She decided to make it easy for him.

"Professor Kearns, I presume?" She stood and held out her hand.

He smiled warmly and gripped her hand, shaking it firmly. "You presume correctly. And call me Matt. Not even my students call me Professor Kearns."

She motioned to a seat next to her and he sat down. After a few minutes of polite chat about the weather and the city, Matt leaned forward.

"So, Carla, the CDC wants to speak to me. Should I be alert and alarmed, or remain quietly confused?"'

She smiled and waited another minute, as the coffees were set in front of them, until the waiter had disappeared. "I've seen your résumé, Matt. You've been around, so I doubt anything I could say would alarm you too much. But I think we're the ones who are confused, and that's why we need your help."

She sipped her coffee. "Do you know a Professor Pieter Jorghanson?"

Matt frowned, then shook his head.

"That's okay; he isn't exactly a household name, even in your academic circles. He used to specialize in anthropology for the University of Santa Barbara. You see, Professor Jorghanson traveled down to the jungles of South America recently, stayed for three months with an undiscovered tribe of natives, and returned a few weeks ago with a fantastic tale and a rather unique specimen. It seems there has been a bit of an adverse biological repercussion as a result of the visit. We need to shut that down."

Matt tilted his head. "Oookay … and now the million dollar question – how does that affect me?" He flashed what he obviously thought was his most winning smile. Carla sipped again and watched his face. He was wary, but interested. She leaned forward, holding his gaze. "Have you heard of the Gran Chaco jungles in South America?"

Matt leaned forward as well, and lowered his voice. "Paraguayan or Southern Brazil Boreal?"

Carla smiled. "Brazil, Pantanal region."

He whistled. "Heavy going – some of the thickest jungle on the planet."

She nodded, thinking that she'd been right about him. "Sure is. It seems Professor Jorghanson found a previously undiscovered tribe who inhabit the area. Over the past twenty-four hours I've been given a crash course in indigenous South American dialects and writing systems. My basic understanding is that a race's writing is supposed to be the representation of their language, usually expressed through a set of symbols. But strangely, the language and writing don't really marry up. Jorghanson's discovered tribe, the Ndege Watu, read and write a language that, according to the scholars I've spoken to, isn't really their own. It's like the writing was taught to them ... we think perhaps by the very first Incans."

Matt sat forward, his eyes wide. "Wow."

"Exactly." Carla exhaled sofly. "Our problem is, we need to know what these natives were saying, writing ... even thinking. And we need to know now." She paused, looking down at her cup.

Matt waited for her to continue. Finally, he opened his hands, palms out. "And?"

Carla continued to hesitate, wondering whether she should tell him any more just yet. While she tried to think, Matt leaned forward and spoke softly.

"You still haven't told me why there is such urgency, or why you and the CDC are involved. This adverse biological repercussion you mentioned – was there some sort of infection that Professor Jorghanson brought back?"

Carla looked at him for several more seconds, then made her decision. She nodded. "You're partly right. There is no infection – it's more like an infestation. It seems the specimen Jorghanson brought back had a few passengers, and now they, and their offspring, have escaped. Our problem is parasitic. And the parasite, like the specimen, is – was – something not seen by modern man ... probably ever. Perhaps excluding the Ndege Watu."

Her face became more serious. "It's moving faster than we can – using us as the vectors. Think about all the people you would come into contact with in a week, or even in a single day – going to work, to the shop, on public transport – dozens, maybe hundreds? And then of those hundreds, extrapolate that again by the people would they come into contact with, and then again, and so on. We call it a contamination shockwave – it moves out in a ring from the ground zero patient, and keeps traveling until it's stopped or burns itself out. That shockwave has already started, and that's why we're involved, and the reason for the urgency."

"But it sounds like you're planning a trip ... to the Gran Chaco? You might as well be dropping yourself into hell."

"Then hell it is. It'll be a lot worse than that if we don't get this under control. We need to find out how the local Indians survived, or lived with the infestation. Something down in that jungle kept them safe, and kept the parasite under control. But up here it's missing. Believe it or not, we're in a race, one the CDC needs to win. And I certainly don't have time to drag along a full team of linguists and camp out in some jungle hothouse for a month. We need one person, one all-round expert." She leaned forward and grasped his wrist. "We need you."

* * * * *

Carla retrieved a folder tucked down by the side of her chair and laid it flat on the table. She rested her hand on it. "We need answers."

Matt was intrigued, but there was no way he could suddenly up and go, especially for a week or two. He thought about the best way to let her down. He knew a few linguistic specialists he could recommend. He glanced at the folder, curiosity burning now. Maybe, for now at least, he'd see if he could help.

He reached out, but then stopped. Carla had a hand firmly on the folder but her head was turned. She smiled at a mother and daughter at a near table. The little girl was trying to sit a small doll down beside her cup of hot chocolate, all the while scolding the doll for taking too long, and wagging her finger at it like a mother would.

"Ah, Carla." Matt cleared his throat.

Carla continued to watch the girl. But the smile she once had began to turn down slightly at the corners and her eyes moistened.

"Carla?"

She quickly turned back to him.

"Someone you know?" Matt asked.

"No." She shook her head. "Just... reminds me of my daughter." She blinked and a frown momentarily creased her forehead. "Madeleine."

Matt thought about continuing the topic, but there was something in the woman's expression that warned him that maybe family, or this relationship, might be out of bounds.

Instead, he nodded toward the folder. "So, you want me to read something, a map, you said? I can certainly try, but I have to tell you, it can take hours, days, or even weeks to extract the meaning from some written languages – if they can be read at all." He reached across and slid the folder out from under her hand. "Can you tell me anything else? I'm intrigued now, and believe me, context helps."

She smiled and lifted her cup. "We'll see." She sipped, watching him over the rim.

"A test, is it?" Matt raised an eyebrow and opened the folder, spreading the contents on the tabletop. There were photographs, and a small device with a cord and an earplug on one end – a recording of something, he assumed. He lifted the first picture and grunted softly.

"Picto-language – but a more modern variant, of an ancient dialect. Wow, these guys are good." He looked up. "This is modern, right, not a copy of some earlier writing images?"

"Near as we can tell, it's only a few months old." She sipped again.

"Hmm. Looks Incan." He snorted. "Looks Incan, Olmec, Sumerian, and a bastardized form of Mayan. In fact, it looks quite unique – more like art than language."

Matt placed the photograph on the table and pointed to an image of a gross head with a tongue protruding. "The sign for eating, I think. Like Incan, but not quite right. It might have been once, but has now evolved into something quite different. Obviously idiographic, but I'm not sure about the phonetic relationships." He sorted through each of the pictures of the language, nodding and muttering to himself from time to time.

He looked up at her and she nodded, raising her eyebrows, waiting for him to go on.

Matt reached for the tiny earpiece and stuck it in his ear. He picked up the small silver box, pressed a button, and swiveled a small dial. As he listened he frowned slightly and lifted one of the photographs to glance at it before closing his eyes and tapping it on the table as he listened. "Glottal stops, clicks, whistles – a little like the African bushman, but longer consonants. I also detect the use of a morphosyntax a little like the local Pirahã tribe. Hmm, this'd take a while to unpick … but it could be done."

"Well?" She drew the pictures back and rested her arched fingers on them.

"Well. That … is not a map." He sat back.

"It's not directions?" Carla frowned. "Godammit – we didn't get the original. Okay, what is it then?"

"A shopping list and … a recipe, I think."

* * * * *

"Think of it as the first ever master class in cooking." Matt watched with amusement as the CDC woman's face went from anger, to acceptance, and then on to humor, as she finally realized that the joke was on her.

"The danger of making assumptions, right?" She smiled ruefully for a second before getting serious again. "But you can read it?"

Matt spun one of the images around and pointed to the photograph. "Most of it. Look, the sign for fire, for eating, for a valley that's either behind, or hidden, or underneath something. These symbols here mean flowers or plants, and these mean a wall, or barrier. I'm obviously not one hundred percent clear, but the context is that it's a valley that's hard to find or to get to, and might be blocked by a barrier. Okay, also the sign for bird, and – hmm, for teeth. That's a little weird, teeth and bird together. It'd be better if I could see the original drawings, but based on what I can see, it's no real location, and no explanation or cure for your problem." He sat back. "I guess it doesn't help much."

Carla gathered up the photographs. "Well, it confirms two things; one we already suspected." She slid the pictures back into the folder and finished her coffee.

"And the other?"

"The other is that you're the real deal, and you'll be coming with us." She smiled without humor.

Matt drained his cup and set it down, not looking at her. "Yeah, well, about that. You see ..."

"Professor Kearns, this ..."

He held up his hand. "Now, I'd love to help, but ..."

She leaned forward, cutting him off. "This is not a request."

Matt gave her a sympathetic smile. "I'm flattered that you think I'm the only one who can help you, but I'm not, and further, I'm just not available right now. Besides, I'm not sure I can do much more." He sighed. "Look, I know this is important. I promise I'll look at it as soon as I can. That's the best I can do, I'm afraid."

Carla smiled, flashing a line of perfect white teeth. But there was little goodwill in the smile – more a shark-like menace.

"Golly ... you promise?" The smile disappeared. "Professor Kearns, under the national sequestration laws, if we, the CDC, determine there is an imminent threat to the domestic American population, we have the right, and the capability, to sequester any item, asset, record, or individual for as long as we deem necessary." She stared him down, as confident and assertive as a New York tax attorney going in for the kill.

Matt swallowed, suddenly realizing that the attractive woman with the big gray-blue eyes was used to getting her own way.

She smiled again, this time warmer and softer. "Please, Professor Kearns – Matthew – this is important. I really want you to come with us by choice, not because we made you. And by the way, it's not my problem, it's our problem."

Matt knew she had thrown him a bone to make him feel in control, just as he knew that the hand squeezing his balls wasn't his own.

Carla pulled her chair a little closer to the table and reached across to grasp his forearm. "Matt, I mentioned we are in a race ... it's against the clock. An opportunity to be placed right at the source has arisen and the CDC intends to take it. Believe me, it took a lot of arm-twisting to make this happen, so we can't afford to be indecisive right now."

"But what do you expect me to do? Talk to these Ndege Watu? It would take me weeks to even learn the rudiments of their language. The writing, I can probably pick up, but anything else? I'll need more time."

"We leave in twenty-four hours. You can study on the way." She stood, tucking her folder under one arm.

Matt shook his head. "Not a chance. I've got to …"

"No, you don't. You're already packed, and the university has agreed to grant some additional leave while you are on secondment to the CDC." Her gaze was unwavering.

Matt's mouth was hanging open, but no words came as his mind worked like a wheel spinning in soft sand.

Carla smiled as a dark Taurus pulled up to the curb.

Finally, Matt's brain started working. "What about Meg? She's staying with me."

"By now, she'll be on her way home." The gentle, confident smile remained in place.

The Taurus's side door opened and a young woman exploded out, yelling something back into the car. She marched down the street toward Matt, shoulders hunched and fists balled. He noticed that her feet were still bare.

"On her way home, you say? You obviously don't know Megan." Matt noticed that Carla's smile had dropped and her brows had drawn together.

The driver got out of the car and opened his arms, hands out, and shrugged. Carla swore.

"Just what the hell is going on, Matt? This goon walked into the house and just started putting your stuff into suitcases. Then he gave me this, and told me to get dressed and go." She threw a rumpled piece of paper onto the table. Matt picked it up and unfolded it – it was a coach class ticket back to Asheville.

"Coach? Hmm, clearly money's no object." Matt looked from Carla to Megan. 'Honey, meet Carla Nero. Carla, this is Megan Hannaford. Carla here has asked whether we would like to take a little trip with her."

The CDC woman's face was like stone as she kept her eyes on Matt. "Don't do this, Matt. It's not a game."

Matt swallowed; the woman's eyes were like lasers. *In for a penny*, he thought. "You want my help – she comes." Matt knew that inviting Megan might make his involvement too irritating or difficult – it could be a deal breaker. At least, that's what he hoped. "She has an encyclopedic knowledge of ancient writing styles, is an excellent biologist, has walked the Kokoda track, and she's probably fitter than both of us put together." He shrugged. "I need her."

Carla looked the young woman up and down. Megan met her gaze and held it, matching her intensity. Matt briefly thought about ducking for cover.

"Oh, I'm coming." Megan looked at Matt, her jaw clenched. "Where?"

Matt smiled. Megan was combative, and was digging in even though she had no idea what the trip involved. Someone had just told her she couldn't do something – bad move.

"Dr. Nero?" The huge driver stood behind Megan, looking like he'd be more than happy to wrestle her back into the car.

Matt spoke over his shoulder to the hulking man. "Don't even think about it." He turned to face Carla, wondering what he would do if the driver tried anything.

Carla tapped a finger on the table for a second or two, ignoring the younger woman's ferocious stare. "I don't have the authority to endorse your ... girlfriend's travel. Besides, this is no Contiki tour, with cocktails and paper umbrellas. Professor Kearns, you know where we're going. People die, or sometimes disappear, down there. You want to put your friend at risk?"

Megan pulled up a chair and sat down, leaning into Carla's face. "Listen, lady. I've climbed Lizard Head Peak in Colorado – thirteen thousand feet of crumbling volcanic plug – *solo*. I've dived to three hundred feet using an experimental hypoxic gas blend, and I've been in many tropical jungles besides the Kokoda. But I'm not here for a pissing contest. What the hell is this all about?"

Carla studied Megan's angry face, then smiled. The shark was back. *Uh-oh*, thought Matt. If Carla tried to slap Megan down that would ratchet his girlfriend up to supernova level. He needed to throw in a circuit breaker.

"Two choices, Carla – either we both go, or neither of us does. Don't think of it as an intrusion or a hindrance. Think of it as double the help."

She swung around, shaking her head, her face carrying a hint of warning. "You really don't know what you're asking."

'You're right about one thing. I certainly don't know what the hell I'm asking for. So, if you want our help...' Matt shrugged and took Megan's hand. Megan smiled back, and then turned to Carla with a look that said *checkmate*.

Carla shrugged and nodded, almost sadly. "I see I'm outnumbered and outgunned. If that's the price of your assistance then I have no choice but to accept your terms, Professor."

"Really? Uh, thank you," said Matt.

"Damn right," Megan threw in, her jaw still thrust forward with hostility.

Carla reached down and pulled another folder from a slim briefcase. "Professor Kearns – Matt – I'm going to lay my cards on the table." There was a hint of a smile.

Matt smiled back as his brain worked to catch up with what had just happened. A few minutes ago, he had been trying to get out of the trip, then somehow he found himself demanding to be taken. How did that work? Matt had a sneaking suspicion that he was the one who had really been outgunned.

Carla slid the folder across the table, keeping one hand on it. "Before I show you this, please remember that within US borders, we have great authority when it comes to protecting our nation's health. I'm sure I don't need to tell you that this is confidential. One word, and there will be enforced incarceration until we deem the threat to public health to have abated." She locked eyes with Megan. "Agreed?"

Megan held the woman's gaze, breathing deeply. Matt could feel the waves of anger rising off her. He sat as still as stone, waiting them out.

Seconds passed as the two women eyeballed each other, until Carla raised one eyebrow, her smile never slipping.

"Whatever." Megan went to grab the folder, but Carla didn't move her hand.

"*Agreed?*" She tilted her head.

After a few more seconds of compressed lips, Megan muttered "fine," then snatched the folder and flipped it open. *Round one to Dr. Carla Nero*, thought Matt.

Megan immediately recoiled. "Jesus Christ! What the hell is this?"

Carla's face was devoid of emotion as she nodded slowly. "That, my dear, was Professor Jorghanson." She spoke without looking at the images. "Forty people he came into contact with are also dead – a trail of bodies leading from the airport to the taxi rank and his hotel. The same goes for another seven people in and around a private quarantine facility in LA. Added to that, we have over eighty people in a negative air pressure isolation unit – a warehouse, really ..." She looked from Megan to Matt. "... and all are expected to die in the next few days."

Matt looked down and flinched. "That many? But what the hell could do this? You said it was a parasite? But how? What?" He gritted his teeth as he looked at the way-too-clear photograph. A body was laid out on a metal table, stripped of its skin. Meaty, glistening, with blue and red veins and arteries, stringy sinew and streaks of fat shining wetly under the harsh lights of a white tiled medical examination room. It was the face that unsettled Matt the most. The features weren't fixed in shock or agony, but instead held an expression more like ... surprise. It was as if Professor Pieter Jorghanson, even in death, still didn't understand what had happened to him.

On another table, in a large silver bowl, sat a pile of gray, rubbery-looking material. Matt winced, realizing that it was the man's skin. "What a ghastly way to die."

"They all died like that. The parasite that came back on the specimen is a form of burrowing mite. It exudes an enzyme that liquefies the protein in the subdermal layers of its host – liquefies them for consumption. In the process, it literally flays the host alive ... *from the inside out.* The only upside – for want of a better term – is that the nerves are the first thing to be short circuited, so the process is actually quite painless."

"Painless? How the hell do you know that?" Megan pushed back her seat and walked a few paces away from the table.

Carla watched her go, but there was no smile on her face now. She turned back to Matt. "Professor Jorghanson had age-related macular degeneration, cirrhosis of the liver, and a mild form of recessive morbilli virus. He probably contracted the more benign strain of measles as a kid, and his system stored it instead of eradicating it. Regardless, he was still a fairly robust man." She held Matt's eyes. "You see, we know he wasn't in pain at the end, because Professor Jorghanson was still alive when he was brought in ... like that. The decorticating process didn't kill him – it was the shock and fluid loss that did."

She closed her eyes for a second or two and drew a deep breath. "At least now we know what we're dealing with. Still, by the time we get to an infested victim, the subdermal insult is ... significant. The patients are being kept in an induced coma until we can work out a way to do comprehensive skin grafts – if they live that long."

Matt shuddered. He didn't want to see anymore, but Carla pulled another photograph from her folder and laid it on the table. This one showed an enormously magnified arthropod creature – teardrop-shaped, with a serrated head, powerful-looking crab-like legs, and several fleshy looking dewlaps trailing behind.

"Public enemy number one – *sarcoptes scabiei primus* – the scabies mite." She pulled a face. "'Primus' meaning 'comes first'. This little monster is perhaps the first ever scabies mite, hence the tag."

"You're kidding. Scabies? As in, what sailors from the fifties used to bring back after an exotic holiday?"

Carla snorted softly. "Yes, and no. It's a recognizable parasite, but not one we've seen before, other than trapped in fossilized amber." She tapped the photograph. "This little critter eats and lays eggs ... and that's all it does. The near-microscopic size of the mite, plus the fact that an infested individual can be carrying millions of mites, makes transference fast and easy. You do the math."

"But scabies is treatable." Matt pushed the picture back toward her.

"Sure it is. A five percent preparation of permethrin or a twenty-five percent dose of benzyl benzoate in a solution should kill 'em every time ... but not these monsters. The only effective thing we've come up with is DDT, and as it's a subdermal infestation, we would need to inculcate the insecticide, once the mites are on, inside the host. We'd also need to perform mass spraying of the open environment to tackle the free-range variety. By the time the enviro-freaks ever allowed that to occur, half the population would be infested, or dead. Bottom line, we've got months – maybe weeks – to find something that will be fast, effective, and have minimal effects, both to us and the environment."

She sat back wearily. "Something in their natural habitat kept these things in check. Otherwise, the Ndege Watu, Jorghanson's specimen, and just about every living creature down there would have been skinned alive. I'm betting that the natives know what that something is, and I need to find out."

Matt nodded, more in sympathy with the problem than with any actual understanding of how it could occur. "It's a nightmare, but you said you had to twist arms to make this happen. For heaven's sake, after seeing these pictures, who in the hell do you need to convince?"

"That's our problem. The CDC has no jurisdiction outside of the American continent. We don't have time to make formal requests to foreign governments, who could vacillate while we burn with infestation. In fact, they're more likely to slap a ban on us for stealing their property."

"You mean the specimen?"

She nodded. "We need to join a group already authorized to travel to the Gran Chaco Boreal. There's a private expedition leaving tomorrow. We'll be leaving with them."

Matt glanced over his shoulder at Megan, who was sitting on a low wall, staring at the ground. He wondered if she was still determined to accompany him. "This private company, do they know where to go? And the danger the mite presents? I'm guessing they're some sort of global medical team. Medical Corps International or Médecins Sans Frontières, someone like that?"

Carla laughed. "I wish. Not even close. Before he died, Jorghanson sold the location and rights to the specimen to a Mr. Maxwell Steinberg."

Matt sprang forward. "You're shitting me – *Dinosaur Kingdom* Max Steinberg? I loved that movie! But how is he even allowed to be involved, given the danger?"

"Mr. Steinberg is aware of the risks, and doesn't see them as a problem, not when it comes to locating 'the find of the century'. People like Steinberg regard problems like this as things to be negotiated away or bulldozed over." Carla's hand curled into a fist, her anger palpable.

"Steinberg's argument is that there are more bugs on the average person's pillow than on the specimen, and that more than five thousand people die every year from food poisoning, so our little problem is nothing to be too concerned about. He can be very persuasive, especially when he's making eight figure donations annually to both political parties." She tilted her head. "But he has his uses. Though the CDC has no power outside our national borders, we certainly carry a big stick within them. If he wants to bring something back, he better play ball. We can use him, just as he'll try to use us."

Matt nodded, trying to come to terms with the politics and dynamics of a side of government he rarely saw. "And the original specimen?"

Carla looked grim. "Now destroyed, but not before it succumbed to the burrowing mite itself, and managed to contaminate a lot of innocent people. Steinberg blames us for not getting it into some sort of treatment sooner." She snorted. "You see, it was taking the specimen out of its environment that signed its death warrant. No modern man has ever come into contact with this bug. In fact, excepting Jorghanson's lost tribe, perhaps no human has ever been affected by it. The thing is a living fossil, a primordial remnant."

"That's the bug, but you said it was a passenger? On the 'specimen' you destroyed? What exactly was this 'specimen' you keep referring to?"

Carla half smiled, but her eyes were sad. "What was it? It was a magnet, and one causing a stampede that we need to get in front of. Our primordial parasitic remnant was living on something just as ancient. And given that the parasite could have been a factor in the demise of the dinosaurs, I think it's appropriate that it was found ..." She glanced briefly over her shoulder, perhaps to see where the waiter was, before placing a final photograph on the table. "... found existing on the body of another living fossil. The specimen was a living archaeopteryx, the first bird, and we need to find its home before we end up like the dinosaurs."

CHAPTER 4

Maxwell Dodi Steinberg belched as he drank his imported beer and looked out over the choppy Malibu surf. He leaned his hand against a sheet of the toughened curved windows that ran the fifty feet around the living room of his clifftop mansion – four furnace-toughened three-quarter inch sheets, invisibly bonded together, each costing more than your average Rolls Royce.

He peered down at the rooftops of his neighbors – aging movie stars, rock promoters, and business tycoons. He could have bought them all a hundred times over – not bad for a skinny Jewish kid from Arizona. He belched again, then swallowed the beer-flavored acid that came up with the gas.

Steinberg was pissed off. He was one of the wealthiest and most powerful movie producers in the world. His special effects movies had grossed billons of dollars, and he counted A-list celebrities, presidents, and Tibetan spiritual leaders amongst his inner circle. So he could afford to – and did – pay a fortune for the rights to Professor Pieter Jorghanson's prehistoric bird ... and then the CDC freakin' went and destroyed it – and cremated what was left! Even though it was dead, he could have had the bones reconstructed. Movies were one thing, but merchandizing and surround marketing sales were where the real money was.

He put the bottle to his lips, thinking. Alive would have been best – better a living fossil than just another dead one.

He sucked heavily on the freezing beer and picked up a pile of papers from one of the cream leather couches. He still had the professor's notes, and a map to the village, which was a start, at least. As far as he was concerned, he was counting down to launch. He'd lead a team down to the jungle himself. He'd find Jorghanson's Garden of Eden-cum-Lost World, even though the old boy had managed to succumb to some sort of jungle mange. He'd seen the photos – *yecch*.

Steinberg gulped more beer and snorted. He'd make sure he was better prepared. He'd take jungle specialists, paleontologists, an entomologist, a medical doctor, plus enough fucking DDT to level the entire Amazon if he needed to. For his sins, he'd also been told he had to take some CDC pencil-neck, who now also wanted to bring a linguist – sheesh. What, they didn't trust that his language expert would tell them what he found out? He snorted again – of course he fucking wouldn't! He toasted his reflection in the glass, turning side-on and sucking in his gut, and thinking he should probably put some pants on.

Steinberg's mind whirled at the possibilities. Talk about fiction turning into fact. It was a goldmine and a dream come true, all rolled into one. He didn't need the money, but he certainly liked the attention and respect that came with being a winner. And that respect, baby, was global respect.

His people had smoothed a path with the Brazilian government. Visas were approved, and local guides, and anything else he needed, would be provided. Funny what a couple of hundred grand dropped into a few Mickey Mouse bank accounts could get you.

Respect, yeah, that's what it freakin' got you.

CHAPTER 5

Matt sat in the back of the Cougar AS532 and dozed. The flight in Max Steinberg's Gulfstream G550 from LAX to Brasília International Airport had taken twelve hours. After a quick customs check on the tarmac, they were escorted directly to a big green military helicopter, which would take them to the Mato Grosso Plateau, part of the Brazilian Highlands. It was an ancient tableland that fell away to flood plains called the Pantanal, the largest continuous wetland on the planet. These flood plains at their darkest heart contained the almost inaccessible Gran Chaco, one of the largest unexplored places on the planet.

Matt felt a hand on his leg, and opened one eye to groggily peer around the cabin. He felt like crap – he didn't travel well – and probably looked like he felt. The twin-engine chopper could take twenty fully kitted soldiers, but today its cargo was less than half that. Glancing around, Matt could see that the warm cabin and long flying time was having the same effect on most of his companions. Other than a single brusque movie producer, the group consisted of scientists, specialists, and a formidable-looking guide – or maybe bodyguard – Kurt.

Kurt was the only one who seemed fit and alert. He had spent much of the early ride explaining the specifications of the helicopter to Megan. Matt noticed that he suddenly became very tactile when talking to her, using his hands to illustrate the flight characteristics of the craft, and touching her shoulder, arm, and eventually her leg. *Creep*, he thought.

Matt had listened to Kurt expertly describe how they would coast along at a hundred and fifty miles per hour, well within the chopper's potential of more than one eighty. The bodyguard had gestured port and starboard, at the housed engines – a couple of Turbomeca Makila 1A1 turbo shafts that could punch out 1589 horsepower on command, he had intoned solemnly. Then he had nudged her and winked, and lowered his voice to a conspiratorial level – apparently it'd last about twelve seconds against one of Uncle Sam's Black Hawks, and even less against an Apache. These last nuggets necessitated a good-natured grab of the knee. Matt had groaned and sat back after that.

He felt his eyelids drooping again, until he felt the hand on his leg start to dig in, like a claw. He opened his eyes to see Megan leaning toward him. He pulled back one cup of his headphones, and she placed a finger on his ear, then rested her chin on the hand. This allowed her voice to be carried to him more via vibrations than by sound waves. It worked. You didn't have to shout, but you did need to concentrate.

"Twenty minutes." She looked excited.

Matt nodded, and swallowed down a moment of queasiness. As a specialist in ancient languages and remnant civilizations, jungle came with the territory – jungles, dry deserts, and once, the frozen Antarctic. But he'd take a desert over a jungle any day. The odd scorpion, sand viper, and dry heat were easily preferable to millions of seething, crawling, sliding things with way too many legs. Added to that, he already knew there was something down there, almost microscopic, that literally burrowed under your skin and flayed you alive. What's not to like? He swallowed again, and tried to pull his lips into the semblance of a smile.

He looked around at his fellow passengers, who were slowly being roused by the ever-energetic Kurt. He hadn't needed to nudge Max Steinberg – he was another traveler who didn't seem to sleep on flights. Come to think of it, Matt wasn't sure he'd even seen him blink yet. Steinberg was all grizzled baldness and skinny-armed paunch, fifty-something and, so far, uncommunicative, seeming to prefer a slim computer tablet to human dialogue. He had only grinned once, more shark than human, revealing a gold tooth just off to the side. It looked incongruous amongst his polished Hollywood teeth, and Matt wondered why he kept it.

The producer's fingers darted over the screen, flicking away images as rapidly as they appeared. The few times he had looked up, his eyes had darted over Matt, Carla, and Megan, then moved on as though the trio had been analyzed, categorized, and then dismissed. It was the look of a man who probably had multi-million-dollar movie stars kowtowing before him, and didn't need any more pissant scientists.

Matt shifted his gaze to the man seated on the movie producer's left. Joop van Onertson was a Dutch paleobiologist specializing in ornithological evolution, and the all-round go-to guy for early species analysis. He had spent the first twenty minutes of the trip trying to explain the pronunciation of his name to Kurt and Steinberg. It rhymed with soap, he had said, with the "J" taking a "Y" sound – Yope. But it didn't stick. After being called Jewp, Jop, and even soap, he gave up, telling them to call him Joe.

The small entomologist sitting beside him had been listening to the struggles of Joe-Joop with a face like stone. The Chinese scientist was a leading expert on entomology with parasitological specialization. Carla had acknowledged the man, and later told Matt she knew of his reputation, and was glad he was with them.

Xue Jian Dong hadn't bothered trying with Kurt and Steinberg, obviously realizing that Xue would have been an articulation bridge too far, and Dong was just asking for an earthquake of derisive mirth. He simply stuck out his hand and said, "Jian" and smiled flatly. Later, as his eyes had slid across to Carla and Matt, he looked skyward and shook his head. Matt liked him immediately.

During the introduction process, it became immediately obvious to Matt that Steinberg's team had been organized for him, not by him. It was clear that he was meeting a lot of his handpicked experts for the first time. That suited Matt just fine; it meant that there was hope that any findings or decisions would be objective, and not simply Steinberg's paid-for answers.

Close to Jian, John Mordell, MD, had risen to his feet, placed both hands in the center of his back, and stretched. Silver-haired and daytime-TV handsome, he was a practicing doctor who had worked with allied forces in both Afghanistan and Iraq. When he spoke, his accent was cultured English. Matt wondered where he and Steinberg could have ever crossed paths. Matt couldn't decide if he was relieved or concerned that Steinberg had brought an English battlefield surgeon on the expedition.

The last two members of the group were "as different as grease and butter," as Matt's grandmother used to say. One was an academic peer of Matt's, Dan Brenner, head of Linguistics at Stamford. He was a star in the paleolinguistics arena when Matt was just starting out, and if not for the early offer from Harvard, working with Brenner was probably where Matt would be today. The slow-moving older man had been strangely standoffish, and Matt couldn't hide his disappointment. If there was one person on the trip, other than Megan, who he could have expected to have a rapport with, it was the avuncular academic. Brenner must have been over sixty-five years old by now. Matt hoped that, as Brenner's career approached its winter, he didn't begrudge Matt the fact that his was only at spring.

The final member of their group was their Brazilian guide. Like a small dark bird, his eyes constantly moved over the group, the cabin, his hands and feet. One foot constantly tapped, as though his body coursed with a form of agitated electricity. It was hard to guess at his age – his skin was smooth and hairless, but his eyes had a yellow tinge that spoke of campfires and a native Tupi heritage, rather than jaundice. Moema Jesus Paraiba looked nervous and hangdog, and Matt wondered exactly what he already knew about their mission.

Matt turned to Carla, who was furiously sending and receiving text messages on her smartphone. Her face was grim. Matt suspected she was probably getting updates about the state of the epidemic back home. She cursed softly, then exhaled between tight lips. She was an impressive woman. Already she had engineered a truce with Meg, rebuffed the silver fox Mordell, stared down Steinberg, and put Kurt firmly in his place. Steinberg had brought six men, not including himself, but Matt felt sure that with Megan and Carla, he already had them outnumbered.

Matt swiveled to look out of the porthole window at the rapidly approaching land. They were to be dropped off at the base of the plateau. One moment there was reassuring stone only a few dozen feet below them, then they passed over the plateau's cliff edge. His stomach lurched as he watched a waterfall pour itself, in slow motion, hundreds of feet to the forest floor, its thick spout of water mostly turning to a shimmering mist long before it reached the frothing pool far below.

They would follow the stream until they came to a clearing cut out of the massive green tangle of plants, spend a single night at the campsite, and be ready for an early start the next morning ... an early start into the thick heat of the Gran Chaco, and to its very heart – the Boreal – one of the last secretive, primordial areas in the world.

They dropped quickly, and the enormity of the continent's flora rose up around them, overwhelming and intimidating. Matt marveled at the giant trees – green, mushrooming skyscrapers, their monstrous canopies rising hundreds of feet in the air. Colossal kapok, ficus, and giant mango – everything grew big down here. There were rats the size of small pigs, and snakes that could swallow a horse whole.

Matt didn't want to think too much about the creepy big-small things ... like two-foot long centipedes, or the Brazilian Wandering Spider, which was the size of a large man's hand, venomous as a cobra, and prone to roaming the forest floor at night and curling up in dark spaces during the day, such as a handy termite mound, a rotting log, or some unlucky camper's sleeping bag. He shuddered and held tight to the seat as the craft slowed and then hovered for a few seconds, like a giant metal dragonfly about to settle on a palm frond.

As soon as the wheels touched, Kurt was on his feet. He helped lift backpacks and equipment into place near the door before bulldozing his way toward Megan. He grabbed her pack and slipped it over her shoulders. As she turned her back on him so he could adjust the straps, she looked at Matt and winked, her amusement plain.

Kurt slapped both her shoulders and announced she was ready to jump, before adding that he'd have to take her skydiving one day... oh, and Matt, of course, if they were still together. This last was said through flashing white teeth. He gave her shoulders another squeeze, and she thanked him and walked unsteadily under the weight of her pack to where Matt was standing, holding his pack on one shoulder.

"That's odd; I wonder why he didn't offer to help me?" Matt raised an eyebrow.

She laughed softly, then said, with mock earnestness, "Well, it's nice to meet a real gentleman once in a while."

Matt pulled a face and leaned in close. "Yeah, well, just watch out. He looks like the kinda guy who believes there's only a fine line between cuddling and holding someone down so they can't get away."

"Ooh, what big green eyes you have, Professor." She grabbed his shirt and pulled him forward so she could kiss him. He forgave her teasing immediately.

A hissing clank interrupted them as the side door was thrown back and the Gran Chaco Boreal pushed its way into the cabin, bringing with it a tidal wave of sensations – cloyingly sweet flowers, rotting vegetation, decay, and spoiling meat somewhere close by.

Heat and humidity washed over them. Up on the plateau it had been roughly eighty degrees and about fifty percent humidity, but down here, in the real jungle, where the geography and towering plants trapped the moisture and held it like a thick blanket over the lowlands, the humidity jumped to around ninety percent. Matt groaned, as if house bricks had just been placed in his pack. Though the actual temperature might not have been much more than up on the plateau, it felt a hell of a lot less comfortable.

Matt leapt to the ground then turned to help Megan, who had already dropped down beside him. She walked forward a few paces, then stopped to turn and look at her surroundings. She spun, holding her arms wide and grinning.

"Wow."

Matt frowned, noticing that her words were indistinct. After the steady drone of the chopper blades, muffled by headphones, the cacophony of noise from every single thing that could squawk, croak, chirrup, or scream was deafening.

He inhaled the damp, wet air, and exhaled loudly. He'd better get used to it – they'd be there a while. *Adapt or die*, he thought wearily, paraphrasing Darwin.

Matt followed Megan as she walked toward the clearing that would be their camp for the evening. His shirt was already hanging limply, damp and uncomfortable, and a cloud of gnats had formed around his head, attracted by the salty perspiration that was beading on his forehead. Yep, adapt or die.

CHAPTER 6

CDC QUARANTINE STATION, LOS ANGELES

Doctor Francis "Hew" Hewson, Carla Nero's second in charge, prodded one of the growing lumps that had appeared on the neck of the female patient. She had presented herself for intense aggravated itching and loosening of her skin, and had been quarantined immediately. However, in the last few hours her new symptoms – the swellings – had doubled in size. Dr. Hewson had to suspect that the protuberances were linked to the infestation outbreak.

He looked down at the sleeping woman, little more than a girl, and sighed unhappily. The mega-dose cocktail of metronidazole, crotamiton, and mebendazole being fed directly into her system was keeping the spread of the parasites under control, but it wasn't killing them. It was if the anti-parasiticals were just holding the invading army behind a chemical wall that would soon be overrun. Hew knew the chemical compound only bought them a few more days at most. Eventually, the invasive parasites would overwhelm her system, and if they didn't, the harsh drugs would probably destroy her internal organs long before they eradicated the intruders.

Wearing Perspex goggles and a sealed clean-room suit, Hew prodded the lump again. It wasn't hard, like an epidermoid or sebaceous cyst, but soft, the size of a fingernail, and only slightly red. He turned to a metal table, wheeling it in close, and grabbed a glass slide and a scalpel, intending to lance the eruption and examine the results under the microscope.

He held the slide below the growth, expecting a dribble of dead biological fragments to be expelled by the woman's immune system. There would probably be nothing more than a build-up of pus, dead bacteria, and phagocytes, just like a giant boil would contain as the body battled an infection.

He made an incision in the side of the lump, intending to delicately cut halfway through the skin and then lift it away, like a lid. To his surprise, however, as soon as he pressed with the blade, the small mound burst.

There was nothing there – no blood, serum, or even pus. Nothing ran from under the cap. Indeed, it seemed hollow. Hew continued slicing through the skin, then, using tweezers, lifted the lid free. Inside was a small, dry crater, descending no farther than the subdermal layer of the skin. *Like a dry blister*, he thought, and turned to swap the scalpel for a powerful magnifying glass on an extendable arm, a strong halo of lights around its edge. He brought the lens in close and squinted.

Hew swore softly into his face mask and moved the lens to the side. With the added light, even with the naked eye he could now see the particles rising in a fine mist – a micro-dispersion plume. It could be nothing else. There were nano-sized particles rising, and Hew prayed they weren't what he thought they were.

Grabbing a swab, he dabbed it into the dry hole, and then wiped it across the slide. He carefully slid it under the microscope platform and fiddled with the magnification to clarify his image.

Sonofabitch. Eggs – and now they're airborne.

CHAPTER 7

The evening was hot and humid. Even though Matt had applied enough insect repellent to deter even the most persistent six- or eight-legged blood-sucking pests, they still hovered just a foot outside of the chemical forcefield, as if they knew that his body would soon wash away his defenses and a spot of salty skin would be theirs for the taking.

Kurt and Moema had dug a fire pit and got a good blaze going for the evening meal. Dinner had been baked ham and flatbread, both cooked in the ashes, with salad vegetables followed by tinned fruit and washed down with revolting coffee. It was probably the last cooked meal they'd have on their trek. Kurt had assured everyone that there'd be more than enough food to supplement, and eventually totally replace, their rations. Water wasn't expected to be a problem in a rainforest, and purification tablets had been handed out, along with instructions on how to use them to disinfect their water. Add little white pill and shake – simple. It made the concoction taste like a swimming pool, but at least you didn't contract dysentery and end up squirting half your bodyweight out through your ass.

Matt had left Carla and Megan talking to Jian. He was delighted to see that the women had found some common ground – the last thing he wanted was a split in his own camp when they were already outnumbered. He knew Megan would force him to take sides and, given he had to work with Carla, it would have meant several weeks of hell ... and more of the same when they got home.

He wandered over to where Steinberg's linguist, Dan Brenner, was sitting away from the dry heat of the flames, smoking a kretek cigarette – a habit Matt remembered he had picked up in Vietnam, on one of his many field expeditions in search of the mythical mother-root language. The smell of cloves, tobacco, and other mixed spices reminded Matt of crowded Asian streets, bright lights, and honking cars.

"Professor Brenner," Matt paused, waiting, as the older man simply exhaled a plume of smoke. "Mind if I join you?"

Brenner continued smoking. Matt frowned. *Okay, awkward*, he thought. "It's nice to see you again ..."

Still nothing. Matt stuck his hands in his pockets. "Uh ... is there a problem? Something I'm not aware of?"

Brenner turned and regarded Matt with half-lidded eyes. The look didn't just carry indifference, or professional snobbery; it held contempt, disdain, and barely suppressed anger. The stare hit Matt like a physical force. He almost took a step back, but instead he waited, holding the gaze.

Brenner looked away. "No, nothing, if losing ten years of your life's work counts as nothing."

Matt's brow furrowed even further. "Excuse me?"

Brenner sucked on his cigarette, worked the smoke around in his mouth, then blew it out through compressed lips. "My paper on the ancestor language. That work was valid and evidence-based. It took me ten years to trace my way back up the paleo-lingual lines of the Southern African Capoid peoples. And then through the Nilo-Saharans back to the potential proto-language – it was the monogenesis of all spoken tongues." He paused, and pointed at Matt with his cigarette, the motion ending in a stab.

He continued, his words squeezing out through clamped teeth in barely suppressed fury. "Ten long years to reach my conclusion, and it took you ten fucking minutes to obscure and demolish it … and then you encouraged my work to be gang-raped by your teenage cheer squad. Unprofessional, discourteous, and damned downright academically vandalistic!" He turned away, his lips a thin line.

Matt sat down in front of him. He rubbed a hand through his long hair, pushing it back up off his face. It stayed, slicked by perspiration and insect lotion.

Now he understood the man's previous coolness. He dimly remembered the paper – it hadn't seemed a big deal at the time. It was the responsibility of the scientific community to peer-review papers, and question them where necessary. That was just the way it worked. It forced the author to respond to any challenges to their conclusions with a forceful and factual defense. Sometimes, minor flaws in logic were found, and sometimes, just sometimes, the author had to go back to the drawing board. It had happened to him, and, he'd bet, to every scientist who hung their work out to be road-tested by the academic marketplace.

Matt remembered that many scientists had agreed with Brenner. Perhaps they shared his belief in the common language ancestry theory, or perhaps they were simply awed by the enormity of his academic status. Matt wasn't, and being young, he had no time for being polite. The fact was, he just didn't buy the theory. No matter how persuasive the man's argument, the proposition didn't work.

Matt had written a small and simple rebuttal, and posed a few questions. He expected a polite response, and maybe a professional debate. Instead, he got silence. After that, it was as if a swarm of academic locusts had been unleashed on

Brenner's work. It seemed the questions Matt had asked were good ones. Unfortunately, Brenner had no good answers.

Those academic locusts had shredded Brenner's paper. At the time, Matt thought it weird that the linguistics giant had never defended himself. He just seemed to surrender. After a little while, Matt had forgotten about it, and moved on. Not Brenner, it seemed.

Matt cleared his throat. "Professor Brenner, I just asked some obvious questions. You needed to have the answers. We all do, that's why we hang our work out in the daylight. If no idea ever got challenged, we'd have automatically believed the Earth was flat, or that mankind was solely responsible for climate change." Brenner exhaled more smoke, watching Matt. He dropped his cigarette into the damp soil and ground it out.

Matt slid forward a little. He tried to keep his tone conciliatory. "I read all your work, and there were some terrific ideas there. I wanted to believe, really I did, but I just couldn't." Matt waited a few seconds, but the man still gave him nothing. He felt exasperated. "C'mon, Professor Brenner, you hypothesized that the ancestor language had its genesis nearly one hundred and eighty thousand years ago. But that's improbable, and impossible to prove. Given the millennia that had passed, every single word would have been altered, changed, substituted, or even just dropped. There could never be any recognition of what it used to be."

The older man lunged forward, his face coming within inches of Matt's. "Bullshit." The sounds of the forest stopped for a few seconds, and every member of the camp swung to look in their direction. Fortunately, the forest forgave them quickly and resumed its chorus, making it impossible for the group to listen in.

Matt wiped spittle from his face as Brenner pulled his lighter and another cigarette from his shirt pocket. He pointed the lighter at Matt like a gun. "The analysis was empirical.

Humans were fully anatomically capable of language and communication at that time, and the matrilineal ancestor would have had the intellect, as well as the physical capability, for sophisticated communication. We started banding togeth-er – how do you think they managed that?"

Matt shook his head. "Wolves band together. So do lemmings. Look, I just think that modern man of about fifty thousand years ago, and by that I mean sapien-sapien, or at least Cro-Magnon, would have been better equipped to produce complex speech. I never said that there wasn't communication prior to that – just not a real language, ancestor or otherwise."

The older man leaned back, looking a little deflated.

Matt inched forward. "Professor, I ..."

"Fuck off!" Brenner stuck the cigarette in his mouth and got to his feet. He looked down at Matt, and for a moment it seemed as though he was about to say more, but instead he just made a disgusted noise in his throat and strode away.

Matt sat for another few seconds and then sighed, standing and sticking his hands in his pockets. He wandered back to where Megan, Carla, and Jian sat, temporarily postponing their conversation to watch him, hoping for an update on the flare-up. He sat down and started drawing on the ground with a stick.

Megan put her arm around him. "So, how's your day going, champ?"

"Had better." He slumped, resting his chin on his hand, and stared into the fire.

Carla leaned around in front of Megan. "What just happened? I thought you guys were about to come to blows. Are you going to tell me that the profession of linguistic expertise is akin to some sort of contact sport?"

Matt snorted and flicked the stick into the fire. "Nah. I re-viewed a paper of his years ago. It was a pretty good piece of work, and it seems it was to be Brenner's defining moment – the cherry on his linguistic cake, so to speak. But I found a few flaws and asked a couple of simple questions. They were just supposed to initiate a discussion – it happens every single day, to every single academic – but instead it started a wholesale collapse of his theory. He hasn't forgotten about it."

"Obviously." Megan narrowed her eyes in the direction of Brenner – in her book, Matt's enemies were her enemies.

Jian grunted. "It is disappointing when we find that our idols have feet of clay."

Matt laughed without humor. "Feet, legs, and up to the armpits, I'm starting to think. Well, I can guarantee I'll be off his Christmas card list this year."

Megan smiled broadly. "I'll send you two to make up for it." She kissed his cheek. "So, Henry Kissinger, who are you going to make friends with next?"

Matt nudged her with his elbow and turned to return her kiss. "I was thinking about going straight to the top, and spilling hot coffee on Max Steinberg's lap. Anyway, enough about my social skills. What have you guys been talking about?"

"Mitigators." Carla glanced briefly at Jian, as though seeking his approval to proceed. He nodded, and she continued. "Nothing in Professor Jorghanson's notes indicated there was any physical problem with the specimen he brought back, or the native population, or any other animals in the vicinity. His notes were a little vague on the actual location of the creature. He did refer to a wall of flowers and thorns, and a hidden sacred place, but he didn't actually find the bird himself – one of the tribe caught it for him. After that, there's nothing until he is on his way home."

Carla gazed into the distance – she seemed to be seeing the dead academic's notes as she spoke. "Anyway, somehow, between the time he boarded the flight and the time he disembarked, something switched on the parasites. They went from what we think was an annoyance, to something far more communicative and deadly."

Jian nodded. "We believe there was a biological balance, and that something was holding the parasite in check within its local environment. Dr. Nero mentioned mitigators. What we are looking for is something that mitigated or attenuated the mite – slowed or stopped it from killing its host. Generally, effective parasites try to form a balance with their host – killing it does not benefit the parasite. Some additional factor was added, or removed, which turned the *sarcoptes scabiei primus* from an effective parasite to an ineffective one."

Matt remembered the images of the skinless Jorghanson. "Ineffective is not the word that jumps to mind. So, we're looking for that mitigating factor – that makes sense. What do you think it could be?"

Jian shrugged. "It's impossible to know yet, but we do have plenty of exemplars we can use to model our suspects. We actually know a lot about our natural environment's existing biological retardants."

"Retardants – sounds like we're looking for a fire blanket," said Megan.

Carla took over. "Sure; we're looking for anything that obstructs or decelerates the mite's aggressive potential in the local area."

Megan was nodding. "You mean like some sort of natural insecticide?"

Jian nodded once. "Very good, and yes, that is the number one contender. But it could also be bacterial. We know that a microorganism called *bacillus thuringiensis* produces toxins that act as a larvicide against caterpillars, beetles, and mosquitoes. So, another contender." He held up a hand, counting on his fingers one by one. "It could also be a reciprocal parasite like a nematode, or perhaps an entomopathogenic virus. We might also be looking for a predator;

there are wasps so small that they prey on greenfly eggs." He shrugged and spread his hands, as though signifying the size and complexity of their search.

Carla took the baton up again. "At this point, anything and everything is on the table. It might be in the flora population – sap, bark, pollen ... After all, some plants produce chemicals that can stun pests. After eating geranium leaves, black beetles can become stunned for twenty-four hours, rendering them vulnerable to attack from other predators. Other plants produce a natural birth control; they can engineer forced termination of an egg-clutch, or even render an insect infertile. We know this because we are exploring all of these avenues to try and mimic the natural defensive capabilities of plants, and allow us chemical-loving humans to reduce the amount of toxins we are pumping into the earth."

Carla leaned forward and rubbed her face, then pushed her hands up through her damp hair. "So, we have a lot of options to sort through, and not a lot of time." She shrugged, and half of her mouth turned up in a wry smile. "Or it could be something we don't recognize, and don't even know to look for. But we're here, and at least we have the opportunity to search at the source. At a minimum, we need to find a local animal that has an infestation of the primus scabies mite, and then analyze the parasite's internal chemistry to try and detect some sort of unique trace in its system that will give us a clue to what we're looking for."

Matt nodded slowly, beginning to understand the enormity of the task. He spoke softly. "I hear Steinberg simply wants to catch a live archaeopteryx, get some footage, and then head straight back home. What happens if he finds his specimen quickly, and you haven't found your answers?"

Carla seemed to think for a moment before answering. "Then there are three options. One, we all leave together –

jump on the Steinberg express, and forget about why we came in the first place. Two, we convince everyone to stay here until our job is finished. It'd mean twisting a lot of arms, and I'm pretty sure we don't have enough physical, legal, or financial leverage to achieve that. Or, three … and then there were three. We stay, finish our job, and find our own way back."

"Four." Megan spoke without taking her eyes off the fire. "I'd stay too."

Carla looked at the young woman for a moment, then nodded. "Good."

They sat in silence, each watching the fire as it consumed the pile of damp wood. After a few minutes, Carla drew in a deep breath, and exhaled slowly. "Damn jungles – we shrink them by about fifty million acres a year." She snorted derisively. "Ninety percent of West Africa's rainforests are already gone forever. Indonesia's could be fully logged out by 2020. We're mowing down the greater Amazon at the rate of a football field a second. These places are our lungs, and the wellsprings of some of the world's greatest cures … but also the source of some of its greatest killers." Carla leaned back, her face grim.

Jian nodded. "Yes, this is true. Like Pandora's box. As we push back the jungles and enter previously untouched areas, we are finding flora and fauna that harbor devastating illnesses and parasites." He sat for a second, lost in thought, before turning to Matt and raising his eyebrows. "Or perhaps these things are finding us."

"You mean things like Ebola?"

Jian laughed. "Ebola?" He laughed again, and shook his head. "Ebola is a Hollywood bogeyman – a microbiological Freddy Krueger. It's probably killed more chimpanzees than it has humans. But things like malaria … we have lost our fear of it. We pop a couple of tablets before traveling, and think it's all gone away, when in fact it's still killing over three-quarters of a million people a year. If we don't read about it, or see it on TV, it just doesn't exist. The fact is, there are a thousand other things that have crawled, flown, and slithered out of the jungles that are inimical to human life. We guard against viral and bacterial incursions, but we are not as vigorous in our defense against parasites." Jian looked across at Carla, perhaps expecting her to object, given her role with the CDC, but instead she continued to stare into the fire.

Jian lifted a canteen from between his feet, unscrewed the cap, sipped, then held it up. "Clean water – we take it for granted, but in some countries it is a rare thing. Water can be a killer. Parasites love it, and love to find their way inside our bodies. Schistosomiasis bores into the skin, and lives in the blood. Guinea worms can enter your system via dirty drinking water and eventually burst from your body as a giant toothed worm several inches long. Then there's leishmaniasis, cryptosporidium, giardia, chagas disease – the list goes on."

"You see, Professor Kearns, the jungle is a wonderland for we entomologists, but sometimes the tiniest creatures can cause the most damage, and must be treated with the utmost respect." He held up a finger, then reached into his pocket and pulled out a small pocket-sized smart-pad and started to open pages, searching for something. He stopped, half-smiled at the screen, then turned it around for the group to see. "And sometimes the things we entomologists find are not so small ..."

The image on the screen showed a single wasp – black and grotesquely armor-plated with spikes and a shiny yellow-and-black carapace. Its jaws were enormous and hooked at the tips. It was positioned next to a soda can, and the creature was easily the length of the can.

"The newly discovered Indonesian Warrior Wasp – found on the remote island of Sulawesi. It's five inches long and mostly eats other insects and slow birds. However, it also managed to blind one of the researchers before they could capture this one to study." He motioned to the other team members. "Mr. Steinberg thinks he is looking for the Garden of Eden, but perhaps he will find something a little less benign." Jian smiled and pushed the device back into his pocket.

There was silence for a few seconds, then Matt turned to Megan. "Glad you came?"

"Pass me the insect repellent," she shot back, looking queasy.

* * * * *

Moema Paraiba muttered and paced in the shadows. A native Tupi, descended from the once-mighty Tupinambá, one of the oldest indigenous peoples in the country, he felt alone and strangely afraid in his own land.

His people had been in South America for thousands of years, and had seen empires rise and fall. He knew the jungle, knew its secrets … and he knew that where the karaíba, the white ghosts, wanted to go, was madness.

He had not wanted to guide them into the dark heart of the jungle. He had told Mr. Max that he knew the way to the area, but that some places were off limits, even to his people. He had also said he couldn't understand the strange picture writing of the Aîuru tapy'yîa people who lived there, and that he doubted he would be able to communicate with them. He actually wanted nothing to do with them – he had heard of the small and ugly tribes that lived in the area, had heard the legends of cannibalism, strange diseases, and the grotesque things that were only kept from the katu-taba, the good people, by the wall of pain.

He paced back and forth, muttering to himself. Many years ago, his grandfather had told him and his brother the story of when he was a young man. He had joined a karaíba expedition to look for gold in the deep jungles. The bosses who were with them had used guns on the small tribes, and made them flee before them. But he had also told of coming to a mighty cliff wall covered with thorns. It was both deadly and awesomely beautiful. Along the canes bloomed flowers of the deepest red – each looking like a tiny fist of blood. His grandfather had said he could smell their perfume from many paces back.

The karaíba had captured one of the local Aîuru tapy'yîa and forced him to show them the way inside the wall. Only the bosses went through, six of them, while Moema's grandfather and his Tupi brothers had waited for them.

It had only taken a few hours for the screaming to start – first in terror, then in pain – soaring up above the enormous barrier. His grandfather had fled back into the jungle, and had not stopped running for days.

Moema had wet his pants when the old man described the gruesome sounds he had heard, and the sounds of something big colliding with the barrier. The old man had told him that while running, he realized that the gods had created the giant wall of thorns to keep something terrible in.

He shouldn't be doing this. He muttered and paced some more, hoping that when he came to stand before his gods, he would not be judged harshly for his transgression. He shook his head; he was making the same mistake as his grandfather, but he had been warned, so this was worse. He stared off into the darkness, wondering if he should stay. It would take him many days to get back, but at least he would get back.

He cursed and spat into the jungle. Aiyee, he needed the money. Jobs were hard to come by, or he'd already be slipping through the trees back to the foot of the plateau. But he'd be left with next to nothing – the boss-man Mr. Max had been smart enough to pay him in instalments, with the largest portion to be paid on their safe return.

His eyes slid across to the largest group of the karaíba, huddled together around a map and what looked like small television screens. The large one treated him like a slave, and he was sure that sooner or later he would strike or kick him if he had the chance. Moema knew of men like this – always brave and strong when they had a stick, a gun, or money.

He glanced at the women. Their faces were so pale and long, not the perfect honey-colored round ones of his people. He wondered if they ever smiled. He sighed; this had seemed like a good idea back home. Moema turned and caught his breath. Standing right in front of him was one of the karaíba, the one with the long hair who always sat with the horse-faced women.

"He-rêr a'ê Kearns – I am Kearns, a teacher." He held out his hand.

Moema blinked. The man was speaking old Tupi – and very well. He nodded and mumbled his own name, and took the offered hand, pumping it, but not looking the white man in the eye.

Kearns spoke again, in the language of his forefathers. "You look nervous. May I join you? I might be able to help."

CHAPTER 8

LOS ANGELES DOMESTIC AIRPORT

Albert Dusche drove the baggage cart across the hot tarmac. There were only a few late suitcases and packages left to load, and frankly, it was just as well. Just about every other asshole on his shift had called in sick – night sweats and a nasty rash, apparently.

Fuck me sideways, what was happening to this country? His father had fought in Nam, lived on jungle rations, and crawled through mud, blood, and minefields. These days you get a couple of pimples and you gotta stay in bed for a week. No wonder the Chinks and Aye-rabs were kicking our asses every which way to Sunday.

He slowed the cart, the small amber light on the rear post indicating his presence on the runway. He climbed out and rolled his shoulder before walking to the conveyor belt, pulling on his gloves as he went. He leaned one hand on the metal edge and yelled up into the dark aircraft hold. "Yo!"

There was a responding "Yo!", then a head appeared – Ruiz – giving him the thumbs up. "Hey, my man, Dusche-bag. Let's go."

Fuck you too, wetback. Dusche sauntered back to the cart and grabbed the first bag, swinging it heavily up onto the moving belt. He moved like part of the machinery – grabbing, turning, and chucking, then back again. The next bag was brand new, and he slammed it down hard, just to give it a little character. Something crunched and tinkled inside. *Oops.* He laughed cruelly. Sorry grandma, no perfume this year.

He grabbed the handle of the next bag and tugged, grunting from the effort. His hand slipped as he swung it around to the belt – *heavy mother*, he cursed. Inside the canvas gloves, his fingers were wet with perspiration. Dusche looked at the remaining bags – all soft casing and no sharp edges – then pulled his gloves off and tossed them onto the cart's seat, waving his hands around for a few seconds to dry them.

Smells like old socks and vinegar, he thought, wrinkling his nose as he caught a whiff of his fingers. Time for new gloves.

Barehanded, he grabbed the last two bags and threw them up onto the moving conveyor, standing with his fists on his hips and watching them roll up into the dark hold. Ruiz appeared like some sort of cave-dwelling mammal, grabbed the bags, then disappeared inside the hold to stack them in their secure places.

Dusche flexed his fingers; they felt strangely bloated and tingly. He held one hand up, turning it over, and frowned. It was coated with something that looked like brown grease. He sniffed, then pulled his head back. *Yecch* – smells like sugared shit. Filthy fucking bags – people transport all sorts of crap these days. He wiped both hands on his pants.

"See ya," he yelled over his shoulder, not caring if he was heard, and jumped back into the luggage cart.

Ruiz never noticed that the handles on the last two bags were streaked with the same brownish grease that coated Dusche's hands.

Neither did the handler at LaGuardia, or the owner of the bags, or the taxi driver.

CHAPTER 9

Matt returned to where Carla, Megan, and Jian were sitting on the far side of the fire and formally introduced Moema, even though the native Brazilian had shaken each of their hands at the start of their journey. This time Matt used Moema's full Tupi honorific title, firstly in the old language, and then in English. Moema nodded to each, almost bowing.

Matt leaned in close to him. "Would you like me to translate, or is English all right?"

Moema nodded. "English, but some words you can please translate, He-rêr a'ê Kearns."

Matt sat down in front of his three traveling companions, his back to the fire. He motioned to the packed earth beside him and Moema also sat.

"Moema was telling me that he does not like where we are going. He said it is pûera – a bad place." He turned to the young man, who nodded his agreement. Matt continued. "He has heard tales of the deeper parts of the jungle where we are heading and wants us to be warned, and think very long before he takes us any farther."

Megan turned to Matt. "What are the tales he's heard? Is it the disease?"

Matt nodded toward Moema. "You can ask him Megs; he speaks English."

Megan grimaced. "Sorry Moema, I wasn't thinking. Can you please tell us more about the stories you have heard?"

He shrugged. "I do not know much. Only what I have heard when the elders gossip, or what my grandfather told me when I was a child. When he was a young man, younger than I am now, he traveled deep into the Gran Chaco and found the Aîuru tapy'yîa – the Ndege Watu. They are said to be a very, ahh …" He turned to Matt and made a show of putting his fist out of sight under his shirt, whispering to him. Matt found some English words he could use – hidden, secret. Moema nodded and continued. "The Ndege Watu are a very secret people, and do not like any intrusions."

Matt leaned forward. "Did anyone talk to them?"

Moema shook his head. "My grandfather, he said they were not like us; not … real people. They ran away after the karaíba fired their guns at them. But that was good as it is said they are eaters of men's flesh, so …" Moema pulled a face. "My grandfather also said they found the wall of thorns, but he did not enter. Perhaps that is why he lived. The legend has it that anyone who enters, other than the, uhh, clean ones will die."

Megan inched forward on her tree branch. "Did no one return from behind the thorns?"

"No one."

"What do you think happened to them? Did they not find their way out, or …" Megan trailed off.

Moema shook his head forcefully. "My grandfather said they screamed."

Carla's head snapped around. "They screamed? How long were they in there?"

Moema held up one finger. "I think, maybe one hour."

Carla turned to Jian, frowning. "That doesn't sound like an infestation of mites – even a mass infestation."

Jian nodded. "That's right, and besides, we are expecting them to be in some sort of benign state in their natural environment – at least, we hope so. Most interesting indeed."

Carla reached out and touched the Brazilian's forearm. "Mr. Moema, have you heard of any sickness where the skin itches?"

Moema's eyebrows shot up, and he laughed softly. "In Brazil jungles, it is rare not to itch – there are many plants and insects that can cause this problem." He shrugged. "We just live with them."

Carla shook her head. "No, no, let me rephrase that. Are there any insect afflictions …"

"Afflictions?"

She tried again. "Ahh … illnesses, sicknesses, where the skin can be become … loose." Carla pinched the material of her sleeve and wobbled it back and forth.

Moema looked upward and bobbed his head from side to side as he thought about the question. "There is one caterpillar, the ybyrá, that has hairs that can make the skin, first itchy, and then break open all over in sores. Some people have died."

Jian nodded. "Lonomia – I know it – contains a powerful anticoagulant. Nasty open rash, and in rare cases, causes bleeding into the brain. Not our suspect here."

Moema shrugged. "Sorry, that is all I know."

"That's okay, it's very helpful Moema, thank you.' Matt patted the young man's shoulder. "Did you ever tell Mr. Steinberg your grandfather's story?"

"Yes, and I also told him that I would not be able to speak to the Aîuru tapy'yîa even if we found them, but he said just to get him there, and he will look after the rest."

"Damn the torpedos, and full speed ahead," Megan muttered, glancing briefly over to where Steinberg and his group were chatting and drinking coffee. She leaned closer to Moema. "This hidden place really frightens you, doesn't it?"

Moema looked at her for a few seconds, then his brow furrowed. "Yes ... no, I am not scared."

"No one said you were. I think you're very brave." Matt added quickly.

Moema nodded and his expression brightened, perhaps feeling as though he his machismo had been validated. "Even the loggers and drug runners will not pass through the deeper areas of the Boreal. There are no riches there, just the black jungle, and the thorns, and death. It is forbidden, but I will take you as far as I can. Like my grandfather, I will not enter." He looked sadly across to Matt. "I wish you do not enter either. I do not want to be just like him – the only one to survive."

"Wow." Megan's eyes were alive with a mix of fear and excitement.

Jian looked at Carla and raised his eyebrows. She sat back, frowning, and Matt could tell what she was thinking – either she had underestimated the parasite, or whatever was behind that wall might be even worse.

* * * * *

Later that evening, Matt and Megan grabbed some time away from the group, sipping antiseptic-tasting coffee. The fire was making Matt's eyes dry and his eyelids heavy. Despite having to sleep rough, he reckoned it'd be about five minutes before he was out cold.

He watched drowsily as John Mordell shone a small light into Max Steinberg's ear – probably checking for fungal infections. A thousand quips came to mind. None of them would have endeared him to the movie producer or his large bodyguard. Matt yawned.

Megan leaned into him. "So, what do you make of this hidden jungle, professor? Superstition and a little local

Brazilian charm, or do you think there really could be a secret place sealed off behind a giant wall covered in thorns?"

"Brazilian charm?" Matt snorted. "I think there is something there – Moema was genuinely scared, not just putting on a little theater for us Americanos. But they must be pretty good thorns to create a lasting physical barrier."

Megan sipped her coffee and pulled a face. "Pretty good physical barrier? That's an understatement. The creature that Jorghanson brought back was supposed to have died out over one hundred million years ago, and is somehow supposed to have been shielded for that amount of time – by some sort of wall or cliff covered in plants? Bullshit. Matt, I respect your opinion, but not even I'm buying that. There's no plant living today that is going to live that long. Even the granddaddy of them all, the Bristlecone pine, can only live to about five thousand years, and we're talking millions here … lots of millions."

Matt shrugged. "Yep, it's a puzzle all right. But there is a precedent. Don't forget that the Wollemi pine was found thriving in a valley in eastern Australia after it was thought to have been extinct for two hundred million years. So, I agree, no individual plant can live that long, but its species, its progeny, could survive."

Megan raised one eyebrow. "Maybe. I guess it doesn't have to be the same plant. If it's a climber, the old canes could provide a lattice for the next generation, and so on. The cage's bars could just keep regenerating."

"Exactly … and we keep finding biological time machines, and creatures living within them that we thought had fallen off the evolutionary chart. The fact is, the specimen Professor Jorghanson brought back shouldn't be alive today, but something kept it alive in a unique and isolated habitat. The clues all seem to fit, when we start to see them in some sort of context."

He nudged her. "Take the Wollemi pine, found in a hidden valley, neatly protected from forest fires and other external influences. The tree was a prehistoric remnant – the last time we saw it, it was pressed into Triassic stone." Matt sipped his coffee, made a guttural sound and spat the vile mouthful back into his cup. He threw the dregs into the fire. "Now imagine if that Wollemi pine's valley wasn't open at the top. Instead, imagine it was enclosed by a massive barrier, creating a living cage. What else might be shielded in there, and survive because its habitat was preserved, and no new predators could get in?"

Megan seemed to think for a minute. 'Okay Sherlock, but you're forgetting something. You're only thinking about new predators getting in. What if the barrier stopped old predators from getting out? Remember Moema's grandfather's story about the screaming."

"Old predators? If that was true, what could they be?" he said sleepily, staring into the flames for a few moments. He stretched and yawned, then got to his feet. "I can't think straight. I'm tired."

"Not too tired, I hope?" Megan grabbed his belt and dragged herself up beside him.

"For you? Never." He grabbed her around the waist.

CHAPTER 10

Matt woke early. His bladder felt the size of a basketball, and his dreams were becoming dominated by images of waterfalls. He'd held it during the night rather than risk stepping outside in the dark. He didn't think he'd be very popular if he just stuck his dick out and hosed the ground out front of his tent.

Matt crept forward in the cramped little tepee and peered through the zipped mesh front. It was still a murky predawn, and there was a low mist hanging over the ground. The fire was now a smoldering heap of silver, lumpy ash. The occasional ghost of smoke leaked out of the pile.

It was quiet – eerily quiet. Throughout the day, the noises of the jungle were almost overwhelming. Rushing shapes pushed through undergrowth, swung through trees, or burrowed into leaf litter on the ground. Then at night, the unseen nocturnal denizens took over, and the sound of pursuit and capture, eat and be eaten, screeches, screams, and whoops were even more intimidating. But then at dawn, when the nightshift and dayshift switched over, there was a brief period of silence and stillness that was hauntingly tranquil.

No better time to take a piss. Matt fiddled with the tent zip. He had taped it down the previous night to ensure nothing could wriggle through the minute gap between zipper head and tent floor. He lifted it slowly upward. The sound of zipper teeth unlocking was like a canvas sheet being ripped in the muted dawn.

He stuck his head out – warm, green – it reeked of composting humidity, but above all, it smelled ... alive. He stepped out, stood straight, and stretched, feeling his vertebrae pop. Throughout the previous day he had done little more than travel, sitting for most of the time. It still felt like his body needed to decompress. A nice trek through the Amazon jungle will sort that out, he thought darkly.

Matt pulled his boots on and, in shorts and t-shirt, briskly walked a few paces away from the camp and ducked behind some palms – far enough, he hoped, for modesty and silence, but close enough to be heard if he had to call for help.

He lifted one leg of his shorts and aimed into a spiked bush. He stood for a few seconds, waiting. Nothing – vapor lock. Ever since he was a kid, whenever he needed to go the most, it took him ages to start the flow. But once it started ...

The stream arced into the bush, drilling into its depths and causing some small creature to scuttle away to dry safety. Matt tilted his head back and sighed with assuaging pleasure. After a few seconds, he opened his eyes, sensing movement on his periphery. His stream stopped dead, and the ensuing sting made him wince. He spun around.

"And she's happy with that?" Kurt stood just a few paces away, already fully dressed in his fatigues, and carrying an armful of wood.

"Ahh, yes, I guess." Matt felt his indignation surge as he turned his back to try and start pissing again. A few dribbles splashed the toes of his boots. He strained harder.

He knew Kurt had his eye on Megan, and even though he hadn't fully explored where his relationship with her was going, and there'd certainly been no talk of long term between them, he'd be damned if he'd let Doc Savage start hitting on her.

He heard Kurt come even closer. His stream automatically shut off for good. *Fuck*. He still had a little more pissing to do, and tossed up whether to give up, or pretend to still be going so he could keep his back turned to the bodyguard-slash-jungle guide.

Kurt spoke, so close behind him that he could have been looking over Matt's shoulder. "Be careful hanging the old baloney pony out for too long down here, Professor. The heat and smell of the salts will bring the jungle mosquitoes – one bite and the sensitive skin down there will swell up like a balloon. The trick is to keep waving your hand over it as you go."

Oh, shit. "Right, right, thanks." Matt started waving his free hand over the top of his penis. He heard Kurt leave, laughing softly.

Matt rolled his eyes and stopped waving. Very funny. *You got me this time, asshole.*

* * * * *

Matt sauntered nonchalantly back into the camp, keeping his eyes on Kurt, who was stacking wood on the fire, trying to coax the ash back into a blaze. *And of course he'll be able to do it*, Matt thought sourly.

Kurt looked over his shoulder at Matt and winked. Matt gave him his best and most sarcastic smile in return, then knelt to duck back into his tent. Megan was up and pulling on a t-shirt. "Where's my wake-up coffee?"

He looked shocked. "So sorry, I'll get right on to room service – would you also like some pastries?"

She nodded royally. "Yes please, a fresh baked croissant would be fine." She lunged forward, pushing him back onto the thin air mattress, and kissed him hard. He felt himself swell – even without the mosquito bites.

"Coffee'll be a few minutes – GI Joe is just kick-starting the fire."

She pulled back a few inches. "Kurt?"

"Mmm-hmm." He went to kiss her again but she started to sit up.

"He's all right." She continued dressing.

"All right, all right, or do you mean ... *all right*?"

She laughed. "Just all right He's a bit like a cross between a boy scout and a big puppy – big, fun, but not too bright."

Matt nodded, not fully reassured. He would have preferred she compared him to a lizard, or a hog. Something slightly less cute than a puppy.

Megan flicked out one long leg to pull on a boot. "So, first day's full trekking into the mysterious black heart of the Boreal." She pulled what she thought was a spooky face. "Apparently there's only a real track for the first few hours, and then ..."

"I get it; then it's into the wide green yonder. Who told you that?" He lifted himself up on one elbow.

She looked at him for a few seconds, then slowly lifted three fingers to her forehead in a boy-scout salute.

"I see." He couldn't hide his annoyance.

"Forgeddaboutit. You're my one and only Action Man." She pulled on her other boot, then went to duck out of the tent, but he grabbed her.

"Not so fast; one more kiss before we start the day. By this evening, we'll both be physically smashed."

She allowed him to pull her back and lay her down. "I can go for that – if you're quiet." She rolled on top of him and kissed him deeply. "But I can't agree to just one kiss."

Truth was, he planned to be as noisy as he could manage. He wanted Kurt to hear the no complaints bit he mentioned. He smiled and eased her shorts down.

* * * * *

Later, Matt and Megan joined the group for a cooked breakfast of leftover fried ham, beans, coffee, and some rehydrated
orange juice – antiseptic flavor, of course. There was
something extra cooked in amongst the beans. It tasted like
potato, but was purple. Moema had called it a Kenke, which
Matt had assumed was some sort of local yam. *So, the local
foraging has begun,* he thought.

While the group was gathered together, Max Steinberg got
to his feet and cleared his throat. "Good a time as any for the
morning's briefing. I hope everyone slept well?" He grinned,
and for the first time Matt noticed that his teeth were a mix
of blinding white, gold, and silver. This told him two things.
One, this was probably why the man rarely seemed to smile,
and two, perhaps it's not just his teeth. Perhaps the entire man
is metal inside – a robot sent from the future to make movies
and annoy the CDC.

Steinberg held out his mug to Kurt, who immediately
refilled it. Without waiting for a response to his question, he
went on.

"It will take us about a week, give or take a day, to reach
the area where we believe our predecessor encountered the
indigenous tribe. Those days will be extremely hazardous,
and our guides," he nodded to both Kurt and Moema, "will
be talking to all of you about the rules. I don't need to
mention that you should avoid wandering off from the group,
and don't touch or eat anything that the guys haven't checked
out first." He paused, looking at each of them individually
and nodding, as if expecting everyone to reply with a nod and
a "yes, sir!"

He pointed to Kurt, who was holding what looked like
a solar light for the garden – about a foot in length, with a
bulb at one end and a plastic spike at the other. "We will

be leaving GPS markers as we go. Although the heavy forest canopy means we're invisible to visual satellite imagers, our mission will still be tracked and mapped, in case we need to call for help – God forbid." He grinned briefly before once again becoming serious.

"This here is base camp. Where we're going is inaccessible from the air. The jungle treetops extend nearly two hundred feet straight up, and do not lend themselves to helicopter landings, so … no chopper is going to be able to land, or even hoist us out. We need to make it back to this point – as I said, our base camp." He grinned his shiny smile once more. "Should be a walk in the park. Oh, and by the way, when we leave, we leave. If you want to wander off or get lost, then please make your own arrangements for traveling home." He raised his eyebrows, looking at each individual in turn. No one doubted for a second that he was serious. Beside him, Kurt smirked and looked at Matt.

Steinberg motioned to his large bodyguard, then stepped back a pace. "If you please, Mr. Douglas."

Kurt nodded to his boss, then stepped forward with his hands on his hips, looking like a big-game hunter about to re-gale them with tales of bagging a killer rhino in Kenya. "How many of you have been in a jungle before?" Most hands were raised. "Good. Okay, now, how many of you have been in the Amazon jungle before?" All hands went down except Matt's, which Kurt ignored. "Well, this is real life down here. Sitting in an air-conditioned office in New York, or eating sushi in California is not living … this is."

Matt heard Jian groan under his breath, and tried hard to suppress a laugh, knowing that he was already on Kurt's shit list. He didn't fancy making the guide a real adversary, espe-cially given that he was twice Matt's size.

Kurt squared his shoulders and paced, keeping his eyes on the group. "There are no jungles like the Pantanal. This here is one of the last unexplored areas of jungle left in the world. The Amazon is roughly four million square miles. Two hundred and fifty of those are still just a green question mark on a map. That's where we are now. I guarantee none of you will forget your time in the Gran Chaco Boreal."

Matt could tell he was warming to his role – a closet martinet. He nudged Megan, but she ignored him. Kurt had her attention one hundred percent.

Kurt stopped pacing and stood with his legs planted and arms folded. "The round trip should take no more than twenty days, depending on what we find, and how long we need to kill, capture, or catalog our specimen."

"Excuse me. I'd like to remind you that before anyone handles the specimen we need to examine it. That is, if you ever plan to get it back into the United States." Carla, sitting ramrod straight, directed her question past Kurt to Max Steinberg.

"Yes, yes, yes." Steinberg waved his hand dismissively, as though shooing a fly off his lunch. Carla tried to hold his gaze, but Steinberg turned away, bored with the line of questioning. He nodded to Kurt, who cleared his throat. Matt saw Carla's eyes narrow and her jaws move, as though she was grinding her teeth. He could read the annoyance and distrust, plain on her features. He also wondered briefly who she was referring to when she said "we".

Kurt went on. "Remember where you are. Things live and die fast down here ... and they die hard. Sure, people enter the Pantanal and come back to tell the story – Mr. Jorghanson showed us that. But for every hundred assholes who wander into the Gran Chaco, only a few ever come back. And Mr. Jorghanson also showed us what can happen to those who do come back. He disrespected the jungle, and it caught up with him ... rather unpleasantly, I hear." Kurt paused and studied their faces before continuing.

"Okay team, here are the rules. Rule one – down here I make the rules. That's all you need to know for now." Kurt grinned. "I'll tell you the rest as we go. Listen to them, follow them, and hopefully we all find what we're looking for and be home in a few weeks, sipping champagne and toasting our success."

He looked across at Moema and motioned for him to approach. The Brazilian had been standing to one side of the group holding a large roll of paper. Kurt took it and let it unfurl, then handed it back and had the smaller man hold it up, acting as his human clipboard, his small brown fingers clamped around each upper edge. It was a large satellite image of the jungle. Though it showed rivers, some lumpy mountains, and shadows of depressions that could have been valleys, basin plains, or just bad lighting, it was largely green – just green. Kurt tapped the center with his knuckle.

"Basically, we're here … and we need to get here." He moved his finger a couple of inches.

It didn't seem like much of a hassle, Matt thought, when you looked at it from a few hundred miles above.

Kurt tapped again. "We will need to push through plenty of virgin jungle, on foot, of course, and without a track. We will also need to cross a river. We're heading into the wet season – it hasn't hit yet, but the river will still be fast flowing, and as you've probably noticed, we didn't bring a canoe."

Matt raised his hand. "Will we make them when we get there?"

Kurt laughed and pulled an incredulous face. "Do I look like MacGyver?"

Matt nodded vigorously.

The biologist, van Onertson, looked confused and mouthed, "Who?" to Matt, before shaking his head.

"No, Professor Kearns, we will be finding shallows and wading … and yes, there will be piranhas, leeches, and crocodiles." Kurt smiled as Matt's eyebrows shot up. "In fact,

there's half a dozen species, ranging from the tiny dwarf cai-
man to the big black river crocs. They can be twenty feet long
and as wide as a Buick. And once the wet season hits, you've
really gotta worry. That's when they tend to move up and
away from the rivers. Makes for a nice surprise, having one
of those big fuckers poke its head into your tent at night."

He grinned at Matt. "That'd sure interrupt any sweet lovemaking going on." Kurt straightened, and Matt felt his face
go hot. "Okay, if we respect the jungle, it might just respect
us back. We pack up now, and I'll do an inspection before we
set off in …" he looked at his wristwatch, "… thirty minutes.
Questions?"

Joop tentatively raised his hand. "How will we know when
we've arrived?"

Kurt shook his head and his lip curled momentarily in
derision. "Arrived? Jewp, we've already arrived."

To his credit, the biologist didn't give up. "But is there an
actual destination? How will we know when to stop trekking?
Will it be when we find the Ndege Watu, the specimen, or
when we run out of patience?" He raised his eyebrows and
tilted his head.

It was a good question; Matt had been wondering the same
thing. He doubted they'd come across a sign that said, "You
are here", with a big red arrow pointing to the ground. Also,
lost tribes tended to be a little shy – they were funny like that.
That's probably why they were lost in the first place.

Kurt started to speak, but Steinberg stepped toward the
front of the group and laid his hand on the bigger man's
forearm. "We have Mr. Moema Paraiba and we have
Jorghanson's trip journal, which details the coordinates of
his starting point, and gives the directions and timing of his
travels. From that, we are able to form a basic travel plan.
The rest is in the hands of old lady luck. We need to find the
Ndege Watu so they can show us the way to the home of the

fantastic creature Dr. Jorghanson brought back, God rest his soul... the creature our CDC friends destroyed."

Steinberg avoided looking at the bristling Carla. His mouth was turned down, almost wistfully. "That's if we can find them, and if we can persuade them to show us the way ... and if we can find another specimen ... There are a lot of 'if's. But by being here, onsite, we give ourselves a good chance of success. Sitting home in LA, we give ourselves nothing more than interesting dinner conversation."

Most of the group nodded. They knew he was right. He turned and raised his eyebrows at Kurt, who looked again at his watch.

"Ladies and gentlemen, final inspection is now in ... twenty-six minutes."

CHAPTER 11

CDC HEADQUARTERS, DRUID HILLS, ATLANTA

The CDC headquarters was an enormous modern building with an impressive double curved frontage on Houston Mill Road. But the impressive façade masked its true character, which was better identified from the rear. It was a disease-fighting factory, complete with industrial piping and high-intensity incinerator smoke stacks.

Doctor Francis "Hew" Hewson sat in a long white corridor, bored but still nervous as he waited to be called. He gazed at the rows of historical photographs on the walls – probably intended more as intimidation than decoration.

The CDC was created under President Roosevelt in 1942, during World War II, as the Office of National Defense and Malaria Control. Malaria had proved a major problem for the US troops fighting in jungles, and was hitching a ride back to the States when the wounded warriors returned home.

The office changed its name to the Center for Disease Control and Prevention, or CDC, in 1992. Its multi-billion dollar budget and expanded brief meant it had now become the nation's watchdog for almost everything, from food poisoning and occupational health and safety to modern bioterrorism.

Hew stared hard at the double wooden doors, willing them to open. His foot tapped on the ground and he shifted in the hard seat. Just twelve hours ago he had forwarded his research and results, along with his concerns, to the office of the director. Within an hour he had received a short reply; a few sentences that boiled down to "get here now and explain yourself."

He expected, or hoped, that headquarters was as alarmed as he was. Now it was his job to fill in the details, and perhaps be involved in spearheading some sort of national operation.

His foot tapped faster, from heel to toe now. He wished Carla were here; this was her domain. He leaned forward onto his knees and rubbed his face, thinking of his boss. She would march in, pin them with that gaze of hers, and then blow them out of the room with her forceful logic.

He sat back. Unfortunately she was down in the jungle, so it was up to him. He hated this part – the politicking, the negotiating and the selling. He guessed that dozens, maybe even hundreds, of scientists and doctors in the field had raised alerts, but probably few had requested what he had – national mobilization. Now it was up to him to justify his request. *Dammit*, he thought again. *Carla should be doing this. She'd twist these guys around her little finger. If only I'd ...*

The thought froze in his brain as the doors opened soundlessly, and a smiling woman motioned with her finger and then breathed a few sentences he couldn't quite hear. Why did she need to whisper? Was the Pope inside? Hew got to his feet and swallowed, making his prominent Adam's apple bobble on his thin neck. The woman turned and disappeared inside, and he followed.

Several older men and women were standing around talking quietly, pouring coffee into good-quality bone china. The lengthy wooden table running down the center of the room held piles of notes in front of each seat. As Hew stood waiting, he could see his research on top of the pile.

The smiling woman silently moved her lips again and led him to the front of the room. Sunk into the table was a recessed electronic panel and a small screen. He looked it over for a few seconds then nodded – he knew what was expected. The panel contained various plug-ins for a dozen different types of media. He pulled a stack of paper and a small memory stick from his briefcase and inserted it into the appropriate jack. Immediately the screen came to life.

Hew's fingers moved rapidly over the small keys as he found his information. A flicker from behind told him that his technical fumbling was working – whether he liked it or not, his presentation had begun. He swallowed once again, and sucked in a huge juddering breath. *You never get a second chance to make a first impression*, his father used to say. Better make the most of it. He worked to slow his breathing.

The woman leaned in close and placed a glass of water next to his hand. He strained his ears. She smiled, her lips opened, and he waited for something: "good luck", or "you'll be fine." Instead, she whispered, "please be brief," then turned to one of the silver-haired men and whispered something to him. The man glanced briefly at the screen, then nodded to the woman.

His gaze returned to Hew, and he spoke, his voice deep and warm. "Dr. Francis Hewson, ready to commence, I believe?" His silver eyebrows were raised.

Hew nodded, and gave a weak smile.

"Good man. My name is Dr. Thomas Mason; I have the fortunate – some would say unfortunate – responsibility of being lead director of the CDC." As he spoke, he walked back to the long table and sat at its head, at the farthest point from the screen. Responding to the signal, the rest of the group ambled over, balancing cups and saucers as they came.

Hew nodded and smiled some more. He knew the name, but had never seen the man in person. Mason was large and barrel-chested. That could have meant a matching barrel stomach, but that was expertly hidden by the expensive tailoring of his suit. He looked like he'd be quite at home sipping wine at Martha's Vineyard, or heading up a large corporation in New York, or anywhere in the world, really.

The older man had a commanding air, but Hew wasn't going to call him "sir" just yet. He needed to create a sense of authority – he needed them to respect him, and, more importantly, listen to him. He tried to think of how Carla would deal with them, then he nodded to the older man and spoke with as much gravitas as he could muster. "Dr. Mason."

Mason motioned open-handed to the screen and sat. He didn't bother introducing anyone else, and no one seemed in any way inclined to be introduced. The motion was clear enough – begin.

Hew coughed into his fist and stood back from the screen. He folded his arms, then immediately unfolded them. His nerves were beginning to overcome his attempt at coolness. He lifted the electronic click pointer, and cleared his throat.

"Ladies and gentlemen ..." Nerves made his voice higher than it should be. He made a conscious effort to compress his vocal cords and take it down a few octaves. He started again. "Ladies and gentlemen, we have a serious problem."

* * * * *

Jimmy Ruiz slowed as he came to the border crossing. Maria had his American employment card and their passports ready on her lap, but crossing from the USA into Mexico was never a problem. Judging by the small number of cars banked up, their wait would be little more than ten minutes or so – nothing compared to what they'd encounter when they returned.

Ruiz kept the windows up and the air conditioning on full blast. Already the outside temperature was pushing ninety degrees, and a yellowy haze lifted dryly from the dust and exhaust of the idling vehicles. He touched the temperature knob again, managing to find another hair's breadth of turn in the dial.

Maria pulled her shawl a little tighter around her shoulders and sneezed theatrically. She had given up asking him to turn it down, instead sitting in irritated, rugged-up silence. Now she had reached the final stage of protest – the physical demonstration of her discomfort by feigning illness.

Ruiz ignored her. There was no way he could turn down the cooling artificial breeze – it was the only thing giving him relief from the damned itch. His skin crawled, from the roots of his hair all the way down to his greasy scrotum.

He shifted in his seat, winced, and cursed under his breath. A few days back he had visited one of the local brothels after downing a few beers with his friends. His favorite girl, all big hips and long red hair, had made him feel special, and young, instead of pushing forty with a growing gut and thinning hair. If she had given him something ... he cursed some more, this time the soft words passing his lips.

"What?" Maria broke her silence and turned with a scowl.

"Nothing, my sweet." He shifted in his seat and sniffed. He needed a shower; he stunk.

* * * * *

Hew had been speaking for around fifteen minutes, and had only just covered the suspected origination point of the parasite, its primary symptoms and multiple transmission

Carla, you should have been here, he thought. HAN, the primary Health Alert Network, was a countrywide program that was used to disseminate information nationally at the state and local levels. It could reach over ninety percent of the population via a messaging system that transmitted health alerts to over one million health and authority recipients.

Hew packed his things away. *It was better than nothing*, he thought. He heard Mason speaking again and turned.

"You've done your job correctly, Dr. Hewson. You have raised the profile of the threat, and for that we thank you. However, at this point the mortality rate, or even the transmission rate, is not of sufficient significance to warrant a threat level change. We are also aware that your senior colleague is already looking for a biological retardant at the source." Mason pushed his chair back but didn't rise. "So, for now, we'll monitor the situation. Thank you for your time."

Hew nodded and noticed that, wraith-like, the whispering girl had returned to his side. She led him to the door and stood back, holding it open and smiling. At the door he paused for a second and half turned, thinking about Mason's comments. *Not of sufficient significance.* Mason hadn't seen … none of them had seen the lumps or the potential aerosol spread of the infestation. None of them had seen the raw skin after the epidermal layer literally slid off the physical frame. Sure, the patients weren't killed immediately, but the idea that they could recover … or even be expected to live? That wasn't living.

The woman whispered something to him, and Hew rounded on her. "Speak up, will you?" He pushed open the door and marched out.

CHAPTER 12

Matt marveled at the strength of the small Brazilian man. He was a good foot shorter than Steinberg's burly bodyguard, but he managed to carry twice the pack weight. It seemed to Matt that where Kurt was Crocodile Dundee, Moema was a little brown Hercules.

Carla had told him the packs mostly contained demountable cages, and some camera equipment. Luckily the cameras were little more than the size of a shoebox, including long-life batteries. In Moema's grandfather's day, they would have had to carry suitcase-sized boxes and tripod legs. Matt had offered to help, but Moema had just looked confused, then smiled and shook his head. Matt knew not to press him – he was paid to do the job, and was certainly strong enough, so any offer to lighten his load might have been viewed as a question about his masculinity.

They had been trekking for over six hours, and Matt felt small streams of perspiration running under his long hair and down his face to join up with the rivers on his torso before continuing down through his groin to flood his socks. His clothing had long given up trying to absorb the sweat and was now doing little more than adding to his personal weight and discomfort. The salty bath also meant that insect repellent had to be reapplied hourly, otherwise the constant swarm of tiny satellites circling his head would land for a quick meal. Matt hated to think what the chemical onslaught was doing to his system, but preferred it to being injected by some parasitic jungle microorganism in a bug's saliva.

He let his eyes wander to the treetops overhead. As they traveled farther into the heart of the Boreal, it became darker – not from increasing cloud, or evening fall, but from the tree canopy, which became further enmeshed, forming a single ceiling of dark green. Shoals of small monkeys seemed to travel with them, running across the upper branch balconies and constantly scolding the humans for their intrusion, and occasionally lobbing soft rinds of fruit in their direction.

Megan was in her element, Matt noticed, walking along with her gaze directed to the green sky, mouth turned up in a broad grin. Occasionally she would dart to the side of the track or get down low to stare at something under a rotting log or growing on a tree trunk. She continually fell behind, and when Kurt turned back to glare, it was usually at him. Matt would just shrug and grin. If Kurt wanted someone to yell at her, he could do it himself.

The path was narrow and squashy underfoot – little more than an animal track, and surprisingly dry. However, the wet season would soon commence, bringing drenching rains that could last for weeks at a time without any corresponding relief from the heat. Matt couldn't wait – there'd be moss, mold, and other exotic fungal infections growing like coral from between their toes and behind their ears.

Matt sped up to walk just behind Carla. For the most part, walking side-by-side was impossible on the narrow pathway.

"Damned hot."

"Don't worry, you can cool off in the pool this evening."

Matt groaned good-humoredly. The thought of a cool swimming pool, even a frosty beer, was too much to bear. "That would be heaven right about now. Any word from home?" He'd been watching her repeatedly tap away on her smartphone.

"Unfortunately, no. Communications are getting a little patchy. I trust my people in the field – it's up to them now. They need to document the cases, treat the afflicted, and, where necessary, raise appropriate alerts with head office. I don't think … I hope we're not at any sort of critical juncture just yet. I'd prefer to have a natural treatment, or develop something simple and with as few side effects as possible, before we have to resort to a barrage of chemicals." She looked across at him with a half smile. "We'd cure the population, but would probably get sued for the next fifty years."

"Ungrateful sods."

She laughed. "We're only ever fully protected under special legislation if the government deems it to be a high probability threat to life – basically, take it or die."

"They can do that?"

She turned and smiled without humor. "We can do a lot if we need to, Professor Kearns." Her jaw was rigid. "If we find a treatment, I'll make damned sure people take it. Did you know that with all the vaccinations we have available today, vaccination rates in the West are dropping to pre-1950 levels?"

"That's weird. Why is that?" Matt glanced at Carla. Her face was hard, but there was sorrow around her eyes.

"Bottom line, we think we know better. I certainly did. I didn't get my child vaccinated for pertussis – whooping cough." Carla watched her feet as she walked, her words lifeless. "At six, Madeleine should have recovered with standard antibiotics; instead she developed encephalitis, and died in agony. My husband – ex-husband – and I were too trendy, too clever, to bother with vaccinations. We paid the ultimate price."

Matt now understood the woman's drive. It was more than a calling – it was her penance.

"I'm sorry."

"It was a long time ago."

Matt saw that Carla's jaw was set, but her eyes had welled up. "Carla, if there's anything…"

She shook her head quickly, and looked away. Matt got the message; the topic was closed. They marched in silence for another twenty minutes before Carla's tight expression eventually eased.

Kurt called a halt at the base of a large tree, pulled his canteen from his belt and took a small sip. He rescrewed the top and lifted his chin; it looked for a minute as though he was sniffing the air. "River coming up soon, ladies and gentlemen. Once we cross that we get into uncharted territory."

Matt leaned in close and whispered to Carla. "I thought we were already in uncharted territory."

Kurt glanced over at Matt. "Only uncharted on our maps … but once we cross the river … uncharted on his." He nodded toward Moema.

Matt gave the big man a flat smile. *Great, hearing like a bat as well,* he thought.

"Hey." Megan caught up with them. After hours of hiking she was still walking as easily as when she started. She was using a long stick as a walking staff, and she tapped Matt's leg with it as she went past, heading off the path and leaning up against the trunk of an enormous tree.

She tilted her head back. "This is like a wonderland."

Matt smiled. "Yep, the happiest kingdom on earth."

She craned her neck forward. "Hmm, that sounds a little sarcastic … or perhaps just world-weary. I haven't been on as many trips as you, Indiana, so to me, it's all fantastic." She pulled the rolled bandana from her head and wrung it out, raining salty drops down onto the rotting leaves at her feet.

Megan went to lean back again when Jian came out of the brush and roughly pulled her forward.

"Hey!" She stumbled and then swung around, raising her walking stick in his direction. But Jian was already on her, slapping her furiously.

"What the fu—" Matt grabbed at the small entomologist, but pulled back when he saw the crawling mass on Megan's shoulders.

Jian continued his attack as Megan shielded her head. "Aztec ants." He swatted at the half-inch insects, some stubbornly clinging to the damp material of Megan's shirt with their sharp, hooked feet. In another few seconds he cleared the red and black mass and pulled her up. Megan did a little shivery dance, and stuck out her tongue.

"*Yecch.*" She continued to shake.

Jian pointed at the tree. "Sorry, but that's a cecropia tree. It has a symbiotic relationship with the Azteca Alfari ant – very aggressive. Anything deemed to be attacking the tree triggers the hive's warrior response." He pointed at the tree with a twig; by now every leaf tip and stem was bristling with the spindly insects.

Matt looked at her and raised his eyebrows. Megan just shook her head. "It's still a wonderland. And besides, they were probably just as scared of me as I was of them."

Jian grunted. "One thing insects do not know is fear. Lucky for us, they are small." He backed up as the ants started to take small leaps from the leaf tips toward his twig. "Otherwise, life on this planet would be very different."

CHAPTER 13

Forget it. Matt gave up and walked in sullen silence, his thoughts the only voice left to chide him for trying to engage Dan Brenner in conversation. The professor refused to offer any more than grunts, and the odd flat-eyed, indifferent stare. After a time Matt had dropped back a step or two, vowing to empathize a little more in future before banging out his professional opinions on another man's life's work.

It was mid-afternoon when, ahead of them, columns of misty sunshine broke through the green ceiling, announcing the river. The waterway was a tributary of the Mamoré River – relatively small, but still a good fifty feet wide, moving sluggishly. Kurt unclipped his holster and moved cautiously along the bank until he found what he was looking for – a slight lumping in the water from one bank to the other. He conferred with Moema, who nodded once, then he had the small man take a length of rope, tie it around a tree and wade in.

Matt gritted his teeth in apprehension. Bottomless water always scared him. Even though the coffee-colored water only came up to the Brazilian's waist, the thought of something hiding just beneath the surface, in all its toothed or spiked glory, made his stomach lurch.

After a few minutes Moema was safely on the opposite bank. He quickly set about tying the rope around another tree, creating a handrail for everyone to follow. Kurt waved to the small guide and then turned to the group.

"Single file, follow the line, hang onto the line, do not stop or step away from the line." He pointed to the river. "Just below the surface we have a silt pile. These are temporary underwater bridges. Something gets wedged in the river, debris builds up against it, and then silt covers it. It'll be washed away in the next rain surge, but for now, it means we don't need to swim."

The big man had a smirk on his face. "But be warned – either side of that silt pile its get deep … and big things hide in the deep. So, let's not go swimming." He turned and whistled to Moema, waving him back.

"Grab all your gear, 'coz we aren't making two trips. I'll go first, followed by Mr. Steinberg. The rest of you follow."

Max Steinberg handed Kurt his computer bag and other personal effects. Moema picked up a pack, looped it over his shoulders and then lifted another large box up onto his head.

Matt turned to Megan. "Seems the rule against making two trips doesn't apply to the hired help." He pointed to the river and bowed. "Ladies first."

She turned and smiled. "Just don't be last. You've seen what happens in the movies to the last guy on the jungle trail."

Matt waited with Moema. The small man looked surprisingly comfortable despite the hundred pounds of gear on his head and back. Matt pulled a face. "Hope there're no crocodiles."

Moema looked at Matt for a few seconds and then shook his head. "No, not here." He turned back to the water. "They get eaten."

Matt frowned, replaying the comment in his head, and then dismissed it. He mustn't have heard correctly. Megan had just set off, pulling herself across on the rope, and now it was his turn. He took a deep breath and lowered one foot into the water, feeling his boot squelch into the mud and sink a good four inches. He kept his eyes on his girlfriend's back as he carefully placed one foot in front of the other.

He inhaled. The smell rising in mist-like vapors reminded him of mud and perfume – the damp soil, combined with the pollens and sap from a billion trees and flowers that had touched its surface now rode the water on their way to the coast. At one point something bumped his knee and he froze, tensing his muscles, expecting the grind of large jaws to come at any second.

A prod in the center of his back from Carla, crossing behind him, unlocked his muscles and he started to move again. He let out a small, sheepish laugh and turned to make some sort of self-deprecating joke when just behind Carla, Dan Brenner grunted and then splashed heavily into the water up to his neck. His face looked ashen, and in an instant he went from looking confused to terrified. The linguist winced and screamed shrilly, his head whipping beneath the brown surface of the water, as if he had fallen into a deep hole.

No, not fallen. *Been pulled.*

Kurt yelled for everyone to get out of the water, and Moema dropped his pack and raised a long machete over his head, his eyes wide. Matt could hear the little man yelling a single word: yacu-mayma, yacu-mayma, over and over. Matt automatically translated the word in his head – *mother of the water.*

Something huge lumped up at the brown surface. There was a flash of shirt, and then it was gone, pulled down deep again. John Mordell, the doctor, dove toward the swirling water, and then, for some reason unfathomable to him, Matt did the same.

He swam with his eyes tightly closed – the coffee-colored water would have done nothing but fill them with grit if he'd opened them. He swept his arms back and forth, searching for the professor amongst the debris and mud, and was rewarded when he briefly touched an elbow. He grabbed it and reached out with his other hand, but where he expected to grab another portion of arm, he instead felt a muscular, scaled hide – thick as his waist, and as unbreakable as a tree trunk.

Moema's words echoed in his mind. *Mother of the water.* His hand slid down to Brenner's, and the linguist's fingers clasped weakly onto his own, but the leviathan muscles that bound him tightened and rolled, and the fingers were pulled away. Matt's lungs were near bursting and he broke the surface.

"Snake!" He was spluttering and startled to see he was a good twenty feet away from the bank and in the center of the river.

Kurt yelled for him to swim, and Moema pointed frantically to the bank. Gunfire erupted as Kurt fired several rounds into the murky water, making little geysers of brown shoot up around him and causing the birds and monkeys overhead to scream their outrage and rip away in the upper branches.

Matt waved his hands. "Stop ... he's here." He dove again, but could find no sign of the man. This time when he came to the surface Megan and Moema were there, Moema with his long blade still held aloft. Megan grabbed his collar and dragged him backward, coughing and spluttering, until they made it to the bank.

"Shit, shit, shit." Kurt marched up and down the sloping mud, his gun at his side.

Matt retched water and mud, and wiped grit from his nose. "I felt him ... it had him, a snake, a giant fucking snake."

Megan brushed his wet hair off his face while Moema sheathed his long blade and stood up, his eyes on the moving water.

"Snake, yes, these are the waters of the yacu-mayma. It can grow longer than twenty men, and as wide as a pony. It is gone now ... Mr. Brenner is gone now," he said.

"But, he was still alive, when …"

Moema shook his head. "Not anymore by now – he will be crushed; the yacu-mayma will squeeze him soft, and then devour him whole. I think it will be doing this in its lair … now."

Megan stood up and planted her hands on her hips, her chin jutting out. "We need to retrieve that body, and then pack it in. Party's over, Steinberg."

Kurt took a step toward her. "Retrieve the body?" He pointed a finger at her chest. "Listen …"

"Kurt." Max Steinberg stopped him and nodded to Megan as he took a few slow steps toward her.

"This is a tragedy, and we shouldn't make hasty decisions when emotions are running high." He came a little closer. "We'll try and send a message to the authorities. However, if we do 'pack it in', we'll miss the last of the dry season, and have to leave it until next year to try again." His mouth turned down and he shook his head almost sadly. "I'm afraid I won't be doing that. So, my team will be pushing on … today." He shrugged. "But by all means, you, or you and your little team, wait here for the authorities to arrive … if they arrive."

Megan's mouth dropped open and then snapped shut, her jaw set in determination. Matt groaned, knowing what was to come, as Steinberg turned away, talking softly to Kurt.

Megan turned to Carla, but the scientist looked away. Matt knew her frustration would boil over, and she would do or say something she, and then probably he, would regret. She marched over to grab Steinberg's elbow and whipped him around. "Wait a minute, not everyone agrees with you …"

The movie producer tore his arm free, but his face remained calm. He smiled and raised his eyebrows. "Really? Ms. Hannaford, do you really want to vote on it? Okay." He turned to the assembled group.

"Anyone who wants to turn back or stay here, please raise their hand." He looked along the faces, as each person looked down or away. John shook his head sadly, as did Jian, who mouthed *sorry* in Megan's direction. Joop's mouth opened for a second before his gaze slid away and his mouth closed without a word. Steinberg shrugged. "Sorry."

"Fuck you." Megan turned to Carla, who had her eyes downcast. Steinberg spoke up. "Dr. Nero?"

She looked up, her eyes going from Steinberg to Megan as she shook her head. "He's dead, Megan. Nothing we can do for him."

"But ... it's too dangerous. More of us will die if ..."

Carla held the young woman's angry gaze. "I warned you this wouldn't be a picnic. We knew what we were signing up for. Megan, I'm sorry, but a lot more people may die if we abandon our search now."

Matt got to his feet and put his arm around her shoulders. "Let it go, Megs."

She looked down and shook her head violently, then shrugged out from under his arm, walking away a few paces.

Matt looked back along the group, stopping at Max Steinberg. "Can you at least pretend to be sorry one of your team just got killed?"

Max Steinberg frowned and walked a few paces closer to him. He nodded, his face the picture of contrition. "You're right, you're right. I'm sorry, Professor Kearns." He put his hand on Matt's shoulder and looked into his muddy face. "Are you okay? That was very brave of you, son."

Matt shrugged. "It was instinct. I just hope that someone would do the same for me."

Steinberg nodded gravely. "Of course. I just hope we don't need to." He smiled. "However, there is some good news." He slapped Matt on the shoulder. "You just got a promotion."

CHAPTER 14

Matt noticed that the farther they tracked from the water, the more Moema's demeanor changed. The guide slowed, became more cautious and particular about his movements. Even Kurt had loosened the strap over his gun. Together the large bodyguard and the small Brazilian would walk carefully forward, then one or the other would pause and stand listening for several seconds. Matt found it unsettling and painfully slow. The addition of the heat, humidity, and things nipping at his exposed legs made it freaking agony.

Even Max Steinberg had commented about the feeling of being watched. Moema had nodded, and responded that in the jungle, there were always a thousand eyes watching – every day, every night. It hadn't made any of them feel any more secure.

A small opening in the undergrowth gave them room to spread out a little and rest. A waist-high mound seemed to grow in the center of the clearing, like a giant green boil on the earth. Kurt climbed to the top and stood like a captain at the bow of his ship, surveying the path ahead.

"Let's take a few minutes." He looked at each of them. "I don't need to remind you not to wander off – this is Ndege

Watu territory. We need everyone's eyes and ears focussed from now on. If they're here – and they probably are – let's hope we can communicate with them." He looked at Matt pointedly. "But first we need to make sure we don't scare them off, or give them a reason to attack us."

Megan leaned in close to Matt, having regained some of her spirit after the river encounter. "Looks like it's all up to you now."

Matt snorted softly. "No pressure." He turned to her with raised brows. "Besides, you'll be helping."

Matt looked past her and saw Moema pacing around the edge of the clearing. Often, he'd move a little way into the jungle to examine something before continuing his slow sentry walk. Matt left Megan with Carla and followed the guide for a while before the small man turned to him.

"Signs of the Ndege Watu?" asked Matt.

Moema exhaled through his nose, then shook his head. "No, nothing ... but there should be, He-rêr a'ê Kearns. The Ndege Watu are not just in the jungle, they are part of the jungle. They will know we are here. But I can see no sign of them. This is strange."

Matt looked around at the green wall surrounding them. "Hmm, you said they were shy. Maybe they are staying hidden."

Moema shrugged. "Yes, maybe I think that."

Matt watched him for a moment. He didn't believe the little man thought that at all.

* * * * *

"Get down." Kurt froze and then hunched over out front. Behind him, Max Steinberg, Matt, and the line of scientists got down on their haunches and tried to blend into the undergrowth. Matt watched the big man as his eyes slid across to something beyond the next stand of trees, fronds, and vines. He turned, put his finger to his lips, pointed at Matt and Moema and waved them forward ... slowly.

When they reached the front of the line, Matt could see what the guide had found –they were about to break through into a broad clearing, the red, hard-packed earth dominated by small round huts with tightly thatched roofs.

Moema grunted his observation. "No fire." Matt understood his concern. For a tribe as primitive as this, fire was hard to create. It was probably up to one or more individuals to keep the spark burning in the communal fire pit. This one had gone out.

Kurt turned to Matt. "Say something, tell them, hello."

Matt furrowed his brow. "I have no idea how to say hello." He looked at Moema, but the small man just shrugged and turned back to the village.

Kurt shook his head. "Fucking great." He pulled his gun from its holster.

"Wait, let me try something." Matt walked forward and tried to make an approximation of the sounds he had heard on Jorghanson's recording. Matt had been able to identify some conversation threads he thought he understood. He tried to lower his vocal cords to make the unique Ndege Watu sounds. The vocalizations came out like a series of whistling clicks.

They waited for a few minutes, but there was no reply.

Matt tried again. Once more, there was nothing but silence ... almost. After a few more seconds, there came an almost imperceptible sound from one of the huts.

Moema tilted his head. "Maybe someone."

Kurt nudged Matt. "Say hello again."

Matt half turned. "It's not ..." *Ah, forget it.* There was no point trying to explain the Ndege Watu expression of friendship to Kurt. He made the small series of whistle-click sounds again.

They waited, but, other than the soft sounds from inside the hut, there was no response or reaction.

"Okay, that's it, we're going in – stay low and on your toes." Kurt pushed through the final barrier of green, and entered the camp. Matt wrinkled his nose at a strange odor, like decaying meat, old flowers, and spoiling food.

Kurt crept toward the hut where they had heard the noise, and turned to wave them closer with his gun.

"It stinks ... dirty bastards." He held the revolver up and went to step in front of the open entrance, but Matt caught his elbow and pulled him back.

"Let me." Matt stepped out, repeating the few phrases he had memorized. He crouched in the opening of the hut, and blinked to try and help his eyes adjust to the darkness. "Hello?"

There was an explosion of movement. A small boar burst from the tent, trailing stinking entrails in its jaws. Matt fell backward. "Shit!"

Kurt stepped over him, ducked his head into the hut, then immediately pulled it back out. He turned to Moema. "Dead. Check the other huts."

The small man nodded and scurried off, his long blade in his hand. Kurt grabbed Matt's forearm and pulled him to his feet. The guide yelled for John, no longer worried about silence.

"Doc, get in here, we got a body."

John came from out of the jungle, immediately followed by Carla, then Megan.

Moema returned and Matt could see that his normally coffee-colored face was slightly ashen and his eyes wide. "More Ndege Watu – men, women, children; all dead. Maybe thirty – all tribe, I think."

Kurt grunted, showing no emotion. "Go around the perimeter and see if there is any sign of another tribe, or something else coming in or going out. Be on your guard."

Moema looked confused, and Kurt clarified. "Be careful."

The small Brazilian nodded and disappeared, just as John went to duck into the hut.

"Doctor." Carla bustled up to him and handed him a pair of rubber gloves. John nodded his thanks and pulled them on, then they both entered the hut.

Kurt looked at Matt, his mouth turned down. "So, everything gone – waste of fucking time." He sauntered back to talk to Max Steinberg, and Matt hung in the doorway with Megan at his shoulder. Matt saw her watch the big man walk away. He turned back to see the doctor and CDC scientist go to work.

The hut was a scene of human carnage, but Matt guessed that was largely due to the scavenging boar. There were two bodies, one larger than the other, with missing limbs, eyes and nose eaten away, and its abdomen torn open. The smaller one was primarily intact, save for the open torso – the softer entrails were always the first to be taken.

Matt winced. The smell was rancid-sweet and the buzz of large agitated jungle flies in the small humid space made him pull his damp handkerchief from his pocket and hold it over his nose and mouth.

In one corner – the only untouched part of the small hut – there were half a dozen soft-looking bags – skins that had been sewn into a balloon shape and then continually worked and treated until they looked soft and supple. Matt pointed to them. "Maybe something they ate or drank – weird-looking water bags. Maybe we should check the local streams for algae or some other type of contaminant."

Carla reached across to pick one up. It had rings of small stones sewn in around its edges and some type of carved bone stopper in the opening. She grunted softly, uncapped it, lifted it to her nose and waved it back and forth under her nostrils for a second or two. "Dry and odorless." She held it up.

"Strange decoration for a water bladder; not sure if it was for food or drink, but good workmanship. We can check their sources later." She dropped it back in the corner and turned back to the body.

"Heavens, I've never seen anything like it; look at this." John gestured over the adult's brow, and spoke softly to himself. "Prominent brow ridge, low vaulted cranium, receding chin … could this be a local genetic trait, a predilection for deformity?" He moved to the smaller figure. "It's the same – not as developed, but the same. If this is representative of the tribe, then these guys are not just primitive, they're primordial throwbacks."

"Let's not get ahead of ourselves, John. What can you tell me about the cause of death?" Carla said.

"Okay, right, it's just …" He bent over the larger body and gently prodded the skin with two fingers, then looked in the mouth and peeled back the eyelids, checking the soft tissue for discoloration. Meanwhile, Carla parted the thick black hair, peering at the scalp and leaning in close to look at the strands.

"Good; no dermal lifting, no sign of parasite infestation other than some local hair lice." She sat back and watched John lift the remains of the stump and prod the flesh of the armpit. He raised his eyebrows. "Swollen, and the skin is mottled." He pulled open the mouth again and then tugged on the facial cheek, making the lower lid droop. "Conjunctive eye, blue-gray spots in the mouth." He looked at Carla, but Matt spoke first.

"Measles."

Behind Matt, Megan snorted without humor. "That's been our gift to indigenous populations for over five hundred years."

Carla sat back on her haunches and nodded. "True. In 1592, two-thirds of the native population of Cuba was wiped out by an outbreak, one-fifth of Hawaii's population in 1850, and so on and so on. It still kills millions globally." She rubbed her forehead with the back of her arm.

"There are twenty-one different strains of the virus. Some are nothing more than a mild inconvenience to us." She turned to Matt. "Remember Jorghanson and his recessive measles strain? Not so recessive down here." She peeled off her gloves and stood up.

John did the same. "These bodies are probably still highly infectious. Probably not to us, but definitely to any other indigenous person who comes into contact with them, and maybe even to ..." He turned to look over his shoulder.

"Got it." Carla nodded toward their guide. "I've got some antiviral that I can give Moema as a preventative. But you're right, we should bury them."

Matt looked around at all the huts. "Moema said there were about thirty bodies – we'd need earthmoving equipment."

John threw his gloves into the hut. "Then burning it is. But ..." he winced as he spoke. "I'd really like to take a sample back."

"Sample?" Matt frowned. "Of the measles strain?"

John shook his head. "No, no ... a sample of the morphology – just a skull."

"Huh?" Matt pulled a face.

Carla waved her hand in John's direction. "I'd like to see the paperwork trying to get that back home ... especially given what we're currently dealing with. Forget it, John."

"This could be big. I don't even want to mention the word 'Neanderthal', but ..."

"But you just did. John, there are many physical traits that are extreme and influenced by nothing more than the environment. Take the Mbenga Pygmies of the Southern Congo. They're all waist-high to us, and their height has been attributed to low levels of ultraviolet light, leading to reduced vitamin D, which affects ...'"

John finished for her. "Bone growth."

Carla nodded. "Also, their soil is low in calcium – double whammy."

John shrugged. "There isn't always a simple explanation. After all, there's no such thing as a living archaeopteryx, right?" He gave her his best smile. "I'll scour it – no biological traces, just clean bone, I promise."

Carla half smiled and tilted her head. After a few seconds she nodded. "I love an optimist – especially one who turns out to be a head-hunter. I still say you'll never get it back into the States."

"Thanks." John turned back to the body.

"Professor Kearns!" Jian's shout came from the far end of the camp, and Matt and Megan jogged over to find the entomologist. They passed the last huts, went through a narrow passage in the vegetation, like a green corridor, and then entered another small clearing. This one was meticulously cleared of debris, and at its center stood three stone totem poles, each ten feet high and completely carved with raised glyphs. Matt had seen some like them in Jorghanson's sketchings. He knew his mouth was open, and he couldn't stop the smile from spreading across his face. The intricate detail was magnificent – even more so now that it was before him and not just in stylized, two-dimensional sketches.

"*Beautiful,*" he whispered. They were more art than language.

Megan nudged him. "I wish you'd show me that sort of adoration."

"Wow. *Wow.*" Matt ignored her, walking slowly around each column, occasionally stopping and fingering a particular raised pattern, symbol, or image. The carvings wrapped all the way around the poles, the story being told in a sort of spiral. Matt could see that each had pole been carved over a long period of time, as the glyphs closer to the bottom were encrusted in lichen and of a slightly different style to the ones at the top – the story, or message, started at the base and worked its way upward.

Kurt and Steinberg came up behind him. "So, not a complete loss after all."

Matt frowned and spoke without looking at the movie producer. "Depends on your perspective – they're all dead. So, I think a big bloody loss, for them at least."

Kurt snorted. "Yeah, caused by that asshole Jorghanson, I hear."

"That's enough, Kurt." Steinberg looked at Matt with a somber expression. "Of course you're right. We should be more respectful." He paused for a moment, then immediately brightened, flashing his golden grin. "Tell me you can decipher them."

* * * * *

Matt and Megan heaved the last body onto the pyre, throwing their gloves in after it. The group had made three large fires and added the bodies one at a time to ensure they were fully carbonized. In a matter of hours, the Ndege Watu would be nothing more than memories – the lost tribe now fully lost to the world.

Matt worked with lost races and language fragments, and knew that what he and other scholars could decipher from their work, no matter how imperfect the translation, would now be the only chance this strange and primitive native group would get to tell their story – to impart their knowledge, and tell them their secrets, their loves, fears, and legends.

What a waste. Matt remembered Carla's words about the disease being our gift to primitive tribes for centuries. *We might as well have just used a machine gun,* he thought glumly.

John was pounding a stake into the ground at the base of a tree. He then tied one of the tribe's skulls to the stake with a nylon cord, threading it through the empty eye sockets. He moved quickly, completing the job before Moema could see him at work on his grisly task. He finished by covering it with leaves, and some soil, and then stood to pull his gloves from his hands and stretch.

He noticed Matt watching him, and nodded toward the small mound. "The bugs will clean that down in a few days. Hopefully the larger animals won't be able to carry it off." He shrugged. "We'll see."

It was getting late, and Kurt was calling for camp to be set up around the totems, as this was the closest clearing that was dry, level, and away from the stinking ash of the burning bonfires.

Joop stood examining one of the bladders from the Ndege huts, his face drawn into a tight frown. He lifted it when he saw Matt approach.

"Strange. It's definitely animal, but I cannot identify it. Might be some sort of reptile, given the long cell structure, but ..." he shrugged.

Matt grunted. "Sleep on it – maybe you'll work it out?"

The jungle around them was strangely quiet – either the flames or the alien noises they made scared the local fauna away. Or perhaps it was a respectful silence for the passing of such a large number of forest souls. Lying in his tent, it took Matt hours to drift off to sleep, his mind haunted by images of coughing natives and the skinless scientist who had unwittingly delivered death to them. Beside him, Megan tossed and turned and murmured in her sleep, perhaps sharing the same nightmares.

The next morning was uncomfortable – muscles complained, mouths were dry and tasted of ash, and eyes felt gritty from lack of sleep. Breakfast was roasted local yams, and something Moema brought in from the jungle to cook. It could have been poultry, reptile, or even a type of meaty fungus. It didn't matter. That morning, food was nothing more than fuel, and most of them chewed and swallowed like automatons.

Matt finished eating and stood, stretching. He walked a few paces to the green corridor leading back into the camp and turned to see if Megan wanted to join him. His heart sank a little when he saw that Kurt had already taken his seat, and that the pair spoke animatedly. Jealousy burned a little and Matt turned away, walking the few dozen paces back into the open compound.

Small ghosts of smoke lifted from the center of the funeral pyres, which were now little more than oval scars of damp ash, like sores with silvery crusty scabs on the red earth. Matt stretched again and drew in a breath. It was odd – in amongst the odors of old roasting meat and damp ash, there remained an underlying hint of flowers, still strong despite the fact that there were few open blooms in the vicinity. Those plants that did feature large purple or green trumpet-like flowers were near odorless to him. He ignored it, putting the smell down to spoiling vegetation in the huts.

Jian and Carla passed him, already locked in conversation. Each of the team had been allocated tasks, but much of what happened with the expedition hinged on what Matt could find out from the Ndege Watu totem poles. He and Megan would pretty much spend the day seated before each of the poles, unraveling the words, sentiments, expressions, and general essence of the age-old artifacts.

At least, that's what he thought he and Megan would be doing.

Matt jumped slightly as Steinberg called his name too loudly. He came out from the green corridor with Kurt and Megan in tow. Matt noticed that the big bodyguard held a small brown satchel monogrammed with calligraphic initials. *PJ* – Pieter Jorghanson.

Steinberg held out his hand and Kurt handed the slim pack to his boss, who in turn passed it to Matt.

"Here, it's all the material we were given by Jorghanson. He, uh, departed before we could really talk to him about any of it in any detail. You might find something useful in there to speed up the translation."

Matt took the satchel. "Thanks." He flipped it open, noting the mini-discs, half a dozen small string-bound books, and a slim electronic tablet that played movie content. He looked up and nodded. "Okay."

Steinberg shrugged. "Well, you're part of the team now, so no secrets." He paused, hardening his gaze. "From anyone." He turned and sauntered off.

Kurt saluted Matt with one finger, gave Megan a winning smile, then followed his boss. For a minute Matt expected Megan to follow, but instead she came and put her arm around his shoulders.

"No pressure, champ?"

He moved out from under her arm. "You know how it is – it'll happen when it happens." He glared at Kurt's back for a moment. "So, you've joined the A-Team then?"

She ignored him and pointed to the satchel. "What else is in there?"

He watched her face for another moment, before deciding to shake off his petulant mood. "Let's see." There was no reason for him to carry on being surly – she was his girlfriend, but it wasn't like they had even talked about getting serious. Still, he felt he was somehow competing for her, and it burned him.

He sighed, opened the satchel again and began sorting through it, drawing forth several small leather books bound together with an elastic band. He opened the first.

"Trip diary." He began flicking through the pages, quickly passing over the early stages of the man's travels. He finished the first book and shuffled it to the back, then opened the next … and then the next.

"Okay, here we go. Jorghanson making contact with the Ndege." He went to the next book in the small stack. "Looks like language classes, day one." The ink drawings were of the totems, with Jorghanson's carefully handwritten notes beside them. It was obvious the man was struggling to understand the language, and their writing was totally beyond him.

"Hello … looks like he found his Rosetta Stone." There were detailed drawings and a description of one of the members of the tribe, a female, pointing to the symbols and mouthing specific glyph's meanings. There were long interpretations of the sounds and words – *ank-arg-okah*, *eban-kken*, *doo-arnoh-da* – the list went on. Matt spoke the words slowly.

"It's like a blend of a written form of ancient Olmec, but spoken with a different tongue – as if the images are being interpreted with an accent." He turned to Megan, who was frowning.

"Megs, imagine if we found an English manuscript from the 1500s, and struggled through reading it aloud – it'd sound damned different to how the original author meant it to sound half a millennium ago."

He shook his head. "It's not making sense." He started to flip through the pages of the notebook again. "Come on man, give me something."

Then he stopped, the frustration in his knitted brows easing, and a smile spread across his face. There it was, the key Matt was looking for. Jorghanson's drawings now had directional arrows showing how the woman would point at a symbol, image of a face or animal, and make the sounds for the glyph, and then move her hand across to the next pole –

not to the next symbol on the same pole. The key was which image was interpreted next – all the poles were to be read together. "Bingo – it's not what you read, but the order you read it in. They key is knowing how it fits together."

Matt couldn't help the admiration creeping into his voice. "Simple, but complex – one image by itself is like a letter … but read all together, they become something more."

He grabbed Megan's hand. "Let's go." They headed back to the smaller clearing, where the totem poles were. He slowed in front of the poles and walked along them, then came back to the center pole. Matt put the notebooks down and took a few steps back.

He snorted. "You almost had it, Professor Jorghanson. I bet he thought she was just showing him the images for his own education, trying to teach him their language. In fact, she was probably breaking all the tribe's taboos and actually reading it to him." Matt walked along the line of poles again, then pointed to one. "Here … I think it starts here."

Matt laid his hand on one of the symbols, then moved to the next pole to touch another, then on to another, his lips working silently as he pulled the meaning from the ancient patterns.

"'The Old Place', or 'the First Place' …uh, let's go with the Old Place. Okay, 'the Old Place where the giants live … should not be entered by …' something here that could refer to anyone who is not blessed or clean … maybe cleansed. Anyway, it goes on to say: 'Take not the unclean meat, lest the anger of the gods takes from you all that covers you.'" He turned to Megan. "All that covers you – could that mean your skin?"

Wow, Megan mouthed. "Just like Carla's bug."

Matt clapped his hands once. "I think this could be it, Megs."

"I'm getting Carla, she'll want to hear this." Megan took off.

"Wait, I haven't …" But he was too late. Sighing, he walked along the poles, reading as he went. "The Old Place … entering the Old Place, but from where? Where is this Old Place?"

Fronds and branches were beaten aside as Megan led a panting Carla into the clearing.

"You've got something?" Carla was sucking in breaths, even though she couldn't have come more than a few hundred feet. Matt guessed her excitement and anticipation were taking her breath away more than her lack of fitness.

"Maybe. I think so … I can read the totem poles – they mention angry gods taking your skin. They also mention an Old Place, where giants live."

"Promising. Are you sure?" Carla straightened as her breathing returned to normal.

Matt shrugged. "We'll never know if I'm right, will we? The authors, or at least the caretakers, of this language are all dead. So I'm all there is right now."

Carla tilted her head. "Okay, okay, professional pride aside, tell me what you've got. Where is this place?"

Matt looked back at the poles and shook his head. "Well, that's the million dollar question, isn't it? I don't know yet. I need to read more of the totems – front and back."

Carla nodded and looked around, as if searching for a place to sit.

Matt hunched his shoulders. "Might take a while."

Carla shrugged and sat down on a patch of thick grass. Steinberg and Karl pushed into the clearing.

"We just heard, well done. So, what can you tell me about the bird?" Steinberg slapped him on the shoulder, then stood with his hands on his hips. Jian and Joop joined them.

Matt looked hard at Megan. "It's a bit premature for high-fives just yet. All I've managed to decipher is something that might be about the infestation … or rather, its effects. It might not be related at all. It's going to take me a while, so I ..."

"We don't have a while, son. The wet season is right around the corner. Believe me, you do not want to be trapped here, or trying to hack your way back through this jungle, with a million gallons of water dumping on you every minute of every hour."

Kurt grunted and nodded, and then turned to Matt as though he was addressing a slow child. "Ever seen the giant Amazon leech?" He raised his eyebrows.

Jian grunted. "*Haementeria ghilianii* – I have; very big."

Kurt snorted, keeping his eyes on Matt. "I'll say it's very big. Very fucking big at eighteen inches ... and it just loves the wet season. And let's not forget about footrot to the ankles – makes athlete's foot look like a small blemish. You can actually lose toes." He turned and winked at Megan, who smiled and shook her head in a *shame on you, you big lug*, type of way, then turned to Matt, imploring, as if urging him to get with the program.

Matt raised his eyebrows. "Yeah, you know what? I think I have encountered a jungle leech before." He noticed Carla smirking.

Matt looked at the row of faces, all waiting on him. He exhaled slowly, feeling himself deflate. "Look, give me another few hours ... and give me some peace and quiet, okay?" Matt went to turn back to the poles as Megan shooing the others from the clearing. He half turned.

"Everyone."

Megan's mouth fell open and she stared at him for a moment before turning on her heel and storming back through the green fronds.

* * * * *

Matt sat cross-legged and stared up at the poles. His own notes were open beside him on the soft, fleshy grasses. He believed he had drawn some of the translation from the strange symbols, leering faces, and interlocking lines and dots, but it still refused to make any logical sense.

"I wish Professor Brenner was here," he said to one of the moss-covered faces. "Or Megan. Why did I kick her out?" He already knew the answer. *Because I'm a jealous asshole, that's why.*

He picked up his notes and examined the sketches he'd made. He had summarized the glyph-strings into three logical – as far as he could tell – story lines. The first referred to an Old Place that was "hidden" or "behind" something, and called the "blood jungle". *Sounds inviting*, he thought grimly. It was where the "teocuitl" was kept. Females or untested warriors were forbidden to enter. Only the special elders of the tribe were allowed there, to hunt.

The second story string told of water and people with what looked like two heads, swimming. Only one head was covered in hair. A depiction of their gods, maybe? There was also the sign for washing, or cleansing. Washing away the dirty water, or cleaning themselves before entering the water?

Matt pushed his damp hair back off his face, and exhaled through the side of his mouth. He looked at the final string of characters. It talked of the "land of giants" – represented by tiny human-like characters shown next to what were either tree trunks or the legs of huge beasts. Hmm, there were no elephants in South America … at least, not for about ten million years. He scratched his head and looked at the last few images. Flowers – that was all, just pictures of blooms.

He put down his notes and spread them out, like a pulled apart comic book, then leaned forward, resting his chin on his hands, and let his eyes move over them. As the sun rose high in the sky, Matt continued to simply sit and stare.

Occasionally he would rearrange the sketches, or stand to pace around the poles. Then he'd make more notes, and then pace again.

Eventually he slowed, and then stopped, freezing mid-step. To anyone watching he would have looked like a machine that had wound down. His gaze was directed at the ground, but his focus was nowhere near the clearing he was in. Matt's gaze had turned inward as he let his imagination take the images in intuitive leaps and bounds.

In a flash, his muscles unlocked and he darted back to the image of the men with two heads.

"Maybe." He started to grin and nod. "Just maybe."

He ran back to the huts.

* * * * *

Megan spun to face Matt as he rushed back into the small camp.

"Maybe." He darted past her, his enthusiasm pulling her after him, and also drawing Carla, Jian, and then the other members of their group.

He went quickly to his small pile of gear and retrieved the drinking bladder he'd found in the Ndege hut. He peered at the stopper, and then turned it over to examine the seals before facing the group, now assembled in a half circle behind him. He held it up.

"You know, I thought these might have been used for food or water. But the nozzle and stopper looked strange. I couldn't work out what it was actually for until I remembered a remote tribe up in the north-eastern tip of Papua New Guinea. Their village is on a natural lagoon that flushes out every tide, and deposits shellfish into a deep gutter at its edge. The young men dive down to the bottom to collect them ... they stay down for ages, and not just by holding their breath – they take another lungful of air with them." Matt held up the bag, and put the nozzle in his mouth.

Carla went to stop him. "Don't do that, remember the ..."

Matt shrugged. "I've had measles." He put the nozzle back in his mouth and blew – the bag inflated. He took it out, and the bag remained inflated. He nodded. "Yep, that's what I thought – it's not for water, it's for air ... just like the New Guineans." He held the bag up, now ball-shaped, and shook it. "This, ladies and gentlemen, is an aqualung."

He waited. Some faces were blank, some were creased in confusion or disbelief, but a few were smiling. *Of course.* He let the silence stretch for a few more seconds before continuing.

'I've translated what I can, and so far the totem scripts tell of the Ndege race that has lived here since the beginning time. According to the poles, they are the guardians of the teocuitl and something called the blood jungle." Matt swung the bag in his hand. "Somewhere, there is a river, lake, pool, or some body of water, where the Ndege dive down and pass through into their hidden sacred land." He looked at Steinberg. "Through to where your specimen came from."

"Teocuitl?" Megan tilted her head. "That name is familiar. That's early Incan, for ..." She trailed off, looking excited.

Matt nodded. "I think so. The language is a mish-mash of ancient South American flavors, spiced with some of their own inflections. The word looks the same, but I might be pronouncing or translating it incorrectly. Hell, I could be translating it all incorrectly."

"Teocuitl – gold?" Megan folded her arms.

Matt nodded. "More precisely, the Aztec word for excrement of the gods, but yeah, gold."

"Gold?" Kurt's eyebrows shot up.

Steinberg was grinning broadly and nodding his head. He looked like he was about to break into applause, and in fact he brought his hands together in a single clap. "Well done, my boy. So, all we need to do now is find it … ah, find the way in, I mean."

Matt nodded. "The way in, the way under, the way through …" He shrugged.

Steinberg turned to Kurt, his face becoming serious. "We set off tomorrow morning. Find me that water source."

CHAPTER 15

Dr. Francis Hewson watched the sealed dump trucks move single file toward the rear of the massive Atlanta CDC buildings. He swallowed, feeling his Adam's apple bob on his neck. It hurt from the dryness – nerves, he guessed.

The board had recalled him twelve hours ago – events had proved him right, and now valuable time had been lost. He looked again at the line of trucks – it wasn't just time that had been lost. He glanced at the rear of the building, where the professional façade gave way to more industrial architecture. Smoke stacks pushed out plumes of grayish smoke – there were no illusions about what this part of the complex did. The factory was designed for just this type of scenario.

Hundreds of bodies were being burned every day now. The public had been told it was due to lack of cemetery space, but this was only partly true.

The bodies were seized by teams in hazmat suits, zipped into airtight bags, and then quietly transported here, or to one of hundreds of new disposal facilities dotted across the country. The glossy black bags were unnamed, unloved, and simply tossed onto a conveyor belt to be fed into the heart of an industrial furnace, where they, and their millions of hungry passengers, were consumed in an instant.

Hew looked a little farther down the block, where another row of trucks was pulling out of a side exit, undoubtedly now empty.

"Off for the next pick-up, eh boys?" he muttered.

The double doors opened behind him, and the silent woman beckoned him in with a nod of her head. As he passed by, he leaned in close to her.

"I guess we're all staying silent now, aren't we?"

CHAPTER 16

Matt sat between Carla and Megan and watched as Kurt spread a green map out on the flattened dirt. Moema squatted beside the map and used a stick to point at different invisible landmarks. As far as Matt could tell, the map was almost useless. It showed endless lumpy green, and only the largest of rivers appeared as slim lines between towering tree canopies, woven together by millions of years of chasing the sunlight.

Megan nodded at them. "I suppose if anyone can find water, it'll be Kurt."

Matt groaned and rubbed his head. Carla looked at him momentarily, and then shrugged. "Doubt it; more like Moema."

Megan tilted her head. "Well, it's not home turf for either of them, so we'll see."

Carla nudged Matt, mischief in her eyes.

He grunted. His first instinct was to offer little more than a disinterested shrug. But then he decided he wasn't going to play the surly boyfriend just because of some teenage game Megan was playing with Kurt.

"Well, for what it's worth, I think the water, or the water entrance to this Blood Jungle or Old Place, or whatever it is, may be something like a sinkhole – a small pool of water only a dozen or so feet across."

"Maybe it's underground." Megan lifted her chin to try and see where Kurt and Moema were pointing on the map.

"Maybe. Anything is possible. I just get the feeling it's somewhere that is generally inaccessible. A tunnel behind a waterfall, a sunken cave, a river – it could be anything. Who knows, it might be something we can't even imagine." He got to his feet.

Megan and Carla followed him as he walked over to stand at the edge of the map.

"Anything interesting?" Matt asked.

"Nothing," said Moema.

"Maybe," said Kurt.

Matt glanced at Megan, who raised her eyebrows and smiled. He waited a few seconds for Kurt to continue – he didn't.

"Ah, any clues for us city folk, Kurt?"

"Not yet, leave it with me." Kurt didn't look up, continuing to stare at the impenetrable green map. Matt felt like they were being dismissed – fine with him.

Megan squatted. "Can I help?"

"Megs, I don't think ..."

"I don't know, can you?" Kurt gave her a boyish grin.

Matt stifled a groan and clamped his annoyance behind clenched teeth.

Carla leaned in close to him. "Easy, cowboy."

Megan frowned at the map. "You need to cross-reference this against the satellite images – have you got them?"

Kurt snorted, but with good-natured humor. "Sure, but they're worse than useless – nothing but green on green on green. Don't expect to pick up something clever like sun reflection, it just won't happen."

She smiled winningly. "Humor me, I've done my geography homework."

Kurt looked at her for a full ten seconds before he shrugged and turned to Matt.

"Can you get me my tech-pad, in the large pack?" Before Matt could snarl something back, he turned back to Megan. "It's not real time. The satellite is way out of range, but …"

Matt stomped away and managed to pull almost everything from the pack as he dug through it. At the bottom he found an unopened pack of Trojans. "Be prepared, huh?" Disgusted, he went to fling them out into the jungle, then paused. *That might be worse*, he thought. "Asshole." He pushed them back to the bottom, punched the packet once, and pulled the slim technology pad from its folder.

"Here you go." He flung it Frisbee-style to the big bodyguard.

"Careful." Kurt frowned as he caught the slim computer, and Megan scowled up at him.

Matt mouthed *what?*, then turned to watch as Kurt switched the device on and called up some data images. He tapped at some more keys and located a small red dot in a sea of endless green. "This is us, as of about twelve or so hours ago. We're still around the same area now."

"May I?" Megan took the small screen and then clicked one of the dropdown menus to see what options he had. "Okay, good."

She flicked over to 3D view and tilted the image, so they were looking at the landscape from slightly to one side.

"I knew it." She showed them the results.

Kurt's head blocked Matt and Carla's view, and they had to jostle to see what Megan had found. She pulled down the menu again, found the geographical contour lines, and added them to the image. Distorted blue lines appeared all over the green landscape. For the most part they were spread wide, indicating little change in the landform, but toward one section the lines started to bunch, just a few miles from the small red dot. She pulled the image back a few hundred miles.

Matt saw it. "Oh my God."

"Yep." She pulled back another few hundred miles, and there it was – the lines were forming gigantic contour rings.

"Impact crater." The land looked to be consistently flat up close, but in fact, there was a significant depression, and not all that gradual. The crater's wall formed a barrier, possibly only a hundred feet high and less than that across, before it fell away to the floor of the geological depression. The crater wall was steep, almost vertical on both sides – high, but potentially climbable.

Matt slapped his thigh. "Unbelievable. You are good."

She turned and grinned. "Not just a pretty face, huh?"

"What is it?" Kurt grabbed the pad and turned it around. "What am I looking at, some sort of hidden valley or something?"

"Bigger. Valleys are small – this thing looks to be twenty miles across, easy. But you're right about it being hidden." Matt pointed at the screen right under his nose. "That, sir, is a crater; possibly hundreds of millions of years old, and exactly what we are looking for."

Megan nudged Kurt in the ribs and took the small screen back, looking again at the display options. She found the thermal imaging, and started to check for variations. Sure enough, the temperature inside the crater was a few degrees cooler than outside. "Only a few degrees, but something in there is keeping it shielded. Could be a water source ... a big water source, like a lake."

"It's like a different landmass; an island within a continent, where the flora and fauna could be sealed off from the land out here – like some perfectly preserved game park." Matt zoomed in. "And I'd say that the nearest edge of the crater is about five miles ..." he turned and pointed, "... thatta way."

* * * * *

Matt had spent the last fifteen minutes updating Steinberg, and correlating their discovery to his recent translations. When he was finally able to break away from the producer, he wandered back to their small campsite. The group had been instructed to pack light, preparing to travel fast and minimally encumbered in search of the crater wall.

He didn't know why Steinberg couldn't have gotten the information from his trusted bodyguard, although Kurt had made himself scarce recently. Coming back, he saw Carla and Jian in conversation, close to where his and Megan's gear was stacked but not stowed away. He saw that Megan hadn't quite finished – distracted by some new wondrous thing, he guessed.

He looked around. "Hey Carla, where's Megan?"

Carla looked up briefly and shook her head. Jian did the same. Matt circled the small area to where John and Joop were sharing a joke with Moema. "Hey guys, have you seen Megan?"

Joop nodded. "Maybe ten minutes ago; she and … she, went to look at something in the jungle."

John wouldn't look him in the eye. Matt felt a funny fluttering of trepidation in his stomach. "Okay. Ah, which way did they go?"

He was greeted by silence. Matt saw that Carla had ambled closer, her hands in her back pockets. He turned to her. "Well, I'm assuming Kurt was with her … which way?"

Joop shook his head. Carla spoke. "Forget about it Matt; she'll be back in a minute or two. Get ready, we're leaving soon."

He swore softly, feeling his face go hot from embarrassment. He doubted they were just looking at something in the jungle, and he doubted anyone else thought that, either. He crossed to his pack, thinking through the dozen or so things he felt like doing to Kurt. Matt pulled the unnecessary items from his pack, lightening his load, and dropped them to the ground for later retrieval – this would be their secondary base camp.

It only took him a few minutes. He eyed Megan's chaotic mess. "You can do your own." He straightened and looked out at the jungle, suspicion growing with every passing second. He continued to mumble softly. "Nice one, taking my girl on a jungle date – think you're pretty hot shit down here, don't you?" He saw that Kurt's pack was neat, but open for a change – his mind whirled.

Matt looked over his shoulder at his fellow travelers and, seeing that they were absorbed in their own tasks, moved quickly to the big guide's pack. He dug down, deep, to where he had seen the pack of condoms.

He felt stupid, paranoid, and like a jealous teenager. His hand closed over the small box, and he immediately recoiled in shock. The new packet was now open.

He dropped the box as his heart sank, and he backed away, feeling an unfamiliar mix of humiliation and defeat.

* * * * *

Matt was by himself, back with the totems, when he heard Kurt and Megan come back into the Ndege compound. He looked back down at his notes, but couldn't concentrate, didn't see them. Instead, he saw his girlfriend in a hundred different acrobatic positions with Kurt. He felt ill.

He sighed. Forget about being chased by a Kraken beneath the Antarctic ice, or a giant missing link on the Black Mountain. This was different, this hurt in ways that went beyond the physical.

"Get, your pack. We're moving out soon."

Matt spun, and saw Kurt standing behind him with a toothy grin.

Matt just glared. Kurt waited a few seconds, and then jerked his thumb over his shoulder.

"Come on, Professor. Time to get physical. Come and help your future wife." He grinned again.

The sarcasm and suggestive tone were too much for Matt. "Why don't you just fuck right off, asshole?"

"What? Hey." Kurt pulled back. "What's up with you?"

Matt got to his feet, and before he knew it, found himself right up in Kurt's face. "Are you deaf as well as dumb, huh? I said fuck off, before I ..." Matt's anger, frustration, and humiliation took over. He threw a roundhouse punch that only managed to complete half its arc before the big man jerked sideways, moving way too fast for someone his size. Kurt's retaliatory punch hit Matt square on the jaw, and then the lights went out.

* * * * *

The party moved forward in a single file. The path they followed was heavily overgrown, although it was probably only a few days or week since the Ndege had stopped using it. The jungle's insatiable hunger for open ground was matched only by its tenacity, clinging to every thread of material or patch of bare skin.

The humidity crushed down on them, adding weight and years to their frames. After an hour, the track broadened briefly, and Megan caught up to Matt.

"That looks like it hurt."

Matt didn't try to respond – doing so would send a deep ache from his teeth to his ear.

"Hmm, a lot of deep thinking going on – everything okay?" She nudged him.

He kept his eyes on the ground as he walked, mumbling in return. He could feel her watching him as he continued to ignore her, feeling her gaze intensify. He glanced up briefly and saw that her smile had dropped away.

"So what's up?"

He spun around, the accusation on his lips, but he couldn't bring himself to speak the words – not now, not here. He knew that the last thing the group needed was a couple of kidults fighting over bruised egos – well, one bruised ego, anyway. He turned away, flinging words over his shoulder.

"Nothing." He sped up, leaving her behind, regretting it almost immediately.

He came up next to Moema, hoping to distract himself by practising his language skills, but the small man seemed agitated and on alert. His eyes were round and his shoulders hunched.

"Okay?"

"Okay?" Moema echoed, clearly not understanding his question.

"Sorry, I meant are you feeling okay? You look ... concerned."

Moema straightened. "I'm not scared."

Matt nodded and waited. Moema put his head down and walked on for a few seconds, then looked up at Matt and at the treetops hundreds of feet overhead. His eyes came back to Matt, the worry still visible. "Can you not feel it? Smell it?"

Matt inhaled deeply through his nose. Amongst the ever-present odors of the jungle, he could smell the pervasive sweetness he had detected back at the camp. He nodded.

"I can smell something sort of sweet. Do you know what it is?"

Moema shook his head. "I don't know, but it is getting stronger ... and I feel like the ghosts of the Ndege are with us." He gave Matt a crooked smile.

Matt just raised his eyebrows, knowing not to make light of the man's suspicions – or his superstitions. He knew

Moema was doing his best to put on a brave front, but he undoubtedly believed that the spirits of the dead tribe were walking with them. And in the Amazon's dark center, not all spirits had a reputation for being friendly.

Moema looked up at Matt again. "I don't think I am happy I came now." He put his head down, walking quickly and leaving Matt behind, clearly signaling that the conversation was over.

"Making friends again?" Megan and Carla were walking just behind him and had obviously been watching.

Matt spoke softly. "He's scared."

"Oh great ... of what?" Megan's voice carried a hint of sarcasm.

He still couldn't look at her. "Don't know. Maybe just his superstition, but one thing he's right about ... that damned smell is getting stronger."

"Thank God it's not just me. Phew. That is one cloying odor." Carla blew air out through her lips, as though to disperse the sickly-sweet smell.

"Well, I reckon we'll find out what it is soon – we must be getting close to it." Megan sniffed loudly.

"Sooner than you think ..." Matt stopped suddenly, causing the women to collide behind him.

The group fanned out. Kurt was standing off to one side with Steinberg looking around.

"That is some barrier." The path they had been following simply ended at a wall of thick, woody vines covered in crimson flowers. Every inch of the knotted canes was covered in thorns – some as large as a finger, some the size of hairs. They all looked sharp enough to pierce even the toughest clothing, let alone skin.

Matt leaned forward. "There's your smell ... the flowers. Any ideas?"

Carla leaned in closer, examining one of the formidable canes. "Never seen anything like it."

"Moema, have you seen this before?" Matt noticed that the guide had dropped back a pace or two.

Moema turned around slowly, his face pale. "No, I have never seen or heard of this plant anywhere in the jungle." He shrugged. "But I have never been this deep into the Gran Chaco before." He turned back to the vine wall. "It is as my grandfather said: the wall of thorns and the tiny fists of blood."

"It's so quiet." Megan looked around. "There aren't even any bugs."

"Strange." Jian joined them. "I noticed the same thing. No insects. The Amazon should have hundreds per square foot, but there's no sound and no movement."

"These flowers are beautiful. I'm going to name them ..." Megan reached out to grasp the neck of one of the open crimson blooms. "I christen thee ..."

Matt reached out. "Don't." In his haste, he bumped her.

"Ouch!" She jerked her hand back. "Thanks."

Megan turned her hand over and looked at her fingertips, where a dot of red welled up. "Those suckers are sharp."

"Sorry, I was trying to warn you. These plants look like they've developed some pretty powerful defenses."

"Well, no need to be so clumsy." She winced. "Yowch, still stings." She gripped the base of her fingers and squeezed.

Matt stepped back. "Maybe Kurt can suck the poison out for you."

"What? Oh, fuck you too." Megan shook her hand as if it was hot.

"No, looks like he's fucking *you* too."

Megan slapped his face, and then grimaced, holding her wrist as if her hand was broken – but not the one she had struck him with.

Jian whipped a magnifying glass from a pouch pocket and held it up to one of the canes. "Interesting, the thorns have become more erect, and directional – toward us – perhaps in response to our presence." He leaned in a little closer. "Not good – there is fluid being exuded at their tips. Professor Kearns, I think your comment about defenses is very accurate."

Megan started to shift from foot to foot. "Jeezus, I'll say it's not good." Megan held out her hand to take another look; her brow creased with concern. The fingertip was purple, and beneath the skin tendrils of red were working their way down to the second joint.

"What the hell is happening?"

Jian's hand hovered over hers, not touching the skin, just trying to keep her still. He looked through the lens, speaking calmly. "It's in the circulatory system and working its way along the veins. Any numbness?"

Megan grimaced. "I wish. It's fucking excruciating."

The group crowded around, and John pushed his way toward her and grabbed her wrist. He turned to them. "Give us space ... *now*."

Everyone took a step back. Jian kept his eyes on Megan, but spoke loudly. "Everyone stay back from the thorns, they're carrying some sort of defensive toxin."

John lifted her arm, which now looked like it was encased in a purple glove. "Keep this elevated." He crouched, opened his bag and pulled free a small pellet-like vial of clear fluid with a yellow plastic cap at one end. In his other hand was a pencil-like device, which he loaded the pellet into. He stood, grabbed Megan's arm again, and in one swift movement jabbed the device into her bicep, above the spreading redness.

"Antihistamine." When he pulled the pencil back, the tip of a needle could be seen at one end. He tossed it into his bag, and reached up to her face. She flinched.

"Keep still." John grabbed her head and, using one thumb, pushed one eyelid back, and then the other. "Any tightness across the chest?"

Megan's lips moved, but nothing came. She staggered. John held her as her eyes rolled back into her head and she fell onto his chest.

"Megs!" Matt rushed in to support her.

"Lie her down." Matt eased her down, pushing Kurt back as he rushed in to help. "I got this."

John got down on one knee beside her. "Just give us some air here, Kurt." He looked at Matt. "She's in shock. That's one powerful and fast-acting toxin."

He felt her pulse. "Going like a train." Her arm was now red to the shoulder. "It's moving too fast. Can't let this get to her heart, or it …" He frowned as he counted her pulse.

Megan started to buck, and froth appeared at the corners of her mouth. "Hold her down!" Matt and John leaned on her as she jumped and bucked for several seconds, then stiffened like a plank of wood, then fell quiet. John quickly leaned forward and listened to her chest.

"Goddammit, her heart's stopped!"

"It what … it what?" Matt felt himself begin to panic.

The doctor ignored him and spun to his bag. He rummaged furiously for a few seconds and emerged with a long hypodermic needle. He held it between his teeth as he ripped open her shirt, then grabbed the syringe and banged it into her sternum with a thump.

He dropped it immediately, placed both hands on her chest, and started to pump.

Matt held Megan's hand, talking softly but urgently to her, coaxing her, pleading with her. He felt how dry the small hand had become.

John counted to three, pumping as he went. He counted again.

Matt squeezed her hand. "Come on Megs, don't do this. Come on."

Steinberg leaned in over them. "Is she dead?"

"Oh, fuck off." Carla shoved him away.

John cupped her mouth, leaned forward, and blew air into her lungs. Megan coughed. He pulled her up.

"Water." He held out his hand and someone put a bottle into it.

Megan gasped, then sipped at the bottle being held to her lips. She lifted one hand to her chest.

"I hurt ... all over."

"Sorry, my dear, CPR bruises ... but it saves lives." John lifted her hand – the angry purple was still under her skin, but the red tendrils had stopped growing up her arm.

"Hmm, interesting toxins. Could be like the Spanish Mala Mujar, or even the cholla cactus. That monster literally throws its spines at you."

Carla kneeled down and examined the fading stain on Megan's arm. "What do you think – some sort of cytotoxin?"

John shrugged. "Volatile oils, resins, alkaloids, glycosides – take your pick, any or all – can't tell out here."

Matt cradled Megan's head and helped her sip some more water. She turned slowly toward the doctor, still groggy. "Thank you."

John nodded, almost bowing. "My pleasure."

Megan started to get to her feet, Matt under one arm, Kurt suddenly under the other.

Jian tilted his head toward the wall of thorns. "I think climbing the wall is not such a good idea."

* * * * *

Steinberg and Kurt wandered farther along the base of the thorn wall. Steinberg clasped his hands behind his back and looked up at the colossal barrier.

"Thought it was too easy." He turned to his bodyguard. "Could we burn it?"

Kurt's mouth turned down and he shook his head. "Too wet. Also, fire might not destroy the spikes, but just harden them."

Steinberg grunted and looked skyward to the tree canopy hundreds of feet overhead. "Couldn't get a chopper in here even if we wanted to."

"They wouldn't even see us," Kurt said.

"Kurt, bring me all the spare batteries. I'm going to try something." Steinberg spun on his heel.

* * * * *

The heat was oppressive, and it was only late morning. By the afternoon, it would be like a steam bath, and there were no showers to wash away the grime and grit. Already Matt could feel pimples coming up along his jawline. He pushed his long hair back off his forehead – for the first time in years, he wished he had a crew cut.

He sat with the group around the edges of a small clearing they had made by flattening out the soft grasses and fronds. Their clothing was dripping wet, but they had mostly stripped down to the minimum; the lack of insects meant they could safely remove clothing without applying an odious coat of tropical-strength insect repellent. Even Megan sat in just her bra and shorts, her arm still discolored from her encounter with the stinging vine.

The odor of the blooms was ever-present, filling their nostrils and invading their consciousness. They simply sat and absorbed it, rested, and waited.

Steinberg entered the clearing and waited at its edge until Kurt joined him. They spoke briefly, then the big bodyguard came to the edge of the group and planted his legs.

"Well, it's pretty obvious that we can't climb the wall." He paused, looking at each of them. "We can't cut it away, burn it, or pull it free. We can't get a chopper to drop us over the edge – we think the thorn wall might extend up into the canopy over the crater, meaning we'd be dropped right friggin' into it."

Matt stood, interrupting the theatrical delivery. "So, the bleeding obvious – we're back to where we started. We need to find the water."

Almost disagreeably, Kurt nodded. "Yeah. If that's how the Ndege went in, then that's how we have to follow."

Just behind him, Steinberg fiddled with a small silver box with extra power cells bound to it. He looked up. "About two hours."

Kurt turned and nodded his acknowledgment. "If the natives used the water to pass through the vines, and maybe under or through the barrier wall, then it has to be close – this is where the trail led us. So we have two options – left or right. We break into two scouting teams – myself, Joop, and Jian on one, Matt, Carla, and Moema on the other.'

Megan got to her feet, but Kurt shook his head. "Sorry Megan, you rest. Dr. Mordell's orders."

John nodded gravely. "And I get to keep you company."

Kurt looked at his watch. "We'll travel an hour out, and then turn back. If we don't find anything the first time, we'll take a late lunch, then set out in the afternoon for a longer search."

John cleared his throat. "Obviously, you need to stay well back from the thorn barrier. It might also be a good idea to keep a keen eye as you travel, in the event that it extends into the jungle. It nearly killed Ms. Hannaford with a single spike. Multiple punctures with more of the toxin introduced into the system would undoubtedly be fatal."

No one spoke; no response was needed.

They packed in silence – just some water, and a single-dose shot of both adrenalin and antihistamine in the event of a spiking. *Not much of an armory*, thought Matt.

Kurt took the left path; Matt and his team went right. They hacked a new trail at least ten feet farther back from the wall. Matt started out with the blade, but knew that in a few minutes he'd have to hand it over to Carla, who quickly surrendered the blade to the wiry little native. Though Moema was of smaller stature than even Carla, his strength and stamina surpassed the combined efforts of the other two.

They worked together like a machine. Matt would hack a central hole through the growth of about six feet. Carla would step through it, chopping away the vines and fronds at ground level, and then Moema would take over to blister through about twenty more feet.

Progress was slow – about a foot every one to two minutes – and it wasn't long before Matt held up his hand, breathing like bellows, face burning from exertion, and shook his head. "I'm beat. I need a break."

They sat together on the trail they'd made, leaning back against the thick greenery. It was like being in a green cave; silent, except for their breathing or the occasional drip of sap from some severed plant stalk. Matt sipped water, and spoke with his eyes closed.

"How long have we been going?"

Carla looked at her watch. "Forty-five minutes, give or take. We've got to head back in fifteen."

Matt sat forward, his head down, just in time to watch a huge drop of perspiration fall from the tip of his nose.

"How far did we get – a mile?"

Carla snorted. "Maybe a hundred feet. I'm thinking unless Kurt found something, we'll be back out again this afternoon."

Matt groaned, feeling the ache across his chopping arm and shoulder.

Moema got to his feet. "It's not a problem for me; I will take over."

Matt shook his head. "No, no, I'll be okay. Just give me another minute." He looked up and grinned. "And Carla is just getting her second wind."

Carla held up her arm, flexing her muscles, then lay down on the slashed grasses and fronds.

Matt laughed softly. "Maybe another couple of minutes." Carla gave him the thumbs up. He sat watching her for a second or two, thinking it had been a while since he saw her try to make contact back home.

"Any luck getting through to the office?"

It was Carla's turn to groan as she pulled herself up into a sitting position. She lifted her canteen and sipped.

"No, still getting a lot of static. I've been thinking about that. When I started out doing fieldwork with the CDC we did a job assisting with a cholera outbreak in a small place called Vredefort, in South Africa. The whole town was inside a massive two-billion-year-old impact crater. Even after that amount of time, the rocks were still magnetic – the asteroid had a huge iron content. It even caused our watches to run slow." She turned to him. "So, if this is a crater, then maybe it's the same deal."

Matt nodded. "Makes sense. We need a stronger signal then. I saw Steinberg has a Zubion940 – a bit more grunt there."

"Yeah, right. I reckon he'd rather see me inside another giant snake than help. Things will be fine back home. My colleague, Francis Hewson, is one of my best – he'll keep things under control." She looked down at the ground for a moment. "But I reckon he'll be hoping we come back with some answers." Her face became serious. "Or we may not come back to the same place we left."

She looked up at him, and seemed to think about what she had just said. "Yep, he'll keep it under control."

She brightened. "So, speaking of being under control ... are you?"

"Huh, under control, me?" He turned to her, confused.

"I mean, everything okay ... with you, and, you know?"

"Megan? Oh, sure." After a minute, he shrugged. "We're not married, you know."

"Of course not – modern woman, huh?"

"Maybe. Look, Carla, she's free to do what she wants. We're good friends, and ..."

"Well, when she was hurt, you looked like you were about to have a breakdown. You might be doing your best to fool yourself, but it won't work on me. Just good friends? Pah." She smiled knowingly. "Give her time, and just relax a bit, okay?"

"She's not really my girl, she's ..." He let his words trail off, then simply nodded.

Moema, who had been sitting to one side, patiently waiting for them to recover their energy, got to his feet and rolled his shoulders. "Bit more cutting now?"

"Yep, good to go." Matt got slowly to his feet and held out a hand to Carla. She got up just as slowly, and he stretched, feeling the tightness across his back and neck. If they came out again this afternoon, he reckoned he'd be bedridden tomorrow. *Bedridden*, he thought, and almost laughed. What bed?

Moema started to slash away at the green wall at the end of the tunnel they had carved out of the green tangle. Sap flew into the air, causing Carla and Matt to stand well back. Matt sucked in a deep breath; he'd take over again in another minute. He turned briefly to look back along the way they'd come, and sighed with relief; at least it'd be a quick trip back.

* * * * *

The return trip was as easy as they expected, and in just a few minutes they were back at their entry point. Megan sat cross-legged with John, but got to her feet when she saw Matt. She smiled, and seemed about to go to him, when the look on his face stopped her. She turned to Carla instead.

"Anything interesting?"

"Nothing but sore muscles." Carla rubbed her arm.

John stood and took her hand, guiding her to a mound of vegetation he had fashioned into a soft seat. She smiled her thanks and sat down, exhaling long and slow. He bowed in return.

Moema and Matt stood, dripping perspiration, in silence. Matt could feel Megan's eyes on him. He nodded at her.

"How's the arm?"

"Arm? My arm's okay." She waited, still watching him.

"Good ... good." He could feel Carla watching him, and felt like a jerk, but he wasn't ready to give up just yet. *Ego is a dirty word*, as the Skyhooks once sang. The awkward silence stretched on.

Suddenly they heard something crashing through the jungle toward them. Matt spun around.

"Someone is coming – fast." Moema pointed to the other green tunnel, which Kurt and his team had opened.

The big bodyguard slowed as he came down the path he had created. When he got to the clearing he stopped and bent over, hands on knees and blowing hard. He looked up, grinning.

"We found it."

* * * * *

Following Kurt's broad back, they stepped out into a clearing roughly fifty feet across. At its center was a black pool of water, still as glass. It was an almost perfect circle, tree roots snaking into its depths, shaded above by the impenetrable green canopy.

"Looks deep." Megan flipped a small white stone into its center. The stone shimmered for a few seconds as it dropped, becoming indistinct and then disappearing from view.

Kurt knelt and flipped open his backpack. He fished around for a second or two and retrieved a glow stick. He bent it in the middle until it made a cracking sound and began to glow a brilliant yellow-green. He threw it in after Megan's stone. It sank – five, ten, twenty feet, then became a glowing dot, which also faded away.

Kurt grunted. "Looks deep because it is deep. I think it's a sinkhole – got to be a cave somewhere down there."

"Great, a cave, and full of water, too." Matt felt his stomach lurch. He'd had experiences with caves he'd rather forget. Things lived in caves – big things. He was several feet back from the edge, but he leaned forward carefully, as if his toes were on the rim, and stared down into the blackness. In the heat and humidity of the jungle, the cool water should have been tempting, but black water, silent and deathly still, conjured up images of something lurking below. Unseen, but watching – waiting for them to step in.

"Smells funny." Megan bent down, her nose almost to the water. "Hard to detect, being so close to the thorn wall, but it smells like a cross between rosewater and iodine." She reached forward.

"Stop." Megan froze, cringing at the sudden command. In the quiet space, devoid of the normal jungle noises and enclosed by towering trees and fern fronds, the sudden sound made everyone stare at Carla.

"Just wait. The water does look tainted; it could be the flowers, or the thorns and their poison that's permeating it. Could be as toxic as battery acid. We need to do tests."

Steinberg's face screwed up tight. "Oh bullshit, Ms. Nero. We already know the Ndege used to dive into it." He turned to his bodyguard. "Kurt, drink some."

Kurt's eyes went wide and his mouth fell open as he turned to the movie producer in horror. Steinberg nodded firmly, and then motioned to the water.

Carla shook her head. "We know the Ndege dove into water, but not if they dove into this water."

"Oh for God's sake, there's freakin' tree roots in it. Kurt ..." He jerked a thumb at the water.

Grumbling, the big man stepped forward and got down on one knee, staring into the depths.

"Don't, Kurt ... please." Megan shook her head, and mouthed *don't* again when he looked up at her.

Matt snorted. "Freedom of choice – let him." He felt Carla's glare burning the side of his face.

Kurt grinned and winked at Megan, then stabbed a hand into the watery depths. He frowned, and fished around just below the surface for a few seconds, before slowly pulling his hand out.

"This gets better and better." He held up a small object – gold. Megan rushed over, followed by Jian and Joop, while Matt and Carla waited on the other side of the pond.

Steinberg, the shortest, was crowded out at the rear. He raised his voice. "Let me see that." Kurt hesitated for a second or two before tossing the object to his boss.

Steinberg snorted in appreciation. "Looks old – an alligator maybe."

Curiosity got the better of Matt and he wandered over, staring hard at the item. It was certainly a piece of gold, thumb-sized, and only slightly crusted with minerals. It had a long, dragon-like face, round eyes and a tongue lolling in the typical ancient Indian style.

"Alligator? No ... something much more fearsome than that. I think it's Quetzalcoatl, the feathered serpent god." Matt held out his hand to the movie producer. "May I?"

Steinberg tossed it to him, and Matt grabbed it and held it close to his face, examining the fine detail.

"Beautiful. This little guy has been around for about two and a half thousand years. Both the Incas and Aztecs had a similar deity. Quetzalcoatl was a feathered serpent, a flying reptile, even a dragon, and was the symbol of death and resurrection." He looked across to Carla.

"He traveled to Mictlan, the underworld, and created a world, our world, from the bones of the previous races, using his own blood … and skin."

Carla nodded her understanding, and Matt tossed the small idol back to Steinberg.

"Feathered serpent, you say? Funny, that's sort of what we're looking for." Steinberg threw it back to Kurt. "Keep it."

Matt saw that Moema was frowning so deeply that his brow was nearly touching the bridge of his nose. He looked like he was about to challenge Steinberg's gift-giving, and Matt thought he'd better try to intervene first.

"Um, Mr. Steinberg, that object could be part of the missing treasure of the Incas. You can't give it away. It belongs to the people here."

Steinberg's eyebrows lifted. "Missing treasure?"

"Well, yeah. Legend has it that after the fall of Vilcabamba – the last hidden city of the Incan empire – the ruler at that time, Atahualpa, ordered his people to carry the last treasures of his empire off into the jungle so that the Gold-Eaters – the Incan name for the Spanish invaders – could never feast on their wealth. They've never been found."

Steinberg looked engrossed as he listened, and soon smiled. He turned to Kurt and nodded.

Matt suddenly realized that mentioning treasure in his attempt to appeal to the man's altruism was probably the wrong tack to take. *Wonder if it's too late to mention a curse,* he thought, glancing briefly at Moema, whose teeth ground behind his cheeks. His frown deepened when Kurt polished the small idol on his chest, grinned, and stuck it in his pocket.

"By the way, the water's fine." He sniffed his fingers and shrugged.

Carla was scooping some into a couple of small vials. She shook one and lifted it to stare intently at the swirling residue, then tucked them both into her kit.

"So, what now? The breathing bags?" Matt pulled one of the Ndege's skin bags from his backpack and let it unfurl.

Steinberg looked up from the small silver device he was tapping away on, shaking it. "Piece of shit." He pressed a few more buttons, then smiled at Matt.

"Be my guest, Professor Kearns. But I'm not keen to place my lips over something that's probably crawling with some type of disgusting disease."

"It was measles, and we're all safe. I only brought one." He tossed it to Kurt. "Probably your man's job to be first."

Kurt looked at it with disdain, then his eyes lifted to Matt. "Me? Dive in there, with a bloody giant animal's testicle sticking out of my mouth? Don't make me laugh." He turned to Steinberg. "Boss?"

Steinberg looked quickly at the small silver box he held. "A lot of distortion now, but in five minutes, put a flare up." He looked up at the dense canopy. "Maybe a few, just to be sure."

Carla shook her head. "It'll never make it."

Kurt lifted a flat metal case from his pack just as the electronic device pinged in Steinberg's hand. He nodded to Kurt.

Kurt opened the case, which contained a stubby revolver and half a dozen fat, copper-jacketed shells. He loaded a plug into the flare gun, and stuffed the rest in his pocket, then looked up, firing at the spot where the branches appeared to be thinnest.

The flare sped away, rising over a hundred feet, before striking the thick branches overhead. It pinballed around for a few seconds before exploding in a burst of orange light underneath the canopy. Matt and the group were brilliantly lit up in the semi-gloom as it fell back to earth.

Kurt wasn't put off. His expression grim, he mechanically reloaded and fired, reloaded and fired, and then again twice more. Two of the four shots managed to punch through the dense canopy and disappeared from sight. Almost immediately, there was an answering series of pings on Steinberg's communicator.

"Take cover folks, we got incoming."

They hugged trees, just as a tea chest-sized box crashed through the leaves hundreds of feet overhead, and thundered off huge branches on its way to the ground. Matt marveled at their aim – a few dozen feet to the west and it'd be on the thorn wall.

A second or two later, the box pounded into the thick underbrush. It didn't explode, but Matt could feel the dull thump beneath his feet as it hit the soft, loamy soil. Kurt charged off, and everyone else followed.

Matt nodded with admiration. "Good aim – the pilot, I mean."

Steinberg shrugged. "The chopper was having trouble getting a fix – magnetic distortion everywhere – so I had them drop half a dozen. Fucked if I know where the rest ended up."

Kurt and Joop dragged the box back to the edge of the pond, and the bodyguard took his longest knife from its scabbard and hacked at the rope. Matt recognized it from his time in Antarctica; it was caving rope, strong and elasticized – perfect for binding a box that would be dropped from several hundred feet.

Kurt threw the ropes to one side, flipped the catches up and lifted the box open. Matt, like the rest, crowded in, curiosity overcoming his antipathy toward Kurt.

Inside, there was a top layer with foam packing material cut into perfect shapes for the cargo. Eight strange-looking helmets nestled in custom-made compartments. Matt leaned forward – full face masks, with a small canister set on the side of the Perspex faceplate – individual breathers. Kurt lifted one free, and touched a small stud on the side. Immediately, a bright light came from a coin-sized LED bulb embedded on the brow ridge. He threw one to Matt.

"This one can be yours … if you can pull yourself away from the thought of wrapping your lips around that big ball bag." He winked.

Matt felt his face go hot, but he ignored the barb, and instead studied the helmet. Steinberg clapped his hands.

"Good. Light lunch first, and a rest – and then we explore."

* * * * *

Matt sat with Megan and ate some of the dried mystery meat, along with some local vegetables that Moema had found. There was awkwardness between them now.

"How's the hand … and finger?"

She lifted her wrapped hand and looked at for a second before carefully unwinding the bandage. Matt could see that most of the redness was gone, but there was a small, crusted black hole at the tip of her finger, where the thorn had pricked her. The skin looked dead.

"*Yecch.*" She flexed her fingers, examining the wound. "Not nice. Imagine falling into those thorns – even if you survived, which is unlikely, you'd look like a walking pincushion."

He nodded. "I bet the Ndege knew about those thorns, and I bet they also had some sort of remedy for the poison. We lost a lot when they were wiped out."

She looked toward the massive wall covered in thorns. "And I bet they knew exactly what's behind that crater wall."

He picked up a small round pebble and tossed it into the dark pool. "What else could they have told us, and shown us?" He sighed. "Passed into history, extinct – and probably only weeks before we got here. It's a damned shame."

"Yeah, that's what usually happens when one advanced culture meets another that's less advanced – one ends up losing everything. It was obviously why Atahualpa hid his gold from the Spanish." She gave him a crooked smile, then reached out to take his hand and squeeze it. "Nothing you could have done."

He smiled back, and took his hand back. Her smile dropped. She looked down at her hand and squeezed her finger. A small drop of clear fluid appeared in the crusted hole.

"Hmm." Megan rewrapped her hand. "Hope it's okay to get this thing wet."

"What? No way – forget the finger, you just suffered a heart attack and had a needle jammed into your chest. You are not going deep-sea diving. Forget it."

"Diving in a pond, you mean." Megan's eyes narrowed. "So now you care?"

Carla, who had been resting nearby, groaned and wandered over to where the doctor was chatting with Joop.

Matt watched her go, then turned to shake his head. "Megan, even forgetting about the possible dangers we might encounter, if it's a deep dive, the pressure alone will stress your circulatory system."

Matt looked over at the doctor, trying to get John's attention.

"Hey!" Megan grabbed his arm and wrenched him around to look at her. "I don't know what the hell's the matter with you lately, but don't you fucking dare try and stop me. I'm going."

Matt spluttered, seeing the volcanic glare and the determination on her face. "I'm only—"

"You're only acting like a prick. Who are you?" She got to her feet.

"Wait." He brought his hands together in a praying motion, almost begging her. "At least not on the reconnaissance dive this afternoon. That way, we can judge the depth. Let's at least find out what we're in for."

She ground her teeth, and he reached out to touch her leg. She stepped back.

"We'll see."

* * * * *

Matt was fairly fit, and a good swimmer, and since he had discovered the relationship between the bird and the water, Steinberg had designated him Kurt's dive buddy for the first swim. By then it was about three in the afternoon, and already the sun was dipping a little in the west.

Steinberg had only just returned to the group after swearing loudly at his phone for a while. It seemed that something, either electronic or human, wasn't obeying his instructions.

The semi-gloom around the pool was stickily oppressive, but Matt still couldn't find the enthusiasm to step into the cool water. By now he and Kurt had stripped to their shorts. Matt was fit and in decent shape, but Kurt's shoulders bulged with power and were crisscrossed with old scars, testimony to numerous adventures – or maybe a taste for S&M. He glanced at Megan and winced, shaking the thought from his head.

Kurt looped his belt around his waist, and paused to lift his huge hunting knife from its scabbard. He pulled a condom from his pocket, opened the seal, and rolled it down over the handle. He noticed Matt looking at him.

"Old jungle trick – keeps the pommel and its contents dry."

Matt felt his face go hot. He looked at Megan and caught her watching him, but she turned away before he could smile. *I'm an asshole*, he thought.

"Just a quick reconnoiter. If there's a way through, check if it's negotiable, and then return. Capiche?" instructed Steinberg.

"Ottenuto," Matt played along with Steinberg's kitchen Italian. Steinberg just looked blank.

Ropes were wound around their waists and Kurt put the facemask on his head, pushed up on his forehead. He looked across to Matt, all business now.

"Ready?"

Matt nodded and the big bodyguard held out his fist for he and Matt to knock knuckles. Matt recriprocated, the shared danger overriding any residual coolness between them. They stepped into the pool at the same time.

It was cool. Matt knew it was probably about seventy-five degrees – it was just that it felt cooler, given the sultry ambient atmosphere out of the water. He waded in farther, to his knees, then his waist, then stopped and looked down. The rock platform at the edge suddenly fell away into nothing. He felt his stomach lurch at the thought of something down there, staring up at him. His mind played tricks, creating shadows within shadows; monstrous tentacles moving in the depths, eager to clutch at him, to squeeze the breath from his body, and rip the flesh from his bones. This was made worse by the knowledge that beasts like that really existed.

They're not here, they're not here, he repeated silently. Matt shuddered, then shook his head quickly to throw off the disturbing thoughts. He looked across to Kurt and nodded, then took a deep breath before pulling his mask down, fiddling with the breathing canister, and switching on the small light. He could feel his heart racing as he sucked in fast breaths, wasting his oxygen.

"Professor Kearns."

Matt stepped back, momentarily alarmed.

Joop waved. "Don't forget to repressurize your ears if you go deep." He made a show of pinching his nose and blowing his cheeks. Matt nodded and mouthed, *thank you.* He stared into the dark water, feeling his nerves tighten.

"Good luck." It was Megan. He looked around and she smiled at him ... just him. She threw him a kiss with her bandaged hand.

Thank God that was meant for me, he thought. She calmed him. Kurt leaned forward into the water and glided out to the center, seemingly oblivious to any danger. He floated on his back, waiting for Matt.

Matt allowed himself to fall forward into the water. He kept his face down, allowing his light to penetrate the depths. His breathing was loud in his ears as he hovered over the bottomless void. He could see he was at the center of a huge stone column that fell away into a nothingness that his ineffective light did nothing to penetrate.

Minute particles drifted across the beam of light, but except for a slight reddish tint to the water, it was extremely clear. The small motes floated past and then down. As he concentrated, Matt saw that they were being tugged toward one side of the column. He lifted his head and paddled to Kurt.

"There's a current ... deeper down."

Kurt gave him a thumbs up, and then dove.

Neither of them had swim fins. Matt had to swim hard to keep up with the bigger man, and to fight against the buoyancy that continually threatened to drag him back to the surface.

As they got deeper, the dim light from above quickly disappeared. When they were only a dozen feet below the surface, Matt looked back up to see a mirrory mirage view of his companions at the edge of the water. The bottom was still well out of sight, and he kicked on to catch up with Kurt.

Matt swam toward the rock wall, preferring its partial protection to hovering over the bottomless black pit. He floated for a moment, trying to slow his breathing, and realized he had been unconsciously holding his breath.

He was torn. Part of him, the cognitive thinking part, wanted to know what was down there. Sinkholes were like time capsules. Anything that fell or was thrown in lay undisturbed on the bottom for thousands, maybe even hundreds of thousands of years. There could be all sorts of interesting archeological relics just out of sight. But the more primitive part of his brain rang loud with warnings about what else could be down there. A crawling sensation traveled up his spine.

He followed the rock wall down, running his hand along its sides. It was strange. Some parts of the wall looked hewn, with extraordinary flat surfaces – far too perfect to be naturally occurring geology.

He slowed his descent. The flat surface started to show definite chisel marks, which became recognizable shapes – writing.

With the Ndege gone, Matt could only guess at how the writing had been formed – either underwater or when the level was somewhat lower. He drifted back a few feet to take in more of the message – absorbing the glyphs, images, and impressions. The ancient language was complex, and took skill and patience to unravel.

"Let not ... the unclean ... pass back to the land of man." As Matt tested those words against a few other possible translations, he saw that Kurt's light had disappeared. In a panic he kicked himself downward, following Kurt's rope into the gloom.

The blackness made Matt feel claustrophobic. He could have been at the bottom of the deepest ocean trench, so complete was the darkness. The small pipe of light from his mask did little to dispel the eerie nothingness surrounding him. His rational mind knew he was no more than twenty-five feet below the surface ... the problem was, his imagination was trying to stop him from believing it.

He continued along Kurt's rope, pausing to repressurize his ears before swimming on. At about thirty feet he was feeling the pressure of the dive, and his muscles were becoming fatigued from the strain of swimming and keeping his body below the water. Kurt's rope veered toward the wall and snaked its way into a huge horizontal hole in the column, heading under the massive crater wall. Matt paused for a second or two, sucked in a huge lungful of compressed air, and then followed.

He pulled himself along Kurt's rope, not caring now if he was causing additional drag on the tether. He was over it. The oppressive darkness was making him feel tiny, alone, and extremely vulnerable. Kurt and his rope were the only links to his own world.

Suddenly the rope went taut, and then slack in his hands. Matt's eyes widened as he realized that Steinberg's bodyguard had somehow become untethered. Matt had a moment of indecision, wondering whether he should continue, when he realized that he could see something farther along the tunnel... without using his light. There was a tongue of green up ahead. He swam on.

In a few seconds, he saw a shimmering disk above him as he rose to the surface. His head broke through into another humid landscape, Kurt's rope dangling uselessly in his hands.

Large hands grabbed him under the shoulders and lifted him free. Kurt plonked him on the ground and then stood back and waved his arms in a theatrical arc.

"Welcome to paradise."

EPISODE 2: PARADISE – a world within a world

CHAPTER 17

Megan pushed her wet hair off her face and turned to the green walls of the strange jungle. "We're through the looking glass." She straightened. "It's so … different."

Matt sat with Carla, Joop, and Jian just a few feet away, drying off. He paused to look around again. "Different" didn't begin to describe how dramatically the vegetation had changed from one side of the crater wall to the other.

Before them were all manner of ferns and fronds – fat bromeliad, gingko, and unidentifiable trees, nightmarish twisted shapes covered in bark that was like dark scales, or damp hair. Other trees, if that's what they could be called, were rod-straight, and rose hundreds of feet in the air. They were like dark columns without branches until they reached an umbrella of ferns at their very tip. Most were draped in dangling vines, many with pendulous fruits or huge seed pods, and red-veined leaves as wide as a handspan.

Megan turned to grin at Matt. "It's beautiful."

Matt stood up for a better look. At ground level there were fern fronds, both broad and fleshy tongues and rapier-like straps. Sliding over them was an almost transparent cotton candy mist, just touching their tips.

He turned slowly. The huge wall behind them continued in both directions, an enormous barrier that disappeared into a distance that Matt already knew stretched for over twenty miles. On the crater basin wall, it was hard to tell where the cliffs ended and the vines began, so completely had they meshed together.

Megan squinted into the distance, shaking her head in awe. Matt turned to the group. Behind him, Steinberg and Kurt talked softly. Kurt held a handful of plastic and Steinberg listened, then nodded. Kurt was their only guide now – they hadn't been able to convince Moema to follow them through.

"Hey." Matt motioned with his head. "Look up." They all did. "The canopy is intertwined with the thorn vines – the trees here are a vastly different species, and the vines have managed to grow all through them. Pretty effective way to keep things out – a cage with poisonous bars."

"Pretty effective way of keeping things in, too," Carla observed.

Megan lifted her arm, looking at the healing finger, and then at the skin on her forearm. "It's kinda nice ... that soft red glow from the light passing through the flowers. It's like permanent twilight from a red sky."

Matt looked along the thick canopy. Megan was right – the red flowers were crowding the ceiling for as far as the eye could see. The fading sun passing through the diaphanous petals cast a soft glow, like a red scarf thrown over a lamp.

"This has got to be a new species," Joop observed.

"Or a very old one," said Jian.

Matt turned to Megan. "Anyone want to guess why the Ndege called this the blood jungle?"

"Yeah, well, I certainly hope that's the only reason." Carla's brows had come together. "At least the heat isn't as bad ... still humid, but more like a giant natural greenhouse."

Matt shook more moisture from his head. "It's awesome – misted atmosphere, isolated and separated – in a word, it looks and feels ... primordial."

"Primordial?" Steinberg's voice close behind him made Matt jump. "Perfect – that's exactly what you'd expect when searching for a primordial specimen, wouldn't you say?" Steinberg looked around. "Seen anything yet? Ms. Nero, Ms. Hannaford?"

Megan turned to the jungle. "No, not yet. Plenty of movement farther away from the crater wall. I think anything living here has learned to give the wall and the thorns a wide berth. We've all heard movement in the thicker underbrush – nothing flying, though. Looks to me like a pristine jungle – it could have been this way for millions for years. Perhaps even long before ..."

"And it's all ours." Steinberg looked from Megan to Matt. "Well done."

"You're joking, right?" Megan's hands were on her hips, her chin forward.

Steinberg shrugged. "Oh, I mean from a corporate perspective."

"Not even," Carla added.

"We'll just buy it – it's empty land as far as Brazil is concerned."

Matt snorted. "Good luck with that. By the way, there was something interesting on the way down, carved into the wall – more Ndege writing. It said something like: 'Let not the unclean pass back to the land of man.'"

The silence hung for a moment, then Steinberg made a circling motion in the air with his finger. "And ... that's it? These guys actually talked like this all the time ... in riddles?"

"These are meant to be warnings," Matt was annoyed by the sarcastic tone.

"So, clean of body, clean of mind ... maybe clean of soul? Which is it? Or is it all of the above?"

"Don't know yet. They're not exactly around to ask."

Steinberg grunted. "Neither is Dan Brenner, more's the pity."

Matt ignored the jibe.

"What do you think, Matt?" Carla tilted her head. "Could it be about the thorns, or something worse?"

"Oh shit – remember Moema's grandfather telling him about the screaming?" Megan looked over her shoulder at the jungle.

Matt shrugged. "I don't know what their definition of 'unclean' was. Maybe there was some sort of purification process they used to perform, either out there, or before they returned."

"Possibly some sort of protection against a threat, real or imagined." Carla grunted. "We need to keep a lookout for any more Ndege writing."

"It's too bad the Ndege are gone," said Megan. "If it was something other than spiritual, we're going to need to piece that cleansing process together. Could be vital for treating the infestation."

"Too bad indeed." Steinberg clapped his hands once, and made a show of looking at his watch. "We're losing light, and it's too late to investigate today, but first thing tomorrow, we'll be hiking into the crater jungle. No one will be forced to go. In fact, I insist that everyone thinks carefully before deciding to come along. After all, we're not sure what it is we'll find in there."

Steinberg smirked as he studied their faces. Matt knew that they'd all go; no one had come this far to stay behind and mind the bags.

Joop cleared his throat loudly. It was rare for the tall man to speak. "I think ... I think this is important, what Mr. Steinberg has said. This jungle might be an example of an evolutionary partition – a physical separation of the old world from the new. Things can be snap frozen in an evolutionary stage as long as environmental, predatory, and geological conditions do not change. Alternatively, whole new species could have evolved. Any jungle is dangerous, but I believe this jungle is more so, as there is an element of the unknown, unexperienced, and unpredictable, making it extremely alien to human life. We have no idea what we could encounter, and should think hard before we proceed."

Megan leaned in close to Matt. "Cool."

Joop became more animated. "Mr. Steinberg, if you can get a signal out, then you should try to organize for more resources. We should have a full team with the proper equipment."

"Seriously? You're getting cold feet, Professor van Onertson?" Steinberg pulled a face. "The Ndege had been coming in here for who knows how many generations, and the only thing that fucking killed *them* was *us*." He roared with laughter, which echoed down at them from the canopy overhead.

Joop pursed his lips, and repositioned his glasses on his long nose.

Carla folded her arms. "I'm going in, but I agree we need more resources. Might I remind you of why I'm here? There's a significant parasitic infestation occurring in the United States – something never before seen by modern man. Who knows what else is in here." She stared hard at Steinberg. "You should make the call."

Steinberg looked a little uncomfortable. "Can't."

"Why not?"

He grinned sheepishly. "Battery's dead."

"Oh fuck." Megan turned away from him.

Steinberg shook his head and pulled a face. "Lighten up. There's a spare back at the Ndege camp. I just didn't think I'd be spending quite so long on the phone to the chopper pilot ... or my scriptwriters. Got a big movie coming up, and what do you know, the world doesn't stop turning just because we're down here."

His head jutted out on his thick neck. "We set off tomorrow morning and if all goes to plan, we'll be heading back by the afternoon. Maybe even sooner, if we get lucky – who knows? Okay with all of you?"

Carla sat back down, waving him away. Steinberg turned his glare on Megan, who nodded. He went from person to person. No one opted out.

"Good." He turned, mumbling to Kurt about dinner, and sauntered to the other side of the pool, away from the group.

* * * * *

Matt woke sore across the shoulders and back, with a raspy throat. He had been tossing and turning, his dark dreams a frightening montage of buried tunnels and things pursuing him through age-old labyrinths in a freezing underworld. He sat up and rubbed his face, then pulled his hands away and sniffed them. He could still smell a slight odor from the water in the sinkhole.

Megan groaned and rolled onto her back, a small, regular squeak coming from her blocked nose. It was just after dawn, and even though the sun was up, in the eternal twilight under the canopy it was still dark, and would remain that way for at least another hour.

Matt could hear movement from outside their tent – probably Kurt, stoking the fire or trying to find something edible for breakfast. Much as he wanted to avoid the big bodyguard, Matt needed to go and relieve himself.

He came out into a surprisingly cool and misted atmosphere. Kurt turned and nodded, an armful of sticks at his side. He waved his hand, indicating the mist that surrounded them. "As we expected; must be a large, cool body of water interacting with the warmer air ... or is it the other way around?"

Matt half smiled. "You were right the first time – invection fog – warm air over cooler water."

Kurt grunted. "And how's sleeping beauty? Any further ill effects from the thorn jab?"

Matt shook his head. "No, I think she's okay. John will look her over again, though. Problem is, she wouldn't tell us even if we asked. She's pretty wilful when she wants to be."

Kurt dropped the sticks in a pile beside the smoldering fire. "That's good. Bad ju-ju, those freakin' thorns – never seen anything like it." He stretched. "You're a lucky man. Woman like that ... I wouldn't be bringing her down here." Kurt raised his eyebrows and then kneeled to softly break sticks over his knee, piling them onto the red-gray ashes of the previous evening's fire.

Matt thought about ignoring him, and turned to survey the best place to empty his bladder. Then he turned back.

"And did you? Leave your own girl back home?"

Kurt laughed softly. "I left dozens of them back home. I like to spread myself around a little."

Matt winced.

"She why you took a swing at me?"

Matt groaned, and thought about lying. "I thought maybe, that you two ..."

Kurt stopped what he was doing. "Seriously? Me and Megan?" He shook his head. "You think I'm fucking crazy? Listen, I've got enough to worry about without putting the moves on some guy's girl in the middle of the Amazon jungle." He snorted. "Don't worry about it; she's only inter-ested in you."

Matt turned, sucking in one cheek. 'Thanks ... I was just ..."

"Forget it." Kurt went back to snapping twigs. "So, why are you here?"

"Here, now?" Matt turned back, confused by the question.

"Yup. Down here, in the Grand Chaco. What's in it for you? I get why Max's team is here – the big bucks. I get why Dr. Nero is here. And of course Ms. Hannaford is here because you're here. But you? What brought you here? Steinberg ain't payin' you, and this is no garden tour."

Matt felt a little embarrassed to admit that Carla basically forced him to come along. He tucked his hands into his back pockets. "Helping Carla out, I guess."

"Saving the world?" Kurt looked up, grinned, and started to coax the fire into a flame.

"Maybe. I've seen what this parasite can do to people. It's serious – Steinberg should respect it ... and Dr. Nero."

"He let you come ... that's more than he usually allows. The man certainly knows how to get his way."

"Yeah, he pays for it." Matt snorted, and looked down at Kurt breaking twigs. "And you? Just here as a hired hand; Steinberg's muscle?"

The big man shrugged. "I've been with Max for ten years. I helped him when he went looking for the Persepolis vaults in Iran." He looked up. "Got him to shelter in a sandstorm and then carried him out of the desert."

"That was you? That was all over the news."

"Yep ... been pulling him out of storms, fires, and fights ever since." He got to his feet. "He's one of the toughest men I know; self-made, works and plays hard, and sharp as a tack. I've seen the guy reduce agents and megastars to tears." He gave Matt a half smile. "He's not a bad guy, when you really get to know him. Self-absorbed, a little arrogant, but overall, you can count on him to do the right thing."

Matt nodded, not convinced. "So, you think you'll catch him his specimen?"

Kurt looked out into the jungle, and then nodded. "I've tracked and caught all manner of species. If that lizard bird is in there, I'll catch him one." He turned back. "Once I do,

I can promise you that I'll be doing my darndest to convince him to pack up and ship out. The rainy season is a bitch, and I certainly don't fancy sleeping under waterfalls."

Matt nodded. "I hear that. I hope you're right – and I hope Carla finds her answers, too. Otherwise she might not leave."

A loud fart emanating from the tent set up a distance away from the others made Matt raise his eyebrows. "His master's voice?"

Kurt laughed softly. "I'll take him a coffee ... ah, in a few minutes, when the gas cloud has cleared." He paused. "One thing ... for Dr. Nero's sake – you'd better convince her to leave when we all do. That's something else I know about Mr. Steinberg – he won't wait, and he won't come back for anybody."

* * * * *

The sun was climbing higher in the sky and huge columns of filtered light dropped down into the jungle around them. The group had eaten a small meal of dried meat and black powdered coffee, and was eager to start the day.

"Hey!" Kurt's voice was hushed but forceful, and froze Megan to the spot, just as she was about to move into the line of fronds edging the true jungle beyond the pool. She looked like she was about to argue when Matt pulled her back.

"He's right. This is no time to be separating. Remember, we're a long way from home, Toto." Matt grinned harmlessly, seeing the annoyance still on her face. He suddenly wondered why he had intervened – it would have been much better if she were pissed off with Kurt.

She rolled her eyes, but came back to the group, sitting down again. She looked at her arm – red from the soft glow.

Matt watched as Kurt set about unpacking some of his bags. Collapsible cages were put to the side, a long case –

which he opened briefly – displayed a long-barreled rifle with telescopic sight, broken down into individually packed segments. A tranquilizer, Matt suspected. Next came ropes, soft netting, and some small plastic canisters with what looked like ring pulls.

Carla had joined Jian and Joop and together they examined their own equipment. Matt suddenly felt about as useful as a barrel with a hole in it.

Megan got to her feet, pulling him up. "Let's see if we can help."

He groaned; she went straight to Kurt.

She crouched. "So, we catch one or two of the archaeopteryx?"

Kurt kept rolling up nets. "Sure ... and anything else that looks interesting."

A little different to what he said to me, Matt thought. It made sense though. When Carla found out, he didn't think she'd be too impressed with even more potentially harmful ancient species being hauled back to the States.

Megan nodded. "Oookay, and then what? How are you going to get them back through?"

"Through the water? Oh my God, you're right." Kurt slapped his forehead, eyes wide, then grinned. "Don't sweat it; we got that. The Ndege gave us the idea. We'll sedate them, wrap them in a plastic bag, and then pull them through. They should survive the ten minutes or so underwater, as long as they're unconscious and in an air pocket. But just to be sure, we'll grab a few spares."

"You're shitting me ... spares?" Megan's face contorted, and this time Matt decided to let her at it. He saw Joop crouching down a few feet away with a magnifying glass, running it up and over the fronds of a small green palm. He backed up a step, away from the fireworks.

The evolutionary biologist looked over his shoulder at Matt, looked past him briefly at Kurt, then winked and ducked in past the first line of fronds. Matt glanced back at the camp and then quickly followed.

Joop moved in about a dozen steps, in a crouch, and when Matt caught up he pointed to a massive column-like tree trunk in the distance. It must have stood seventy feet, with branches at its very top. It looked to be covered in fur, or thick fibers.

When Matt caught up, Joop pointed up at its heavily ferned top.

"Looks like a giant tree fern, doesn't it?"

Matt nodded.

"And it is … in a way. But not one you or I would come across. I think it's a cycadeoid. Possibly even a *Williamsonia* cycadeoid." He looked at Matt, his eyes glowing. "These trees, if you can even call them that, were some of the first tall plants in the Cretaceous forests."

"Wow, so it's not just the fauna that's anachronistic," Matt said.

Joop grinned. "I think I'm in heaven." He fiddled in his bag, not taking his eyes off the enormous trunk, then lifted a small pair of binoculars to his face.

"Yes, yes, there's no doubt, the cone pods are there … enormous." He handed the glasses to Matt and spoke softly, describing what Matt was looking at.

"A magnificent ancestor species, and the forefathers of the modern cycads. They were remarkably successful for tens of millions of years, but found themselves too specialized when events caught up with them. Two things occurred – their environment altered, causing the massive continent-covering forests to shrink. And their reproduction technique also became too specialized." He nudged Matt, and pointed to the very top of the tree. "You see the giant cones? Like spongy footballs. Well, they needed large beasts to eat them and then transport the seeds away in their gut.

Worked perfectly – the seeds would be dehusked and then deposited at another site, already embedded in their own pile of fertilizer. Problem was, when the larger herbivores started to die out they were left stranded, and so evolved into the smaller species we see today."

"They look hairy." Matt handed the glasses back.

Joop looked again. "So they are – and not like existing cycads at all." He shrugged. 'But the main thing is, they're here."

"Here, and still alive ... in the crater basin." He turned to Joop. "Because of the big herbivores?"

Joop shrugged, giving him a wry smile. "Maybe, maybe not – perhaps over the many millennia they could have found another way for their seeds to be dispersed, yes?"

"Well, if there could be big herbivores, there could be things that eat big herbivores." Matt looked around at the red-tinged jungle, now full of lurking shadows. "Let's get back; best if we stay together. I'm sure Kurt and Steinberg would regard it a hanging offense to wander off right about now."

"Yes, yes." Joop waved vaguely and continued to peer up into the massive green umbrella's top, a grin splitting his face below the field glasses.

Matt waited for him, looking around at the weird plants that crowded in around them. Close by on the jungle floor was a green pod, roughly twice the size of a football, with strappy leaves rising from around its edge, each one tipped with red dots of glistening color. A beetle the size of Matt's little finger was edging its way up one of the straps, toward the candy red tips. Matt leaned closer and could see that the small flowers were crested with tiny drops of liquid – nectar, he guessed.

The bug looked to be sucking it up, but when it went to change positions, it found itself stuck. As Matt watched, more of the flower tips closed in on the beetle, and then when it was hopelessly stuck, the leaf started to roll back, encasing the beetle, cigar-like. The strappy plant slowly coiled back toward the green pod on the ground.

Ugh. Matt stepped back. The football had now split open in an excellent semblance of a floral set of jaws. The strap, along with its tightly held prey, disappeared inside, and the jaws closed.

Matt shook his head. He grabbed Joop by the shoulder and tugged. "Definitely time to get back."

He pushed through the fronds to their small camp in time to see packs being slung and a neat pile of additional items next to his own kit. Megan looked at him and grinned.

"You're on carrying duty – one of the capture nets."

"I volunteered, did I?" He lifted the soft rope mesh – roughly six feet square, with slight additional weighting at the edges, probably to allow a fanning effect if thrown. He practised for a moment, then swung it over his shoulders like a mesh cape.

"Perfect fit. And what do you get?" He stood with his arms folded.

"I get to supervise you, spider boy. C'mon, briefing time."

Steinberg stood with one foot up on a small crate, looking like Admiral Nelson on the bow of his lead ship. He had his fists at his waist, and even though he was one of the shortest people in the group, he managed to create the impression he was looking down on everyone.

"Ladies and gentlemen, this may be dangerous." He stepped up with both feet, balancing precariously on the box.

"Everyone must work together." He looked pointedly at Carla, as if she were a gatecrasher at a private party. "Our job is simple; we net the specimen, drop or push it into a cage, and then deposit it, or them, back here at our base camp. If there is time, we will head back out for a brief exploration, and see what other specimens we can locate. However ..."

He paused again, head tilted, eyeing the small assembled group. This time there was a hint of a warning in his tone. "There will not be time for individual exploration. If you wander off and get lost, you may find yourself here for a very long time." He grinned, as if he was joking, but Matt remembered how cold the man had been after Dan Brenner's death, and didn't doubt for a minute that Steinberg would leave them behind.

He went to step down, then hesitated, and turned to them again. "By the way, you have all signed nondisclosure contracts regarding this find. Regardless of what you think, in effect it belongs to me. Its whereabouts also belong to me, and while you are down here on my watch and under my care, your very livelihood belongs to me."

He smiled again, but there was no warmth in the curl of his lips. He motioned to Kurt as he stepped down.

"Mr. Douglas, if you please."

"Thank you, Mr. Steinberg." Kurt had slung his assembled rifle over his shoulder. Matt recognized it now; he'd been right – the gas-powered, skeletal black frame fired a hypodermic tranquilizer dart, and was accurate as hell. *Good*, he thought. He'd prefer Kurt hit his target the first time.

Kurt cleared his throat. "No one wants to be here longer than they need to. I want a smooth location, capture, and transport. To that end, we'll need to run through some practise sessions."

Megan leaned in close to Matt. "Lesson one – net go over bird."

Matt rolled his eyes. "I wonder if they bite?"

"You've seen the teeth, right? Shit yeah." She leaned back as Kurt raised his voice.

"For this first run, Mr. Kearns will be in charge of capture, Mr. ... ah, Joop will secure the specimen in one of the cages. Everyone else will be tasked with carrying what we need and spotting. Any questions?"

There were none.

"Good. By the time we set off in … thirty minutes, we should all be working together like a machine." He motioned to Matt.

"Professors, let's go."

Matt took the net off his shoulders and hung it over one arm. Megan nudged him.

"Big job for a little man." She winked. "Make me proud."

For the next fifteen minutes Matt and Joop swung nets over small tree stumps, crates, and each other. Each time, the mesh flowed a little more freely and gave better coverage. At the end of their short session, Matt would swing the net, cover his target, and then he and Joop would rush forward to secure their prey in a cage. All up, each capture only took about two minutes.

Steinberg, who'd been watching, looked at his wristwatch. "We're ready." The movie producer motioned toward the red-tinged jungle. "Take us in, Kurt."

* * * * *

It only took a few minutes' trekking before they were all enclosed in the strangest jungle Matt had ever experienced. It wasn't as tangled and knotted as the jungle on the other side of the crater wall, and there were certainly more trails – some wide enough to drive a SUV along – but nonetheless, it was very … different.

Joop was constantly lagging behind, examining one plant or another. Matt recognized many of the bark types and leaf shapes, but time and again when he tried to recall a name, he found they didn't quite fit. They were outlandishly large, different, or somehow distorted from the fossils he remembered.

Matt knew he didn't have the botanical or paleobotanical expertise to say for sure, but based on the giant cycad Joop had pointed out, he didn't doubt for an instant that he was seeing archaic remnants, trapped in the eddy of an evolutionary backwater. He was thrilled, but also concerned about the animals they'd possibly encounter.

As they moved farther away from the crater wall, the sounds of the jungle started to increase. More chirruping, squealing, and snuffling sounds rose from behind the primordial green walls surrounding them, their owners invisible, but very close.

They made good time, walking on trails that could only have been trampled flat by large animals. Kurt led them out, followed by Steinberg, with Matt and Joop on capture detail, nets and cages at the ready. Carla, Megan, John, and Jian followed behind.

After another twenty-five sweaty minutes, they pushed into a small clearing. Kurt held up his hand, and Steinberg moved up to his shoulder. Matt and Joop paused, and Matt rearranged the net in his hands, waiting for the call.

Kurt was looking along the secondary branches under the tree canopy. The uppermost branches formed a red roof, woven through with the thorned vines hundreds of feet above them. But a secondary network of branches started fifty feet up, and based on Joop's briefing on the known characteristics of the archaeopteryx, this was where they hoped to find their quarry.

"Don't expect them to be circling overhead – they won't fly," Joop said. "Not like the birds of today. This creature will be more a climber and glider. Our analysis of the fossil remains revealed a supportive bone structure for dorsal muscle mass along the back, with a corresponding deep sternum. It can probably flap strongly, but it's doubtful that its muscle-to-weight ratio will be enough to sustain true flight for more than a few seconds."

Joop slowly scanned the second-tier branches with his binoculars, while beside him, slowly swiveling, Kurt was doing the same with the scope of his rifle. After a few minutes Kurt lowered the tranquilizer gun.

"Nothing."

"Hope we came to the right place, hmm?" Steinberg turned to Matt, his expression flat. He didn't need to speak; Matt could clearly hear the suspicion in his tone.

"Hey, if you're questioning my translation ..."

"Look!" Megan whispered, immediately hushing Matt.

Everyone swung around to Megan, and then to where she was pointing. Standing, frozen and half hidden in the underbrush, was an animal the size of a cat. Its coat was softly speckled, like a young fawn, but where the face of a deer was soft and short, this creature's face was longer and ... unmistakeable.

From behind them, Joop whispered, "Impossible. Eohippus – the Dawn Horse."

The tiny animal could have been a toy, an impression not helped by the fact that it was as still as a stuffed likeness on a storeroom shelf. It had obviously decided that the strange two-legged creatures might not see it if it stayed completely motionless.

"Don't ... move ... a ... muscle." Joop breathed out the words.

Steinberg slowly put his pack down and whispered out of the side of his mouth, "Bullshit. Kurt, shoot it."

"No!" Megan shot back. "It's tiny, you'll kill it."

Steinberg muttered something inaudible, then whispered through clenched teeth. "All right; we catch it. Get up here, Kearns. You too, Mr. Jope."

Matt and Joop exchanged glances. Joop nodded, the anticipation on his face outweighing any better judgment. Matt shrugged and led them out.

He carefully placed one foot in front of the other, slowly lifting the mesh netting as he and Joop closed in on the creature. At fifteen feet away it was still completely motionless, with just one glittering black eye turned toward them. The small horse's head started to turn almost imperceptibly, the small black eye fixing on Matt.

"Easy," whispered Steinberg.

Matt slowed even more. He could now see the animal clearly and marveled at its perfect form and structure. Like a horse, and yet not. The body was more rounded, lacking the long muscular flanks of the modern animal. The ears were shorter, but still upright, one clearly turned toward him, and the feet were totally wrong – it looked like there were three toes at the front of each foot, ending in sharp claw-like hooves, rather than a single rounded hoof.

Small as it was, is still looked fast. With its body still half in the brush, Matt knew that there was no clear shot at the horse. He paused and half turned.

"Someone needs to get behind him, to make sure he doesn't bolt into the jungle."

"I'll do it." Joop's face still glowed with excitement and he stepped out to the side, his eyes locked on the Eohippus. One of the tall man's boots came down on a twig, which crackled and snapped under his weight. The animal's ears flicked once, and it spun away, the jungle absorbing it as completely as if it never existed.

"Go, go, go!" Steinberg pushed Kurt in the back, who in turn nudged Matt to the right, and pointed ahead for Joop. Behind them, the rest of the party surged forward after the tiny horse. In front of Matt, a flattened path opened slightly, and up ahead the animal burst from the brush to race down a few dozen feet of mossy grasses. Matt was still dozens of feet back, but he held the net high and ready. He reckoned he'd only have to partly cover it, or tangle it with the net to slow it down.

The pursuers came together; Joop now at his shoulder and Kurt just behind, cradling his gun.

Matt swung the net around his head once and then flung it at the animal, just as it raced toward a fallen log. The net opened gracefully as it spun in the air, but its slow descent and a snap change of direction by the Eohippus as it reached the log, meant the net landed over empty grass.

Matt cursed and sped up to retrieve the net, thinking he had another throw in him. But like a conjurer's trick, a piece of the log ... detached, and exploded toward the small darting horse, landing squarely upon it and knocking it flat.

Matt braked hard, and someone crashed into his back. Megan's scream was nothing compared to the terrified screech of the small animal. It took Matt a few extra seconds to work out what he was looking at. He flung his arms wide to keep everyone back as his mind assembled the scene into horrifying detail.

What had at first looked like a black, many-fingered hand was in fact an enormous spider – plastic-shiny, muscular, and the size of a dinner plate. Its eight legs were fixed tightly on its prize. Finger-length fangs were inserted into the small horse's shuddering flank.

Matt felt the gorge rise in his throat. The massive arachnid looked deformed, longer than normal, and completely un-troubled by the gathered humans.

"Oh my God, this is unbelievable." Jian's words came short and fast. He pushed to the front and stood beside Matt. "Stay back, this is probably extremely dangerous."

"No shit," added Steinberg from the rear.

Jian got down on his haunches, and Matt did the same, keeping his eyes on the revolting scene. "What freakin' type of spider is that?" he whispered.

Jian shook his head slowly, as if concerned the thing would scurry away. Matt doubted they worried it at all.

"I think ... Mesothelae, or certainly an early order of it. See the longer head? More sausage-like, rather than the modern rounded shape." He snorted in admiration. "The only fossil evidence of these guys was found in China, embedded within a fifty-million-year-old clay pan. Very, very rare – soft bodies don't fossilize well."

"Soft?" Matt thought it looked like giant knot of toughened plastic pipes.

Joop came and carefully knelt beside them. "Amazing. Mesothelae ancestry?"

Jian nodded. "Yes, just what I was thinking – the musculature and basic morphology is consistent with Mesothelae. Also, it looks ground-dwelling, rather than web-spinning, which is also consistent with fossil records. It's just ... its size, and head to abdomen ratio, is puzzling."

"Hmm, my thoughts exactly. I also found some plants that should have died out during the Cretaceous period. I think this place has somehow acted like a vacuum jar for many species for millions of years. The changes might make sense though – within a sealed environment I would expect some evolutionary stranding, and given the amount of time, there would be the possibility of minute genetic meandering – mutations, deformities."

"This place has somehow acted like a vacuum jar." Something about the concept nagged at Matt, but he didn't let his mind pursue the thread. Instead, he looked at the multiple button-sized eyes that stared unblinkingly at the group, and the giant fangs embedded in the still-screaming animal.

Megan made a retching sound that turned into a wail. "Make it stop. Can someone kill it?" She pushed at Matt.

"Stay back." Jian held an arm up in front of them.

"Were they poisonous?" Matt turned to him.

"Not very, we don't think ... relatively. It's just that their size meant that they could pump a helluva lot into their prey. Probably paralyze, temporarily. Might kill you if you had heart trouble to begin with."

Matt exhaled. "If that thing landed on me, I'd sure develop heart trouble."

Jian bobbed his head to see the creature from a different angle. "Then again, it looks different to any fossils I know of. It might have onward evolved – a Mesothelae, but a whole different species. There could be anything in its poison sacs by now."

While they watched, the spider began using its muscular legs to drag the small horse back to the fallen log. Underneath the rotted husk of the tree, they could make out silk webbing. The spider backed its long abdomen into it. Shriveled carcasses of previous meals were deposited like ornaments around the entrance.

Jian spoke softly. "It'll liquefy its prey, and then literally drink the fluids straight from the body. Weird, though – they're supposed to live in burrows, not in the open. Unless …"

Matt waited for a few seconds, his nerves finally giving out. "Unless what?"

Joop answered. "Unless it's a juvenile, and hasn't found its own permanent burrow yet … or is not big enough to contest an existing one."

"Are you shitting me? Are you saying they could get even bigger than that monster?"

"Who knows? Maybe. As I said, we just don't know that much about them. Let's get out of here." Jian rose slowly from his crouch. "Back up everyone, slowly. Let's not startle it – it's probably more scared of us than we are of it."

"I doubt that," Megan said.

Underneath the log, the huge spider seemed to pulse obscenely. Its venom had now been injected, and the flesh within the skin of the small horse was turning to a protein soup, which was being drawn back up through the fangs. Eight coin-sized eyes, the largest pair at the center, seemed to watch the humans with cold disdain.

"Come on, let's go." Jian grabbed Matt's arm.

"Wait." Steinberg held up his hand. "Kurt, can you hit that ugly fucker with a dart?"

Kurt shrugged. "Sure."

Jian spun on him. "This is a creature without an internal skeleton. Your dart might pass right through the exoskeleton."

"Or bounce right off, if it's thick enough," Matt added.

Jian pushed in closer to Steinberg. "Also, you have no idea how that drug, designed for mammalian and avian biochemistry, will affect an arachnid. It might kill it, or just piss it off."

Kurt grunted. "They might be right, boss."

Steinberg snorted. "Give me that." He held his hand for the gun. "I'll try not to kill it."

Megan's mouth turned down. "Frankly, I have no problems with killing it."

Cute little horse trumps big ugly bug any day, Matt guessed. He'd prefer just to leave it alone, but, like Megan, he'd be more than happy with a dead specimen this time. The thought of someone having to carry that thing in a cage strapped to their back was mortifying.

As they watched, the Mesothelae seemed to bunch up behind its prey, leaving just the top of its glossy black head and eyes visible, with the tips of its feet still massaging the body, as if to coax more fluid from the deflating bag of fur and flesh. Steinberg advanced a few steps.

"I do not think this is a good idea." Jian had his shoulders hunched as he watched the movie producer slowly approach the spider.

Sshh. Steinberg turned and brought a finger to his lips, then waved the entomologist away. He lifted the gun to his shoulder.

Either sensing the threat or protecting its meal, the spider reared up on its hind legs, displaying long, curved fangs that looked needle sharp. It hissed.

"Fuck, did that thing just hiss?" Kurt guffawed.

Its front legs opened like a hand, and Steinberg took another step and planted his feet, sighting along the tranquilizer gun.

Twin streams of fluid shot from the fangs and struck Steinberg's legs.

"Wow, did you see that? Now we know what additional weapons the primitive arachnid had in its arsenal." Jian edged forward. "Please be careful, Mr. Steinberg. It would not be wise to allow that fluid to get in your eyes."

Matt shuddered, imagining being blinded by the spider and knowing it was still close by. *Hello, nightmares.*

Two things happened at once: Steinberg fired the gun, making the soft *pfft* sound of air being blown hard through a pipe. Immediately, the spider seemed to collapse and vanish backward, either blown away by the force of the dart, or pulling itself out of the way with freakish speed.

"What the fuck – where'd it go?" Steinberg strode forward.

Kurt leapt over the log and rustled about for a few seconds before stepping back into the clearing. "Gone – I'm sure you hit it." He used a long stick to rake the body of the Eohippus out of the way. The tiny shrunken animal blinked.

"Oh my God, it's still alive." Megan put a hand over her mouth.

"Paralysis toxin," Jian said. "Many ground-hunting spiders use it – it disables the prey, but doesn't kill it. It usually means the spiders hunt things bigger than them – they bite their prey, it wanders away, and they follow. Eventually the prey is overcome, and then ... they dine."

"Ugh, it was being eaten alive. Can we ... save it?" Megan knelt down beside it, her hand hovering over its deflated body.

"Unlikely. The venom will have liquefied its internal biological structure by now." Jian knelt down and examined the puncture wounds with a stick. He pulled Megan's hand back. "Careful you don't get any of the venom on your hands."

"Kill it." Carla spoke softly, but her voice carried a hard edge of authority. No one disagreed.

John knelt down and put his fingertips on its neck. "Very slow pulse. It's basically in a coma. It'll probably go into full respiratory system shutdown any time now."

"Shoot it." Matt wanted it dead quickly.

Kurt shook his head. "Might not kill it. Besides, we need to save the darts." He looked to John. "Have you got something you can give it, Doc?"

John nodded and rummaged in his bag.

"Let's go." Steinberg paused. "Wait – bag it. We'll take it with us. Even if we don't find anything else, at least we'll have this little guy's body as proof something was here."

Joop hesitated. "Ah, Mr. Steinberg, is it a good idea to be carrying dead game around with us? We don't know what type of predators are in here just yet – the Mesothelae might not be the biggest thing we run into."

Steinberg pulled a face and handed the gun back to Kurt. "You'll be fine. Just stay close to the big man with the thunder stick." He laughed and turned away. "Besides, Mr. Joop, you're not carrying it … Jian is."

Jian looked up briefly as he slid the now-dead animal into a bag. "Do you know something interesting about spiders? They have unbelievable eyesight and an even better memory. I just hope it doesn't decide that it wants its meal back." He smiled. "The upside is, it'll probably remember who shot it."

Kurt slung the rifle over his shoulder. "We should keep going. Give it another hour, and then find a place to rest."

Steinberg nodded and waved him on.

Carla helped Jian strap the animal across his shoulders. "We should check the carcass for mites when we're at the rest spot."

Jian positioned the bag squarely on his back. "I get the feeling that mites are the least of our worries in here."

* * * * *

Kurt had managed to get a small fire going, which was no mean feat, given the damp environment in the crater. He had balanced a metal canister on the pile of burning logs, and was boiling water for some very gritty outdoor-style coffee. It'd still be welcome, if only to settle everyone down following their encounter with the spider.

Megan leaned up against Matt, and he was grateful for the physical contact. He was probably as unsettled as she was. They had come looking for a bird the size of a turkey; the biggest threat it posed was a row of tiny cone-like teeth and sharp talons on scaly feet. The Eohippus hadn't dispelled the magic, being small and cuddly and about as threatening as a teddy bear.

But the massive black spider, looking like some freakish Halloween prop with enormous fangs and intelligent eyes, had dispelled the sensation of them being in a wonderland. The red-twilight jungle had lulled them with its paradisal beauty. They knew there had to be predators. *Stupid*, Matt thought. They should have known better. There were things down here that were waking nightmares – scientifically fascinating, but terrifying and deadly.

Matt now knew that this was probably why the Ndege left all the warnings. They had no need for gold, or additional hunting land. It was more likely that they were trying to save lives. Matt sighed and turned to kiss the top of Megan's head. She made a small contented noise and relaxed even further.

The group sat in silence, each person probably wondering what else was hiding in the depths of the red-hued jungle, what else was watching them right now.

Matt finished his coffee, leaving the last mouthful, which was nothing more than coarse coffee grounds and foreign bodies. He flicked it away and got to his feet, rubbing his itchy scalp as he did so. He held out his hand to Megan.

"C'mon, let's see what Carla and Jian have found."

Jian and Carla had set up a makeshift laboratory, their portable microscope resting on a backpack, flashlight balanced to shine its beam into the reflector mirror to compensate for the half-light of the crater's interior. Beside them, an array of sample tubes lay open, awaiting their guests. Both scientists wore gloves.

Jian carefully ran a knit comb down the crumpled body of the small horse, then shook its contents onto a slide with a drip of water at its center. He handed it to Carla, who was kneeling behind the backpack. She slid it into the cradle of the scope and immediately started to twist focus wheels, her lips pursed in concentration.

"Anything?" They squatted down, careful not to block any of the meager light.

Carla nodded, without taking her eyes away from the lens. "Oh, they're there all right. Not many, but what I would call a proximate normality for a parasitic species."

Megan leaned forward. "So why aren't they stripping this little guy and everything else of its skin? Looks healthy to me … at least, it did until the spider started sucking it dry."

"Yep, well, that's the question, and that's why we're here. Jian?" Carla moved back from the scope, allowing the entomologist to examine the parasite.

He focussed the instrument and then scraped more of the dust-sized arthropods onto the slide. He grunted. "Primitive form, and from what you tell me, exactly like the invasive specimens back home." He changed the magnification and focussed in on the sample. "I would like to do an autopsy."

Megan snorted. "I'd love to see the autopsy table for that gig. I'm guessing nano-technology?"

Jian turned, his face deadpan. "No, I have very steady hands."

Megan's jaw dropped in disbelief, until Jian's face broke into a smile.

"Of course nano – electron scanning. These scabi primus are between 0.5 and 10 microns – almost invisible to the naked eye. Their internal structures are beyond this microscope." He moved back from the eyepiece. "We need to look at the blood from the Eohippus now."

"Need help?" Matt squinted at the work Jian was doing.

"I'll get some blood." Carla withdrew a syringe from her pack. She paused. "And Matt, you can give me a hand. The arteries are pretty much collapsed, and may also be contaminated from the spider venom, so we'll need to go into the spine. Grab some gloves."

Matt crouched beside Carla, who showed him where to hold the animal – stretched out with its backbone facing up. He held the small animal in place while Carla carefully inserted the needle into its back, between the largest rear spinal discs. She pulled back the plunger, withdrawing a small amount of deep red blood. Matt scratched his ear against his shoulder.

Carla looked up at him. "Itchy?"

Matt froze for a second, and then responded cautiously. "Yes."

She nodded. "I bet we all are. We've picked up a few passengers."

"Oh, shit." He let go of the horse and went to put his hand to his head, then paused, guessing his hand was probably crawling with the things after touching the horse.

"I knew it. My scalp has felt like it's crawling ... and also some other, more ... vulnerable, places."

"Me too," Megan added.

Jian grinned. "In here it's just a normal infestation of the scabie mite; we can treat that easily before we leave. We just have to find out why this same parasite is acting normal within the crater, but becomes super aggressive back home."

From the other side of the clearing, Steinberg belched loudly, threw the contents of his cup into the bush behind him, and groaned to his feet. "Let's go, Mr. Douglas."

Kurt had been checking the darts for his gun. He now also had a handgun holstered at his belt. "You got it."

Matt wandered over. "Where did that come from?"

Kurt turned, followed Matt's gaze and lifted the gun to show him.

"Heckler & Koch. No jamming, fast load, and very little recoil. Oh yeah, and a shitload of stopping power. I've had it all the time, but packed away. Just thought after seeing the spider, and how territorial it was, we might need to do more than just try and put something to sleep." He slid it back into its holster and nodded toward Jian. "You heard our two experts. That spider probably wasn't the biggest of its kind. I'm pretty sure I hit it with the dart, and it sill walked away. If its mommy comes looking for us, I don't want to be stuck with little more than a fancy blowpipe and a handful of needles – I want stopping power." His eyes narrowed. "That spider also made me wonder what else could be living in here." He grunted, then turned away.

Matt couldn't argue with the man; he had been thinking the same thing. The gun made him feel better, but only slightly. A full team of HAWC Special Forces might do it … or, even better, to be back in California, lying beside a swimming pool with Megan.

Steinberg called them all together, and Matt jumped as Megan's hand alighted on his shoulder.

"Ooh, cool it, Mr. Nervous." She slid her arm through his, and they wandered over to the group. As they joined Joop and John, they saw that Kurt had his long blade in his hands and had uncapped a small lid on the pommel. Inside was what looked to be a tiny compass – no wonder he had wanted to keep it dry. *This guy is definitely old school*, Matt thought.

The bodyguard frowned, shook the compass, and then peered at it again. "We keep heading east – I think this is east – in as straight a line as we can manage." He looked up, waiting for any other suggestions or arguments. There were none. It was probably as good as any other direction. He continued.

"This allows us a couple of options on our return. We can loop back and cover different territory, or, if we need to move at speed, we can retrace our existing trail. Like before, we're going to take it slow; I'll lead out, but I want everyone to keep a lookout above, beside, and below the lower foliage line – seems there are a few anklebiters in here."

Kurt looked over at Carla and Jian, who were still absorbed by their tests. He raised his voice. "Dr. Nero, this is for all our benefits."

She spoke without looking up. "We're staying here; this is too important. The Eohippus has the mite. We all have the parasite on us by now, but it's not as aggressively invasive as the species back home. We need to complete our tests to find out why."

She looked up and smiled disarmingly before Kurt or Steinberg could respond. "We'll be fine." Her head dipped back down to the sample she was working with.

Kurt shook his head, his hands now on his hips. "Dr. Nero, I don't think that's a good idea. We have no idea what other predators exist in here. Might I remind you, you are not armed."

Jian looked up. "Not true. We have mankind's greatest weapon – fire." He nodded to the small burning pile of logs. "We'll keep it burning, with a few long sharpened sticks for backup. Pick us up here on your way back."

Kurt looked across at Steinberg, who just shrugged, his face twisted into an *I don't give a fuck* expression.

Megan leaned in close to Matt. "I don't think we should let them stay, or at least, we should stay with them."

"I'm net man," he said.

"Okay, then I'd better stay. Those guys are gonna be so focussed on their work, an elephant could come and sit behind them and they wouldn't notice." She glanced briefly at Jian and Carla, before turning back to him with a half smile. "Nerd blindness."

"I don't know, Megs." Matt felt torn. He didn't want anyone to stay behind, and definitely didn't want Megan out of his sight. But he didn't like the idea of her going deeper into the crater, either. His mind raced. "Look, I really need you with me. If we find any more script from the Ndege – warnings, or anything else, we need to decipher it immediately."

She grabbed his chin, pulled his face toward hers, and kissed him. "No we don't. You deciphered the totems by yourself – I was just there as a sounding board. Come on, Matt, you're the languages genius, not me. Anyway, I'll probably be safer than you will."

"What?" Matt's voice caused a few heads to turn. "Stop selling yourself short. Look, you're not staying. I need you with me, end of story."

Megan started to walk toward Carla and Jian. "Bullshit, Matt. They need me, you don't. And don't try that *do as your told* crap on me."

Carla looked from Matt to Megan. It seemed like she was about to object, but Megan quickly waved her away. "Anything could creep up on you two geeks, and you wouldn't hear it. I'll keep a lookout for spiders, or anything else." At the mention of spiders, Carla simply nodded.

"Good, then it's settled." Megan folded her arms and looked from Matt to Steinberg.

Steinberg shrugged. "Fine with me; let's go."

Megan walked back toward Matt, arms still folded. Her smile was supposed to be one of triumph, but it carried a hint of nerves. "See you at supper time."

Matt returned her crooked smile. "You make sure you're here when I get back, okay?" He brushed the hair off her defiant face.

Her expression softened. "And you just make sure you come back ... in one piece."

He kissed her quickly and she gave him a small push. "I'll be fine."

"Come on, Romeo, we're gonna be gone a few hours, not a few months." Steinberg guffawed at his crack.

Looking into her eyes, Matt realized he really cared for her. It didn't matter if she was impulsive, sometimes a smartass, or even if she had snuck off with Kurt. He loved her, and he was determined he wasn't going to lose her. He half turned to Steinberg. "Give me a minute."

He also realized he didn't owe Max Steinberg anything. They had come to find a remedy for the infestation, not to track some long lost dinosaur bird for an overly rich Hollywood enfant terrible. Carla was the reason he came down here, and he was the reason Megan did. Steinberg and his gang could go to hell.

"Matthew, Professor Kearns, are you ready?" It was Joop this time.

Damn, he thought, *gotta go*. But if there was any consolation, it was that if there were more clues, he might find just as many answers on their trek as Carla and Jian would through their microscope.

He kissed Megan again quickly, then turned away. "Coming." He started to jog after the disappearing team into the jungle.

"Hey." He stopped at the sound of Megan's voice. "Don't be too long, buster."

"I'll bring you back a dinosaur." He grinned, waved, and then ducked into the red foliage. Inexplicably, he held his breath for a second as he became submerged in the red-hued jungle once again.

* * * * *

Matt plodded along, lost in his own thoughts, methodically following the man in front of him. The crawling sensation he felt on his body was somehow made worse by the knowledge that it was caused by something actually living on him, feeding off him – something potentially lethal.

He sighed and scratched. The going was extremely slow. Kurt had taken to simply pushing the tangled green chaos out of the way where possible, and only resorting to carefully cutting or chopping through it when necessary. It cut their speed to next to nothing, but it allowed them to hunt in comparative silence. Well, as much silence as five blundering bipeds from another world could muster.

Matt hoped they'd stumble upon another animal trail soon, and just as he stepped over a particularly elastic vine, it managed to loop over the toe of his boot, causing him to stumble a pace or two into the thick undergrowth. Matt went down onto his hands and knees and something hidden in the thick growth crashed away from him, causing him to pull back so quickly he pulled a muscle in his neck. He shuddered; visions of a squat, black body held aloft by eight shiny looking legs were fresh in his imagination.

Matt had traveled beneath the dark ice of the Antarctic and climbed to the peak of the Appalachians' Black Mountain, both times searching for mankind's hidden secrets, and both times encountering things that were horrifying and deadly. But it was the eyes of the spider that haunted him, the primitive part of his brain refusing to see the creature as anything other than coldly intelligent – a predator. It made his skin crawl.

John dropped back a step. "You okay?"

Matt wiped his hands down, and picked up the fallen net. "Yeah sure, just fell. Something was in there. I scared it ... and it me."

John laughed softly and slapped him on the shoulder. He continued walking, with Matt following just behind. "We are the outliers here. Makes me think that, even though the natives made small forays into this place, modern man probably hasn't ever set foot in here. This place is as unique as it is remote – and beyond valuable to modern medicine." He turned and looked at Matt from under lowered brows. Matt nodded, not really understanding the man's point, but the thing that nagged at him bubbled to the surface again.

"John, something that Joop, Jian, and now you referred to – this place being unique, and a vacuum jar for ancient species. If it's just within these walls, why did the Ndege look so ... primitive? So much so, you're going to try and get one of their skulls back home."

John nodded, and pulled at his lower lip. "Strange, yes. The Ndege had some racial characteristics that certainly looked ... retrogressive, and they lived outside of the crater walls. However, they'd been coming inside the crater for countless generations. I'll need to do some DNA extraction from the teeth, but I don't have the answer right now." He suddenly looked up. "Cross breeding?"

"Huh?" Matt frowned.

"Maybe cross breeding with an older species within these walls? It's a wild theory, but everything about this place defies logic. Maybe there is a tribe in here that are true dawn people – now wouldn't that be something worth finding out about?"

Matt's eyebrows shot up. For a paleolinguist, the opportunity to meet with a race that was proto-language, or even pre-speech altogether, would be unique, and extraordinary. He shook his head. "We'd need to stay away from them, even if they did exist. Remember how the Ndege were wiped out? We might do the same to them, and everything else in here. I don't want to be responsible for bringing this place to an end."

John nodded. "It could be vice versa, of course."

"Well, hopefully Carla and Jian are getting to grips with that," Matt said.

John nodded thoughtfully, and dropped back to walk beside Matt. "Yes, Dr. Nero, she's a very competent woman." He nodded, as if agreeing with his own assessment. "How did you meet her – a professor of linguistics and a CDC specialist?"

Matt shrugged. "Long ... no, actually a short story, I guess. She was leading the field team investigating the infestation outbreak. There was a lost language involved, and the potential to have to communicate quickly with the Ndege. She needed my help."

"She needed the best?"

Matt snorted. "We were in the same city when her logistics shortfall became apparent. A mutual friend recommended me ... and the rest, as they say, is history."

John's mouth turned down while he contemplated the information. "Yes, very competent woman. I would expect she'd seek out the best ... and damn well get it." He seemed to think for a while.

"Is she, uh, would you know if she's ... single?" He immediately shook his head. "Forget I asked that; none of my business." He cleared his throat and put his head down, picking up speed a little.

Matt sped up to keep pace. *Nothing like love or sexual attraction to turn us back into awkward teenagers*, he thought. Matt smiled up at the tall, urbane doctor. He liked the man; there was something old world and gentlemanly about him.

"I'm not sure, but if you like I can find out."

John tapped his long nose with a finger. "Thank you, but on the Q-T, Professor Kearns. Don't want to make anyone feel awkward."

Matt returned the gesture. "Got it." They walked a few steps farther, or rather, slid and pushed through the hole being created by Kurt out front.

"Okay, my turn; how did you and Steinberg come together? It doesn't really seem like the pair of you have that much in common."

"I have been Max's private physician for a number of years." He turned and smiled. "So, I guess I know him better than most people – inside and out."

Matt made a mental note to pull back on any overt criticism of the film producer in front of John. "He can be a bit prickly, but generally he's a good man. He knew that I had been on jungle treks before, and even did some work in the deep Congolese jungle. He asked me if I'd like to join him, and then offered me enough money to retire. And like you said, the rest is …"

Matt raised his eyebrows. "The guy definitely seems to get his way."

"Go easy on him. He's okay, when he's not being competitive or trying to show everyone how smart he is. There's been very little for me to do; he's surprisingly fit, and except for a few doses of the clap over the last five years, he's a strong as an ox – a small one anyway. The guy makes movies, and he's damned good at it."

"Yeah, I've seen most of them," Matt said. "He's certainly found enough material for a dozen new movies down here."

"That he has." John turned and smiled. "I wonder who will play you – Brad Pitt, maybe?"

"Please. I'm sure they can find someone good-looking," Matt shot back.

They trudged on in silence for another twenty minutes. Matt decided he needed some fluid replacement. The perspiration was running down his neck, along his spine, and making his ass crack greasy. He wished he'd remembered to bring salt tablets – he knew he'd need more than just fluid by now.

He sipped his water, looked up, and then froze as he almost crashed into John's back.

"What is it?" he said in a stage whisper.

"Kurt's seen something."

The big guide had his hand raised. As they watched, he went into a crouch. Matt didn't know if that meant another spider, but he had been on high alert ever since that thing had disappeared into the brush.

Kurt stayed down, but edged forward a dozen feet. Matt was relieved to see that his focus was toward the upper branches. He followed his gaze.

At first he saw nothing, but then he let his gaze travel a little higher. There – movement. One, two, three, four avian shapes on a horizontal limb. The creatures scuttled along, bat-like, using feet and tiny hands on the ends of strong, feathered wings. They looked nothing like the decrepit creature in the pictures Carla had shown him back in Orange County.

In the soft light of the red flowered canopy hundreds of feet overhead, their plumage was an iridescent blue-green, tending to a light brown on the head and legs. They moved along rather clumsily, their feet gripping the bark with heavy talons. There were scales just visible below the plumage. Just like Carla's creature, the head was blunt, more reptilian than avian. Even from this distance, Matt could see their serrated beaks.

Kurt spoke over his shoulder. "Kearns, Joop, get up here and get ready. I'm going to take one down."

Matt burrowed forward and tried to gauge where the animal would fall – probably about fifty feet to the east of them, unless it managed to fly while tranqued. He pulled the net from around his shoulders and held it in both hands.

Kurt aimed, the gun barrel rock steady. There was the sound of air being pushed through a pipe, a squawking hiss from overhead, and then all four of the archaeopteryx swooped – not flew, but sort of glided away in different directions. Matt thought they were all going to loop away into the jungle, but one crashed heavily into the foliage at ground level – obviously the tranquilizer had kicked in.

"Bingo. Boys …fetch."

Matt resisted the urge to yell *yes, bwana*, and settled for some griping under his breath. He and Joop pushed and grunted their way toward the spot they thought the bird had fallen from the sky. There was no track, and all they had to rely on was their sense of direction, with Kurt yelling curses and coarse directions from behind.

As it happened, they needed neither. Just ahead there was a hissing, squawking commotion from the undergrowth. Matt and Joop slowed, net and cage at the ready. Zeroing in on the sound, Matt paused amongst the last long threads of grasses and pushed some fronds out of the way.

It was there – one red eye, like a glittering ruby, swiveled toward them. Matt flung the net. The archaeopteryx tried to escape, but its limbs refused to obey, and it simply flopped miserably, squawking loudly under the mesh. One of its wings looked to be held at an awkward angle.

"It's injured … hey, watch out." Joop pushed Matt out of the way just as several dark objects swooped low from overhead. Lying in the grass, they looked upward. The group of archaeopteryx had landed in the trees just overhead. They stared down with a beady-eyed ferocity.

Joop nudged him. "Seems his pals haven't given up on him. Let's get this guy into the cage and quiet, and then get back to the group."

Matt pulled the net toward Joop. Small claws came through the mesh, and the creature's toothed bill set to work picking at the tough fibers. Joop had the door of the cage open, and he stuffed the protesting animal in quickly, careful of the sharp teeth and claws trying to snag anything within reach.

A large, iridescent feather remained on the flattened grasses. Matt picked it up. *Beautiful*, he thought, holding it up and allowing the muted light to highlight its shimmering, metallic coloring. He frowned and held it close to his face. Moving around on the small strands was what looked like dust – *ugh*. Matt knew exactly what it was. Thoughts of sticking the feather in his top pocket evaporated instantly. He flicked it back to the ground.

"Let's go." He wondered how Megan was doing with Carla and Jian.

* * * * *

Kurt watched Matt and Joop struggle back through the thick undergrowth, holding the caged bird between them. He ignored the crawling itch on his body. He was a jungle man; he'd put up with worse in his time … much worse.

"It's injured." The paleobiologist lifted his end of the cage as he approached.

"Badly?" Kurt raised his eyebrows.

Joop shook his head and shrugged. "Don't think so. Maybe a sprained wing, but it's in pain."

Kurt nodded, but ignored the entreaty – he couldn't do anything about its pain right now. Still, the ugly little bastard might go into shock and die. Might be a good idea to have a backup. Besides, they were here, and once he headed back, he'd prefer to keep on going … all the freakin' way home.

He didn't want the boss to decide to press on further into the center of the crater. He couldn't shake an unsettling feeling. The spider had been weird enough, and he'd encountered plenty of life-threatening animals, insects, and parasites before, but this place made him feel different – unsettled and on edge. It was about as alien, or rather, primitive, as you could get. Mankind wasn't supposed to exist in this jungle, and he had a feeling it might decide to object.

Fucked if I'm coming back anytime soon, he thought. "I'm going to take another one – maybe a breeding pair." The small archaeopteryx flock had been following them in the upper branches, hissing down at them.

"Good thinking," Steinberg responded.

"Breeding pair? How the hell will you know if you've got two of the opposite sex?" Joop's face had creased into a disbelieving frown.

Kurt stifled an urge to laugh in the man's face. Instead, he simply grinned. "That's why we brought you, isn't it?" He turned and sighted the glaring birds along the barrel, then paused, senses alert. He had acted as bodyguard, guide, lead trekker, and hunt master for a number of people over the years. He was successful because he had developed a hunter's ear – it didn't take him long to program into his brain the usual sounds of a particular forest or jungle. Anything outside of that, no matter how minute, would ring an alarm … like now.

There was something moving through the jungle – slow, but not stealthy … not yet. He couldn't be sure if it was a lone animal, but he knew it was big, and it sounded heavy – elephant-sized, at least. He clicked his fingers at Matt and Joop, getting their attention, and motioned them back in behind him.

He turned and put his finger to his lips, waving them down into a crouch. They all squatted and eased into the undergrowth, trying to make themselves as invisible as possible.

The shimmering reptilian birds overhead stopped their hissing and squawking. Looking up, Kurt could see where their attention was focussed – on the sound. It was moving closer. He put the rifle strap over his shoulder and drew his handgun.

"What is it?" Steinberg whispered, moving up behind him.

He half turned, whispering himself now. "Something's coming … something big. Get down and stay quiet." He gave the man a push.

Steinberg fell back into the lush growth, and Kurt squeezed behind the massive stem of a rubbery plant with pendulous purple fruit. He looked down at the pitiful gun – it could stop a man with a single shot, but if it was an elephant, and he hoped to God that's all it was, it'd do little more than piss it off.

He slowed his breathing and waited. He felt as though they were in a jungle within a jungle. Tall banyan trees, hundreds of feet high, were interspersed with the massive branchless trunks of cycads rising like hairy columns above a secondary jungle. Like a massive greenhouse, oversized palm fronds, lianas, and other plants that defied description grew to fifty feet or more; their car-sized glossy fronds dense and water-filled.

A crushing sound to his left made him whip his head around. A hundred feet away, two palms were being flattened; their waist-thick ribbed trunks bent over and their heads came down just behind the wall of green that separated the men from whatever was approaching.

"Get ready." Kurt could feel the perspiration run down his temples and onto his neck, joining the rivulets heading south on his body. Not all of it was due to the heat.

A snort, a deep grunt, and a smell like shit and rotting meat. *Damn*, he thought. *Fucking big carnivore* … but what type? Nothing he knew of was that big. The plants continued to give way, heralding the creature's advance. Kurt gripped the gun tighter.

An inhuman screech made him jump. It had come from at least half a mile away. Suddenly all the sounds of the jungle ceased. The screech came again, and it had a secondary effect – whatever had been approaching them changed course and sped up, bullocking its way toward whatever beast had cried out, the sound of challenge, pain, or distress too enticing to ignore.

Kurt exhaled, long and slow. Only then did he realize he had been holding his breath. He licked his lips, which had gone bone dry from his rapid breathing, and turned to his boss.

"We're done for the day."

CHAPTER 18

Something screeched and Megan jumped to her feet. "Shit – that was close. I should check it out."

Carla looked up briefly. "No. If you're here to help, you can do that by keeping a lookout. And you're right; it was close. So if we need to pack up quickly, three pairs of hands are better than two."

Jian sat back and rubbed his eyes with a forearm, careful how he used his gloved hands, which were smeared with Eohippus blood. "They are exactly the same parasite. I just can't determine the cause of their hyper-aggressive attack on the epidermis."

Carla nodded and rubbed her itchy scalp, then went back to looking through the scope. "We expected that; I always thought that the difference would be in the environment, not in the animal population or the arthropod parasites. But take a look at this ..."

She shuffled out of the way and allowed Jian to look through the scope.

He twirled the dials. "Normal blood cell shape, normal serum."

"Keep looking." Carla leaned in closer.

The entomologist changed magnification, then pulled a face. "I see it." He moved the slide a fraction and squinted back down the lens, then looked up at her. "What is it; spoor, maybe?"

"Maybe. But if we drew some blood from a different animal, or better yet, a different species, and saw that same micro-fragment, wouldn't that be informative?" She raised one eyebrow.

Megan joined them, their conversation piquing her scientific curiosity. "Something interesting?"

The scream exploded out of the jungle again – closer this time – and Megan cringed. Something was being torn apart literally a few dozen feet away. "What the fuck is that?"

Carla looked up and pulled a face. "I don't know, but it sounds like it's having a bad day." She went back to her work, but looked worried.

Megan grinned nervously, and was about to respond when they heard the sound of trees being pushed aside only a dozen feet from their clearing. She frowned – it had come from the opposite side to the loud screeching. *Something else?* she wondered.

"What was that?" Carla whispered, getting to her feet.

Megan vainly hoped it was Matt and the guys returning, but the sound had been so heavy, so …

The crushing of trees came closer and then something nightmarish pushed into their clearing. Megan had a fleeting impression of massive horns and teeth, tiny eyes in a skull too wide for the brutish body. It was a rhino, skinless bear, alligator … nightmare, a melange of beasts welded together by massive plates of muscle and sinew.

Jian leapt to his feet and screamed in Mandarin, fear causing his English to escape him.

Carla grabbed Megan's hand and crabbed backward as the huge creature descended on Jian. Megan pulled free from

Carla and lifted the only thing she had to throw – the microscope.

It shattered on the massive snout, but the piggishly small eyes never left Jian. The creature came into the open space, its bulk filling the enclosure. Megan heard screaming – her own voice. The sound hurt her ears.

* * * * *

The trek back was slow, cautious, and nerve-racking. Kurt stopped at every thicket of dense jungle that didn't afford a complete view of the area, fearful of what could be hiding just behind the curtain of deep green. It was a difficult job, as the lower growth was high and thick enough to hide a double-decker bus. However, no one complained.

The big bodyguard raised his hand, and the group crowded up behind him. They had been following their own trail back to the campsite, and now had come to a jungle crossroads. Kurt waved them forward, and they stepped out onto a veritable road – the ferns, fronds, and vines had been flattened, and a fifteen-foot wide path had been ground out of the jungle.

Kurt called Joop forward; everyone followed. He pointed at several additional marks and indentations.

"Thoughts, Professor?"

Joop walked back and forth for a few seconds and then looked up. "Quadruped. Big – possibly fifteen to twenty tons. Not pad-footed like an elephant, but claw-toed."

Kurt nodded. "Great. Four-footed and fucking big as a house."

Joop frowned and crouched, examining one of the footprints. He put his hand on the massive pugmark. "Strange." He shook his head, looked back to the group and shrugged.

"I don't know what it is, or even what family it might be associated with. Certainly not a contemporary animal, and not a reptile." He grinned at Steinberg. "Shall we get the nets ready?"

Matt peered down at the deep indentation. "Maybe one of your lost herbivores that's spreading the cycadoid seeds?"

Joop nodded. "Has to be – there have been very few, if any, large carnivores that were quadrupeds. Most of the saurians were bipedal, and the distant mammal record is free of anything this large."

"Wait here." Kurt jogged down the broad, flattened pathway, traveling a good hundred feet before yelling to the group. Matt was the first to join him. He was on one knee by a relatively small pile of cone-shaped packages. The smell was a giveaway – dung.

Kurt didn't look happy. "It's what I thought, and what I smelt a while back – carnivore."

Matt looked at the brownish-green bulbs. "How can you tell? Looks like elephant shit with slightly less vegetable matter. I can see some large plant fibers in there."

Joop answered from behind him. "Not plant fibers, crushed bone shards. He's right; it's carnivore spoor all right – longer and thinner, denser and tapered at the ends due to a more effective digestive system. Very little energy remains in the waste. Also, the smell is a giveaway – an abundance of sulfides."

Joop looked around, listening, then turned back to Kurt. "It didn't bother hiding it – means it certainly isn't afraid of much."

Kurt grunted. "Mega predator." He turned to Joop. "Well? Give me something?"

Joop looked pained. "I don't … it just shouldn't … exist. I have no idea what it is."

"Fucking experts." He turned to Steinberg. "We are not equipped to deal with something this size – we're bottom of the food chain here. I suggest we take our bird and head for home—"

The screams came from the west – everyone knew who they belonged to.

Matt took off blindly, sprinting down the flattened track. From behind him, he heard Kurt's voice, ordering him to stop. Then came the sound of pounding feet.

* * * * *

Matt made good time on the open path. He hadn't thought what he would do when it came to an end – when he came face-to-face with the gigantic, unidentified predator.

Kurt was just behind him, the large man's longer legs easily matching Matt's pace. The rest of the team were strung out in a line behind them. He knew he was being foolish in the extreme, but logic had vanished even before the last note of Megan's scream had died out.

He literally fell into the clearing, dragging in deep breaths and trying to make sense of the scene.

"Megan!" He went to charge off again, intending to do a loop around the perimeter, but a huge weight crashed into his back, flattening him.

"Stay down and shut up."

Matt grunted from the weight – Kurt had him pinned. He tried to turn over, wrestling with the larger man.

Kurt pressed his forearm across his neck. "You'll get us all killed, you dumb fuck. You know better than this."

Matt dragged in a few deep breaths, and soon his oxygen-starved brain started to see the irrationality of what he was doing. He nodded, and Kurt stood, dragging him up.

The rest of the team came into the clearing cautiously.

"Blood." John examined a huge pool of sticky material already being covered by flies from above and worms coming up through the sodden, loamy soil.

"Human?"

"No idea. But little coagulation, so it wasn't spilled all that long ago." He looked at the three-foot wide stain and looked around. "That looks about it. Doubt it was a mortal wound, judging by the amount of blood, but certainly deep. They could have escaped, unless …" He pursed his lips.

Matt finished for him. "Unless the victim was carried off."

"Well, perhaps, but animal attacks, especially savage ones by large predators, cause a lot of pattern spraying of fluids …"

"Thank you, doctor." Kurt had been walking the edge of the clearing. He came into the center of the group. "The creature came in where we did, and went out through there." He pointed. "I also see the beginning of an additional entry from two or three people who went into the jungle there, before the rest was flattened by the beast's pursuit."

Matt ground his teeth. "They went in, and the creature followed." He felt the knot in his stomach tighten. "So, we go after them." Matt started to walk toward the exit path.

"Whoa there, Professor, we're not talking about dropping down to the local 7-Eleven to pick up some groceries here. We need to think about this. Not everyone should go. That path is headed into the interior, and this is not a benign place, if you haven't already noticed. We go back to our base camp at the pool, obtain additional supplies, and then we see who needs to undertake a rescue attempt, and who needs to return through the sinkhole." Kurt turned to Steinberg. "Maybe send Moema back with a message."

Steinberg nodded. "Sure, I can do that."

Matt couldn't believe what he was hearing. "Are you fucking crazy? Every second counts here. Fuck the supplies, fuck the bird, and fuck you."

Kurt walked over and put a large hand on his shoulder. Matt batted it away but the big man stayed in front of him. "I need ammunition Matt; we should also take the flares – if not for signaling then at least as another potential weapon. I'll go with you, but the objective has got to be to save people, not throw more bodies into a meat grinder, so to speak."

He waited, staring into Matt's face. "When we find her – and we will – I want to be able to help, *really* help ... don't you?"

Matt's gut roiled, but he knew Kurt was right. He looked down at his watch. "Still a lot of daylight. Okay, let's get the supplies." He spun and headed for base camp – fast.

Matt was moving quickly back along their partially obscured trail. He dripped with perspiration, and his face, arms, and legs were lashed and scratched by jutting branches and hooked tendrils from plants that reached out to bind him as he bullocked his way through.

He would have run all day and all night if need be – the thought of Megan being pursued, or worse, in some prehistoric jungle made him feel sick. He was first to the clearing, and he immediately fell beside his pack, rummaging through the pockets, pulling out food bars, water, anything he thought might be useful.

Kurt crashed down beside him and did the same. He spoke without looking up. "Go through the other bags as well – take spare food, flashlights, and anything we can use as a weapon. Also bandages, iodine ..." He paused. "And take a pack – we don't know how long we'll be out."

Matt stopped stuffing things into his already full pockets, closed his eyes for a moment, and settled his breathing. His mind whirled and nerves clouded his thinking. He needed to calm down and focus if he was going to be of any help. He thanked fate that at least Carla and Jian were with Megan.

Steinberg lumbered into the clearing and bent down, hands on knees, red face puffing and pulling in long, ragged, wet breaths. He called to Kurt and waved him over. Matt watched as he spoke to his bodyguard, who frowned and craned his neck toward his boss with a look of incomprehension.

Joop joined Matt, packing his bag. He motioned toward the movie producer.

"I think he wants to go back, now … and he wants Kurt to go with him."

"Bullshit." Matt's jaw clenched, and his eyes narrowed as he watched. "He'll just slow us down. As far as I'm concerned, that prick can go anytime he likes."

Joop grunted. "Yes, but not Kurt; we need him if we are going to find our colleagues."

Matt stopped packing and stared at the pair. Kurt now had his hands on his hips, and Max was jabbing his finger into the man's chest. Kurt was shaking his head, but his eyes were downcast – Matt guessed that Steinberg's will was wearing him down.

Matt stood, announcing loudly, "We're ready. Let's go." His eyes were on Kurt, waiting to see what he would do, but it was Steinberg who responded.

"I'm afraid you'll need to carry on without us. Although, a better suggestion is we all head back, and rally a larger party to perform a more formal, better-equipped rescue."

Matt nodded slowly. "And that would take how long to organize?"

"No more than a few days – weeks at most." Steinberg looked away from Matt's fiery gaze.

"But …" Matt felt his frustation overwhelming him. "But, you're covered in the mites. You can't go back yet."

Steinberg swung back, looking bored. "Got plenty of DDT wash, and a change of clothes waiting. We'll be fine; let's get moving. Kurt?"

Kurt was standing slightly apart from his boss, looking out into the jungle. He turned slowly, his face grim.

"Max, I think you know that in a few days, there might be no one left to rescue. If it was you lost in this place, would you want us to abandon you?"

"No one is being abandoned, and I don't like your tone, Mr. Douglas." He turned to the group. "What I'd want is for someone to make a courageous decision that was best for everyone. It is grossly irresponsible to risk everyone, and I won't do it." He shrugged, looking regretful. "Sorry Professor, I'm in charge. You can take whatever supplies you need, but you'll need to go on alone from here."

Matt's mouth dropped open in disbelief, and then his fists balled. He could feel the blood rushing to his head. A hand came down on his shoulder.

"Not alone; I will also stay and search for our friends." Joop slung his pack over his shoulder.

Steinberg shrugged, indifferent, until John also came and stood beside Matt. His face wrinkled in surprise. "Ah, fuck, John, don't be an ass."

John sighed. "Maxwell, I know and you know that the amount of blood in the clearing indicated that someone is going to need me. I've got to go with them."

The movie producer seemed about to argue, then his mouth turned down in disappointment. "Okay, okay, fine. Good luck to all of you."

Matt wasn't prepared to give up just yet. "Kurt, we need you."

Kurt kept his eyes on the ground. He grimaced, then shook his head slowly.

Steinberg took this as a rebuttal to Matt's request. "As I said, good luck. Come on Kurt, we should be going while there's plenty of light left." He turned again to Matt. "Once we're away from the interference, we'll call in some support." His brow creased in sympathy. "I think you'll appreciate that we can't wait for you at the Ndege village."

Matt crossed to stand in front of the big bodyguard. "Kurt, he doesn't need you; we do. Moema can guide him back."

Kurt lifted his head and made eye contact for the first time.

"Don't make this more difficult, Professor Kearns. Joop, please assist Kurt in getting the bird bagged for transport through the sinkhole." Steinberg pulled his facemask from the pack and checked its light.

"He's right."

Steinberg froze. Kurt continued to hold Matt's eyes, and for a moment, Matt wasn't sure who he was referring to.

"Moema knows the land here better than I do. I led all these people in, and I'll damn well lead them all out." Steinberg got to his feet, his face turning red. Kurt went on, now facing his boss. "Bottom line, if it was you lost in this place, I'd damn well come and find you."

"Fuck it." Steinberg went to slam his facemask on the ground, just stopping himself at the last moment. He charged up to Kurt, muscling Matt out of the way, and took hold of the big man's forearms.

"I'll give you twice the bonus I offered." He paused. "Triple." He smiled in what he thought was his most disarming fashion. "Come on, Kurt, you know we don't have the equipment or people for a full-scale search. And we certainly don't have the right armaments." He nodded at the lone gun on Kurt's hip.

Kurt stepped out of the man's grip. "They're competent people. If they've stuck together, maybe we can find them all quickly, and be back by morning." He looked at Matt. "But if they're scattered, then I'm afraid we can't spend more than a few days searching. Agreed?"

Matt looked away, while the others nodded their assent. He wasn't leaving without Megan. Sure, they had some problems, but there was no way he could live with the knowledge that she might have been alive, and for the want of an extra hour, or day, or however long, she could have been found.

Kurt turned to Steinberg. "Good luck."

Matt watched the movie producer for a few more seconds. The man was still slightly red in the face. He looked at Matt and shrugged, his mouth set in a wry smile.

Matt smiled back. "You'd better pray we find them. Because you'll never get that bird back into the States without Carla's approval. It's simple really – she doesn't come back, the bird doesn't go back. And it will have all been for nothing."

Steinberg's eyes burned into Matt for a few seconds before his smile returned.

"You let me worry about that, sonny. But I'll tell you right here and right now, I could have a team of fifty jungle specialists and medical experts here in two days. Just think about what you're doing. If you're still looking in two days, you'll regret this. I just wanted to help."

Matt shook his head. He knew Steinberg couldn't give a fuck about him, or any of them. "Good luck."

He turned and followed the others into the red-hued jungle. To Matt, it now looked like hell.

* * * *

Megan tore madly through the green walls, fighting the vines that clung to her skin and wrapped around her limbs. They whipped at her body and face, making her look like the recipient of a severe lashing. Fear pushed her on. She sucked in air and threw her shoulder into a dense clump of green, breaking through, with Carla landing on top of her.

"What happened ...?" Carla wheezed.

"We're out of it ... I think." Megan levered herself up on her hands and knees, breathing deeply. She spat more of the mashed green plants from her mouth. Every now and then, something particularly unpleasant would end up on their tongues, with Carla doubling over a mile or so back and throwing up.

Megan wiped the sweat from her eyes. After the chaotic tangle of the jungle it was a strange scene – there was no undergrowth for what looked like several miles. The landscape was still punctuated with the same huge tree trunks, as thick as houses, towering hundreds of feet into the air and still meshed together beneath the ever-present red roof of thorned vines. But underneath, at ground level, the grasses were only a few inches high.

"Looks like a park," Megan observed.

"More like a paddock that's been grazed – by large herbivores." Carla kneeled beside her.

Megan got to her feet, surveying the open ground. She turned her head and strained to listen for any sounds of pursuit, then swallowed and used her sodden shirt to wipe her face. She helped Carla to her feet. "Do you think it's still coming?"

Carla turned back to the jungle. "Maybe, but I think it'll be … preoccupied with Jian for a while."

Megan continued to stare into the dark jungle. "He might have got away …" Megan trailed off. In her heart she knew the entomologist hadn't stood a chance. He knew what he was doing when he got between it and Megan and Carla – sacrificing himself. The thing had descended on him and crushed him to the ground with a clawed foot the size of a manhole. Its jaws had opened wider than anything she had ever seen in her life, and then descended slowly toward the screaming man's head. That's when they had turned and fled – she still felt like a coward.

Carla squared her shoulders, trying to pull herself together. "We can't take the gamble that it will give up. I say we keep heading inward for a few more miles, and then try to loop back."

Megan turned to look out over the flat ground. Except for a few good-sized lumps, like pitcher's mounds, it was relatively flat. At a jog, she reckoned she could cross it in under an hour, easy.

"Ready?"

Carla pulled a face. "I don't like it – it's too open."

"We've got a head start. This open ground will extend it. I say we go for it, leave some clothing at the other end for it to play with, and then start looping back. That should take it miles away – and I want that freak as far from our camp as we can get it."

Carla grimaced, obviously unconvinced. "Okay, but don't slow down for me."

Megan took a step, then froze. "Wait."

A single creature that looked like a labrador-sized armadillo waddled into the clearing, stopping to eat something it had found in the grass. It then continued on, untroubled. More of the animals followed, until there were about a dozen of them.

"There are your herbivores, I think." Megan pointed. "Well, if they're okay, we certainly will be." She turned and gave Carla a nervous grin. "And besides, if that big mother chasing us enters the clearing, I'm betting we can run faster than any of those little sawn-off guys."

And with that, they started to run.

CHAPTER 19

Steinberg looked down at the strange bird in the cage next to him. It cocked its head and glared back at him. He leaned in close and it backed away, hissing, and dropping a few shimmering feathers. He stuck a finger into the cage and slid one out, lifting it and twirling it in his fingers, delighting in the way the light played on its iridescent highlights.

"You know what, buddy? It's all your goddamn fault."

The bird continued to watch him suspiciously. He rummaged in his pack and pulled out a tiny plastic bag, placing the feather inside and then sealing it. "That's for Kurt's hat, payment for selling me out, when we get home … if we fucking get home from this goddamn shithole of a jungle."

He pushed the bag into the folds of Kurt's pack and then sat back on a rock at the edge of the pond. The humidity was still oppressive, and he flicked small stones into the black water, the heat making it look almost inviting.

He stared hard at it. "I can do this." He pulled the facemask onto his forehead and lifted one of the larger plastic bags, gauging how much air he'd need to include for the bird, and how much extra weight he'd need to compensate for the additional buoyancy. He tried to remember how long the swim was, and whether there were any bends or twists in the underwater cave.

He shook his head, lost with the complexity of it all. "Fuck it. This wasn't supposed to be my job, you know. Someone could drown." He looked at the bird and grinned. "And guess which one of us that's likely to be."

He laughed without mirth, and flicked one of the stones into the cage, eliciting a satisfying hiss. "I bet you taste like chicken." He laughed again, the guffaws quickly turning into heavy breaths, more from nerves than fatigue.

"Ah, fuck." He pulled the mask off his head.

* * * * *

Kurt slowed and then stopped. He didn't need to raise his hand; everyone froze. They knew the dangers of following the huge animal's trail, and that being alert could be the difference between life and death. Kurt had holstered his gun, but Matt knew from the way his hand constantly hovered nearby that it could be in his hand in the blink of an eye.

Matt had cut a tree branch, about six feet long and sharpened at one end. It needed fire-hardening, but it was sharp enough to penetrate flesh, and long enough that he felt it would keep something at bay, at least for a short period of time. Joop had done the same and John held some sort of bent club, a little like a boomerang.

They eased forward, one slow step at a time, over broken trees and bent palm fronds, until they stepped out into a clearing of depressed grasses. It was a bowl-shaped enclosure that had been pressed flat, as if a large dog had circled before settling down with a bone. Which is almost exactly what had happened.

Joop jammed a hand over his mouth, and Kurt swore softly. He drew his gun and then turned to John.

"Can you find out who it ... err, was?"

Kurt and Joop stayed at the edge of the clearing while John walked forward. Matt was right on his heels, silently praying it wasn't Megan.

The pile of offal was obviously the less palatable bits of a body – intestines, larger bones, and gristle. There was no sign of anything else, except for a red abraded ball-like object at the clearing's edge. John made for this, and, without any hint of disgust, picked it up and turned it over.

Matt winced – there were no features left, and it was impossible to tell who it had been. It looked like something had tried to grind the meat from the hard bone of the skull; large gouges had been carved into the tough bone of the brow, which still flapped with a few scraps of bloody hair.

John grunted. "Male – Jian."

Matt exhaled. Despite the horrifying loss, he couldn't help feeling a little relieved. "Are you sure?"

John nodded. "Yes, I'm sure. Poor chap – stronger jawbone, more prominent supraorbital ridges – definitely male."

Kurt spoke softly from behind them. "We can't stay here, this'll draw scavengers … and more predators."

Matt turned quickly. "Only one body, and no sign of Megan and Carla."

Kurt nodded, and pointed to where the grasses were compressed at the far edge of the clearing. "They've got a head start, but time is against us."

Joop joined them; his face looked green. "Poor Jian."

Matt looked back down at the mess. Jian had been obliterated. Probably eaten alive; nothing left but his guts and head. *Maybe I should say something*, he thought, searching for the right words.

Kurt had already started walking. "We don't want to be here anymore. C'mon."

John patted Matt on the shoulder, and then used it to get to his feet. "He's right. Our priority is the living now. Let's find our friends."

Matt knew they were right. There was nothing anyone could do for Jian, and nobody was even going to spend five minutes trying to bury the remains. Find Megan and Carla and then get the hell outta here, that was the plan ... the only plan. He grabbed his spear and jogged after them.

* * * * *

The massive beast moved like a Mack truck through the tangled undergrowth, pausing to lower its head and inhale. The small animals it followed had left stomach fluid on the soil surface, and it was sharp with fear and fatigue.

A long, leathery tongue snaked out to lick at the miniscule drops. It wanted them – it had tasted one, and the meat was soft and salty, with no bony plates, spines, or stinging poison sacs. It wanted more. It would gorge itself on the creatures, and then return to its lair and regurgitate the meat to consume over a number of days.

It lifted its head, too large for its body, the skin drawn tight over the large knobbly, box-like structure. Megan had thought it a cross between a deformed rhino and a crocodile, a monstrous dinosaur, but the reality was it was related to neither – it was something far more primitive than the ancient saurians.

It sniffed deeply, inhaling the scents still hanging in the humid air. Small eyes stared hard into the misted landscape, but they were not its primary sense. It shook its bulk, small parasites falling free from shoulders fifteen feet from the ground. It was twice as long as it was high, and its twenty-ton bulk was supported by column-like legs ending in broad clawed feet, each with articulated toes. It could stand on its hind legs for short periods of time, and grip things if it needed to. It sniffed again, its long head coming around to fix in one direction.

The mouth opened almost half the length of its skull. Its ancestry was akin to that of a reptile, but with warm blood its family sat somewhere in between mammals and reptiles on the distant evolutionary scale. One day it would evolve into something very different – smaller and more benign. But in here, it was a mountain of talons, teeth and horned bone, one of the crater's fearsome rulers.

Saber-like teeth, still strung with gristly tendons and fragments of clothing, snapped together as it moved its bulk forward slowly. It was capable of short bursts of speed, but would preserve these for when its prey was in sight.

It followed the scent trail, which gave it a clear path forward in the red-misted landscape.

*****

Steinberg sat on a rock and chewed at a stick of dried mystery meat that Moema had prepared a few days back. It was salty and tough, but high in energy and, he had to admit, quite tasty. But he struggled to enjoy his meal as his thoughts tumbled and fell over each other.

He grimaced and rolled his shoulders, the movement doing nothing to ease the discomfort he felt over his torso. He was itchy as fuck, and wanted a warm bath. He looked toward the calm water. He could try and swim back through; he could do it. He'd need to convince Moema to take him back without the rest of the team. The Brazilian might baulk, but so what? He could try and make it by himself.

He looked at the bird, holding its ruby red gaze for a few seconds before exhaling slowly. "Who the fuck am I kidding? I wouldn't last a day."

He ran stubby fingers up across his thinning pate. That Kearns guy was right; once he got to the US, how was he supposed to get the animal back in? He threw his head back. "I need some fucking help here."

His voice bounced off the crater wall and he sat forward, biting another chunk off the meat. He looked across at the cage; the bird was looking intently at the meat in his hand.

"What, you want some? Or are you thinking about ripping my eyes out?" He snorted and broke off about half an inch of the tough meat and tossed it into the cage. The bird watched it drop, and then bobbed its head to fix its eyes back on him.

Steinberg sat back, looking at the bird. "Don't trust me, huh? Not many do. Go on, it's good."

The bird lowered its head to the morsel and snapped it up, chewing in a very un-bird-like fashion – more like that of a dog.

"Good?" Max watched it for a few seconds. "So, ugly bird, what should I do?"

The bird swallowed and then lifted its head, puffed up its luminescent feathers, and shat on the cage floor.

"That's your only opinion?"

The bird cocked its head and looked past Max out into the jungle.

Max grunted. "Yeah, that's what I thought." He took a larger piece of the meat and tossed it into the cage. "Be here when I get back." He grabbed a pack, stuffing in a water bottle, knife, and anything else he thought might be of use, then stood and turned to the jungle, took a single step, then paused, looking back over his shoulder. He returned to the other packs and removed the breathing apparatus from each one, stuffing them all into a single bag, along with some of the remaining meat.

"In case they get back first; now they'll wait for me ... whether they like it or not." He laughed croakily, then dragged the bag to the jungle's edge and hid it under a pile of fallen branches before lifting his own pack and throwing it over his shoulder.

"Just keeping them safe, okay?" He winked at the bird, which regarded him coldly with its ruby red gaze.

***** * *

From behind a wall of fronds, she silently watched the giant move clumsily from the clearing. The two-legs was similar to her, but larger, more cumbersome, and was a strange skinless-pink. Once the sounds of its departure receded into the jungle, she moved quickly into the camp, rummaging through the bags and boxes, stopping to peer in at the caged bird. She knew of the animal from the jungle, but never ate them, as they tasted bad.

The bird hissed, and she hissed in return, slapping the cage and eliciting even more agitated sounds from inside. The bird dropped its chunk of meat. She immediately jammed two small dark fingers in through the bars and snatched the morsel from the cage floor, stuffing it into her mouth. It was good.

She sniffed deeply, moving her head to inhale all the odors of the camp. There had been more of them. Moving cautiously to the pile of logs and fern fronds, she easily found the bag the tall one had secreted. Tearing it open, she found more of the meat, and some other strange things inside. She decided to take them all.

The skinless giants were even stranger than the brown skins that used to come every full moon.

The bag was heavy, but she was strong. She followed the pink giant.

***** * *

Megan could have made it to the other side in twenty minutes, running flat out. Although her body ached and her lungs burned, adrenalin and fear powered muscles that were still long and youthful. However, behind her, Carla's breathing was ragged, and she half-loped, her body running on reserves only. Megan slowed to allow the older woman to catch up.

"I said ... don't wait ... for me." Carla gasped out the words.

"Save your breath and keep—" There was a screech, and Megan's head whipped around. She slowed further.

She was sure it had come for the herd of small animals. But they all seemed to be there, just frozen and looking slightly confused. She slowed to a walk. "Did you hear that?"

Carla looked at the jungle perimeter, a massive green wall bordering the clearing. "Of course. Maybe just a—"

Another screech. This time the small animals were clearly agitated, moving back and forth, a chittering noise rising from their huddle. One of the small beasts made a break from the pack. It had crossed about twenty paces of open ground before there was a blur of movement and it simply ... disappeared. Megan frowned, not sure what she had just seen. One second the animal had been there, the next there was a terrified scream, and then it was gone.

"What ... what just happened? What the hell just happened?" Megan stopped and swung left and right. Carla came up beside her and the women stood back-to-back, dead center in the massive clearing.

"I don't know – it just ... went. And look, the pack ... it's smaller now. I'm sure of it."

The animals' small eyes were wide. Even from that distance, the women could see how terror made the whites show clearly around the orbs. Instead of fleeing, the armadillo creatures had formed into a tight knot of bodies, armored shoulders and heads pointed to the outside and young at the very center. Like a many-legged beast they edged toward the side of the jungle they had come from, but as they came close to one of the manhole-sized mounds the women had observed, the mound itself flipped up like a jack-in-the-box, and long black shiny legs shot out and grabbed one of the small beasts, dragging it inside.

"Oh shit, it's more of the goddamn spiders."

Carla groaned. 'Worse, they're fully grown – look, it's the size of a Rottweiler."

Megan's head whipped around as she noticed that they were about ten feet from one of the mounds. Looking down, she could see silken lines leading from the lump – trip-wires. She was sure if she approached any further, she would be able to see the tips of feet, each resting lightly on a thread, and the lid open just a crack so that eight alien eyes could fix firmly on her.

Her heart thumped in her chest. She could almost feel the spider's unblinking gaze and knew that the powerful, elongated body would be waiting, hard carapace-covered muscles coiled in the darkness, ready to spring out and grab her, inject her with venom, and then drag her down to be sucked dry like the Eohippus. She almost vomited.

"We can still make it. We need … to keep moving." Even to her own ears, her words sounded shuddery and small. Megan grabbed Carla's hand and together they walked toward the far side of the clearing, giving the mounds as much clearance as they could manage.

Even though the light was dimming, they could pick out the numerous mounds. Luckily for them, it seemed the massive arachnids were territorial, and demanded a certain amount of space between their burrows. Megan was confident they could navigate without coming too close to any one of them – besides, they had no choice.

The women edged along slowly, and Megan saw that the armadillo creatures were now down to just over half of their number – *poor things*, she thought. They had been bunching tighter and tighter. Suddenly, as if some point of final compression had been reached, they exploded outward, compact bodies and short legs racing toward the jungle edge.

Good for them, Megan thought as she alternated between watching the beasts and keeping her distance from the mounds. The fleeing animals, still keeping their young in the center of their herd, lifted her spirits and convinced her that she and Carla should do the same – sprint, rather than creep along. They needed to get out of there – the thought of being trapped in the open when the giant monstrosity that had attacked Jian was still behind them, was a nightmare.

"We should also—" The words had barely left her mouth when some of the closest spiders launched from their burrows. Three of the many-legged horrors, each the size of a large dog, moved at a frightening speed toward their prey. Long, muscular bodies easily overtook the smaller animals and huddled over the screaming beasts, burying finger-length fangs into their armored hides and then dragging the jerking animals back to their lairs.

"Oh no, no, no – they're coming out."

* * * * *

The women ran. Megan felt like she was flying as she belted across the open ground, fear giving her wings. Carla managed to stay with her for the first few hundred feet, but then started to fall behind.

Megan veered slightly, angling to avoid one of the mounds. They weren't that far from the jungle edge now. As she looked over her shoulder she was horrified to see two of the trapdoors behind them fly open and a pair of massive black shapes burst from their burrows. The things were a chaotic blur of long legs and bristling determination. She felt like crying as she tried to accelerate.

"Keep going!" Carla screamed. Megan could see she looked about to stop. *No way – fucked if anyone else is going to sacrifice themselves for me today*, she thought, and dropped back slightly to allow Carla to catch her.

Megan grabbed Carla's arm. "Follow me and do as I do."

The closest spider was now only about fifty feet away. Its black glossy eyes were like small pools of obsidian atop a muscular, humped thorax. Another fifty feet back came the next one.

Megan swerved, dragging Carla toward one of the remaining trapdoors. When the sound of the creature's scrabbling feet was loud in their ears, they ran across the silken mesh of tripwires. The reaction was immediate. As the lid flipped back, she and Carla swerved sharply, and the spider behind them leapt. It was intercepted in mid-air by the approaching monster – she was right, the things were territorial, and the encroaching spider had issued a challenge that could not be ignored.

While the two giant arachnids wrestled on the ground, the last spider closed on them. Megan ripped at her shirt, bursting buttons and tearing it from her back. In one swinging movement she turned and flung the damp material behind her. The garment opened in the air like a parachute, and by instinct the spider leapt on the moving object, burying its long fangs into the sodden material.

They sprinted the last few hundred feet and dove into the undergrowth. Megan immediately rolled to her feet and snatched up a broken length of tree branch, turning and pointing it sword-like in front of her.

She waited – seconds passed, but there was nothing. No sound of pursuit, no multiple-legged monster bursting through the hole they had cleaved as they dove through the wall of jungle – nothing but silence.

"Did ... it ... give up?" Carla was dragging in ragged breaths, unable to raise her head from the ground.

Megan peered through the hole.

There came a maelstrom of sound and, as she watched, the spider raced back toward its burrow; it dove in and dragged the manhole cover shut, disappearing like a magician's trick. It had looked ... panicked.

Her breath caught in her throat – she could now see the reason for the noise and frantic activity. The massive monster, the devourer of Jian, had entered the clearing.

* * * *

Megan scrambled down the embankment of a stinking river that bubbled up out of the ground. Carla arrived next to her in a roll, covered in mud and debris. She stayed on her knees, sucking in huge breaths and spitting out mud-speckled sputum. She coughed, then vomited onto the soil, forcing up nothing but stringy bile, streaked with mud.

Megan shook her head. "It's a freakin' swamp." She turned back, and then stood up, peering one way, then the next. "I don't know – should we go around?"

Carla just lay on the ground, groaning. "I guess so …" She closed her eyes.

Megan squinted out over the pools of shallow, boggy water, broken by huge trees standing on stilt-like roots. The water was a brackish red, and a silver mist hung over everything. She rubbed her forehead with her arm, and immediately felt more perspiration rush to take its place. It ran into her eyes, bringing with it some of the debris she had picked up on her mad dash through the jungle.

She looked over her shoulder and held her breath for a second or two, concentrating on the sounds behind them. It was difficult to make anything out – everything that could chirrup, croak, or scuttle seemed to congregate near the stagnant pools.

Megan turned to look out over the heavily misted water. "So, swamp or no swamp?" As she scanned the wet landscape, a large bird glided toward her, coming in fast. It didn't stop, and zoomed to within a foot of her face.

Megan raised hands to protect her eyes, but the thing hovered in front of her like a toy on a string. The massive insect had two golf ball-sized compound eyes at the front of a two-foot-long body, and long, diaphanous wings, beating so fast they were nearly invisible.

Carla sat up and threw a handful of mud at the enormous dragonfly. It changed direction, heading back out over the water. She snorted. "I think no swamp – bad things live in swamps. Besides, if that creature manages to find us, its longer legs will probably navigate the mud better than ours. Let's try and stick to the drier edge."

Once again, they started to jog. They ducked under hanging vines and trees like fleshy weeping willows, their draping limbs covered in a sticky leaf that had trapped small animals and insects as they passed through the curtains of green. The ground underfoot was beginning to flatten and become spongy as the dry bank disappeared. To their dismay, it seemed the entire landscape was turning into a bog.

To Megan's left, the water was now complete – a massive lake with any opposing bank hidden behind a thick mist. It reminded her of the old Hammer horror movies that had Nessie rise up to roar at some poor Scottish soul who had wondered too near to the Loch after dark.

They plowed on, the soft ground taking its toll on their legs. "We need to rest." Megan stopped and bent over, hands on knees and taking in deep drafts of the stinking humid air. Carla seemed to have found a second wind. She had her hands on her hips and had wandered a few paces forward to survey the landscape. Megan was amazed at her stamina – she was used to jogging five miles a day before breakfast and doing aerobics three times a week. After the rush across the spider field, she had expected to be carrying the CDC woman by now.

Carla turned and shook her head. "I agree we need to rest, but not here, not now." She turned again, peering into the jungle, clearly expecting an unwelcome appearance at any moment.

"We need to find some high, and preferably dry, ground." She swallowed audibly. "And some water." She looked up overhead. The light was fading to a dull maroon – there was little of the day left. "We can't be caught on the ground – maybe we can find one of the banyan trunks we can climb."

Megan groaned, dreading the thought of spending the night in the jungle. She slapped at her bare shoulder – things the size of sparrows whirred and buzzed close by, trying to alight on her sweaty skin. "Okay, a bit more then. But we should also think about looping back soon."

Carla nodded. "Sure. C'mon." She turned and started off again.

Megan followed about five paces behind. She stepped in an ankle-deep puddle, causing a small wave to slosh up over its edge. Something splashed in the lake, and the mist momentarily swirled. "Easy Nessie," she whispered nervously.

The pair slowed now – they had no choice; the boggy ground sucked at their boots and splashed them with slimy water. Every inch was a battle. The smell was becoming sulfurous, and most footsteps elicited a fart of swamp gas trapped just below the surface.

They searched for high ground, or at least a tree trunk so they could get above the stinking morass. Megan plodded on, head down, mostly watching her feet and swerving around the trees that stood on slimy stilts above the boggy mess.

Ahead of her Carla had stopped. "Oh no."

Megan swiveled and then sagged with disappointment. "End of the line – we're fucked." Their muddy trek had ended on a peninsula of brown swampy soil. Excepting their route of entry, there was water on all sides – not just the shallow brackish pools they had been meandering through, but deep water, stained red by the flowers, just like the pond they had entered the crater through. Away in the mist, things splashed out from the bank, and looking down into the shallows, Megan could see small creatures wriggling and jerking in the warm water.

Carla spun, looking around them. She shook her head. "Two options – we try and cross, or we double back, pronto."

"Huh – you mean swim it?" Megan pushed her wet hair back off her face. She looked out over the water, the mist hanging over a surface that seemed alive with movement. Time and again, the water surface swirled and lumped, as if there was a large fish just below the surface. She laughed softly, the notes sounding slightly manic even to her own ears. She shook her head.

"You know, the next time I demand to come on one of your trips, can you be a little more forceful when saying no?"

* * * * *

Max Steinberg grabbed a tree trunk and turned to lean against it. He pulled an expensive-looking silver compass from his pocket and flipped the lid, turning it one way and then the next.

"Fucking stupid magnetic hell-hole fucker."

He snapped it closed and jammed it back in his pocket. He had the feeling he had somehow wandered off the trail he had been following, although "trail" was a flattering description. It was really just a slightly less tangled area of the jungle, with flattened grasses. He was moving so slowly he wasn't sure he'd be able to catch up to the rest of the team now.

He looked at his watch – ten to five – no wonder it seemed a little dimmer, even with the heavy canopy overhead. He'd give it another ten minutes or so and then turn around. It'd take him roughly an hour to get back, with just enough light left to try and swim through the tunnel. Fuck the bird if it drowned. Now that he knew where this place was, he'd come back with a big enough team to net, shoot, or eat every motherfucking thing in this hidden shithole.

He smacked his lips. Suddenly the thought of diving into the dark water and finishing his evening with a hot meal of monkey pie or whatever concoction the little Brazilian whipped up sounded pretty good. He was sure he'd be able to convince Moema to head back – after all, money always talked loudest in these stinking places.

He continued on, no longer in a hurry, taking another bite from his remaining piece of dried meat and washing it down with water the temperature of hot blood. Looking around, he grunted – it all looked strange, and yet familiar at the same time. He paused at a jumble of fallen logs, trying to remember whether or not he had been past here before.

A rustle in the brush beside him convinced him to keep moving. He looked at his watch again – still two minutes to go. Bugger it, he'd gone far enough. He turned on his heel and started to walk quickly back the way he'd come.

He was feeling more unsettled with every step. A thousand eyes watching every second, Moema had said. *Sure feels like it*, he thought, feeling the hairs on his neck prickle. He stopped and whipped his head around, listening for a few seconds.

"Who's there? I've got a gun." He wished he really did as he started walking again, picking up his pace. It was like the time he decided to walk home from a bar to sober up. He'd turned into an alley and within two seconds knew he was being followed. This felt the same, but a million times worse.

The rustling in the heavy undergrowth was only a few feet in, but whoever or whatever it was remained hidden ... and worse, it seemed to be keeping pace with him.

"Fuck off ... I'm a good shot." Max pulled his hunting knife, the ornate silver pommel engraved with the letters "M.S.", and brandished it as he walked. He hoped the silver tooth would be enough to deter whatever giant rat or bug had decided to follow him. In his other hand he held a forgotten morsel of dried meat. He tossed it toward the sound.

"That's all you're getting." He started to jog, muscling his way through strangling vines and fern fronds. The rustling sounds kept pace.

Max sped up a little more, but the undergrowth beside him was pummeled and pushed as the thing worked hard to match his speed. From the sound and force, he estimated it to be the mass of a good-sized dog – maybe a hundred pounds – more than big enough to give him some trouble.

"Shit, shit, shit." He picked up a stick and threw it at his invisible stalker. It hissed – that was it.

"Fuck it." He ran.

Max Steinberg bullocked his way forward, slashing his hunting blade at anything in his path. He knew he was pan-icking, but he couldn't help it. Fuck Kurt for leaving him. He'd fire that bastard when he next saw him.

He paused for a second. Everything looked different. Either the path had shrunk, or he was wildly off course. He charged on. There was an open patch of grass ahead, bordered by a leaning tree that made a perfect hurdle. He ran and leapt, his short legs never gaining enough height to clear it. His back foot snagged and he came down hard.

His pursuer finally burst from the foliage behind him, keen to take advantage of his misfortune. It landed on his legs, pinning them, and Max looked over his shoulder, his mouth dropping open in a scream that his stricken throat refused to release.

"Gah ..." His mind refused to assemble the image, to make words, or to categorize what he was seeing. It looked like a giant monstrous glove had gripped both his legs. Glossy black exoskeletal fingers were wrapped around his lower body, bony knuckles flexing, and on the back of the glove ... eyes.

Fucking goddamn giant spider! his mind finally screamed. The massive Mesothelae was more than five times the size of the one he had shot at on their first trek. Up close, the detail was like something from a mad, drunken nightmare. Its body was long and powerful, a glossy licorice black, and on top of a long, lumpen head, glass-like eyes regarded him with cold, alien indifference. Still face down, he tried to move, but the spider's grip was like steel cable.

The movie producer was hypnotized as he and the spider stared at each other, evaluating, understanding their respective positions – one predator, the other prey. Max tried to turn over and simultaneously slash backward with the blade of his knife. The monstrous creature scrabbled forward and then two fangs as long as pencils penetrated the tough fabric of his pants to slide into the soft flesh of his buttocks. The pain was excruciating, but only for a second or two, then it was quickly replaced with a flooding warmth as the poison started to take effect.

"Fuck no-ooo." The last word stretched, coming out squashy as the muscles in his tongue started to relax. His head and shoulders dropped to the ground. He could see, smell, and hear everything – it was just his muscles that were now held hostage by the venom of the massive spider.

Max could see the ground move under his face, and knew that the arachnid was tugging him into the forest. "Kurt!" he yelled, but only in his mind.

He remembered what Joop had said when they were watching the smaller spider attack the tiny horse – it would liquefy its prey and then drink the fluids straight from the body. *I'm about to become a Max Steinberg milkshake,* he thought morbidly.

He thought he was thrashing, screaming, punching, and kicking, but the frantic activity only took place in his imagination now, as he was dragged back into the thick foliage.

A shadow fell across his vision – a person, was it a woman? Hard to tell. Tiny, naked, and covered in hair, she watched him with indifference for a second or two. *Save me*, his eyes pleaded.

She darted over, but only to pick up his fallen knife. She turned it over in her little hands, then looked back into his frozen face. She held up one palm, the fingers curling up and down. He would have laughed if he could – she was waving goodbye.

* * * * *

"Looks like someone just drove a truck through there." The men stood at the edge of the clearing, looking out over the churned ground. The creature they had been following had broken cover to cross the clearing. Its massive bodyweight and clawed feet had scraped a path across the landscape.

Kurt stepped out, and squatted. The edges of the furrows were still crumbling inward.

"It's not that far in front now."

"Well, what are we waiting for?" Matt stepped out onto the grass beside him.

Kurt rested his elbows on his thighs, looking up at Matt. "Do you think we should consider what we're going to do when we catch up to it? We've got a few sharp sticks, a few knives, and one gun – not much against a freakin' biological tank."

"Yeah, we don't try and kill it – we just change its mind ... or direction."

"Piece of cake." Kurt grinned and got to his feet. He started to walk and Matt went to follow.

"Wait, wait, something is not right." Joop reached out and put his hand on Matt's shoulder. Matt shrugged it free and spun at him.

"What are you doing? I mean, seriously... something is not right? Everything about this place is not right." Matt turned and went to continue.

"Professor Kearns, you won't help your friends by getting killed." Joop took a few more steps. "Look, just look at the clearing. What do you see?"

Kurt had stopped to listen, and Matt turned to look out across the open ground. There was nothing save for a few massive tree trunks and some slight lumps in the grasses, a little like baseball pitcher mounds.

"Nothing," he said.

"In a jungle there is always something." Joop picked up a couple of fist-sized stones from the clearing edge, and tossed one. It landed on the ground and bounced a couple of times before rolling to a stop. He took the next and threw it, obviously using the first as a distance guide. This time the rock flew a little farther and landed near one of the mounds, bouncing and then rolling in front of it. Almost faster than the eye could follow, a black shape launched itself from the mound, grabbed at the stone, assessed it as inedible, released it, and disappeared under the trapdoor it had lifted.

"Holy fuck!" Matt stepped back into the foliage.

"Jesus Christ, that was one of those spiders, except bigger." Kurt had his gun up and was retreating hastily.

"Yes, I thought as much," said Joop. "The Mesothelae were ground hunters, not web spinners. And fossil evidence indicated the spider species liked burrows – open ground is their favorite nesting site. They will have a radial mesh of trip-wire all around their lair – when their prey steps on one they can be out and on top of it in a second."

"Megan and ..."

Joop shook his head, waving his hand. "No, I think they're okay. If the large beast is still following them, they must have somehow managed to pass through."

Matt nodded. "Good. Then so will we … how?"

Kurt started out, gun at the ready. "We follow this big fucker's tracks. I reckon he's flattened or buried anything in front of him. Be ready to fend off any sneak attacks." He looked up at the canopy ceiling. "We're running out of light, so let's pick it up."

As they stepped out of the tangle of vines and ferns, the atmosphere immediately felt cooler against their skin. With every step, they seemed to leave the raucous sounds of the jungle behind. Matt became conscious of his own breathing – raspy and dry. He took a sip of his remaining water, purposely doing little more than wetting his lips and tongue. It needed to last until they got back … if they got back.

They now had a clear path – the land leviathan they followed had gouged the ground before them, crushing or burying anything dangerous. However, they would need to pass by several of the three-foot wide trapdoors, death lurking beneath each one.

The four men moved like a single creature – Kurt at the front with the gun, Matt to the right, John at the left, and Joop bringing up the rear, facing backward as he walked. All except Kurt had sharpened sticks pointed outward.

When they were within twenty feet of a mound, Kurt aimed and fired. It was almost imperceptible, but they all saw it – the lid closed a fraction. The thing that had been peeking out either pulled back from the noise or was hit.

Kurt grunted his approval. "Shoot first, no need to ask questions later."

"I hear that." Matt kept his long stake pointed at the mound as they passed.

Joop gave the group a shove. "We need to hurry; I think I can see movement." He backed into them harder, pushing them forward.

Kurt fired at another mound, with the same effect. "Don't like that, do you boys?" He laughed cruelly, and was about to turn when Joop yelled and banged into them hard.

"It's out … it's coming."

Matt turned and saw the large spider racing across the open ground. Its long black legs were a blur of motion. Immediately, three long pikes swiveled in its direction, with Joop trying to wrestle his way in amongst them. He screamed, his voice getting higher with his rising panic.

"Shoot, shoot!"

"I can't … it's moving … too fast," Kurt replied jerkily over their heads.

In another second the spider was on them, leaping at the closest human – Joop. However, instead of meeting soft flesh, its softer underbelly was impaled on his stake. He fell back, the thing continuing to slide toward him as its weight pushed it down the length of the wood. Matt and John stabbed at it, their pikes barely piercing the leathery hide of its back.

Oddly, Matt smelt bread, the large lumpen body giving off an odor of warm dough. Matt was sure the expressionless eyes were fixed on him as he continued to stab at its long abdomen. Underneath, its fangs were extended, dripping milky venom. Joop screamed again as the thing used its sharp, pointed legs to try and draw him closer to its mouthparts.

The boom in their ears made Matt's heart skip a beat and his ears ring like an air-raid siren. The smell of cordite was sharp in his nostrils, obliterating any trace of the warm bready odor. Kurt had reached between their fighting bodies and fired point-blank into the thing's eyes. It shuddered, and curled into a large ball, still impaled on Joop's spear. He heaved the monster aside and Matt and John helped him stand.

"My spear …"

Kurt checked his gun and turned away. "Leave it. Let's go – double time."

They ran, Kurt firing at anything resembling a mound. He ran hard, his long legs powering him ahead of the group. He spoke without turning. "Nearly there."

Matt watched his side of the clearing carefully, but nothing made a move. As he looked ahead, something amongst the grasses caught his eye. He veered out from the group.

"What? What the fuck are you doing, Kearns?" Kurt's voice was both disbelieving and furious. "Get back!"

Matt darted to the object, snatched it up, and sprinted back toward them. Kurt pointed the gun at him and fired. The bullet whistled over his shoulder. He didn't look back. It might have panicked him even more if he did.

Once he was back with the group, he looked at his prize. It was Megan's shirt – ripped and punctured, but unmistakable.

"Oh no." His heart sank.

John reached over to grab one corner and spread it out. "No blood." He looked hard into Matt's face. "Decoy, maybe? Probably how they managed to cross safely."

Or one of them did, Matt thought miserably. He pushed the thought away and tucked the shirt into his pocket. "I hope to God you're right John, I really do."

Together they passed into the jungle again, the path made by the beast still wide and clear.

✵ ✵ ✵ ✵ ✵

The sound of a tree coming down somewhere behind them in the swirling mists jarred Carla and Megan from their indecision.

"Right, going back is not an option." Carla took a few steps out into the water. Megan rested her hand on her shoulder and waded out with her.

Megan could feel the silty mud squelch under her boots, and small things bumping into her calves. She now envied Carla's choice of longer pants. Plus, Carla was still fully clothed, while all Megan had left was sodden shorts and a filthy bra. *Perfect jungle attire ... if you're in a porn movie,* she thought.

They waded out until the water was up to their waists, still amongst alien-looking trees with massive trunks on stilts that were heavily coated in moss. There was the sound of swirling water from somewhere farther out, and both women froze.

"Shit, I don't like the sound of that," Megan said.

"I don't like the sound of it, I don't like the feel of it, and I'm sure if I could see it, I wouldn't like the look of it," Carla responded.

Megan's head whipped around at the sound of heavy movement from back along the dry shoreline. "And I definitely don't like the sound of that." She took a few more steps. "Rock or hard place?" A small wave lapped up against them, and then continued on, splashing against the muddy shoreline. "I wish we could see something."

More waves pushed against them – larger now, and more forceful.

Carla's voice was urgent. "That's a bow wave. Something's coming ashore – something big."

"Fuck it. I'm not going in any farther." Megan looked back, left, and right – and then upward. "Up."

The huge mangrove-like tree was a difficult climb. Other creatures huddled against the feeder roots for protection and wriggled against their legs when they got in close. The tree was over forty feet high. Its huge branches meant they might be able to climb high enough to be well clear of the water, and also clear of the thing that was approaching along the shore.

Megan pushed Carla's bottom as she climbed. "Keep going – it won't be able to track us into the water. Let's get up above it. Quickly." Carla's boots scraped against the slime-covered wood, trying to find purchase. Megan kept pushing.

In five minutes they had made it two dozen feet into the air. Jockey-like, Megan started to edge along a limb, moving farther out over the water. She'd seen where the branches interwove with one another, and was hoping they could cross to the next tree, farther from the bank, without getting wet.

Carla was behind her. Two-thirds of the way along, their combined weight was causing the branch to dip a few feet. By the time they got to the end, their branch would be hanging below the next. They'd need to go one at a time.

Megan turned. "We're too heavy. Back up."

"Shhh." Carla was peering intently at the shoreline. Megan followed her gaze.

The huge shape that meandered along the bank, head to the ground, sniffing like a giant skinless dog, was a mountain of green-gray muscle. The upper head was all horns and weird protrusions, and underneath seemed to be nothing but teeth and jaws. The hot breath from its cavernous mouth blew the mist out of its path.

It stopped at the water's edge and lifted its snout, sniffing the air. Megan could see that its eyes, sitting on the sides of its head, were tiny in relation to its massive skull. She hoped that meant its eyesight would be weak.

They were just a few feet above its head – if it chose to rear up they'd be easily in reach of its jaws. Megan looked up above her – there was nothing. She'd have to edge back to the trunk. She pointed and mouthed to Carla: *higher*.

Carla shook her head, held up a hand and mouthed: *wait*.

The huge beast turned and wandered a few dozen feet back along the water's edge, then spun back, as though its nose was caught on a wire. The scent of the women was still lingering in the air, even if it wasn't on the wet ground. The creature came back toward them, passing by the spot where they had entered the lake. Megan grimaced and held her breath.

It didn't work. The thing stopped and returned. Small, pig-like eyes stared out over the mist-covered lake. It snorted, then took a step into the water.

"Ah, shit," Megan whispered.

It waded out, quickly reaching the trunk of their tree, then leaned forward to sniff at the scuff marks Carla's boots had made on the slimy bark. Its head tilted back, following the scent, and then turning side-on. One small, piggish eye fixed on Carla, and its mouth dropped open. A noise like the roar of an approaching train exploded up at them.

One huge forelimb came out of the water to rest against the trunk. Mighty talons raked downward, ripping hundred-pound slabs of the soft bark from the tree. The forelimb came up again ... higher this time.

"Climb, climb!" Megan hopped back along her limb as Carla started upward, the tree shaking now, raining leaves and huge drops of red water down on their heads. Megan prayed neither of them slipped – they saw what had happened to Jian.

Carla was surprisingly spry, and was two branches ahead of Megan in a flash. Megan wrapped her arms around the next branch and levered herself up, balancing on the slippery limb, then reached up again, just as the enormous beast reared up on its back legs and thumped against the trunk. It was like a massive bear trying to dislodge a piece of fruit.

The tree tilted in the soft underwater mud and Megan slipped, her arms pinwheeling in space for a few seconds. Her eyes were on Carla. She saw the woman's mouth open, but shock had shut out all sound. It was like being in a momentary vacuum without sensation as Carla swung down and grabbed at her.

The CDC woman locked her legs around a limb and hung on as the giant animal crashed into them again. Megan screamed and swung, pendulum-like, as the tree started to topple, gathering speed as it went. Both women were flung another fifty feet out from the bank. They surfaced in deep water, and paddled quickly back toward the branches of the fallen tree, the half-submerged limbs acting like a cage against the huge creature that now advanced to meet them.

* * * * *

Matt's head swung toward the sound. "That was Megan." He didn't think, just ran. As he sprinted past Kurt, the big man reached out for him, but he was too slow.

Matt dodged and weaved through the jungle, leaping over crushed plant debris and slapping vines out of his path, all sense of self-preservation gone. Megan was only here because of him. He'd seen what was left of Jian, and he wasn't going to lose her to the same fate.

"Megan!" Matt screamed her name, flinging the word from his lips even as his brain told him that silence was the smarter option right now. "I'm coming!"

He burst from the broken tangle of jungle onto the muddy shore of a riverbank and paused to get his bearings, sucking in gulps of stinking swamp gas.

Matt tried to make sense of the shapes on the glassy body of water, but the mist swirled and dipped, a thousand wraiths tumbling over each other. There was no smaller vegetation here, only giant trees that looked like a cross between a mangrove and a banyan. Nothing small had seemed to survive in the oxygen-poor silt. He looked down to the ground, tracking back and forward until he once again found the deep indentations made by something that was probably larger than a bull elephant.

He followed them to his right along the bank, and started to run again, trying to calm his breathing and listen for Megan's voice. Up ahead there was splashing, and the ground under his feet was becoming squashy and waterlogged. The massive beast's footprints were now individual pools filled with brackish water.

A grunt – or was it a voice? He paused and turned his head to listen – more noises, but from behind him now. Kurt, Joop, and John, most likely. Louder sounds came from farther away in the mist – a crash, water falling onto water, and a distant sound, like a cough. He started to run again, splashing through shallow water.

Before he knew it, the water had gone from ankle deep to knee deep. Somewhere, the shoreline had simply finished, and he was beginning to wade. He could make out shapes farther out in the water – they coalesced and formed into something massive, hunched shoulders with a huge horned and lumpy head trying to reach in amongst the branches of a fallen tree.

He could see its objective now. Small heads and shoulders were ducking down and moving away – Megan and Carla. The branches made it difficult for the monstrous animal to snap them up, but it stood on its hind legs, towering over them. If it fell forward it would be in amongst the branches and at its prey.

"Hey!" Matt fought against the water. "Hey, get away from them." He looked around for something to throw – anything – but there was nothing floating, and beneath his feet, just a silken ooze.

"Matt!" Kurt and the others had arrived. Kurt and John splashed out, and all Matt could do was point, his voice high and strangled with frustration.

"Shoot, shoot goddammit."

Kurt raised the gun, but paused, frowning. "I can't get a—"

"Just fucking shoot!" Matt roared.

Kurt let loose three quick rounds at the huge animal. With the distance and heavy mist, it was impossible to tell what struck and what missed, but the sound alone made the beast swing around toward them.

It still stood on its hind legs, like a massive grizzly bear, one small piggish eye fixed on the shoreline. It was doubtful it could see them at all. After another few seconds it gave up and once again turned back to the women. It leaned forward and started to rip branches out of its path, preparing to leap on top of the sheltering humans.

"No!" Matt turned to Kurt, frantic now. "Shoot again."

Kurt fired one more time, then shook his head. "I'm wasting ammunition; there's no effect from here."

"Give me …" Matt charged back at the big bodyguard and grabbed the gun. Kurt released it without a struggle. Matt turned and waded back out, having to keep hopping up off the sediment to stop himself from going under.

"Megan!" He fired the gun over and over, until he heard the clicking of an empty chamber. The ooze beneath his feet had fallen away and he was treading water now. He let go of the gun and started to swim out, with no plan or objective other than to get to Megan.

The massive animal fell forward, its weight causing the partially submerged branches to disappear, leaving some floating twigs, some frantically paddling arboreal creatures, and two floundering women.

One of them screamed, and Matt swam, thrashing at the water, fast closing on them. He lifted his head and saw that Carla was closest, and seconds away from being seized by jaws that would crush her down to the same mess that Jian had become. As he trod water, momentarily transfixed, he saw Megan swim toward the CDC woman.

A hand alighted on his shoulder, making him spin in the water. It was John, his face pale in the gloom of the darkening mist. Matt's mouth worked, but no words came. He could only turn and watch, impotent, useless, spectator to a grisly primordial feast.

"What's that?" John's head whipped around, and Matt followed his gaze. A lump appeared in the water, no more than fifty feet out from the gigantic creature.

The beast ignored sharp branches and dipped its head toward Carla, who dove, reappearing six feet away. The huge animal's assault had pushed the tree farther out in the lake, and with its sizeable bulk, it was now having trouble staying above the water line. It dipped again – bobbing for human apples, its mouth open, trying to scoop one of the flailing bodies up, but the women kept diving.

The lumping in the water occurred again, and then a small island appeared. The glossy island rolled, and one massive eye, easily three feet across, fixed on the scene, and then silently submerged.

"Oh shit, there's something else in here." John pulled Matt back toward him.

The beast attacking the women froze. Its head came up sharply, and then it roared. The women now forgotten, it turned toward Matt and John, and started to power its way toward them.

The island appeared again, becoming a mountain as it surged after the fleeing beast. The new creature's jaws opened wide on a head that was a cross between reptile and whale. Rows of tusk-like teeth grabbed at the fleeing monster's torso, clinging there momentarily before several hundred pounds of flesh were ripped away, and the thing slid back under the water.

The wounded beast turned momentarily, prepared to fight, facing the open lake with its own artillery now brought to bear. Its massive jaws hung open, dagger teeth ready and claws held forward. But there came another surge, as if the lake itself was welling up to consume the standing beast, and it was jerked below the water. When it re-emerged a few seconds later, it was a full fifty feet farther out.

On dry land it might have stood a chance, but the massive thing it fought had no intention of giving it that option. The water was its kingdom – here, it ruled. The beast bellowed again, but this time there was panic and fear in the long, tortured notes. It continued to move away from the shore, pulled by something below the water.

It was jerked hard again, and this time a geyser of blood flew into the air. The attack now began in earnest – an enormous gray body, outweighing its prey many times over, like a huge muscular eel with flippers on each side, clamped a mouth across the beast's back. A huge tail thrashed and churned, propelling itself and its prey out to ever-deeper water. Matt knew what its goal was. Just like modern crocodiles, this thing wouldn't need to fight, it just had to hold on and submerge its prey. The water would do the rest.

The lake was exploding in a maelstrom of thrashing, the two leviathans locked in a death match. Their battle created huge waves, pushing Matt and John closer to the shoreline.

"Matt!" Two small bodies frantically swam toward them. Matt bobbed out through the choppy water to meet them. Megan grabbed him, shaking, and pressing her icy lips to his. She clung to him. "I knew you'd come."

John grabbed Carla just as the last of her energy reserves ran out. He held her head above water as she slumped against him, telling her softly to relax. She shook her head.

"Not here – get to the bank."

Megan tugged at Matt. "She's right – too much blood in the water now."

They swam hard, John using a one-armed stroke, while his other arm kept Carla afloat.

Kurt and Joop met them in the shallows and helped them onto the bank. Megan fell to her knees, coughing and spitting. She looked up at Matt and laughed wetly. "Good times, Kearns."

Carla pointed. "Look."

The group turned back to the water – there was nothing. The lake still rippled, but there was no more noise, no more thrashing of bodies fighting to the death. The battle had been decided, and now, somewhere below the surface, a feast would begin.

Carla rose to her knees, then used John's arm to get to her feet. "Anyone else think we shouldn't be here?"

Megan straightened. "At least I'm not itchy anymore. Either the little critters drowned, or they were scared right off me."

Carla looked up at Megan and then felt her hair. "Neither am I ... but we should be. *Sarcoptes scabiei primus* is not affected by water at all – in fact, bathing can cause them to burrow deeper, actually increasing the itching sensation." She ran her hands through her hair, looking at her fingers, then scraped her scalp with her nails, turning them over to examine what was underneath them. She wiped them onto her palm and squinted at the debris.

Her hands were covered with what looked like soggy dust. "Dead." She looked up again, but her focus had turned inward, analyzing, processing, and theorizing.

"Something in the water." She smelt her hands. "Some sort of suspension – the floral dye, the flower pollen – an infusion of sorts. It must be the red-flowered vines; they're everywhere, in everything in this place. Perhaps this plant type is exuding some type of natural insecticide or retardant."

Matt snapped his fingers. "Of course; the pond we came through. It makes sense – remember the words carved in the stone? 'Let not the unclean pass back to the land of man.' The Ndege left the warning. They must have brought their kills back through the pond, drowning and soaking them, effectively sterilizing them of the mite."

Kurt was craning his neck, looking back into the growing darkness. "Okay, good, we're all clean. Let's go. I don't want to be near the water or out in the open anymore."

Megan wrung out her hair and then staggered a little; still fatigued from the water. She shivered, even though the air was still around eighty degrees.

"Oh yeah." Matt stuck a hand into his pocket, pulling out the sodden and punctured shirt. He held it out to her. "Quick thinking, by the way."

Megan grinned and thanked him with a kiss. She lifted it, looking at the holes. "I was surprised it worked. What a mess … better it than me, though." She draped it over her shoulders.

They set off, huddling close, following the wide track back to the camp. Matt's mind whirled with the implications of what they'd discovered. He turned to Carla. "One thing I don't understand; why did Jorghanson's bird come back still infested?"

The CDC woman shrugged. "Don't know. Maybe he kept it dry, that's why it was alive when it arrived State-side." She shrugged and gave him an exhausted smile. "No one left to ask. They're dead … everyone is dead."

* * * * *

They jogged until night had completely descended, caution now slowing their pace. Kurt was out in front, followed by Joop, then Carla, John, Matt, and Megan. It would still be hours before they made it back to the spot where Jian and the women were attacked. The trip had been prolonged because they had chosen to skirt the open ground where the spiders waited in their burrows – they had been lucky once, but trying to cross in the dark would have been suicide.

A light came on. Joop had placed his flashlight band over his head and switched it on.

Kurt immediately swung at him, whispering through clenched teeth, "Turn that off!"

"Huh? But I can't see." Joop clicked it off, looking bewildered.

"Hey, easy – I was about do the same," said John.

Kurt dropped his head and rubbed a hand through his damp hair. "Sorry, but in a jungle there are plenty of nocturnal predators, so a light is basically a dinner bell. I don't think any of us would relish running into some abomination in the dark ..." he glanced at Matt, "... without a gun."

Matt grimaced – he had dropped it in the lake.

The pace slowed as the jungle thickened. They each reached out to the person in front to stay in contact. The sound of their heavy breathing was masked by the sounds around them – whoops, hissing, and distant thrashing as large bodies came together in courtship, pursuit, or death. It made them feel small, vulnerable, and alone.

They paused only briefly at the place where Jian was attacked. No one suggested they make camp anywhere but back at the pool, close to the deadly but protective cover of the thorn wall. There was little to salvage – already it looked like something had spent time investigating the contents of the abandoned packs and boxes. Carla retrieved a few samples, and then they set out again.

In another hour, Kurt stopped them with a raised hand. He pulled out his blade, letting it hang at his side, and half turned. "Joop, shine your light up here for a second." He lifted the blade, pommel facing upward, and flipped the cap to examine the compass. Joop illuminated the small instrument.

"Hmm, hard to tell with this thing acting so screwy – I'm sure we're going the right way, but we've wandered off our original path. Two options – either we backtrack and see if we can find our previous route, or we continue." He reached up and flicked Joop's light off for him. "If we do continue, it's going to be a little slower and heavier going."

Carla stepped around Joop. "And if we go back?"

Kurt shrugged. "In the dark, there's a chance we'll miss it altogether. Swings and roundabouts, I'm afraid." He paused. "Go, no go?"

The silence hung for only a few seconds. Carla nodded. "We go on ... this way." Heads nodded in agreement.

Kurt turned and pushed into the green growth again, keeping his large hunting knife in hand to slash or saw through tenacious vines and stalks. He chopped hard at a tangle of vines, pushed, and then tumbled forward into a small clearing. The group piled in behind him, but immediately froze as a strange smell enveloped them. Out of the dark came a rattling hiss.

"Ah shit, there's something in here." Kurt got slowly to his feet, holding out an arm to keep everyone behind him. He didn't need to.

By now, their eyes had adapted to the dark, but some things gave off a soft phosphorescent glow. Leaves, bark, insects, and the occasional pair of silvery eyes shone back at them as they traveled. But now, hanging about three feet above the ground, was a dinner plate-sized cluster of glowing eyes, some the size of softballs, others much smaller.

"Permission to turn lights on?" Joop's voice was soft and steady.

"Oh yeah ... easy now." Kurt held up his blade.

Immediately, several pipes of white light flashed bright. It was like a flashbulb going off, temporarily blinding them. A scrabbling in the bushes, and more hissing, drew them all in one direction.

"Oh, God no." Another spider, the size of a dog, all leathery dark skin and hideously powerful, hung on a silken bag the size of a long knapsack.

"No one move." Kurt spoke just above a whisper.

Matt gulped and felt Megan crowd in close to him. He doubted he could move even if he wanted to.

The spider repositioned itself, keeping its multiple eyes fixed on the humans. After another few seconds it seemed to relax and settled back down, inserting its fangs back into the silken bag. Its bulbous abdomen acted as a pump, drawing the liquefied contents up and out of the thing.

Joop swung his light along the length of the bag – something inside glinted.

"There's something in there that looks synthetic ... metal, I think."

John turned his light on too, and the extra illumination provided another view of the prize the enormous Mesothelae nestled upon.

"Is that ... is that a monkey in there?" Megan was leaning over Matt's shoulder.

Kurt backed up, pushing into the group, his rugged features pulled into a grimace. "No, oh God no, I think ... it's Max."

With all the lights focussed on the bag, its contents were now visible. A hideously dried skull and shoulders could be made out. The mouth was pulled open in a rictus scream, and a gold tooth could be seen just off to the side of the jaw.

The bag seemed to wriggle.

"Oh fuck no, fuck no, he's alive." Kurt gritted his teeth, shaking his head. "Help him ... please."

John shook his head. "Impossible. It's just the spider ... has to be."

Carla leaned forward and grabbed Kurt's arm. "He's dead. There's nothing we can do for him. Let's go."

The big guide let her ease him back, revulsion and anguish clear on his face.

Matt looked at the bag. He wasn't sure whether the shrunken eyes actually swiveled to look at him. *It must have been a trick of the light.* But he remembered the small horse being alive when it was nothing but dry skin over bone. Carla could be wrong – Max might not be dead, but she was right about one thing: there was nothing they could do. This was not their world, and fighting one of its denizens in the dark and on its home turf would be beyond madness.

Matt paused as the group backed up – he wished he still had the gun, and just one bullet – not for the spider, but for

Max. He stepped back, and the jungle closed over the grisly tableau. Kurt moved to the front of the group and paused for a moment, breathing in and out and settling himself. He turned on his own light and looked again at his compass, and then at his watch. "This way ... we can't be that far now."

This time, Kurt didn't ask for the flashlights to be switched off.

* * * * *

It seemed like hours later that the noises of the forest started to quieten and the jungle thinned, signifying that they were close to the crater's edge. The six of them staggered into the sterile moat of openness in front of the deadly thorn wall and fell to their hands and knees.

Kurt lay down and put his hands over his face, breathing heavily. "Fucking Max, oh God, I was supposed to look after him. It was my job to stay with him, and I left." He rolled over and knelt, hands on his thighs, and stared blankly at the ground. "I fucked up, and now Max is dead." He crushed his eyes shut.

"Hey ... hey!" Matt sat up. "If you had stayed here, then maybe Max would be alive. But maybe Megan, Carla, and the rest of us would be dead somewhere out in that infernal jungle."

Kurt continued to shake his head, and lifted one large arm to wipe his nose. "I fucked up."

"No, he did." Carla propped herself up on one elbow. "You saved us; you did the right thing. Max should have been with us. From what you've told me, it was his choice to stay here."

After a few moments, Kurt gave her a brief nod. He took out his water bottle and poured some over his face. "I can officially say, that is the worst damned bit of jungle I've ever had the misfortune to live through."

"Nah, I've been in worse." Megan sat forward, managing to keep a straight face for about three seconds. Kurt tossed his bottle at her.

Carla crawled across to the cage and peered inside. The bird hissed back at her. She squinted, examining the animal in detail.

Matt sat up and leaned forward, letting drops of perspiration fall from his brow. He scratched his skin and winced. "I'm itchy again."

"Yep, the jungle is crawling with the mite. The hike back probably reinfested all of us." Carla was finger-combing her hair, then looking at her hands.

Matt got to his feet. "Time for a test, then." He walked to the pond and slid in, fully clothed. He lay on his back for a few moments before letting out a long and soothing, "ahhh". He ducked under again, and rubbed his scalp before rising from the water's edge, his long hair slicked back. He stood with his arms spread.

"Unless the little buggers are holding their breath, I don't feel them anymore."

"Good enough for me." Kurt leapt in, followed by Joop. John waded in with a little more dignity, while Megan chose her characteristic bomb, red water exploding over the pool's edge and spreading about twenty feet. Even Carla, who looked ready to drop from exhaustion, climbed in, a grin splitting her face.

Kurt hovered on the surface. "Damn, that's good." He turned to Matt. "Get the kits. We'll swim through to the other side tonight and make camp over there. I've had enough of this mad prehistoric game park."

"Works for me." Matt wandered over to where he had left his gear and knelt, flipping open his bag. He frowned, and blinked. His pack was empty. He looked around for a second or two, checking to see if the face mask had somehow rolled free. Did he take it out before he left? He shook his head, and pointlessly checked some of the smaller pockets.

"What's going on here?" He looked up to where Megan was at her own kit. "Megs, did I … did I give you my breather?"

Megan shook her head as she looked in her own bag. She snorted in confusion, her brow furrowed. "That's weird; mine's gone as well." She stood, pinching her bottom lip, staring at the empty bag.

"Oh, shit no." Kurt charged from the pool and hurriedly opened his own bag. After few seconds of rummaging he flicked the top down hard and stood with his hands on his hips, looking like he was about to stomp his feet. He stared up into the now ink-black canopy.

"Fuck!" His roar echoed along the crater wall. After another few seconds, Kurt lowered his head, eyes closed, and breathed slowly out through his nose. He opened his eyes.

"Anyone … anyone still have their mask?"

Carla held one up. "Yes – I kept it with me." She checked the gauge on the side of the small canister. "But it's only half full."

"Great – we're fucked." Kurt rubbed his brow hard. He looked at the ground and shook his head. "We have to go back."

"Go back? What are you talking about? Go back where?" Megan was on her feet.

Kurt kept his head down. "Max must have taken them."

"Like hell we're going back. I didn't see any pack full of masks back at the spider's lair, did you?" Matt couldn't help his voice rising.

"Well, I'm not going … no one is." Megan marched over to the edge of the jungle, staring out into its blackness.

Kurt was still staring at the ground. "Believe me, it's the last thing I want to do. He must have taken them, there was no one else." He looked up at Megan, and then to the others. "I'll go alone."

"Why? I mean, why would he take them?" Megan asked over her shoulder.

"Who knows? Maybe to keep them safe; maybe to ensure we didn't go without him. Maybe just to fuck with us." Kurt ran his hands through his wet hair. "We know where he is."

"No way, Kurt. We've already lost two people in here. There's no way we're throwing more lives away. There's no way Max would have dragged a kit full of face masks through the jungle just because he wanted to keep them safe. If he took them – and that's a big if – my guess is he would have hidden them ... close by."

Kurt shrugged. "Maybe."

Carla held up her mask. "Could we buddy-breathe? Share the air and go through one at a time?"

Kurt shook his head. "There's six of us – not enough air for all of us to make it. I'm not even sure there's enough for you." He gave her a weak smile. "One of us could try. But it's a one-way deal ... and we wouldn't know if they'd made it or not." He walked to the jungle's edge. "If there was food in the bag, then something might have dragged it away."

"We need to find it," said Matt.

Carla joined Kurt at the jungle's edge and grasped his upper arm. "Not now, not tonight. We all need some rest."

The big man nodded. "Okay. Let's think about it tomorrow with clear heads. I'm beat." He walked back to the pool and sat down beside it, staring into its depths.

Megan snorted. "Sleep? Yeah, sure."

* * * * *

Carla woke early, the scratching sounds coming from the bird's cage intruding on a beautiful dream of cool clean sheets, pastries, and coffee. She sat up blinking, momentarily disoriented, before the depressing reality sunk in.

She crawled across to the cage, lifted back the shirt that had been draped across the box, and peered in. The strange creature cocked its small reptilian head, red eyes gleaming, then opened and shut its toothed beak with an audible clack.

"A lot of people died for you ... and now ... we don't need you." She smiled crookedly at the strange animal. "Besides, I think you'd like our world about as much as we like yours."

She let the shirt drop back over the cage. Kurt was up and about; gathering sticks for the fire from the clearing's edge. Carla wandered over.

"Morning. How'd you sleep?"

He grinned. "Like a log ... and a petrified one at that. You?"

"Okay." She shrugged. "What's the plan?"

He pursed his lips. "Plan A is to quickly scout the surrounding area. I think Matt's right; if Max did hide the pack, he was too lazy to do a good job of it. He'd have hidden it close by. If that fails, Plan B – I'm going back to the spider's nest."

Carla could see that he meant it. She didn't want him to attempt it, but could see that it had to be considered. She nodded. "Okay then, quick search, then we meet back here for coffee and see about Plan B." She smiled up at him. "Here's hoping we don't need it."

* * * * *

After weak coffee and the few remaining scraps of meat, they agreed that Carla and John would wait by the pool to guard their belongings while Kurt, Joop, Matt, and Megan would grid-search the fifty feet of jungle around their camp.

Kurt stood with his hands on his hips, looking along the line of dense red jungle. "No way Max would have had the time or patience to bury the masks. Gotta be close by. So ..." He turned to the group. "… look for anything covered in leaves, under logs, or even thrown up into a tree."

They nodded and Kurt continued. "Stay close; within earshot of each other. We'll use a crisscross pattern in our search. If we find nothing in the first allotted grid, just move on to the next." He paused, then turned to the jungle. "Let's do it."

Matt had found a slim, six-foot branch, which he used to push shrubbery out of the way and lever logs up to peek underneath. Though they were still close to the thorn wall and animal life was sparse, he still didn't fancy using his hands to flip a log back only to have some fanged or poison-spitting horror spring at him.

The sun was just coming up over the crater rim and the light was slowly reaching the twilight level that was constant in the crater basin. With the sun came the heat. Steam lifted from the moisture that had settled on the leaves and fronds throughout the evening, and soon the oppressive daytime humidity would crush down on them again. Matt stopped to lift an arm and wipe his brow.

"Alright over there?" Megan was out of sight, but her voice carried through the steam – she couldn't have been more than fifty feet away.

"All good – nothing yet. You?"

"Nada," she responded.

Matt moved into the jungle another ten feet, knowing he'd soon be turning and making his sweep back to the camp before starting in on his next assigned grid. He looked up at the branches overhead – nothing, other than that ever-present feeling of being watched. He hoped they'd find something – and not just for the obvious reasons. He knew he wouldn't be able to let Kurt go back into the jungle by himself. Their luck could only be stretched so far.

He pushed his stick into some ferns and lifted the tongue-like fronds, then frowned. There was something there – small, brown, and hairy. He squinted, lifted the fronds out of the way, and went down on one knee.

"Wha...?" He didn't understand the shape ... it looked like ... toes. Still bent on one knee, he let his gaze travel upward, reaching into the fern and parting its branches. A small face stared back at him.

"Jesus." He fell back on his ass.

Large brown eyes stared out from under a ridged brow, regarding him with interest. She came out slowly and he noticed that one hand held a large hunting knife with a silver pommel, engraved with the letters "M.S.".

"Uh, hello." He held up a hand and got up on one knee, not wanting to startle her by getting to his full height.

She came out from behind the ferns, not showing any fear at all. Matt couldn't help staring. The small being was the size of a child – ape-like, hairy, but with the small hanging breasts of a woman.

He kept his eye on the knife – a formidable weapon, even in her small hands. She kept coming toward him, and reached out to take a length of his hair and run it through her fingers. Then she patted his head, stroking the long hair.

She grunted softly and pointed at his head, then down at his body, and then back to his hair. More sounds emanated from her throat, but they were impossible for Matt to decipher.

He touched his head. "My hair?"

She pointed again at his hair and then at his body. "Is it on my body as well?" He shook his head. "No." Then he shrugged and smiled. "Well, only in some places."

The small female frowned and stepped forward, reaching for his chest. Two slim brown fingers went in between his shirt buttons and scraped at his bare chest. Matt felt their roughness, like tree bark – these hands had seen a lot of use.

She pulled her hand out and sniffed at her fingers. Matt pointed at the knife. Shrugging, and holding out his hands flat, he tried to engineer a look of inquiry, mouthing, *where?*

She lifted the weapon and slashed it back and forth, demonstrating her mastery, or perhaps her ownership. She nodded, and tapped her chest.

"Yes, yours ... now. But where?" He made a sweeping gesture out at the jungle, then shrugged again.

She motioned him in closer, and he leaned toward her, trying to keep the knife in his field of vision. She reached up to touch his head again, then let more of his hair run through her fingers, making a soft noise in her throat. She took Matt's hand and lifted it to the top of her own head. The short hair, or fur, was thick and coarse, more like fibers. No wonder she was so curious about his locks.

He stood slowly and dropped his hand to her shoulder, letting it travel down her arm to her hand.

"Come." He started to lead her but she dug her heels into the soil. He let go of her hand and knelt again. She immediately grabbed a lock of his hair.

"I get it, you like my hair." He reached around her, resting his arm behind her legs, and lifted her. She was surprisingly heavy – solid muscle, he assumed. As he carried her back to the camp, the small ape-girl inspected his hair, leaning forward occasionally to sniff at it.

Matt called out as he came in. "Megan, call in Kurt – I've found something ... or rather, someone.'

* * * * *

The small female cowered behind Matt, who was kneeling, all bravado disappearing in the presence of more of the giants. She displayed no real interest in the other team members, or in the objects scattered about. Only when the bird hissed and rattled in its cage did her dark eyes flick momentarily to the creature, before returning almost immediately to Matt.

John and Joop crouched beside her, studying her cranial symmetry. Occasionally, John reached out to try to touch her ear or chin, or turn her head for a better view. She'd slap at his hand, or bare her formidable teeth in his direction.

He shook his head, sitting back on his haunches. "Amazing. Possibly *Australopithecus – boisei*, I think."

Joop nodded. "My thoughts exactly ... but more like *Australopithecus robustus*, or even *afarensis*. We'd need to see a male to confirm it, but the size, morphology, cranium – she could be the embodiment of Mary Leakey's Lucy."

"Three million years and counting." John examined her head again. "Magnificent bone structure – look at that brow ridge."

Matt carefully looked sideways at the doctor. "Sorry John, but this one's still using her skull."

He laughed. "I don't care; I've just beheld a wonder of the world." He looked over his shoulder. "Anyone now want to hazard a guess as to how the Ndege looked so retrogressive?" He looked back, trying once again to turn the woman's face toward him. "I think a few night-time dates with one of these sirens might have done it." She slapped at him again.

"Erk, dirty buggers." Kurt pulled a face.

John ignored him.

"Do you think we can communicate with her, Matt?" Megan edged forward, waving and smiling at the woman.

"I'm not sure. It's not really a discernible language she uses. She vocalizes and uses a few hand gestures, but whether it's words, impressions, or emotive expression, I can't tell." He shrugged. "Give me a few weeks, then maybe."

Kurt snorted. "That we don't have. She's got Max's knife. My bet is she took it from the camp, or his body. I'm also betting she knows where his pack and the masks are. We need to find out ... one way or another."

Megan turned and pulled a face. "What, we torture it out of her? Welcome to Modern Man, now let me pull your fingernails out."

"No." He turned to Matt. "You know what I mean ... we just can't afford to be wasting time." Kurt sighed. "Anyway, we should continue our search; at least tie off that avenue for getting out of here."

Matt nodded. "Sure, but I need Megan; she has a good ear for linguistic consistencies and repetitions. We'll do our best; she might be our best lead to the masks."

Kurt shrugged and walked away, calling Joop and John with him. Matt turned to Carla. "Let's try and jog her memory with a prop. I can use your face mask – a picture's worth a thousand words and all that." Matt reached around to disentangle the small woman's hand from his hair, and moved in front of her.

"Communication 101." He tapped his chest. "Matt." He nodded.

She looked into his eyes, her brown orbs almost black, they were so dark. He repeated the gesture. "Matt." He tapped again. This time, he slowly brought his hand over to her chest, and tapped it. He opened his hands and raised his eyebrows in a questioning manner.

The small being reached out and tapped his chest with two small brown fingers, but made no sound. She reached out to his hair again, then ran fingers lightly over his face.

Megan moved beside Matt, and tapped her own chest. "Me-gan."

The small woman kept her eyes on Matt. Megan moved in closer to Matt and tapped her chest again. "Me-gan." Then she reached across to tap Matt's chest. "Ma—"

In a blur of movement, the small ape woman bared her teeth and screamed. She pummeled at Megan, who fell back, before darting back in behind Matt again.

"Are you okay?" Matt knelt beside Megan.

"Yeah, sure; she just took me by surprise." She grinned. "Something tells me she likes you."

Matt laughed, but shook his head in disappointment. "Those sounds she made didn't even sound like a contextual language. Maybe they don't even have speech." He looked down at the knife still in the female's hand.

"I'm going to call her Eve." He tapped his chest. "Matt." Then hers. "Eve." The large eyes never left his. She lifted the hand holding the knife and tapped her own chest. Matt waited, but no words came, just a momentary shift of the eyes to Megan, then back to his own.

He shrugged, and then looked down at the large blade. "Better de-fang her just in case." He grasped the hand holding the knife, and she let him take it from her. He held it up, pretending to cut himself, and pulling a face. "Bad – dan-ger-ous, dan-ger-ous." He shook his head and put the knife down. She kept her large brown eyes on his face, and he waited. Her lips were twitching, a word coming … almost, and then her eyes slid away as Carla approached.

"Here we are." Carla held out the remaining face mask.

Matt reached up to take it, but the mask was already gone. Like a wisp of smoke the small woman had leapt to her feet, snatched the face mask from Carla's hand, and sprung into the jungle.

"Shit." Matt leapt after her, with Megan and Carla close behind. But as soon as he entered the first line of jungle he knew it was hopeless, as he watched her go from the ground to the trees in a single leap. In another instant, she was gone.

He charged on for another dozen feet in vain, but after a few moments he came back into the clearing, where Megan and Carla stood waiting for him. He stopped with his hands on his hips, head down, groaning. "Great, I can just imagine what Kurt's gonna say."

"What's Kurt gonna say?" Kurt stepped out of the jungle with Joop and John.

Matt exhaled and grimaced. "She, ah, took the mask."

Kurt stared, his face going from sweaty pink to boiling red. "Are you for fucking real? And this is a surprise to you? Haven't you seen the signs at the zoo about letting the monkeys reach out to you? They steal things."

"I knew you were going to say that." Matt shuffled. "She wasn't a monkey."

"Well, Professor, she wasn't a supermodel either. But she was smarter than you." Kurt walked away a few steps, and then turned.

"And now we're all fucked."

* * * * *

The next half hour was spent in a stony awkward silence. Carla came back from the jungle's edge with an armful of wood for the fire. Matt and Megan were talking quietly together, while near the pond, Joop, John, and Kurt stood, arms folded, looking as though they were discussing fantastical ways to pass through several hundred feet of underwater tunnels.

Carla dropped the wood near the still-smoldering fire, then walked over to the bird's cage. She got down and peered in between the bars.

"You know, I think at least one of us should be allowed to get away." She lifted the cage, carried it to the southern edge of the clearing and flipped open the door, then stood back half a dozen paces, watching. The bird's bald-looking head came out and it peered around the edge of the cage, first back at Carla, then toward the thorn wall, before fixing its gaze on the jungle. It bobbled out and then stopped, rigid almost, the way some birds freeze in the presence of prey.

"Go on." Carla waved her hands at the strange animal. It moved away another few steps, then paused again, staring out at the jungle but seeming hesitant to enter the red-hued fronds.

"What's up with you?" Carla shook her head as Matt and Megan joined her.

"Perhaps he's grown attached to you … or the free meals." Megan crouched down and rubbed her finger and thumb together, as though coaxing a puppy.

"Food's gone. If he stays, the next free meal is going to be him. And I think he's been through enough." Carla waved her arms. "Shoo!"

It ran a few more steps, lizard-like, in the quick, darting motion of a reptile on a hot surface. One of its wings was held out, angling down from its body.

"It's still hurt, no wonder it's not flying away," Megan said.

"It should be okay, it was only a sprain." Joop had joined them. He flapped his hands at the small animal and began to chase it toward the jungle. It squawk-hissed at him, hopped once, then did a sharp U-turn, heading back toward the crater wall.

Joop followed in a crouching run. "Not there, you stupid thing, you'll poison yourself."

The bird ran fast. Its clawed muscular legs, usually used for climbing, were powerful enough to get some good speed up, and its cornering ability left Joop well behind. The reptilian bird jinked again, then started to head parallel to the wall. It went under a fallen tree, around a boulder, and then, as if on a string, darted in toward the wall, disappearing through a dark opening at the farthest point of the clearing.

They pulled up short and peered in through the branches. The vine canes were brown, as if dying back, or awaiting new growth, and they looked brittle, with the smaller spines having dropped off and been blown away.

Carla got down low, pulled out her flashlight and held it up. "Hey, there's a break in the wall here ... it's a cave. You don't think ...?"

"What is it?" Kurt had seen the commotion, and now threw himself down on his belly beside her.

She turned. "Maybe another way out?"

He shook his head slowly. "I doubt it; if it was, there'd be more weird creatures out there. More likely a dead end."

Megan held her light high above everyone's heads, allowing the beam to move around the interior from a different angle. Something metallic glinted.

"There's something there – I think it's the masks."

* * * *

Kurt got to his feet. "Oh please God, let it be true."

Megan started to bob and weave at the entrance. Matt knew exactly what she was doing – looking for the best way in. "Oh, no you don't; you've already had one heart attack from this stuff."

She shook her head. "We either go in and have a look, or we grow gills." She turned. "Unless you've got any better ideas?"

He shook his head and grimaced. He knew she was right. "Look, just ... give me a minute."

He backed up and turned, jogging to the edge of the jungle and scouting along the ground. In a few minutes, he found what he was looking for. Coming back, large stick in hand, he stood in front of the opening.

"Stand back." He needed more room for what he had planned.

Matt commenced knocking the dried edges of the vines away from the wall. The desiccated stems broke away easily and fell like needle-sharp snow. In just a few minutes he had cleared a good-sized hole, exposing the deep cave within. He used the other end of the branch, where leaves still clung to it, and swept the shards away from the opening. The thorns may not be lethal now that they had dried, but there was no way to safely test the hypothesis.

"Good work." Megan readied herself.

Matt grabbed her. "Hang on; Megan, please, it might be dangerous in there. I should go."

Megan looked at him as though he had just grown a second head, and wrenched her arm from his. She stared at him, bristling. Matt stared back. After a few moments a small smile touched her lips, and she half bowed. "Sorry ... I'm sorry. I know you're just trying to be my Sir Galahad." She shrugged, and then quickly pulled him close for a kiss before pushing him back a step. "But I'm going."

Matt bowed. "Then I'm going with you."

Kurt lifted his light, squinting over their shoulders. "Looks roomy in there – I say we all go."

Carla nodded. "Works for me – I want to take a look as well. Let's grab the packs." She spoke without looking up. "Everyone got their lights?"

John's voice sounded at the rear. "No, but I'll share yours if I may, Ms. Nero."

Matt nudged Megan and leaned in close to her. "Old silver makes his move," he whispered, jiggling his eyebrows.

John's voice was serious. "Please be careful of the surrounding branches, and also of the thorns on the ground – we don't have enough adrenalin if we get into trouble. One at a time ... and slowly."

***** *

The small figure dropped from the trees and ran toward their camp, scooping up Max Steinberg's knife and then racing, sometimes on four limbs, sometimes upright, to the mouth of the cave.

She skidded to a stop and got down low to peer inside, her face screwed up in terror. She lifted the knife and pointed. "Ba-ad ... dan-ge-rus."

She crawled closer, and pounded the ground. "Ma-tt."

* * * * *

Megan led them in on her hands and knees. Matt followed, having to crawl on his belly. Once they got under the vine and the stone overhang, it was immediately cooler, and larger. The cave quickly opened out into a good-sized room. The brown soil was slightly damp, churned ... and littered with bones.

"Oh shit; do you think it's a predator's cave?" Megan backed up. "Spiders?"

Joop crouched and picked up a long thin bone – a rib – and examined it. "Unlikely; this bone is very old. Animals that are sick or at the end of their life tend to seek out dark, isolated places so they can die in peace."

Their beams of light swung around the cavern. Megan scuffed her toe into the cave floor, exposing the metallic object that had originally caught her eye. She bent to pick it up, frowning as she pulled it from the soil. She hefted it in her hands, feeling the considerable weight.

"Wow." It was a golden rod, decorated at one end with a grotesque face. "Well, this is what was glinting in here. More of the Inca gold?"

Kurt came in close, taking it from her and weighing it in his hands. "Mmm, nice, about ten pounds – two hundred grand's worth, at least."

Matt reached out to take it from the big man, but Kurt lifted his shoulder, deflecting him.

Matt shook his head. "That's a priceless artifact, not just a lump of gold at seventeen hundred bucks an ounce."

Kurt shrugged and let his arm drop, still clasping the rod.

Megan shone her flashlight around. "Look – more carvings." Several beams of light followed hers.

"More advice from the Ndege?" Carla turned to Matt. "Please tell me it says: 'this way out'."

Matt's mouth dropped open. He ran his fingertips in the grooves and along the carved images.

"No ... not Ndege at all." He pointed at some more of the images, beautiful and frightening in their realism and detail. "Far more ornate than the Ndege could ever produce, or copy. Far more ... pure."

"This is ..." Matt smiled, his hand still resting on one of the raised images. "This is why I had so much trouble with the Ndege totem poles. There were always embedded elements that didn't make sense. Now I see why."

Matt pointed to a rounded female figure and turned, his eyes shining. "The Valdavian Venus."

He stepped back to take in more of the carvings, and bumped into Megan. She grabbed his arm. "It's beautiful, but Valdavian? That predates Incan and Aztec, by ..."

He nodded. "By thousands of years, according to archeological records. People have been in South America for over fifteen thousand years. They were mostly small tribes, such as the El Inga, the Chivateros, and the El Abra, but the first real empire, the first great nation, was the Valdavians, about 3500 BC." He pointed to the rounded figure. "I give you their queen – Valdavia."

He opened his arms wide. "This writing ... these messages, they start as Valdavian, then change – they seem to have been embellished by a dozen different cultures and writing styles." He moved from place to place, tapping different glyphs, symbols, and images, and naming each. "Aymara, Cajamarca,

Paltas, Camanas, Aztec, Inca, and so many more." He snorted. "It seems this place was only ever hidden from us."

He rested his hand on a pictoglyph of an angry face, tongue lolling, with either vines or coiled snakes in its hair. "The royal seal of Atahualpa, last great Incan ruler, and his warning." He laughed softly. "Basically, it says, 'touch my shit and you die'."

A screech from the darkness made Kurt swear and Joop drop his flashlight. Matt's head snapped around so quickly he actually heard it crunch before the sting of pain flared in his vertebrae. "Ow ... what the hell was that?"

Beams focussed along the walls, fixing on another passage-way leading farther into the heart of the crater cliffs.

Megan's voice was tight in the darkness. "I think ... it was Steinberg's bird."

John grabbed Carla's arm, guiding her flashlight beam back to the bones. "Joop, you did say these bones were old, didn't you?"

"Yes, but that doesn't mean something hasn't taken up residence in here ... and dragged the fresh ones away," he re-sponded.

Kurt snorted. "Fucking great – no weapons, no way out, and now we can't even claim a single cave as our own." He turned momentarily back to the entrance before swinging back to the dark interior. "We still need to take a look."

Matt grinned. "Concern for the bird, or a bit of gold fever kicking in there, big fella?"

Kurt shrugged. "We still need to find a way out." He raised an eyebrow. "But don't forget, I'm out of a job now."

He headed off into an antechamber, and the group fol-lowed, flashlights sweeping every corner of the narrowing tunnel. The walls now had a single glyph carved every few dozen feet – the seal of the Incan king, obliterating all words or messages that had gone before.

"Wow, these guys sure knew how to keep a secret. I bet they …" Megan's mouth clamped shut. The next chamber in the cave was strewn with human skeletons. Each looked to have been dumped in the cavern, rather than carefully lain, as in a crypt.

The ground around the skeletons looked churned, as though it had been heavily raked by several sharp-pronged instruments. Matt walked in amongst the bones and knelt, lifting a crescent-shaped plate of gold on a heavy chain.

"Priests."

"What were they doing in here?" Carla knelt beside one of the skulls.

John pulled some putrid rags from a carved alcove in the wall. "Maybe guarding this." When the cloud of dust settled, the fantastical objects shone in the combined glare of their flashlights – delicate birds, chains of gold, exquisite statuettes, and tablets with ornate raised symbols.

Matt walked to the alcove. "The gold of the Incas, removed and hidden from the Spanish Gold Eaters. It was thought to have been lost, or just a legend, never to have existed at all."

"They brought it here, and then died with their secret," said Carla, lifting her light. "This place is huge – there must be mountains of the stuff."

"That's good … that's very good." Matt nodded, looking around the cave.

Megan muscled in beside him. "Now who's got gold fever?"

Matt smiled. "No, no, don't you see? If the gold rod you found weighed about ten pounds, then this stuff must weigh …"

"Tons," Kurt finished.

"Exactly – and I can't see how this number of men, or even ten times this number, could have brought that much gold in through the pond. There was no technology then to float, winch, or drag it, so ..."

Carla turned. "So, there must be another way in ... and out."

"Exactly," Matt said.

"Really? Then why are they still here?" Megan asked.

John had been kneeling by one of the skulls. He spoke without turning away from the bones. "Maybe I can answer that." He lifted the skull, staring into its hollow sockets. "I don't think these chaps simply died of deprivation or exposure. I think they were killed." He flipped the skull around, and then turned. "Does anyone have a spare flashlight?"

"I might." Kurt rummaged in his pack. "Here we go." He tossed a small light to the doctor, who switched it on and went back to his examination. "I thought so; the bodies, they've been scored. See here at the base of this skull, I can just see a pre-mortem grinding or scraping, as if something sharp came together." He carefully held the flashlight and brought his finger and thumb together, pincer-like.

He glanced up at the motionless group before shining his flashlight along the floor. "See here – strange, the patterning, looks like tire tracks." He shrugged. "Hey, maybe it was just Steinberg's prehistoric bird wandering about."

Matt turned. The tracks John referred to were especially pronounced at the edges of the cave, the two-foot-wide tread-like pattern seeming to move around aimlessly.

"Hmm, maybe something the priests brought with them, like a wheelbarrow device for the gold." Carla was examining the ground at her feet.

Matt shook his head slightly. "Unlikely. The new world civilizations never invented the wheel, so a wheelbarrow is out of the equation."

Carla looked up. "Well, it looks sort of mechanical ... and I doubt they carried that gold by hand."

"Maybe." John placed a couple of fingers into the tracks, measuring them.

The group stared down at the strange markings. Now that they'd been pointed out by the doctor, it was obvious that they were everywhere.

Matt broke the silence. "Whatever happened here occurred centuries ago." He looked around uneasily, trying to convince himself as much as the group.

"Maybe something followed them in – then left after ..." Carla motioned to the skull in John's hand.

"Didn't see these tracks near the entrance." Kurt spoke over his shoulder as he sorted through the piles of golden objects. "Doesn't matter. As Matt said, the party's been over for hundreds of years." He lifted the pieces, replacing some and selecting others to keep, dropping them into his sagging pack. He half turned. "You know, if we can keep this secret, we can all be as rich as kings – as old Atta-palpa himself. Whatever happened to him, anyway?" He winked and went back to his sorting.

Matt grunted. "Atahualpa, the last great king of the Incas – he was choked, beheaded, and burned by the Spanish after a mock trial. They said he was planning a rebellion, but in reality he was tortured and killed because he wouldn't tell them where he had hidden the last Incan treasure." Matt paused, raising his voice. "Oh, and by the way, if we don't escape, I guarantee it'll be our little secret too, Kurt."

Megan shook her head. "It belongs to the Brazilian government, and I'm betting there'll be claims from a number of other South American countries, too."

"Hey, I won't tell if you won't," Kurt grinned.

"Too late, someone already knows." Matt raised his flashlight to the wall. A face like a devil, twisted in Incan fury, stared down at Kurt with a malevolence that matched the words inscribed below it. Matt spoke the warning. "Those who would seek the possessions of the mighty Incan people shall be torn asunder in this world, and in the underworld for eternity."

"Okay, standard curse then." Kurt pulled a face, and continued to arrange the pieces of gold into his own personal size and weight category. He paused. "Wanna hear a real curse? Try and grab a taxi when you're in a hurry in New York. Now that's a freakin' curse." He laughed and went back to his task.

Carla shone her light farther down one of the passages. "Well, we're here, so we might as well have a good look around, and see if there's any other way out."

"If there is, it must be sealed. Otherwise we'd have had more species interaction between inside and out," Joop said.

Carla nodded. "Sure, but still, let's have a look." She motioned with her flashlight beam. "Through there." This time she led, and John took a few long strides to catch up with her. Matt, Megan, and Joop followed.

Matt paused, letting the others get ahead. He waited for the guide. "Come on."

Kurt knelt, shutting his pack and hoisting it onto his back. He got slowly to his feet, the straps cutting deeply into his broad shoulders. The big man grimaced.

"You okay?" Matt asked, as Kurt walked carefully toward him.

"I got this," he said, giving him a strained grin.

That's determination, Matt thought as he stepped aside for him.

They continued on for another twenty minutes, just the sounds of their own breathing and shuffling in the enclosed space. The earthen floor of the tunnel was still strewn with dark bones. Looking up over their heads, Matt could see that the tunnel they were in was a jagged, torn pipe, around fifteen feet in diameter.

Joop noticed him looking. "It's not a lava tube; not in a crater wall, anyway. More likely a result of seismic activity. South America is quite active – close to the circum-Pacific belt."

Matt nodded. "I think I've heard of that. Any activity recently?"

"Unfortunately, yes. In 2010, an earthquake in Chile killed over five hundred people and is still regarded as the sixth-largest earthquake of all time." Joop looked up at the ancient rips and tears in the rock. "That's probably what happened here at some time in the distant past."

After several more minutes, the walls started to glisten with moisture, and the tunnel was beginning to develop a noticeable slope.

"We must be below ground now." Carla shone her flashlight on the wet wall. "Could be leakage from the pool we came through."

"And it's getting humid." Megan wiped her brow. "I thought it was supposed to be cooler below ground."

Matt reached out to touch the wall. "The stone is warm." He wiped his hand. "It usually is cooler below ground. Joop and I were just talking about it. We're right over where the South American tectonic plates are grinding up against each other. With that amount of friction and pressure, we're probably experiencing some geothermic residue. This place is still geologically very active."

"Let's hope it doesn't decide to erupt," Megan said.

Joop grunted. "It doesn't need to do that to cause problems – just a tiny tremor could shake loose the water behind these walls, or allow a vent of lava to shoot to the surface, or simply close the passage while we're in it."

Megan turned to shine her light on his face. "Thanks, I feel much better now."

Matt spoke from behind her. "You could always wait for us outside – just yell out if anything with more than two eyes decides to pay us a visit."

The tunnel dropped another few dozen feet, then opened onto a broad, flat-floored chamber, once again piled with treasure – chairs of gold, birds, and a type of striped deer, the bands on its back filled with smoky jade. A jaguar with emerald eyes so green they seemed to blaze with life. Other small pieces were embedded with garnet and emeralds the size of a man's thumb.

Kurt rushed forward, emptied his sagging pack, and began selecting gem-encrusted items to replace his less interesting pieces. Matt noticed that there were more bones in amongst the gold, and more of the strange Incan tire tracks.

"Look." On some of the less-churned areas of the chamber floor, a new set of tracks could be seen. Matt recognized them as those of a small-clawed biped – an avian biped. They led into one of the smaller side chambers, and seemed to indicate that the bird was moving quickly.

"Seems to be following the other tracks," Megan said.

"Hmm, really?" said John.

Matt barely heard the doctor; he was drawn to the far end of the cave. The jagged rock was smoother here – not naturally; it had been carved flat. There were pictoglyphs; another message – one he had read before. But this wasn't in the language of the Ndege – it was ancient Incan.

"Let not the unclean pass back to the land of man." He looked at Carla, the words now having obvious meaning.

"They knew. Even then, they knew. They probably had no idea about the mite, but they knew something in here was causing the horrific effects on their skin. The priests knew they needed to bathe in the pond before heading home."

"It was a pretty effective curse." Megan got down low to the ground and peered into one of the smaller side tunnels. "Well, it seems this is as far as we go. Not sure anyone could bring anything large through one of these." She played her flashlight around inside.

"No." Matt kept looking at the flat wall, rereading the glyphs, frowning in concentration as his gaze moved along the smooth surface, and then the edges. "No, no, they left through here."

The team fell silent, their attention firmly on Matt, as he placed a hand on the smooth surface. "This is not a blank wall. Many of the early South American cultures were master stonemasons. And one thing they did well was ... pivot stones." He placed both hands against the warm stone and pushed.

Nothing happened. He moved along the ten-foot section, continuing to examine its edges, looking for clues to the direct point on which the massive stone would twist or flip. He looked over his shoulder at Joop. "Give me a hand here."

Together the two men pushed at the wall. After a few moments, Joop stood back and wiped a damp sleeve up over his forehead.

"Are you sure this isn't just ... a wall?"

"No, I'm not sure. But history – and my gut – tells me this stone should pivot. We just need to find the right place to add pressure. These things were cut to a precision that would have put today's craftsmen to shame." Matt continued to push, working up and down the block.

"Matt." Kurt's voice was soft behind him.

"Just give me a—"

"Matt, it's never going to happen." Kurt's voice rose slightly. "Look up."

Matt stopped pushing and did as Kurt suggested. Almost imperceptibly, the roof of the cavern was pressing down on top of the stone wall. If the block had pivoted once, it certainly wasn't going to do it again. Matt's arms dropped and he turned to lean back against the damp stone. He rested his head there and closed his eyes, letting the air escape slowly through his lips.

Carla ran her hands through her damp hair and made an exasperated noise. "So, now we know why the priests decided to stay."

"Yeah – no choice." Megan walked over to Matt and leaned against the wall next to him.

He turned to her. "A tiny earth movement; not enough to bring the place down, and maybe barely more than a trembling beneath their feet. But enough to lower the cavern roof by about an inch, trapping them ... and us."

"Was worth a shot." She smiled, and reached out to take his hand. "We're no worse off than when we came in here. Besides, we're all rich now, right?"

He laughed softly, squeezing her hand in return. "We're not done yet."

Matt pushed himself off the wall and turned to face it, his hands on his hips. "You know, the reason these guys chose this spot must have been because it was close to the other side ... or at least, close to another naturally formed tunnel that they made use of. In effect, all they did was put a door over it."

Matt backed up, almost tripping over Joop. He moved to where Megan had been kneeling earlier. "I think you had the right idea; we need to check a few of these out."

Matt shone his light around the cavern, lighting up two more of the smaller holes. One of them was about four feet in diameter, the others about half that. It'd be a tight squeeze – probably a belly crawl for most of the way. Matt clicked his tongue. Given the humid atmosphere and the damp ground, the exploration promised to be dirty, uncomfortable, and claustrophobic.

He turned. "So, how do we want to do this?"

Kurt seemed to understand exactly what Matt was asking. "Doesn't make sense to all go into the same tunnel. We should split up – there's six of us, so a two-person team in each." He looked at the group. "I'll go with—"

"I'd like to go with Dr. Mordell, if you don't mind." Carla spoke quickly as Kurt's eyes came to rest on her.

John smiled and nodded to her, beaming with delight. Megan put her arm around Matt's shoulders, and Kurt shrugged and looked at Joop, his eyebrows raised.

"Picked last – reminds me of my school days." Joop shrugged and smiled.

Kurt snorted. "Don't sweat it … I'll even let you crawl in first."

The three teams stood together, checking watches. "I call it ten-fifteen am … now." Kurt waited while they calibrated their watches before continuing. "We head in, proceed for twenty minutes, and then come back to report on what we've found. If all three teams find nothing, we rest up a bit, then go back in for a little longer. If, however, we do find something promising, we still report back at the designated time, but we can then concentrate on the one cave. Sound okay?"

They nodded in unison. Megan looked at Matt, a mischievous grin on her face. "Toss a coin?"

"Nope."

"Arm wrestle?"

"Nope. You want to go first, be my guest." Matt knew that even if he won, Megan would still find a way to go in first. It was just her nature. *Best to save time – and angst*, he thought.

"Thank you." She smiled sweetly.

Carla turned to the doctor. "John, I should go first as well. Only because if I get stuck, you can pull me out. But if you get stuck, you might find yourself staying there."

He gave a slight bow. "Impeccable logic. I'll be right behind you."

Matt looked again at his watch. "Let's do this." He turned to Kurt and Joop. "See you in forty."

Joop gave him the thumbs up. When he turned, Megan was already crawling away from him.

* * * * *

Carla inched along on her hands and knees. It was more than uncomfortable – it hurt. The angle of her body stressed her joints, and the ground was damp and slick, quickly coating her knees, elbows, and hands in slime. The greasy soil smelt vile. She guessed it was rotting moss or lichen, but if she didn't know better, she would have sworn it was some type of feces. The strange tire tracks were everywhere, although they were obliterated as she dragged her body through them.

Behind her, the tall English doctor came slowly on his belly, puffing and pulling himself along, trying to keep up with her.

She paused. "John, you okay back there?"

After a second or two there was a small cough, then, "Sure, this is great fun. Maybe we can stop for tea and a slice of cake soon?"

Carla laughed. "You English sure know how to enjoy yourselves. And it's coffee – we Americans like coffee, remember?"

"And we English laugh in the face of danger, didn't you know?" He coughed again. "I'll start drinking coffee when you guys learn how to make it properly."

After a few more minutes of sliding and pulling their way forward, Carla came to a junction in the stone tunnel. Several smaller caves branched away in different directions. She paused and turned her head.

"There are other caves … too small for us."

"Stick to the main one," John wheezed from behind her.

"Yup." She leaned toward one and closed her eyes momentarily, trying to detect the slightest wisp of moving air on her damp cheeks. There was nothing. She angled her light inside, and squinted. A shining object caught her eye and she reached forward, grasping it. She held it up to her light.

"Ha, it's one of our bird's feathers … I think. Covered in crap, though." She turned it over in her fingers; the quill was red. "I guess this is where our speedy little friend went."

She looked back into the small tunnel, angling her light for a better perspective. Farther in, she could see more feathers. A sinking feeling came into her gut. *Maybe it got caught on the jagged stone, and knocked some of its feathers out,* she thought hopefully.

"Everything okay?" John's voice was right behind her. It sounded strained.

"Probably." She flicked the feather back into the cave and wiped her fingers on her sleeve. "Yeah, sure; let's press on for a bit longer."

The next offshoot tunnel was just as small, and was again filled with unmoving dead air. However, this time a faint sweetish odor leaked out. Carla concentrated, and was sure she could hear a distant clicking noise, coming from far back in the darkness. She brought the flashlight around and shone it into the cave, hoping there was nothing there. She exhaled, realizing she had been holding her breath – empty.

Giving myself the willies. She breathed deeply and wiped her brow with the last clean spot on her forearm, then dragged herself onward.

*****

"You got something?" Matt paused; Megan had come to a halt at a narrowing in their cave.

The answer came back after a few seconds. "Nothing; this place is deader than a dodo."

Matt laughed softly. "You sure that you want to use that analogy in this place? We might still find one of those."

Megan looked back over her shoulder and grinned. "Good. Did you know they became extinct because they tasted so damned good? And I'm starving."

"You're always eating. I don't know how you keep your figure."

"Fast metabolism, and plenty of good sex." She reached back with her boot and nudged Matt in the shoulder, leaving a streak of the shitty smelling earth. "And that's the first thing we're doing when we get out of here ... well, maybe after a shower ... and some food ... and I call my mom. But then, you and I ..."

Matt shushed her.

"What is it?" She froze.

"Did you hear that?" Matt asked.

"No, what?" She waited for a few more seconds. "Don't you dare try to scare me in here, Matt." Then she heard it as well.

"That sounded like ..."

"Carla ... screaming – up ahead."

"Let's go." Megan sped forward with Matt right on her boots.

* * * * *

John Mordell inched along behind Carla. He was feeling his age. He glanced briefly at his wristwatch, grateful to see that they only had another few minutes of exploring time before they would head back. He grimaced; unless he could use one of the side caves to turn, he'd be doing it all the way on his belly again, but this time backward. He'd be a wreck, and if Carla was able to turn around and he couldn't, she'd be staring into his red, agony-racked face the whole way. *How undignified*, he thought.

As he pulled himself forward, he thought again of the cave they had just passed. The smell emanating from its dark interior still unsettled him. It reminded him of something, but he couldn't remember what. Images of the Congo flashed into his mind from the time he'd administered a malarial outbreak there decades ago. Something about the smell reminded him of the Congo, but what? Just when he thought he had it, the connection danced away.

Carla, with her smaller frame, had pulled ahead a dozen feet, and his flashlight beam wobbled as he tried to maintain his pace. He marveled at the woman – her features, her stamina, and her intellect made her his ideal woman. He'd certainly be asking her out when they got home ... or maybe before then. *Best not give her a chance to change her mind.* He squirmed ahead a little faster, hoping to catch sight of her derrière again.

John stopped dead – his boot was stuck. Odd. Suddenly his lower leg felt like he had just run up against a thorn bush. He rolled to his side and pointed his flashlight back down his body. It felt like the hair actually rose off his head when he saw what was stopping him. There was something attached to his leg – some sort of deep-sea creature. The crustacean's appearance was compounded by its fire engine-red body, reminding him of a cooked lobster.

As he watched, it inched forward another half foot to just above his knee. He could see now that the plated body was long and segmented, and what he had taken for thorns were actually spiked legs, dozens of them, working in unison to grip, then release, as the creature wormed its way farther up his body. Several pairs of the spiked legs had hold of him at any one time.

He gagged, feeling cold dribble on his chin. He kicked out, hard, with his other leg, but it felt like he had struck hardened ceramic plating – the creature's exoskeleton was like armor, and his tough boot just glanced off. The thing moved forward another few inches. There seemed to be no eyes, just foot-long antennae that waved and tapped at his legs, as though gently testing for the most succulent portions of flesh. At the bump of his knee, the thing rose up for a moment, displaying mandibles that made his stomach lurch – two needle-sharp pincers on each side of the ten-inch-wide head. But what was between them was worse – serrated mouthparts like a buzz saw.

He kicked again, harder, and then again. The creature re-acted this time, burying its pincers deep into his thigh. He screamed, and went to thrash out with the fury of a madman, only to find his other leg gripped in another spiky embrace. Looking down, he saw that a second creature was making its way up his other leg.

"John, John – are you okay?" He became aware of Carla scrabbling back toward him, and then her light was added to his.

Her scream in his ear pushed his own nerves over the edge, and he roared with pain and fear. The first creature pulled its pincers from his leg and crawled forward onto his gut, its sightless head bobbing closer. Numbness was spreading throughout his limbs, and he could see the creature's mandibles opening as it continued to inch closer to his face.

He looked down briefly, feeling more of the sharp legs on his lower body. As he feared, there were more – many more – of the monsters.

He tried to turn toward Carla. "Get out of here ... go!"

The smell enveloped him, and he immediately re-membered where he had encountered it before – in the Congo, when treating a tribe at the edge of the forest, one of their makeshift hospital cabins had become infested with giant jungle centipedes. The poisonous creatures could only be cleared out with fire.

"Run." He didn't know why he said it – he knew Carla couldn't run, but he hoped she knew what he meant. Her hand reached for his silver hair, pulling on it. She scurried down, having somehow managed to turn her body around – something he knew he would never have been able to do. She brought her face close to his.

"What can I do, what ...?"

One of the creatures scurried up and buried its mandibles into his neck. Another inched closer and passed up over his face, trying to reach Carla. He grabbed at it, hugging the monstrous segments in his arms. He only had strength for another few words now.

"Please ... go."

He dimly heard her scurry backward – she'd be safe. He smiled and shut his eyes, just as something sharp pressed down over his face.

* * * * *

Matt and Megan crawled forward. Their tunnel widened slightly, allowing them to move on their hands and knees instead of their bellies. It was agony on the bony bits of their legs, but at least their progress was better.

"It's shouting ... up ahead. I know it's Carla." Megan kept up her speed.

"It must be an echo. We should go back." Matt still couldn't work out how Carla could have gotten ahead of them. He navigated around a fallen chunk of stone, and silently prayed that another tremor didn't occur while they were stuck in this long coffin of rock.

Megan was pulling away. "No way; I'm sure it's from up ahead." She started to crawl even faster, her words drifting back over her. "These caves must intersect."

"Possibly." Matt had to move faster or he risked losing her. His knees and palms were shredded as he plowed forward. The tunnel was starting to shrink, becoming little more than a pipe of sharp rock. Megan was gone now and his own hoarse breathing blanketed any sounds from up ahead. He squirmed for a few feet, and then ... he was out.

He stayed on his hands and knees, sucking in the cooler air, perspiration dripping from his forehead as he waited for the pain in his extremities to abate. But he was in open space. It was a room of broken rock, glowing from above and below.

Matt stood gratefully and stretched, glancing around. "She's not here." He took a step, then quickly pulled his arms down and squeezed his eyes shut as something gelatinous touched his forehead. He carefully opened his eyes – the cavern was about fifty feet across, and slightly less than that in width. Its roof hung at least four feet above his head, but he had to stoop – long, sticky tendrils, like glowing blue snot, hung down all around him. He'd seen something similar before, a long time ago, in a cave deep beneath the Antarctic ice – a species of glow-worm.

"She must be here; keep looking." Megan crawled over to one of the rock walls, and Matt was drawn to something at the far side of the small cavern. The blue luminescence from overhead was matched by another source of light from the cave floor – a red pool shone from the far wall. He walked toward it and bent to stare into its depths. About five feet down there was a shelf of stone, and then the water disappeared under the wall. Maybe the glow was sunlight on the red water – on the other side of the crater rim.

"This might be it. This could be the way out."

"Carla!"

Megan's voice made him spin. She was kneeling in front of another small cave, its mouth no wider than a large dinner plate. She got down low and turned her head to listen for a few seconds before shining her flashlight inside. She turned to Matt.

"Come here ... quick." She turned back to the small opening, yelling into it once again. "Carla?"

This time there was a response; a wretched moan ebbing from the dark hole. Matt rushed closer, and Megan wedged her head into the hole.

"Carla, Carla ..." She tried to get more of her body into the opening, but couldn't fit. She pulled away, searched the ground, and snatched up a fist-sized chunk of loose rock, then started to pound at the small entrance, chipping and cracking the rim. Within a few seconds, a few pieces had been dislodged. She dropped the rock and plunged her head and arm inside.

Matt quickly grabbed her waist. From within the hole she grunted back to him: "Pull."

Matt dragged his girlfriend back, and, like a long splinter being pulled from a wound, she and Carla were drawn free.

Carla looked wild – hair frazzled, face and body streaked with blood and covered in disgusting-smelling ooze. But worst of all was the expression of abject terror on her face.

She babbled, looking from Megan to the hole in the wall. Then she furiously grabbed onto Megan's arm. "It's John, John." She gulped air into her lungs, then hunched forward and rocked back and forth. "I couldn't ... I couldn't." It was if she didn't know whether to scurry away or throw up.

Megan grabbed her upper arms and shook her. "Carla, Carla, listen to me. Where's John? Is he stuck inside?"

Carla's face was wild and staring. She babbled for a few more seconds, then shook her head and grimaced, squeezing tears down her muddy face. "They got him. We need to, to ..."

Matt went to dive into the hole. Carla pushed Megan aside and leapt for him, screeching loud in the small room: "No!"

Matt froze, and turned to her. She was wild, and clung to him, staring into his face. "They'll be coming. We need to get away from here." She wailed, dragging Matt back. "They had him ... all over him. It was horrible."

"Was it spiders?" Megan kept one eye on the small hole now; Carla's fear was infectious.

Carla breathed in and out deeply, hyperventilating. "No, worse. We need weapons – we need, we need ... fire."

"We need to get back; we'll use our tunnel." Matt looked at it warily, his dry lips moving in a silent prayer.

* * * * *

"Do you think he's still alive?" Matt whispered.

Kurt wrapped a couple of spare shirts around his forearms. "From what we've experienced so far in this hellhole, and after what Carla described?" He shrugged. "Doubt it. But we've got to check." Kurt doused another shirt in lighter fluid, then knotted it tightly around a stick. He had his hunting knife at hand, and even had Megan's golden rod stuck in his belt – a magnificent club for close-quarters combat.

"I should go with you." Matt handed him some matches.

Kurt shook his head, his mouth turned down in thought. "Not this time, but thanks anyway. Besides, if some ugly fuck-er gets in my face and decides he isn't scared of fire, I'll be backing out – fast. I certainly don't want anyone behind me."

"I think you'll find—"

"No." Kurt's steady gaze left no room for argument. He gripped Matt's shoulder and nodded, then turned away, the conversation effectively over.

The big guide stood in front of Carla, looking down into her face. "I'll find him." He tightened a few more straps at his waist. "You were about eighteen minutes in, right?"

She nodded, still subdued from her ordeal. He grunted his understanding, then walked the few paces to the small opening and stood looking down at it. He checked his watch briefly and paused, thinking, then turned to Matt.

"Listen, if I don't come back out, just be ready in case something else does." He took a breath, and then without another word, ducked down and disappeared into the dark tunnel of rock.

Matt watched the halo of light dim as Kurt disappeared. In just a few minutes the cave was dark once again. He turned to Carla and Megan.

"I should go after him."

Megan shook her head. "No, he's right about needing a clear path if he wants to back out. Besides, there's no room to fight side-by-side."

"Yes ... you should go." Carla had been biting her lip, the professional scientist now a sunken-eyed ghost. She sniffed. "He'll need help; he doesn't know what he's getting into. Bravery and stupidity are sometimes the same thing. You should go."

Megan shook her head slowly, and Matt hung his head for a second before looking to Joop for the deciding vote. Joop also shook his head. "I'll go."

Matt snorted. "No, you're way bigger than me – that would be a bad idea." He squared his shoulders, then turned to them. "Get anything else we might need, and be prepared to meet us at the end of the cave at the red pool. Once we have John, we might need to get out of here – fast."

Megan nodded, her eyes welling up. She shoved him in the chest, her face momentarily angry, before grabbing him and pulling him close.

"I love you – be careful," she whispered, and then pushed him again. "Idiot." She turned away.

Matt checked his flashlight and ducked into the tunnel.

* * * * *

Kurt moved quickly for the first ten minutes, then slowed. Sweat dripped from his face to the mire on the ground. Some of the sweat was from the unusual humidity in the jagged rock pipe, but some, he knew, was from the tension. He stopped and listened, calming his breathing so he could concentrate. There was noise up ahead, rhythmic, like rain on a metal rooftop. As he focussed on the sound, it started to remind him more of the clack of knitting needles ... but hundreds of them, all working together. He pulled the fuel-wrapped stick from his belt, and then touched the matches in his pocket. He decided to pull them out as well, to be ready.

He continued on, placing one hand in front of the other, and trying to keep the matches and the accelerant-soaked cloth out of the damp soil underneath him. His light only penetrated about twenty feet, and then the wall of blackness closed like an impenetrable curtain. Now that he was closer, he thought he could also hear tearing, like canvas sheets been torn down the middle. A smell enveloped him – ammonia-sweet, with something else underneath it, metallic and meaty. He knew what that was.

Up ahead, something appeared, roiled and twisted momentarily, then melted back into the darkness. Kurt quickly fumbled for his matches, pulling one of the waterproofs from the box and striking it. It caught and he touched it to the fuel-soaked rag, which flared into an orange tongue of heat.

Kurt squinted from the light, and had to hold it away from his face as it scalded him in the confines of the small cave. He held it out, his fingers locking down on the stick as the source of the noise was lit up on a macabre stage.

John Mordell, or what was left of him, was a moving mass of long, segmented bodies. Sharp, telescoping legs gripped their prize hard, and muscular mouthparts sawed at both flesh and bone. Kurt grimaced; the frantic, bloody mass plugged the entire cave, and while he watched, one of John's arms was detached from his body and hauled into a side tunnel. No sooner had the creature disappeared than another was disgorged from a different tunnel to take its turn in the boiling knot of chitenous plates and needle-sharp mouths.

One of the creatures, at least ten feet long and a foot wide, started back toward Kurt, but a wave of the flaming torch dissuaded it from coming any closer. Instead, it turned, trying to muscle its way back into the pile of meat that used to be Dr. John Mordell.

Kurt's jaws had clamped tight in disgusted horror. A brief, mad idea of trying to use the flame to drive the creatures away from the man was jettisoned, as the thought of sending the many-legged beasts into a frenzy was insane. They only had a few directions to go in – and one was toward him. Besides, Mordell was dead, and he didn't think anyone would be impressed if he dragged a ravaged and limbless torso back to the group – least of all Carla.

Another beast took an exploratory trip toward him, and once again, he waved it back.

"Sorry, John." He swallowed, his mouth dry, and started to back up.

"Ah, shit." Something sharp pinched the calf of his leg. Whipping his head around, he saw the waving antennae of one of the creatures, its long, many-legged body half out of a small cave as the other half made its way up his limb, sharp legs cutting through the tough material, and then into his flesh.

He screamed and kicked, but nothing happened. The hard-bodied creature simply hunkered down over its prize, sharp legs clinging tight, the tips now deeper into his flesh.

He lay there staring at it, knowing that bringing the torch back around would allow the boiling mass of monstrous creatures from the other end of the tight tunnel to descend upon him from the dark.

"Fuck it!" He was trapped.

* * * * *

Matt could hear the yelling from farther up ahead, and once again increased his speed, working already bloody hands and knees into pulp in the tight tunnel. In another few minutes he came upon the bizarre scene of Kurt sandwiched between a large creature that looked like a giant centipede, and dozens more balled up just beyond him.

The beast hooking onto his leg looked enormously powerful, and was only halfway out of a side cave. From the six feet of creature that he could see, Matt calculated that it must be at least twice that length, and probably weighed in at over a hundred pounds. A very formidable predator – especially in the tight confines of the underground tunnel.

"Matt, thank God. Goddamn, get ... it ... off ... me!"

The thing was rearing up, sharp legs still clinging tight to the meat of his calf, and powerful-looking pincers opening wide. Kurt's teeth were gritted, and he kicked back with his boot time and again, but the thing might as well have been made of stone. All he was doing was tearing his own flesh where the legs hooked in tight.

Use the flame, Matt thought. "Why don't you ...?" But then his mouth clamped shut, as Kurt shifted and he saw the moving, knotted mass beyond him – the mass that was only held at bay by the flaming torch, which was rapidly losing its heat and light.

"Get it off ... now!" Kurt's scream smashed into his ears, and he felt himself begin to panic. Matt swallowed down his revulsion and inched forward. Pulling out his knife, he reached out and lifted it as high as the tunnel would allow. Then, aiming for a joint in the segments, he brought it down with all his strength.

There was a crackle-crunch, and his blade sunk in about five inches. The monstrous centipede exploded into furious activity, detaching itself from Kurt's leg and folding back on itself, diving first toward the blade, and then at Matt's face.

Matt recoiled, arms up and eyes crushed shut, waiting for the impact. But there was another loud crunch, and the attack never landed. He opened his eyes to see Kurt's boot jammed down hard on the back of his blade. It was too much for the long creature, which pulled itself back into its lair and disappeared.

The light in the tunnel was a dull orange now – Kurt's torch was exhausting its fuel. Matt didn't wait another second.

"Come on." He backed up, fast. Kurt, as he had promised, came at him at a frightening speed, holding what was left of the flaming torch behind him as he came. Matt only just managed to stay in front.

"Wait, wait, I need a second here." Kurt stopped for a moment, wheezing heavily and holding the torch out behind him. "I think we're okay, I don't think they're following. I reckon they've got enough meat for the time being." Kurt continued to hold the torch out the way they had come, and lay on his side, panting.

Matt gratefully collapsed, looking at his wristwatch. They still had about another ten minutes of tunnel before they could join the group.

"Was … that meat … was it?" Matt lay on his back, still gasping.

"Yeah, yeah, it was Mordell. Those fucking big worm things took him apart." He leaned forward. "Don't tell Carla. I think … they liked each other." He felt his leg, groaning. "Hey."

"What?" Matt looked up.

"Thanks."

Matt nodded. "I just want to go home."

"I hear that." Kurt got back up on his hands and knees. "After you."

* * * * *

"There was nothing we could do; he was already dead." Kurt unwrapped the cloth from around his arms and let it drop to the ground. He wouldn't meet her eyes.

Carla nodded, and then walked away, her head down and arms folded. She didn't cry, or seem surprised. Matt guessed she had expected the worst.

Matt sat down and leaned back against the wall of the cave, Megan beside him, hugging his shoulders. She had given him some water, which he had first poured over his head, and then gulped down in a few big sips. He was relieved to see that everything they needed was stacked at the back of the larger cave. He'd had enough of this place.

"Ready to go?"

Megan nodded and rested her head on his shoulder.

Matt would have liked a few more minutes to rest. He would also have liked to bathe the wounds on his elbows and knees, and he would really have liked something to eat. But after seeing the carnivorous arthropods up close, he knew he couldn't rest until they were out of the caves. They were obviously the things that had made the strange tracks in the soil all around them, and that meant that sooner or later they would come boiling out of the smaller tunnels.

Kurt went back to packing his gold, and Joop stood watching him. He threw a backpack over his shoulders. "A few mementos, yes?"

Kurt kept packing. "Well, no bird, and no job; Brenner, Steinberg, Jian, and now Mordell, dead. Without the gold, it's all been for nothing."

Carla joined them and stood close to Kurt, holding up several vials of red water she had collected from the pond where they had first entered the blood jungle. "No, not for nothing; I came for the *sarcoptes scabiei primus* retardant, and thanks to Jian, John, and even Max Steinberg, I think we've found it." She looked hard at Kurt. "This is my gold."

Kurt smiled and afforded her a small salute.

Matt got slowly to his feet and stretched – it didn't help. Every part of his body ached and stung from abrasions. *Coulda been worse*, he thought, a momentary image of John in the knotted mass of arthropods flashing into his mind.

"Okay, let's go, everyone. I'll lead off, then Megan, Carla, Joop, and then you can bring up the rear, Kurt."

Kurt nodded. "You got it buddy ... and watch the side tunnels, okay?"

Matt grunted a confirmation.

* * * * *

This time, the crawl through the claustrophobic rock pipe seemed to go on forever. They were already fatigued, their nerves were wire-tight, and they were in a damned hurry to be free.

At last, they pushed and pulled one other from the small tunnel and stood up straight in the open cave. The red pool was a little less bright. Checking his watch, Matt saw that it was getting on for late afternoon.

"We need to hurry. I don't want to do this in the dark ... and we're not sure where we'll pop up."

"So long as it's on the other side," Megan said.

Carla knelt at the edge of the pool and scooped some of the water into her hand. She sniffed at it. "Good, it's infused with the red flower – we need to fully douse ourselves. Leave nothing dry – even our backpacks should be totally saturated. We certainly don't want to leave with any mites on our bodies."

The few remaining backpacks were undone and anything sealed was opened – if it couldn't be satisfactorily soaked, it would be left behind. They worked quickly, and in a few moments, they stood ready, looking into the darkening water.

Matt re-slung his pack as Kurt came up behind him, talking softly. "Matt." He had some of the gold in his hands. "Matt, I need a favor. Can you bring some of this through? It's way too heavy for me on my own ... I'll share it."

Matt looked at it dismissively, and shook his head. "I don't need it."

"I do. I can't keep doing this, and I'll be broke now. It's a new start for me ... please."

Megan got up and walked to the rear of the cave. Matt waited until she was out of earshot. He looked down at the gold in Kurt's hands, mentally calculating its weight. He reckoned about seven to ten pounds. It would be a little like a diver's belt, and he was already bone tired.

"Shit Kurt, I'm beat. I've already—"

"Please, Matt. I'll owe you big time."

"You already do." Matt pulled a face, and then took two of the items. "Do not take this as me endorsing the stealing of artifacts in any way."

"Thanks." Kurt bowed slightly, and then straightened and clapped his hands. "Okay, who volunteers to be the scout?" He placed his hands on his hips, knuckles still bleeding from the cave crawl. From the expression on his face, he obviously expected to be nominated.

"Shussh, be quiet." Megan's tone silenced everyone.

Matt turned to where she was down on her knees, her head lowered and tilted, by the smaller cave where they had pulled Carla out only hours before. She turned to him, her face pale.

"They're coming. I can hear them."

Matt rushed over and bent down to listen. From far back there was a familiar sound, like thousands of knitting needles working furiously ... and they were getting louder.

He got to his feet, pulling her up. "We're about to have company." He turned to her. "Ready?"

She nodded. He turned to the rest of the group. "Listen up. Forget the scouting – we aren't going back. Either we come up on the other side of the crater wall, or we end up somewhere else inside ... and if that's the case, it's got to be better than here."

He looked at Megan and smiled. She leaned in quick, kissed him, and then dove into the pool.

Matt looked back toward the small caves. The click-clacking was growing louder now, coming from several of the openings. He guessed their abraded hands and feet had left a blood trail that was irresistible. Death was coming quickly, and their time was up.

"Go, go, go!" Carla and Joop jumped in, disappearing below the surface. Kurt gave him the thumbs up and dove.

Matt took one last look back – his breath caught in his chest. The first creature filled the tunnel mouth, and had a glossy black head on its fire engine-red segmented body. Its antenna waved for only a second before it came at Matt like a locomotive, legs moving so quickly they blurred.

"Shit." He jumped, feeling something scratch at his hair as the extra weight of the gold quickly pulled him below the surface.

Sinking fast, he wished he had taken a larger breath. He had to swim hard to keep from being pulled down and was quickly using up the oxygen in his lungs. In a few seconds, his ears felt the pressure of the depths as he frantically swam under the shelf of rock and toward the dimming light.

* * * * *

Matt broke the surface and dragged in several gigantic, lung-filling breaths. His arms and legs felt like rubber, but he still thrashed hard to stop the weight in his pack from dragging him back down.

He hung on the pool edge for a moment, mentally and physically recharging. It felt good to be free of the oily slickness of the warm cave and the constant itch of the small mites. He pulled himself out and rolled onto his back, the tightly curled grasses beneath him acting like the softest bed he had ever felt in his life.

He slowly sat up, pushing the wet hair back off his face. "Whoa." It was lucky they came up as far from the wall as they did. The crater face, covered in the thorned vines, reached down to the surface of the red pond. If they had come up just a few feet back, they each would have worn a crown of deadly thorns. He let out a long breath and laughed softly. To escape the horrors of the primeval world beyond the crater wall, only to be poisoned at the exit – now that would have been a curse.

"Are we safe?" Carla sat with her arms wrapped around her knees, her hair hanging in strings over her face.

"I think so; I think we're ... out." Megan walked around the edge of the pool, looking at the more normal plant life. She stopped and turned. "We need to find Moema ... if he's still here, that is."

Kurt was already on his feet. "I don't think we're that far away." He looked up at the fading sky, to where the sun was setting, to get his bearings, then pointed. "This way."

* * * * *

Moema was exactly where they'd left him. It was hard to believe, but they had been away less than three days. He was camped out by the original pond, a small fire burning low, and something small and rat-like skewered on a stick suspended over the fire. It smelt ... wonderful.

The Brazilian jumped to his feet, his mouth open, first in surprise, then developing into a broad grin of joy. "I was worried for you." His grin turned to a look of confusion. "Another way out, yes?"

"Long story." Megan fell in a heap beside the fire, her eyes on the cooking meat, the small dry blaze searing the humidity from her face and hands.

Moema looked at each of them. "Where is Mr. Max? Where is ... Jian ... and the doctor John?"

"Dead, all dead, I'm afraid." Carla responded.

Moema sat down. "And no bird?"

"Yes, there were the birds, but … it got away." Carla shook her head. "We don't need them now. Mr. Max … Max Steinberg wanted them, not us."

Moema nodded solemnly. "It was very dangerous, I think."

"Yes, deadly. We're lucky we escaped alive," Matt said.

Moema nodded again, knowingly. "My grandfather's story was true." He looked at each of them. "You were also warned by the Ndege. Next time, you will know better."

"They warned us all right, but as usual, we refused to heed them because we think we know better." Matt snorted. "And there's not going to be a next time."

Moema nodded, but didn't comment. Matt guessed he already knew as much. Moema reached down for a cloth bag and emptied its contents onto the ground. Four more of the rat-like creatures tumbled out, already gutted and skinned. He started to thread them onto different sticks, and then carefully angled them over the small blaze to roast.

Everyone's eyes were on the food. Kurt was the first to break the spell. "Now, it's time for dinner and then we should rest. But at dawn tomorrow, let's get the hell out of here."

He looked at Matt, then at his pack, and winked. Matt guessed that Kurt was thinking about his gold, rather than dinner.

CHAPTER 20

Just before they turned in for the evening, Matt stepped from the jungle after relieving himself and walked straight into Kurt. The big man acted surprised, as if the meeting was co-incidental, but they both knew what he wanted.

Kurt gripped his shoulder and squeezed. "Thanks Matt ... for looking after that gold. I'd never have been able to swim with all of it in my saddle bags." He grinned and pressed Matt's shoulder again, before dropping his hand and holding it out, palm up.

Matt dropped the bag off his shoulder. He'd brought it with him because Kurt hadn't taken his eyes off it. He pulled out the two heavy objects, each gleaming and polished, as if they had been cast just that morning. He looked at them in detail for the first time. One was a warrior, its face in the broad and flat style of Incan metal craft, a war club held down by its side. He'd need to do some research to identify if it was a character of any great status.

The other he recognized immediately, seeing the coiled bird demon. Quetzalcoatl – the bringer of life and death. He smiled. *Appropriate*, he thought.

He placed them in Kurt's large hands – he had to bring both palms together to hold the heavy weight.

"Damn things nearly drowned me." Matt watched Kurt's face, his broad grin of delight as he roughly stuffed each into a bag, and felt his anger rise at the disrespect. "You know, you'll never get those out of the country, let alone through customs. They belong to Moema and his country. The authorities take a pretty dim view of stealing antiquities." He watched Kurt's face darken.

Kurt tilted his head. "We don't go through customs, remember? Once we're on Max's plane, we're home." He patted Matt on the shoulder. "Don't sweat it."

"Yeah, well, the United States became a party to the 1970 UNESCO Convention on the Means of Prohibiting and Preventing the Illicit Import, Export and Transfer of Ownership of Cultural Property. Basically, that means the US government imposes import restrictions on antiquities originating outside of the United States to stop archeological theft."

Kurt just shrugged.

"We're talking fines, huge fines, even jail time." Matt paused. "Look Kurt, you saved our lives, and you risked your own to go back for John, so I'm not going to dump you in it. But you should have a good hard think about what you're doing."

Kurt's face brightened as it became clear that Matt would keep his secret. He shrugged, and his face pulled into a semblance of thoughtfulness. "Okay, little buddy. Once I'm home, I'll drop the Brazilian government a line and tell them about their gold. They can decide what they want to do about it."

He nodded toward the camp. "Let's get some sleep ... and, ah, thank you."

* * * * *

Before dawn Matt felt another body force its way into his sleeping bag. Megan breathed into his ear. "Are you awake?"

"I am now."

Her hand went lower. "Mmm, awake and up, I see." He could hear the playfulness in her voice. He rolled toward her, but knew that lovemaking would be impossible in amongst the group.

"I'm sorry I was such an asshole to you, back when ... but I thought ... you know."

She looked confused, and then kissed him. "I think I know what you mean. And I'm sorry if I seemed a bit of a bitch sometimes ... friends?"

"Hmm," he pretended to think about it. Her hand squeezed ... hard. "Okay, friends, friends."

Soon, the sound of people moving about in the predawn light made the pair burrow down in the sleeping bag for a few more minutes' privacy. They emerged only when someone prodded their bag.

"Coffee's on."

They met Carla at the fire Moema had started, and each accepted a mug of coffee.

"I slept surprisingly well. A hot shower, and I might begin to feel half human again." Carla looked up at the dark wall of the crater lip towering over them, its red blooms fragrant in the still morning air.

"Was it real?"

"Too real," Megan responded.

Carla nodded, still facing the crater wall. Her eyes had a haunted look, and Matt could tell she was thinking of John, Jian, and maybe even Max Steinberg.

"Should we tell anyone?" She smiled flatly, adding, "Who'd believe us?"

Matt thought for a few seconds. "Maybe. There's all the Incan artifacts to consider. Their value to archeologists and museums would be priceless. But I guess they've remained hidden – and therefore, safe – for countless centuries. What government can promise that these days, when museums across Europe and the Middle East have all been looted during times of unrest? Scientists would also love to get in there to study the unique specimens, not to mention the evolutionary throwbacks. The problem is, it's both a Garden of Eden and a Pandora's Box."

Megan shook her head. "Not everyone who came would have noble values. It's been hidden for millions of years, and it could be gone before the end of our lifetimes. Is it worth it?"

Matt thought for a moment and then shook his head slowly. "No ... no it's not."

He turned to Kurt, who stood silently, listening to them. His mouth turned down as he nodded sagely.

"I agree; best to keep it all a secret."

"Ha, so you can come back with a dozen men and a U-haul for the rest of the gold?" Megan shot back.

Moema's head snapped up, now following the conversation.

"Keep it down will you?" Matt said.

Kurt dismissed Megan's suggestion with a wave. "Not a chance. Max is gone, so I am officially retired." He pulled a face. "Come on Megan, I know I'm no saint, but I'm not a complete asshole either. Cut me some slack will you?"

He turned and walked away, snapping his fingers at Moema. "Let's go. I don't think we need to enter the Ndege village again, so we can cut a more direct route home."

Moema glared at him for a moment, but nodded, kicking soil over the smoking fire.

Matt watched him go. "Yeah, well, not a complete asshole." His smile only touched one side of his mouth. He stepped in close to Megan, seeing her shoulders hunched, and looked at her with raised eyebrows.

"Okay?"

She continued to stare hotly at Kurt's back. "I don't trust that guy."

Matt shrugged. "I trust him more now than I did. But I'm glad you feel that way."

She looked skeptical, and he just shook his head. "Forget it. Anyway, he was there for us when it counted. So, 'cut him some slack', we shall. Let's just get home first."

* * * * *

The return trek to the base of the Mato Grosso Plateau was faster than their original trip, as they didn't need to follow antiquated maps, and could also take a more direct route. They just caught the onset of the rainy season, and the last two days were spent walking in pouring rain the temperature of blood. It did nothing to cool them down, and instead just added damp weight to their bones.

They spent the evenings inside their tents, pouring salt onto the blood-bloated leeches that had managed to find their way inside boots and socks, between toes, and even up into sensitive parts of the groin.

Carla kept to herself, jotting notes in her rapidly deteriorating notebook. Matt had tried to speak to her, but she was distracted – in her mind she was already back at home, working on a solution to the mite infestation. He had tried to focus on what she mumbled to him over her shoulder, but when she started touching on synergized butoxides and tanacetum geneses, it became obvious that their fields were vastly different, and she quickly lost him.

The radio equipment was where they had left it, still double-wrapped in oilskin and plastic tarpaulins. Kurt immediately called in the Brazilian military helicopter, and in a few more hours they were watching the giant metal dragonfly gently descend toward them. Matt couldn't help grinning – never had a machine looked so welcoming.

They piled into the craft, gratefully falling onto metal seats and slumping, with Joop falling asleep in seconds. Matt once again looked out of the window as they lifted up past the magnificent green skyscrapers and the clouds of fine spray from the plateau's waterfalls. It was odd – even though the chopper was sealed, as they lifted up out of the Gran Chaco, it was like the air around him suddenly became cleaner, clearer.

Kurt sat up the front, headphones over his large head, talking rapidly. As Matt watched, he saw Kurt's features go from confused to heated. After another few moments Kurt pulled the headphones from his head and stared incredulously at the pilot, who just shrugged. Kurt came back to join the team.

Matt sat forward. "What's up?"

Kurt didn't respond for a moment, his lips tight. He looked up. "We've got a problem."

Everyone waited, their attention fixed on the guide. He went on.

"Seems our ... pilot ..." He motioned to the chopper pilot. "... not that guy, but Max's pilot, is having difficulty organizing immigration and customs clearance."

Matt raised his eyebrows at Kurt, motioning to the weighty backpack in the corner of the craft, and then whispering, "Looks like Moema must have ..."

Kurt looked pained and shook his head. "No, no, the problem is at the US end. They're not letting any Brazilian planes in ... no, nix that, they're not letting anything in, full stop. Seems there's a national quarantine order been called. So Brazil is not allowing us to leave."

"Huh? But I need to speak to my office, and we need to report all the deaths on our expedition. What about Max Stei—" Carla was leaning forward, her eyes wide.

Kurt waved his hand impatiently. "Now is not the time to be complicating things. Did you not hear me? There's a general quarantine order."

Carla looked slightly stunned. "Oh." She sat back. "By who? For what, where?"

Kurt shrugged. "Oh, come on lady, who do you think? By you guys, of course, and for the entire fucking United States."

Carla shut her eyes and put a fist over her mouth, looking like she was trying to process what must have been unfolding in the US.

Kurt spoke wearily. "Steinberg's pilot is trying to negotiate a take-off based on the argument that we are returning home, it's a private plane, and we will not be coming back." He looked at each of them, his gaze steady. "Bottom line, though; we've got to be ready to move quickly." He looked pained. "And maybe not all that legally, if need be."

Megan sat back and half closed her eyes. "I'm guessing that a few days in a five-star Brazilian hotel is now officially off the agenda."

Kurt held up his hands in a helpless gesture. "I think if we don't get out now, we might never get home. Brazil might decide to close its own borders, and then ..." He shrugged. "Look, the plane is on an outer runway, and the chopper will be touching down at a military hangar close by. We can wash off and change there."

Megan groaned. Carla seemed frozen, her eyes unfocussed and her mind obviously elsewhere.

Joop shrugged. "Better than nothing. The sooner we are home the better, I think ... for all of us."

* * * * *

The heat on the tarmac radiated back up at them from the black surface like a frying pan. No one complained; compared to the deep jungle's stifling humidity, near-impenetrable vegetation, energy-sapping ankle-deep mud, and ever-hungry insect life, it was a veritable walk in the park.

Each of the team took turns at the small soapy basin, and then changed into the clean clothes they'd left on Steinberg's plane. They felt cleaner, if not all that rested or refreshed. Kurt's arm strained when he carried his gold-laden backpack, keeping it close as always. He even stood it against his leg when he took his makeshift bath.

Matt walked a few paces out into the hundred-degree heat on the tarmac and squinted as he watched Moema shrink into the distance. He'd miss the little guide. He wasn't so sure that Moema would miss them, but he had been stoic and good-humored, and he had kept them safe.

Matt waved to the speck in the distance. "Thank you."

He sighed. Unfortunately, the Brazilian's good humor had leaked away, and Matt felt responsible. Kurt had paid him, so he had no reason to stay with them anymore. Moema had briefly said his goodbyes, then sought Matt out and shaken his hand. He continued to hold it tightly and stared into Matt's eyes.

"I know Mr. Kurt takes home some of the relics of our ancestors. I know that you know this," he had said levelly.

There was no accusation in the words, or anger, just a simple stated fact. Matt had just stood there with nothing to say. He felt guilty, complicit, and dishonest, even though he wasn't the one removing the artifacts. But he knew about it and did nothing, so he felt just as responsible.

He had tried to apologize, and promised to get them back, but the small man had stopped him. He didn't seem all that fussed, just disappointed.

"They will eventually find their way home – this year, next year, next hundred years … it doesn't matter; they know they will always belong to us. Those who would steal our history discover that the gods and kings always have more than one curse. They always have the last laugh, Mr. Matt."

He had turned without another word, his body now a wavering speck in the tarmac's blistering heat.

Megan had come and stood beside him, watching Moema vanish in the haze. "What was that about?"

Matt had shrugged. "I think Kurt, or all of us, just got cursed ... again." He clicked his teeth and turned.

"Come on, let's go home."

* * * * *

They climbed into Steinberg's Gulfstream G550 and breathed in the deodorized air conditioning. Cold drinks were handed around as everyone dropped into large cushioned chairs. Kurt would use the movie producer's name and account for as long as he could. They figured the man owed him that, anyway.

Kurt had told the pilot that Max Steinberg and the other missing passengers would be staying on for another few weeks, and that they were to leave immediately. This wasn't unusual – Steinberg often changed his plans erratically, and the pilot was used to Kurt taking charge.

In a few minutes the pilot's voice came over the intercom, giving them some flight details and telling them to ready themselves for takeoff.

He told them that he'd been briefed on the quarantine situation and was confident he could negotiate a landing point and facilities for them once they were in the air. His voice clicked off and there was dead air ... for only a minute.

His voice came back on, a little more urgent than before. "Dr. Nero, call coming in for you – a Dr. Francis Hewson. Says it's urgent."

EPISODE 3: TERMINAL STAGE

CHAPTER 21

Maddie stroked Baloo's long white fur from his head all the way down to his tail. The cat hadn't been itself for days. It was probably like the rest of the family – sick and tired of being locked in the house. Daddy went out by himself now – no one else was allowed.

They only ate food from tins, and the occasional lemon from the backyard. Mommy had to put a lot of sugar on them as they were really sour. Maddie hated them – she would have given anything for a blackberry juice poppa.

The cat was agitated on her lap, continually moving, scratching, and pulling at itself.

"Yuck." Maddie held up her hand, flicking her fingers to remove the fur sticking to them. "Baloo, you're shedding. You're going to get into trouble if you make the sofa all hairy again." She watched the cat tug at itself, working the itch. "And you probably have fleas as well." She shook her hand. Some of the hair refused to detach, a gummy residue gluing it to her fingers. "Double yuck." She wiped it on her leg.

Maddie brightened. "Would you like a bath?" She turned the cat around on her lap and looked into its face. "That will make you smell better as well."

The cat groaned and licked itself, its mouth working over-time to expel the copious amounts of hair sticking to its rasp-like tongue. It stopped and seemed to rest, its golden eyes staring up at her. Maddie took this as a sign of assent and got to her feet, placing the cat on the ground, where it lay like a sagging balloon.

"Well, don't you go away, Miss Loo-loo. I'll be right back."

Maddie knew where her old baby bath was, and also her berry shampoo – it'd be perfect. She maneuvered her six-year-old body through the disheveled house, scratching at her own itches as she went. Daddy went out a lot, and Mommy didn't get out of bed much anymore. She took sleepy tablets all the time – because she hated the itch, she said.

Maddie scratched again, turning to speak over her shoulder. "And I think you've given me fleas now as well." Maddie went into the garage and looked under the bench – the bath was still there, with a few of Daddy's tools in it – she could take them out if she was careful. Reaching forward, her arm tingled, and she noticed small round lumps on the skin. She pulled her arm back and stood up, squinting down at the fingertip-sized blisters. She pressed gently against one; it didn't hurt. She pressed again, a little harder. It burst, and then lay flat against her skin. Nothing icky came out, so she ignored it.

Probably Baloo's fleas – she should have a bath as well. Maybe they both could have one together. She liked baths, and cats liked water too, didn't they? She wondered where Daddy was, and tried to remember exactly when it was that he went out. She was sure he'd gone out looking for food, but it felt like a long time ago now.

She reached under the bench for the baby bath – first things first, she thought.

* * * * *

Dr. Francis "Hew" Hewson paced in the small laboratory. He'd been wearing the sealed suit for so long, the high-density polyethylene material was chafing his skin raw. The inner lining of his nose was scabbing and his lips were chapped and split from the dry air that circulated within the self-contained mobile unit.

Hew licked his lips as his stomach grumbled. He was learning to go hours without food and water. The time it took, having to go through the double decon-chambers – first the air blast, followed by chemical misting, and then the ultraviolets – before exiting, only to then have to worm his way out of the rear flap of the heavy suit, made the few sips of fluid through a long straw far from worth it. The amount of time lost was enough to make him swallow down his hunger with a scratchy, dry throat. He needed answers, fast, so he needed to work.

He went to the computer and started typing up his latest results. Thankfully, the board had given up pressuring him for answers, preferring to simply log in and check the notes that he posted every three to six hours. Realistically, there was nothing to report beyond what they already knew. Harsh insecticides and chemical baths worked. Ultraviolet light worked. Many more chemical compounds also killed *sarcoptes scabiei primus* ... and DDT worked best of all for a quick takedown.

But the real problem was the same one that always manifested when treating viruses. Killing a virus was easy ... that is, when they were free range. However, for the most part, viruses tended to hide inside cell walls, where they did the most damage to their host. To kill them there, you had to kill the cell itself – not ideal for the human body.

The same issue arose when attempting to treat an infestation of the mite. The little monster was a burrower, and no matter how effective the external treatments, it needed to be applied directly to the skin. So far, the best-case scenario for individuals who were freed of both the living mites and their eggs was nausea, skin rashes, and respiratory problems. The short-term worst-case scenario was the risk of cancers developing. The long-term, absolute worst case, was that chemical derivates turned out to be significant mutagens, and destabilized human DNA for generations. What was the point of living today if it meant you rendered the population infertile, or worse, gave them a ninety percent chance of severe birth defects for the next hundred years?

Hew snorted. The greener politicians had stopped talking about the debilitating effects to the water table, or DDT residues turning up in the fatty deposits of whales. Any treatment was expected to be a potential hammer-blow to the environment, but it was funny how pragmatism won out when the life in danger turned out to be their own.

Hew stood back and folded his arms within the bulky suit. He looked at the image of *scabiei primus* magnified on the computer screen. It was every horror writer's dream – or nightmare. A bulbous body with a chitenous coat and eight powerful legs, six of which ended in curved hooks, perfect for clinging to both hair and skin. The two legs near the head were smaller and sharper, looking like a combination of machete and chainsaw, used primarily for opening and then burrowing beneath the epidermal layers.

But it was the thing's small head that was truly repulsive. Tear-shaped, with mandibles like twin buzz saw blades, it was perfectly designed for what it needed to do – cut and eat its way into the skin, and then once there, simply keep on eating.

He shouldn't have been surprised that it was proving so formidable. This thing once fed on dinosaurs, so humans must have been a piece of cake ... literally.

Hew sighed in the heavy suit and pulled up some maps of the American contamination shockwave. Color-coded rings representing the infestation spread out from several original points of contact – the airport, the lecture theater in Santa Barbara University, and the Orange County Quarantine Facility. Now, rings covered seventy-five percent of the continent. The spread was slower within the colder climates, and there were a few oases here and there, slightly slowing the spread. He hit a few keys, bringing up a spread projection – ninety percent coverage of the United States in another week. He updated again, this time to see the global perspective – the shockwaves started at the international airports, and rapidly ate up their respective countries. The projection analytics gave the world just ninety days.

Hew closed his red, gritty eyes for a few seconds, wanting to blank out the images before him. In a matter of weeks, the world had been made a different place. Borders had been closed, and no international traffic was allowed. This was by order of the United Nations, and was being enforced by each country's respective military. A limited martial law was already in practise – limited, because venturing out meant doing so in a hazmat suit, and they were fast running out of those, as production of most goods and services had ceased.

Hew wondered what would come next … chaos, he guessed. He turned away from the screen, his shoulders slumping. So promising, so brilliant, so astute … and so out of ideas. He felt about as dumb as dirt. He licked his dry lips again and was contemplating a short break when a series of pings emanated from his computer. He frowned.

The scientist, along with the hundreds of other laboratories working on a solution, had been afforded an enormous amount of seniority and clearance – no request was too great. One of the first things he had asked for was a standing order for all international ports to be on alert for news of Dr. Carla Nero.

Like a flashbulb in his brain, Hew's tired memory lit up scraps of information. The alert had kicked in – somewhere, someone had seen, heard from, or knew something about the whereabouts of his boss.

CONNECT – YES/NO?

He fell against the computer and hit the large square flaring on the screen.

YES.

Immediately, Hew was routed through to an incoming plane.

Please be on it, please be on it, he whispered as the pilot answered.

"Dr. Carla Nero, is she there? Put her on, please put her on, this is an emergency."

CHAPTER 22

"Carla, thank God. What happened? Were you successful? Is everyone safe? How was Steinberg? I hope he doesn't think he's bringing another one of those goddamn birds in here. He'll be shot." Hew took a deep breath, realizing he was talking as fast as his heart was beating.

"Calm down, Hew. Too much has happened for me to answer all your questions now. I think I've got something here – a tincture. I believe it inhibits the growth and hyper-aggression of the mite. In large doses, it may even eradicate them."

"Side effects?"

"No idea. All our equipment was destroyed, so my evidence is line of sight only … empirical, but not confirmed. Now tell me quickly, what is the infestation status? What does the epi-curve look like?"

Hew quickly brought up the screen, already knowing it was useless. The epidemic tracking curve, or epi-curve for short, showed the progression of an outbreak over time. Normally they were either a bar chart or a line curve that had the standard bell shape describing progression – outbreak-escalation-intervention-management-reduction. However, the mite infestation graph was just a straight line, shooting up at an angle of about seventy-five degrees. It had overrun meaningful statistics within a week.

"Off the chart. The data overwhelmed the statistical analysis, rendering the graph outdated even before it was complete. It simply keeps progressing at a geometric rate." Hew sucked in a huge breath, wondering where to start. He shook his head; like Carla, he had too much to say. He settled for a few words. "It's bad – worse than bad and what we feared – they've gone airborne, like a plague. The mite eggs micro-disperse – they're nanoscopic and can be carried on the slightest breeze for miles."

He paused, compressing his lips, forcing the words out. "We've got ... nothing."

He blinked, making a conscious effort to rouse himself from his depression, concern for Carla overriding his own problems. "Carla, you've got to be careful. Things are ... different."

"Okay Hew, we should be at LAX in around six hours," Carla said.

"No, no, you can't land here," he shot back.

"For God's sake, is the local quarantine going to give us a problem? We might have—"

"No, yes ... I don't know anymore. The infestation has gone global – there have been outbreaks in Spain, Italy, the United Kingdom, and we expect most majors to be affected by now. It's not just our nightmare anymore." Hew sighed. "The problem is, the machinery has already been started, and once we call a pandemic severity 5, we commence a process that rolls on by itself."

Hew snorted sadly. "The borders are closed – nothing in or out. We called a Pan-5, and then there was an outbreak in DC ... in the White House itself. They went nuts – panicked. The President and Vice President were taken to secure bunkers at opposite ends of the country – they shut the place down. No one is allowed to leave, no one is allowed to enter, and now we're under nationwide martial law. We are effectively closed for business."

"Hew, for God's sake, we're in a private jet, we can come in on a short runway. Don't worry about the welcome home band, we can just—"

"Carla, it's not that. It's ... the militias watching the airport – they'll stop you from landing, or disembarking, or..." He swallowed, not wanting to frighten his boss, who obviously had no idea what had been occurring in the time they'd been away. "The militias are mostly infested, and some of them are clearly insane. We stopped being able to deal with them ages ago."

"Oh shit," she said slowly.

"Oh shit is right. These protocols were planned and wargamed and computer simulated for decades, and the first time we put them into effect, guess what? We forgot one thing – the unpredictability of the human condition. People don't do as they're told. People basically don't believe the government and want to get out, to get away." He licked his dry lips. "And no wonder, because those who stayed were either killed by looters, or ... changed." Hew drew a breath.

"But how? We haven't been gone long. How did it get so bad, so quickly?"

Hew snorted, remembering. "Fear makes people coalesce into mobs ... and the internet is only too happy to feed their fear. No matter how we tried to control the information, once images started to appear showing the effects of the infestation in full, frightening, bloody color, well, what do you think happened? People shit themselves. Then their fear turned to anger, and they rioted, demanding that we do something – like, yesterday!" His voice rose. "Everyone is so scared of being infested, people are being shot on doorsteps." He was breathing like a marathon runner, the panicked pressure and pent-up stress catching up with him. "Within a few days, we went from the law of the land to the law of the jungle."

He drew in a few deep breaths of artificial air. "It's quieter now; people don't go out. There's no real reason to – the shops were raided, and it quickly became obvious that going out increased your chance of either being infested or shot. The National Guard is out – teams of very large men in blue hazmat suits riding around in sealed jeeps, shooting ... anything – dogs, cats, foxes, you name it. Just animals for now, but ..." He let the implication hang there. He didn't want to spell out what he thought the next steps in Control and Management might be.

Carla's voice was more exasperated than surprised. "Jesus Christ, Hew, I'm so sorry." He heard her laugh tiredly. "You know, you've got to hand it to us humans. With all our sophistication and technology, we're still only one lightning strike away from savagery."

Hew lowered his head; he knew he was out of his depth. He needed help; he needed Carla here. "Yeah ... so, some divine assistance would be welcome right about now." He laughed softly. "Anyway, forget about my day ... how was yours?"

Carla laughed. For the first time, he heard genuine pleasure in her voice – probably relief that he was retaining his sense of humor. "Aw, you know, we went down to a little bit of paradise, ate tropical fruit, and swam in blue lagoons. What else do you do in the Amazon?" There was silence for a few seconds, before her voice grew serious. "Hew, what now?"

"Now? Now, we need you here, ASAP. We need your expertise and management. I just can't deal with everything, and frankly, I've hit more brick walls than I care to admit. Most importantly, we need to run tests on that solution you've got." He paused to gather his thoughts. "We need to get you back to Atlanta, one way or another. You can't come in to a normal airport. We can find a cleared runway close to us – there should be a safe place to set down, but that's all we can do. You'll have to come to us, I'm afraid. Can you do that?"

Hew heard a muffled conversation as Carla discussed it with someone else on the plane. "Sure, just give us the coordinates. And you're at CDC home base, yes?"

"That's right; Lab-6 … hell, we've commandeered all the labs," he said.

"Are … are the streets clear? Safe?" she asked cautiously.

"Yes and no. We'll organize an escort when you get to the outskirts, but there are militias out on the highways, and at night, you'll need to find a safe place. It's a funny world out there – people are scared, people are hiding – people are killing themselves, and each other." He breathed in deeply, feeling concern for her, but also feeling more confident than he had in weeks. "Good luck, and godspeed."

"Same to you … see you soon, hopefully." Her voice faded out, and he lifted his head and closed his eyes. He hadn't told her everything; he couldn't, not yet. Get her here first, that was his priority. He opened his eyes and whispered to the ceiling. "Please, God."

* * * * *

Carla turned to the pilot. "Did you get any of that?"

"Some. So, I guess LAX is out, and we are being directed to … where exactly?"

Carla turned back to the front window. "Not sure … Hew is sending coordinates. But I know it'll be close to the CDC headquarters in Atlanta. How much extra time until we can get there?"

The pilot stared at her for a few seconds before blowing air out through compressed lips. "Well, it was just on five hours to LA. We had plenty of fuel to make that, but if we have to divert across most of the continent … well, I don't think time will be the issue. Either we drop short, or we find a place to refuel." He raised his eyebrows. "These things can get pretty heavy when the engines stop working." The pilot turned back to the cockpit window and seemed to ruminate for a second or two. "Rough down there, huh?"

"Rough? Yeah, a perfect storm sort of rough. And we're about to fly right into it."

"Okay. Do me a favor, then? Ask your man if there are any refueling stations I can use. I only need about a quarter of a tank for the hop, but without that I won't make it all the way."

Carla nodded, pulled the headphones down over her ears, and connected once again. As she spoke to the scientist again, the gravity of the situation became even bleaker.

"Okay, thanks, hang on, Hew." She pulled the phones off her head. "He wants to know how far you can get before you're empty."

The pilot looked at his dash, checking dials and computer screens showing weather, speed, altitude, and fuel, taking them all in and calculating his best chances. "Well, we've currently got a slight tailwind over the central states. If I take us up another few thousand feet, we can probably squeeze an extra few miles out of her. I think I can get us somewhere between St Louis and Memphis, maybe a few miles farther, if we're lucky. You an Elvis fan?"

Carla grinned. "Who isn't?" She passed the information on to Hew, who was obviously relaying it on to someone else. Carla nodded, pushed one of the cups back off her ear, and turned to the pilot. "Okay, he says there are plenty of smaller airports there you can use, depending on how far you get – obviously the closer to Atlanta the better." She put her hand to the headphones, listening.

"They want to know where you think you can get to. If we can get to the city outskirts, they'll meet us and bring us in from there."

The pilot looked at the control panel again, his eyes narrowing. "You know, I've spent some time in Tullahoma. How would that be? If I can make it that far, then at least it's somewhere I'm familiar with, and it puts you about one-ninety miles from Atlanta."

Carla nodded and pulled the headphones back over her ear. "Hew, what about Tullahoma?"

She waited as another conversation took place in the background. A few minutes later Hew came back with his reply. She turned and gave the pilot a thumbs-up.

"Thanks Hew, hopefully see you soon." She pushed the headphones back off her head.

"Tullahoma regional airport it is. You know it well?"

He smiled. "Oh yeah, like the back of my you-know-what. Excellent facilities, nice long smooth runway, rebuilt in 2009 – it'll do just right." He turned and stuck out his hand. "It's Frank, by the way. Frank Janzen. Will you guys be okay once we're down?"

Carla shook his outstretched hand and nodded. "Carla Nero, and yep, there's a chopper going to meet us."

"Good job, Carla, nice to meet you." He continued looking at her, nothing but clear blue outside and the gentle whine of high-powered jet turbines, just audible in the soundproofed cockpit. His face became serious. "So, Max didn't make it, huh? I don't believe he stayed behind." He looked hard at her. "Two questions – what happened, and do I need to inform the authorities and go back?"

Carla sat back and closed her eyes. She shook her head. "He's dead ... same as Jian and John Mordell. The authorities already know." Carla kept her eyes closed, not wanting him to see the lie on her face. "We had nothing to do with it, other than being in a place that was more dangerous than we were ready for." She opened her eyes and turned to him. "There's no reason to go back – there's nothing to go back for."

She sank back into the co-pilot's chair. "It's over. I guess we both found what we were looking for." She shrugged. "Could have been any of us ... or all of us."

The pilot grunted. "I always thought an ex-wife would kill him, long before any old jungle."

She pulled a face. "Old is right."

Frank continued to look at her for a few more moments. She could feel her eyelids drooping. The chair was large, and the sunlight coming in through the tinted windows and bathing her legs was like a warm blanket. She was dimly aware that Frank was speaking.

"Get some sleep. I'll give you a nudge in a few hours, when we're getting close," he said softly.

"First, I need to tell ..." she said, slipping into sleep.

"I'll tell them. You rest."

Carla let her eyes fully close. For the first time in ages, the world and its problems went away.

* * * * *

The hand on her shoulder made her jump. Broken images of a creature with a hundred legs gripping her arm disappeared like smoke as the late afternoon sunlight broke through and dispelled the monsters.

Carla blinked with crusty eyes. "Where are we?"

"We're a little over two hundred miles out from Tullahoma and I'm running on vapors. I've taken us inland. You can just see Memphis coming up on the right." Frank motioned toward the window. "Strange – looks like there are some pretty big fires. The smoke's dark – burning rubber tires maybe? Signal fires?"

Carla leaned forward, watching the multiple columns of dark smoke rise from the city's outskirts for several seconds before exhaling slowly through her nose. She sat back. She knew that sort of emission; she'd seen it before in other countries dealing with major outbreaks – amongst both human populations and animals. It was the greasy dark smoke that came from rendered flesh.

"Crematorium smoke – or, more likely, just mass burnings. Looks like we've been overwhelmed by the numbers and speed." She narrowed her eyes as she thought through the social implications. No one wanted to stand out in the open and grieve anymore; close proximity to other humans probably represented the greatest risk to life.

So quick, she thought. They always expected that if something like this occurred, it would be via a natural or bio-engineered microorganism, not some sort of primordial parasite.

"Thirty minutes out from landing and there's no one answering from the tower. I sure hope we don't have to circle. You're welcome to stay up here with me – or do you want to join your friends?"

Carla was snapped from her reverie. She leaned across to grasp the pilot's arm. "Thanks Frank, but I'll give everyone a heads up about what we're about to go into."

"Okey-dokey. I'm going to try the tower again. See you on the tarmac."

Carla rose and threaded her way back to her seat. Matt was snoring under a blanket. Megan watched her come down the aisle, Joop nodded to her, and Kurt just fiddled with something in his bag.

She took the seat in front of Matt and Megan and half turned. "We're landing in thirty minutes; better wake Sleeping Beauty. We need to talk about what happens next."

Megan simply elbowed Matt, waking him mid-snore. "What is it?"

She nodded toward the CDC woman. "Carla wants to talk."

Carla half knelt on her seat, raising herself so they all could see and hear her.

"By now you all know we're not touching down in LA. We'll be landing in Tullahoma, about one hundred and ninety miles northwest of Atlanta ... where I need to get to."

She paused, looking at each of them – three pairs of eyes stared back; Kurt continued to rummage. "Let me lay it out for you. It's, ah ..." She gave up trying to sugar-coat it. "... it's all gone to shit. The infestation is now countrywide, and there is significant danger. Martial law is being enforced, and I need to get my sample to Atlanta as a priority – that overrides everything else."

"How will you get to Atlanta from Tullahoma?" Matt asked.

"There's a chopper coming for me. You're all welcome to come, and to be brutally honest, it'll be a lot safer for you," Carla responded.

Joop cleared his throat. "My family is in New York. I need to get back to them. That is my priority; I'm sorry."

"Second that. I got a cabin on the outskirts – I'll tag along with Joop." Kurt winked at Joop, who nodded back, obviously pleased with the idea of company.

Matt turned to Megan. "Atlanta's only a few hundred miles from Asheville. Maybe we can hop a ride, and then keep on going when it's safe."

Megan raised her eyebrows and nodded.

Carla looked at each of them. "Okay, we'll see what it looks like when we're on the ground. From what my people have been telling me, traveling unaccompanied is not a good idea right now. In fact, it might be deadly."

"Take your seats and strap in, folks, I'm making my approach." The pilot's voice had the laid-back tone that pilots were renowned for – cool and calm, and unflappable.

"Ms. Nero, can you please join me?" Suddenly, there was an edge to his voice.

Carla tried to keep her face serene as she rose, conscious of everyone watching her. The knots in her stomach started to tie themselves ever tighter.

She closed the small door behind her. "What is it, Frank?"

The pilot's face betrayed nothing, but the edge of concern in his voice gave him away. "I still can't raise anyone in the tower. There should be a dozen people there."

Carla strapped in and leaned forward, looking out at the approaching runway. "Power blackout, maybe?"

Frank shook his head. "Airports have their own backup generators. Tullahoma is no backwater; it's a city with half a million people. Nothin's moving down there. I tell you, something is very wrong."

The plane continued its descent, and the pilot eased back a little. "There's smoke over the runway ... worse, there's fire and debris on the tarmac itself."

"Can we still land?" Carla saw several fires on the runway, some large, some small.

"Lady, we have to land." He took off his sunglasses. "And yes, I think so; this bus doesn't need a long strip."

The plane came around slowly and lined up with the stripes down the runway's center. It was clearer now what was burning – planes larger than their own had been reduced to skeletal bonfires. Luckily, most were pushed to the side. Frank came down softly, the wheels just kissing the runway before he immediately used the craft's port and starboard navigation flaps to gently ease the still fast-moving bird past or around the biggest obstacles.

After a few more minutes he eased back and used the remaining thrust to roll toward the terminal.

"Weird," Carla said in a hushed tone.

The tower was dark – in fact, the entire airport was dead and dark. The silence and desolation was total – broken windows, abandoned suitcases, and the odd piece of paper lifting off to float across the outfield.

"Weird is right." Frank unleashed his belt and leaned forward, looking around the intersecting runways. Large and small fires dotted the edges and spread into the surrounding fields. "Where's your chopper? I thought they said they'd be here when we arrived."

"Maybe we're early." Carla was confused by their non-appearance. If they only had to come from Atlanta, they should have been there with hours to spare.

"Maybe." Frank continued to taxi in slowly, staring intently through the window and barely breathing.

Suddenly, the cockpit door burst open.

* * * * *

"Jesus, man! You want to give a guy a heart attack?" Frank shook his head, continuing to stare intently through the windscreen.

"Sorry." Matt got down beside them, looking out at the deserted airport. "Looks like a war zone. What happened here?"

As they rolled in closer to the terminal, they could see a banner hanging on the front of the wedding cake-shaped building. Two large words were written on it in dripping red paint: GO HOME!

"Wow, now that's a welcome the founding fathers would have struggled to come up with." Frank brought the plane to a halt, letting the turbines whine down to silence.

"Oh God, please no ..." Carla brought her fist down on her knee as she spotted another craft burning.

"That's ... oh no, Carla." Even to Matt the markings were familiar – on one of the still-distinguishable panels a large blue square containing the white CDC logo was buckling.

Within the frame of the cockpit a blackened skeleton could be made out, its head thrown back, blackened jaws hanging open. A few feet away, another body lay sprawled on the tarmac, this one unburnt.

"What the fuck is going on here?" Frank's calm exterior had finally been punctured. He unlatched his seatbelt and got to his feet. "There's a man down there, maybe dead – I'm gonna take a look." He paused, his lips tight, and opened a small locker at his feet, drawing forth a first-aid box. "Stay here." He elbowed Matt out of the way and rushed along the galley toward the exit door.

"Frank, wait." Carla leapt after him, followed by Matt.

Frank unlatched the door and engaged the gangway-lowering mechanism. In a few moments the stairs and railing had unfolded. He poked his head out and looked around.

Matt grabbed at his shirt. "Let's wait until we have some idea of what we're dealing with, okay?"

Frank looked back at Matt, his face stony with determination. "And if that was you or your girlfriend, or Carla lying on that tarmac, son? Would you want me to wait?"

He dislodged Matt's hand and started down the steps. Carla went to follow him, but Matt grabbed her and held her back. Megan and Joop joined them at the door, while Kurt watched through his porthole window.

As the pilot walked cautiously across the tarmac, Carla, Matt, Megan, and Joop walked partway down the gangway, each taking up a position on a different step and hanging on to the person in front.

"Careful, Frank." Carla's call was hushed. He turned and nodded briefly, and then continued to walk hunched and crab-like, his head turning left and right.

The windows of the terminal remained dark and inhospitable. Some were smashed, the glass on the ground below testament to the impact from inside the building. There was the sound of something flapping from behind the row of hangars, and the pop and crackle of burning plastic from the fires. But beyond these noises, there was nothing. No car horns, moving vehicles, or shouts from busy workers, or even bird calls as the day came to a close.

Frank was close to the fallen man now and he eased to a stop, his head whipping quickly left and right – either nerves or intuition urging caution.

* * * * *

Matt turned briefly to the terminal. The dark windows seemed to watch them, frowning with displeasure at the intrusion.

He jolted; there was something there, a quick movement. "What the ..."

"What was it?" Carla was below him on the steps. She turned quickly, saw where he was looking and followed his gaze. After a second she turned back to him. "What was it, what did you see?"

Matt frowned, and stared hard at the broken windows. It was gone now, but he was sure there had been a quick hint of movement on the top floor. Just his imagination?

"Maybe nothing. I thought there was someone at the window."

Joop was highest on the steps, at the plane door, and was craning his neck. "There's nothing there now."

Carla turned back to where the pilot was nearing the body. "We'll need to check it out later." She cupped her hands around her mouth and called again to Frank. "Be careful."

Frank half turned and waved, and then quickly knelt beside the body. He reached down and placed a hand on the side of its neck, then immediately withdrew it as if burned, and turned back to the plane. He swiped his hand across his neck, and slowly got back to his feet.

The crack of a rifle made them all jump as it tore a hole in the silence and then bounced away. Collectively, they snapped around to stare at the terminal for a split second before whipping back to Frank. The man fell like a tree, a fountain of blood shooting from one side of his head.

"Frank!" Carla went to charge down the steps, but the rifle came again, and a thump beside their heads left a single, finger-sized hole in the steel of the plane's outer skin.

"Back inside, back inside, we're under fire!" Matt pulled Carla back, and Megan fell inside onto Joop, who tumbled backward. Matt hauled Carla inside the doorframe just as another shot rang out. This one was better aimed, and carved a divot in the flooring beside Joop's head.

"Scheisse!" The evolutionary biologist rolled and scrambled away.

"Get down!" Matt dove to the floor on top of Megan, Carla landing beside him. More shots drummed metallically against the outside of the aircraft.

Kurt's voice drifted up from the back of the plane. "I'm thinking the 'go home' message was something they expected us to pay attention to." He walked calmly forward, reached around the doorframe, grabbed the heavy door and pulled it shut. The airtight oval closed with a soft hiss.

Carla sat up. "We have to try and help him."

Kurt shook his head. "Nope, he's dead, just like anyone else who steps outside will be."

Carla put her hands over her eyes and rubbed hard. "No, no, no! What the hell is happening?"

"Chaos, I think," Kurt said simply.

She looked at him with red eyes. "We've landed right in a hornet's nest." Carla crawled toward the cockpit. "I'm going to call the CDC. I've got to tell them about their pilots ... and see if they can help us out of this mess."

Kurt pressed a button beside the door and a soft whine told them the stairs were retracting back into the underside of the craft. "No use leaving out the welcoming mat."

Matt sat up and rested his elbows on his knees. "Thanks. At least we're safe for now."

"Don't thank me yet. Those reports were from a high-powered rifle – 99 caliber or better. Smaller caliber will be deflected, but those bigger bullets will pass right through the side of the plane, through you, and then keep going out the other side, fast enough to kill someone else. All shutting the door did was make it difficult for whoever is out there to pick us off with their sniper scope. But they can still hit us."

He looked over his shoulder at the door. "Best we stay low and away from the windows."

Matt leaned toward the cockpit and repeated Kurt's instructions to Carla.

"Got it," she replied.

Joop climbed into one of the seats, but stayed hunched over. "So, now we wait, hmm? For what?"

Megan climbed up in the row behind him. "We wait for Carla to reach the CDC and get another chopper here, I guess. There's food and water for a few days, so if we stay out of sight, we'll be okay for a while."

Another couple of gunshots pinged metallically on the front of the plane, the shooter having sighted Carla through the cabin window.

"I'm fine." Carla crawled back to them, breathing hard. "No more choppers, but—"

"Great, well there goes plan A." Megan slumped, and then sprang forward. "Can anyone fly this thing?"

Kurt shrugged. "I can fly, but just small recreational craft. But that's not the problem ... fly to where, exactly? Besides, there's no fuel for a takeoff."

Megan's face turned red. "To where? Are you shitting me? To any fucking where but here. You know—"

Carla cut her off. "Cool it – there's a military unit patrolling just outside Shelbyville. They're about thirty-five miles up highway 16, and being diverted to us." She smiled. "They'll be here in an hour, give or take."

More bullets struck the plane – front and back. "Shit." Kurt spun and eased down to peer out one of the small windows. "Double shit; we ain't got an hour." He quickly headed down to the rear of the plane.

Matt snuck across to steal a look and immediately felt his heart sink. He eased away from the window. "Here comes the welcoming committee."

Megan, Joop, and Carla leapt forward and peered from the side of one of the toughened porthole windows. Matt knew what they were seeing: a ragged band of people, some in face masks, some in torn hazmat suits, some simply with t-shirts tied around their noses, as if trying to protect themselves from nothing more than a bad smell. Most had guns, but some had shovels, bats, or large pieces of broken brick.

"This is a nightmare." Carla sat down in one of the seats.

Matt leaned over her to look again. "When they said go home, they meant it … ideas, anyone?"

Megan half turned. "Let me ask again. Can anyone else fly this fucking thing?"

Kurt reappeared with two revolvers. He spoke while loading one of the guns. "Carla, get back on to your pal at the CDC and see where those guardsmen are." He looked up at Matt. "Get over here."

Kurt straightened, sucked in a breath, and then grabbed the door lever, twisted it, and pushed the heavy porthole door open. In one swift motion he leaned out and fired several times into the crowd, then smoothly pulled the door shut. He threw the gun to Matt and pulled a box of bullets from his pocket. "You're on reload."

"Where'd these come from?" Matt fiddled with the heavy silver weapon.

Kurt checked the other weapon, now in his hand. "Steinberg's satin nickel-plated Colt 45s. Never used ... until sixty seconds ago. Reload."

Matt looked out the window as yells rose from outside. Many in the decrepit band had thrown themselves to the ground following Kurt's volley, but they were now getting back to their feet. Several remained prone and bleeding, attesting either to Kurt's marksmanship, or his blind luck. They resumed their noisy approach, this time with more caution.

Kurt turned to Matt and smiled briefly, then opened the door again, this time causing panicked shouts from the mob. He did as before, his aim just as good. There was sporadic return fire, but no hits, and the crowd mostly scattered. He pulled the door shut, and he and Matt swapped weapons.

Matt looked out the window again. "That got their attention."

Kurt snorted. "For now. They'll be back. They get closer to the plane and we're all as good as dead." He shouted down to Carla in the cockpit. "Any word on that ground support?"

"On their way," she shouted back.

Kurt looked across to Megan. "The thing is, we don't need to fly the plane, we just need to get the hell away from here. So someone needs to get up there, start this tin can up, and drive it out the gates." He smiled apologetically. "I'm a little busy, so you know I mean you, Megan. Go on, I'll walk you through it."

She nodded, her face a mix of determination and doubt.

"You can do it, Megs. Get Carla to tell the CDC what we're doing so they can meet us. Unless you can drive this all the way to Atlanta," Matt said.

She laughed nervously, then got down low and crawled toward the cockpit.

Kurt ducked down to look out the window, then quickly turned to push the door open again. Five more shots, but only one takedown. He handed the gun to Matt for reload. "Running out of time."

"And bullets," Matt nodded. "I think there's still enough left for a few more reloads."

Kurt shook his head. "Doesn't matter; there's no door on the other side of the plane. As soon as this bunch of Einsteins realizes that, they'll be looking in our windows."

Matt checked again, and saw a mobile set of steps being pushed along the tarmac. The steps started to veer toward the rear of the plane. Their course was obvious. "That didn't take long."

"Yep, I expect our friends will be joining us real soon," Kurt said.

Matt leaned forward. "Anytime's good, Megs."

"How do I ...?"

"Ah ..." Kurt stuck the large gun in his belt and walked quickly into the cockpit.

Matt leaned around the edge of the window and watched the gathering crowd push the metal steps down the runway. More people joined in, some near-naked, all armed with something.

"Welcome home," he said softly as he heard Kurt hurriedly explained the controls to Megan.

"Start-stop-port-starboard ... that's all you need to know. We don't need up or down, or to learn about altitude, weather, hydraulics, or even fuel consumption. We're not taking off, and when we're out of gas, we're out."

He rushed back, pulling his gun out again. "Any change?"

"Still coming," Matt replied.

"Okay." He turned. "Now, Megan."

"Here goes." Her reply floated back to them.

There was silence for a few more seconds, and then a gentle whine could be heard coming from outside the body of the aircraft.

Joop looked down past the rear of the plane. "I think they're going to try to climb up on top of us. What will they do? Try to break in, do you think?"

"Maybe. Maybe just shoot down into the plane until they get lucky and hit one of us. The proverbial fish in a barrel." Kurt got close to the window and looked back along the craft to the engine. "Good, spinning now; takes a few seconds – Steinberg had nothing but the best and this Gulfstream has a couple of Rolls-Royce BR710 turbo fan engines with over fifteen thousand pounds of thrust each. In a few more seconds the gas should kick in and the fans will really start to spin, and then we'll get some go."

He changed his angle to check on the mob. "Better slow them down a tad." He pulled open the door, eliciting animal-like howls, and let go with another six rounds. He didn't have a hope of hitting anyone this time, but it was enough to make the crowd scatter. He dragged the door shut and this time spun the locking wheel. "Okay, time to make it interesting."

He walked to the front of the plane and leaned in beside Megan and Carla. Matt glanced back and saw that the crowd was back with the stairs, about to disappear behind the plane.

Matt got to his feet and followed Kurt into the cockpit. "Kurt, they're behind us."

Kurt reached forward. "I got it – hairdryer time. Hang on." He reached in front of Megan, pressed the ignition, and smoothly pushed the lever forward. A low, muscular roar came from the rear of the plane, and then there was an almighty push as the turbo-powered gas turbines sucked in, compressed, and then blasted a mix of combusted gases and super-heated air out backward.

The crowd pushing the stairs was blown over like leaves in a gale, most skidding down the runway as though across slippery ice, some lying still, flesh red and smoking where the rush of inferno-hot gases and air had bathed their exposed skin.

The plane gathered speed, and he eased back on the throttle, settling into an easy ten-mile-per-hour roll down the tarmac. He stood back, leaving it to Megan.

"Which way?" she asked, smiling at being in control of the large machine.

Carla pointed. "Go straight down. We need to go the length of the runway, and then cross the grass verge. Should be okay – it's been dry lately. Then we need to crash through a barrier and hop onto the highway. Just pray it's not crowded with cars – broken down or otherwise."

Matt looked back down at the rear side windows. The men and women who had been on the tarmac were just stirring, some getting to their feet, others lying still, smoke or steam rising from their prone bodies. None of them made any move to follow.

"No chasers," he said.

"Good, we just bought ourselves some time. That patrol better be where it's supposed to be."

They were all crammed into the cockpit now, Megan and Carla seated and Kurt, Joop, and Matt standing behind. Each offered their own advice for navigating the grass field. They bounced and rocked, and Megan pulled a face, trying to concentrate as she gave a little more thrust to compensate for some of the deeper holes.

"Ach, trees coming up." Megan went to change the plane's angle, but Kurt stopped her.

"Forget 'em; this baby is about ninety feet long and weighs in at seventy-five hundred pounds. Somehow, I don't think we need to be worrying about scratches right now – just plow through 'em."

Megan gave it a bit more thrust and the ten-foot high trees were pushed over or out of the way as she smashed into them. Coming to the end of the field, a wire fence was easily nosed aside, then she maneuvered toward a gap between some shed-like buildings, losing the tips of both wings. "Ouch." She jumped a curb and bounced heavily down onto the four-lane highway.

"Easy." She smiled as she headed down the deserted road, cruising along at about twenty miles per hour. A blinking light from the panel indicated incoming communication, and Carla pulled the headset back on and nodded.

"Hew? Go ahead, I'm here." She turned. "They can see us on satellite. Escort is only about ten miles out now, and closing on our position. Keep a lookout."

Megan snorted. "I think we'll be a little hard to miss."

In a few minutes a broad green vehicle, the only one moving, could be seen roaring down the center of the desolate highway. Megan took one hand off the control column and punched the air. "Captain Hannaford coming in for landing. Thank you for flying with us today." She laughed and started to ease back on the throttle, the big plane slowing and then stopping as the engines whined down to silence. She looked across at Carla. "Well, that's got to be something off my bucket list."

"Not bad – and given some of those bumps, I think you could honestly say you even had it airborne." Carla jumped to her feet. "Less than two hundred miles and we're home ... sort of."

Kurt pushed the door outward and lowered the steps, ducking back inside to grab his pack and heft it up onto his shoulders. Matt saw him grunt with the effort.

He noticed Matt watching and winked. "The one upside to the end of the world – no customs and immigration." He laughed and stepped down, followed by Joop, the rest having already grabbed what possessions they needed.

Kurt stood watching the broad, aggressive-looking vehicle roar toward them. He turned to Matt. "It's an ASV Guardian, I think." He watched it for a few more seconds. "Yep, an M1117 Guardian Armored Security Vehicle. These guys are really ready for war."

The vehicle pulled up alongside the group. Carla could see what appeared to be a small water cannon mounted on top. Two young soldiers stepped out and stood slightly apart. Both of them were armed, looking formidable. The red-headed one seemed to be in charge and motioned to them to stay where they were. The other, who had dark, glistening stubble on his square-shaped head, slowly scanned the surrounding countryside, as if expecting someone else.

Red spoke loudly, staring directly at Carla. "Dr. Nero? Dr. Carla Nero?"

Carla nodded, and he stepped a little closer to her. Matt guessed he already knew exactly who he was looking for.

He gave a small salute. "I'm Sergeant Reed, and this ..." he gestured to his companion, "... is Corporal Metzger. It's great that you could get here, ma'am; unfortunately we've still got a bit to go yet. I need to take you straight to the CDC. The rest of your companions can be dropped off at the base and scheduled for relocation at a later date and time that suits." He looked at each of them. "That will be a secondary priority."

Matt had the feeling the soldier would have been just as happy to leave them by the side of the road.

Carla wrinkled her nose. "Phew, what is that you're wearing?"

Red responded almost mechanically. "Something the lab put together. We call it DeeBee – it's a combination of Deet and benzyl benzoate."

Carla had suspected as much. Deet was short for diethyl-meta-toluamide. It was one of the most powerful insect repellents known, and had been since 1946. The addition of benzyl benzoate made it target specific – it was one of the best topical treatments for burrowing scabies.

"Pretty tough stuff; you guys feel okay?" Carla peered into the young man's eyes. Even from where Matt stood, he guessed the amount the men were wearing must have been eye-watering. Inside the vehicle it would probably give them headaches ... or worse. The young man just shrugged.

"You're going to have to wear it as well ... or one of the sealed suits, which are pretty damn stifling in this weather. The alternative is doing nothing and getting the bugs under your skin, and that ain't too pretty ... but you know that, Dr. Nero."

Carla grunted softly and gave an almost imperceptible nod of her head. She knew the effects only too well. She turned to their group.

"So, suits or spray?"

Megan stepped up with her fingers over her nose and spoke in a pinched squeak. "Wow, that is really rank." She turned her head away, breathed in, and then spoke again. "Okay, better than a sealed suit in this heat, I think. Bathing in this once can't be that bad."

Red walked back to the vehicle and lifted free a canister bottle that looked like a small fire extinguisher. He cleared his throat. "Actually, in this heat, the repellent needs to be reapplied every twenty-four hours. Otherwise you just sweat it off."

"Great." Matt stepped in close to the door of the ASV and felt the heat radiating out of the steel interior. He looked at the suits hanging on pegs inside the vehicle and shook his head. "Cattle dip it is, then."

He lifted his arms and turned his head. "Just like getting a spray tan."

"Pretty much; and that's why you'll all need to strip down. The spray has got to touch the skin." He smiled flatly, his eyes on Megan. Matt noticed that Corporal Metzger had stopped scanning the countryside and now watched them, waiting for Megan to take her clothes off.

If he expected shyness, he was disappointed. Megan was in her underwear in a few seconds flat, arms out. "Let her rip, Ginger."

The sergeant smiled and pointed the nozzle. "Keep your eyes closed and hold your breath for ten seconds while I do your head, okay?"

She nodded and gulped in air. The spray started, and a fine mist coated Megan's face, neck, and hair. He stopped the spray. "Okay, hold out your hands, palms up. I'm going to drench your hands, and then I want you to comb it through your hair." Megan did as requested. While she had her arms up, he worked his way down her body, asking her to turn slowly, like a roast on a spit.

The whole process took a few minutes. On completion, he asked her to hold out her hands again. This time, after drenching them, he told her to scrub it into the places that she still had covered. She looked at Matt and pulled a face – it stung.

One after the other they followed suit, even handing over bags and backpacks so they could be doused. Kurt grabbed the canister so he could personally do the inside of his own bags, being a little shy about anyone seeing the contents.

Together they piled into the back of the large vehicle. It was cramped, and once the doors were closed, red lights came on, giving everyone a hellish appearance. Megan had tied a handkerchief around her face, as the air was stifling despite an air-conditioning unit whining softly in the background. All it did was stir the chemical air around them. Other than the air con, it was surprisingly quiet inside, more to do with the smooth roadway, rather than the vehicle's heavy insulation and armor plating.

Carla leaned forward. "Sergeant Reed, just how bad is it getting on the ground?"

He turned and stared hard at her for a few seconds. "Lately, hard to tell; people rarely come out anymore."

Kurt snorted. "They certainly came out to welcome us at the airport."

The soldier made a noise in his throat, and looked glum. "Yep, real sorry about that. Same thing at the bigger airports – didn't think it was happening at the smaller ones. The healthies aren't keen on planes landing anymore. Seems they blame foreigners for the infestation."

Megan scoffed. "That's crazy; foreigners didn't bring this in, unless you count a primordial bird, and an American biology professor. And what's with this 'healthies'?"

Reed sucked in one cheek. "Got a few tribes now – the uninfested, or healthies, are a shrinking bunch. There are also the invisibles, who never come out, the heavily infested – we call them skinners – and then the most dangerous of all … the bloomers." He sighed. "Dr. Hewson will fill you in. And as for who's to blame; it doesn't matter to the mob – these people don't have a conscience or a sense of logic anymore." He turned back to the front of the vehicle. "We're trying to bring some sense and order, but …"

"But you're outnumbered," Carla finished.

"Yep, a thousand to one. Bottom line is, we lack information. The government is trying to run a phone census – they've got computers to call people and ask them for names of occupants, number of residents, status of health. It's not precise – some people just aren't answering, probably thinking it's just looters checking to see if there are people home." He shrugged. "Streets are pretty quiet now."

Carla pointed to the roof. "So why the water cannon, if there's no need for crowd control?"

Reed squinted at her for a few seconds, then turned back, shaking his head. "Not really a water cannon, Dr. Nero." His expression had drooped. "We sure hope you guys can help. This isn't going to get better by itself." He turned to his companion. "Let's pick it up, corporal." The vehicle accelerated.

Hope ... Carla thought that was the best word to use. She sure hoped they could help.

"Well, first things first – get us home so we can find out if we can."

*   *   *   *   *

Matt looked over the interior of the armored vehicle. There were a couple of metal tanks along the ceiling, both marked with the triple-linked circles of the biohazard symbol, struck through with a red lightning bolt. *More insecticide?*

Sergeant Reed pushed a small send-receiver into his ear. "Got 'em." He removed it and set it down again.

Carla sprang forward. "That's it? Nothing else? Can we talk to some people, and find out what's going on?"

Reed turned. "Not now. This far out, I was authorized to send a three-second burst, either when I had you, or knew I never would. Any more and there's a chance we'd be found."

"Found? What does that mean?" Carla's face was a blend of confusion and annoyance.

"Like I said, things are different now. There are people out there who are looking to take advantage of the situation – either for political, psychological, or religious reasons. They target transmissions, especially military. It's quite easy; they use simple direction-finding techniques that have been around since World War II. Stick a few homemade receivers around the countryside, and then locate the source of a transmission via triangulation. They only need six seconds."

"Why? Hostage taking?" Matt frowned, and the red-headed sergeant shrugged and turned back to study a chart on his lap. Matt guessed the conversation was at an end. He exhaled through his nose in exasperation just as the truck swerved and he fell against Megan. He nudged her. "You okay?"

She snorted behind her handkerchief. "Could be better. Then again, I suppose I could have stayed back home, meaning I'd either be locked indoors or skinned, so, all things considered … yeah, I'm okay."

He nodded; she was right. In a matter of weeks the country had been transformed by something almost too small to be seen by the naked eye. By that, and by fear.

Matt grasped her knee and squeezed. She placed her hand over his and squeezed back. He looked into her eyes, still bright, and smiled. She was strong. He knew they'd make it … they had to.

He turned and leaned toward the two young military men, peering out from behind the toughened glass of the armored vehicle as it roared along the vacant highway, swerving every now and then to avoid a stopped car.

"Do you guys see many survivors? Is that what you're doing out here?"

Reed looked at his companion and snorted soundlessly. He turned back to the road and shook his head. "No … no, Professor Kearns."

Matt waited, but nothing else came. Metzger broke the silence.

"Red, on your one o'clock."

Matt looked out through the heavy glass. There was a mound beside the road up ahead. The ASV slowed a few hundred feet out.

"Bloomer, I bet," Metzger said, keeping his eyes on what looked like a pile of clothing.

Reed grunted. "Got it." He made a quick notation on his chart. "Bring it up on my three o'clock." Reed flipped a panel on the dashboard and an eighteen-inch control board lifted and was angled toward him. There were several buttons, and a small joystick, which he grasped, looking at a small inbuilt monitor. He focussed in on the mound, his fingers moving over the keys. From behind him, Matt could just make out the small screen changing from a standard picture feed of the mound to thermal imaging, then to something flaring blues and black – possibly showing different materials or internal densities. "Warm, solid, organic mass. Confirmation on visual?"

Metzger drove even slower, keeping his eyes on the pile. With one hand he lifted a small pair of field glasses. Although it was only fifty feet away, he squinted, his mouth drawing up. "Okay, I can confirm a bloomer."

"Roger that ... ready to burn in ..."

Matt leaned forward. "What is it?" Everyone behind him tried to crowd forward to see what was happening.

The soldiers ignored them, and Reed continued to speak in an automatic monotone that betrayed zero emotion but plenty of training. Matt craned his neck and saw that the small screen in front of Reed now had a red bomb site target displayed directly over the mound. Reed counted down.

"... 5, 4, 3, 2 ... burn." Reed pressed a button and a liquid whooshing came from behind and over them. Matt's focus was drawn to a streak of red-orange that shot toward the pile on the road.

The flames touched the clothing ... and stuck there. Matt was sure an arm rose briefly from within the giant red flower of heat, dripping material or skin from the sleeve. There was no doubt what the men were doing.

"Holy fuck, that was a person in there ... and I think they were alive." Matt gripped the sergeant's shoulder.

Reed ignored Matt's grip. He took his finger off the button as the inferno blazed. Black smoke rose in a greasy column beside the truck. He turned to Metzger. "Burn complete; move out."

He twisted in his seat, his face stony. "Sit back, sir." He waited until Matt had complied, then his expression eased, now more fatigued than severe. He looked from Matt to the others, who were watching intently, and then back at Matt.

"You asked about survivors, Professor. Well, we sure are out looking for them, but that … that wasn't one of them. They're not survivors, they are already dead, they just haven't stopped breathing. In fact, I think of them as more like dirty bombs. They're walking weapons, biological time bombs who have entered, or are about to enter, a dangerous and infectious stage, which we call blooming."

He turned toward Carla. "Bloomers, skinners – they haven't briefed you on any of this yet?"

Carla spoke softly, her voice only just audible over the revving engine. "About the egg dispersal going airborne?"

Reed nodded. "That's right; some of the living bodies produce vesicles that disperse millions of the eggs. They're small and light enough to be carried on a breeze for miles. Our brief is to ensure that doesn't happen."

"But … you burn them alive!" Megan tried to push past Matt, but he held onto her.

"Alive? Not really – and not for long … seconds, maybe, and it's painless, as the bugs have already short-circuited the body's nervous system. That way they can either eat you from the inside out or turn you into a walking hatchery. Even though your brain has been turned to mush, your body still functions, but it has been programmed to do one thing, and one thing only …"

Carla finished for him. "Produce eggs … to infect more people. And then the cycle starts again."

"Infecting perhaps hundreds more, geometrically growing faster than we can control it."

Megan slowly sat back down. Matt felt sickened, but now understood the logic behind the attacks being carried out by the young soldiers.

There was silence for a few seconds. Reed looked along their faces, his own grim. "This isn't a pleasant job, but these days there are a lot of unpleasant things we have to do ... if we are going to survive this."

Carla's voice was soft. "Sterilization."

Reed nodded.

She looked up at the tanks over her head. "What are you using; thermite?"

Reed raised his eyebrows. "Sort of; thirty-three percent jellied gasoline, twenty-one percent benzene, and forty-six percent polystyrene ... with a thermite initiator."

Carla closed her eyes. "Napalm B."

"Yes ma'am; super napalm – burns at two thousand degrees, and the jelly causes it to stick to its target. There'll be nothing left but ash in a few minutes."

Kurt was sitting in the rear, but his voice carried easily. "I thought that stuff was banned."

Reed never blinked. "It is in warfare, but this isn't war ... it's survival."

Kurt thought about it for a few seconds, and then nodded. "Remind me to keep up my chemical baths, will you?" He sat back.

After an hour of driving in silence, and several more bloomer burns, they reached a fork in the road. Kurt leaned forward from the rear. "We're going through Chattanooga? I could jump out at the East Ridge turnpike. You guys will head south, I assume – down the 75 – and I can keep going on up to New York."

Matt shook his head. "Are you mad?"

Kurt ignored him.

Metzger looked at Reed, and Matt could have sworn he rolled his eyes. He spoke casually over his shoulder. "We'll be staying off the main roads and traveling via the smaller tier-two roads. Less ... ah, debris."

Kurt tilted his head. "Debris? What does that mean? I don't want to go to Atlanta. I can grab a small plane in Maryville, Johnson City, or a dozen other places and be home in few hours."

The driver glanced briefly at Kurt and, seeing his determined look, simply shrugged. "You're not under arrest, and we can't force you to stay with us. I can, however, urge you to reconsider. There are armed militias out there, not to mention the infestation."

"I'll be crossing the country, staying low. I'm trained for that." He snorted. "I'll even take some of your home brew with me and bathe in it, okay?" Kurt looked at Joop. "You with me?"

Joop stared, wide-eyed, for a few seconds, then shook his head, perhaps convinced by the bloomers that being outside was not a great idea right now.

Kurt shrugged. "Whatever."

Reed didn't look unhappy with Kurt's decision. He spoke quietly, checking his maps again. "That's fine, sir. It's your funer— ah, your decision."

Kurt sat back, satisfied. He clutched his backpack, its weight lying heavily across his knees.

"Sure you know what you're doing, Kurt? I mean, is it worth it?" Matt nodded to the bag.

Kurt ignored him. "You guys will have things sorted in a few days – a week at most. I'll be home by then." He snorted. "I promise to keep my doors locked and windows closed. After all, I'll have the magic potion to keep the little fuckers away. And I'll have this ..." he pulled up his shirt, displaying the handguns, "… to keep the larger variety of pest at bay."

Carla's voice was flat. "You'll be safer with us."

Kurt looked indifferent. "Maybe. Then again, maybe a smaller group will attract less attention." His face softened. "Seriously, thank you for your concern, but I'll be more worried about you guys. I'll be home and safe long before you will."

Carla shook her head and leaned toward the soldiers. "You should make him stay."

Reed shook his head. "Sorry, we're not going to do that. He is free to make his own choices – good or bad." He turned to Kurt. "If you find food, grab it. There's nothing left on the shelves now, and you may find you're trying to survive on whatever food you had left behind – if there's anything left of the food you had. There's no public transport, few working utilities, no police force, no nurses …" He shook his head again. "Sir, it's your decision, but if you'll allow me to offer one piece of advice, it'd be to stay away from people – living or dead."

"Got it," Kurt responded, a little too quickly.

Megan looked shocked. "No police force? That's great. I know how well we humans respond when law and order and the constraints of civilization are removed. So, who's giving the orders?"

"For now, the government is still functioning. Congress has gone underground and the president and vice president have been moved to separate and secret locations. Critical infrastructure is controlled under martial law and is still ongoing. We'll be fine as long as things don't stay bad for too much longer."

Matt had to ask. "And how much longer is too much longer?"

Reed seemed to think for a few moments. "A month, maybe less."

Carla sat back. "Better get us to Atlanta then."

* * * * *

The turnpike at Chattanooga looked like it had been barricaded, knocked down, set fire to, and then built back up ...
several times. Metzger bumped up over the guttering to cross
into a field, then slowed under some trees. The ASV braked
and he turned. "Close as I can get you, Mr. Douglas."

Kurt grunted and started to rise heavily from his seat, the
bag weighing him down. Matt grabbed his arm.

"Please Kurt, one last time ... I think you should stay with
us; just for a few days."

Kurt smiled and patted Matt's hand. "You'll be fine." He
looked at Reed. "I'll take some of that magic potion now."

Reed held out a bottle the size of a soda bottle with a milky
liquid inside. "Keep reapplying it every twenty-four hours;
more if you're sweating." Kurt went to take it, but Reed hung
on. "There's enough for about four days. You'd better be
locked indoors by then, sir." He released the bottle.

Carla spoke, an anxious look on her face. "He's right,
Kurt. When you get home, seal yourself in, and keep listening
to the radio." She seemed to think for a few seconds. "And
don't go patting any stray dogs or cats – everything, warm or
cold blooded, could be infested."

Kurt looked at the small bottle in his hands, his face carrying a hint of doubt. He looked back at the sergeant.

"Seeing as I'll be the one on the outside, I'll need this more
than you guys. I could do with a little more."

"Being on the outside is your choice, sir. There is no more."
Reed's eyes never wavered.

Kurt's expression hardened, and his hand dropped to his
lap. For a split second, Matt thought the big man was contemplating asking again – this time with a gun in his hand.

Reed's eye's narrowed slightly. He knew what Kurt was thinking. The hint of a confident smile touched his lips, and after a second, Reed gave an almost imperceptible shake of his head. *Don't try it*, the action said. The smile never left his lips.

Metzger operated the side door, and it swung open. Sunlight streamed in, along with a gust of fresh air.

"Good luck … sir."

Kurt saluted and stepped out. He turned and ducked down, looking back into the armored vehicle's red interior. "I wish you all luck, and …"

Metzger closed the door.

CHAPTER 23

Kurt jogged through the alleyways, staying low and trying to hold his breath. Rubbish was piled high, forming black plastic mountains and valleys on every sidewalk. Lumpy puddles of flesh, all different hues and sizes, dotted the streets. There was a small one with long hair piled on top, and the brightly colored clothing of a child; a larger one with new leather shoes and a wristwatch, and still another with a stained baseball cap. They were everywhere. No one came to clean up anymore, and the dying had simply stopped moving and allowed the bugs free reign.

Other than the odd newspaper page blowing down the street or door swinging on a hinge somewhere, there was no sound. Still, Kurt had the feeling there were plenty of eyes watching him from behind darkened windows and pulled blinds.

He had passed several barricades across streets, and had no luck locating any off-road vehicles to jump gutters or cross fields. His feet hurt, but he was damned if he was going to rest just yet. He paused outside a bike store, considering, for only a second.

Inside, he pulled a new Bear Mountain bike from a rack and rode it out the door, swerving, but gathering speed swiftly. He knew the area, but it seemed almost alien to him. He bumped over some debris, and his back was temporarily racked with pain from the massive weight he carried. It'd be worth it when he got it all home, he thought. He always remembered his father telling him that when people fail, currencies fail, and countries fail, they turn to gold as the basis for trade. He'd be ready.

He stopped at the edge of the airport, sighting a row of small single-prop Cessnas still tied down with their wheels chocked. At least a few of them would be partially gassed up – he only needed enough for an hour's flying time. He looked along the runway; other than some debris, there were no "go home" banners, or any sign of a band of maniacs like the one they'd encountered at Tullahoma. He reached back to feel the gun at his waist. One thing was for sure – this time, he'd shoot first.

He rode slowly between the outer buildings, then stepped off his bike and hid in the shadows, watching, for a good five minutes – there was nothing. The fence around the runways was down. Kurt checked his gun again, and then sprinted for the nearest plane.

* * * * *

Matt peered through the slotted, armored windows as the vehicle roared down the roads on the west side of Johns Mountain reserve. They avoided the main highways, bouncing over dirt fields when the road was blocked. Once in a while Matt noticed a dazed-looking person wandering the dead zones between houses or the stretches of forest. Some were still in clothes, others were stripped bare and running with blood. Some would wave, and some would stand, staring at nothing, as though their soul had already left their body behind.

Reed called out the names for each as though they were on a bird-spotting field trip – bloomers, skinners, comas, rabids. It seemed the mite infestation affected people in different ways. For the most part, it caused the destruction of the dermal layer that had been inflicted upon Jorghanson. Then there were the bloomers, the living egg factories, their bodies covered in hundreds of thousands of budding sacs that would swell and then burst, infecting miles of countryside. The strange thing was, these poor creatures lived the longest, and until they actually ruptured, were the least infectious. It was as if the mites refused to let them die, preferring that they survived and continued to produce new generations of the parasite.

Reed pointed again to a figure standing at a corner and he had Metzger slow the vehicle. It was a man, his skin hanging like red gauze from his frame. He didn't turn to the vehicle and didn't move. He just stood there, mouth open and eyes vacant.

"Coma. He'll most likely stay there until he just falls to pieces."

Reed motioned ahead and Metzger sped away. "Most humane thing to do would be to put him out of his misery." He snorted softly. "Not enough ammunition."

"That's horrible." Matt grimaced.

"That it is, sir. But I'll tell you what's more horrible. Seeing what happens when a pack of rabids attack sad sacks like that. The rabids stopped being human long ago. There's just a single base instinct left in them – to feed."

"They eat them?" Matt rubbed his face, then regretted it. "Ah shit." The insecticide stung his eyes, which were already watering from the vapors inside the cabin.

Reed continued to talk softly, describing more denizens of their new world. There were other types of infested, too. Some were using powerful medication to slow the spread of the mite. Usually they ended up brain dead and stripped of their skin long before their bodies succumbed. But many managed to get organized, anger and resentment burning hotly through their veins. These were the militias, the mobs that saw the government as being responsible for their plight. These were the ones that Reed and Metzger feared the most.

Matt squinted through the thick glass as they slowed at a road junction. There was a boarded-up building that could have been a store once; he saw a shape in the doorway. Matt frowned, trying to concentrate on the figure. He caught a glimpse of disheveled and stained clothing, and a head swathed in bandages, Egyptian mummy-like. He blinked and they had passed it.

He turned to the group in the back of the ASV, but no one was paying attention. Most looked lost in their own thoughts, or were dozing in the vehicle's chemical warmth. Carla leaned forward to Reed.

"How much farther?"

"As the crow flies – around eighty miles, but the way we're going, add another fifty to that. Sorry, best we can do, but it gives us a better chance to avoid built-up areas. Things are a little crazy in there right now," Reed said.

Carla nodded. "Do we have enough fuel?"

Reed nodded. "Just. We've stripped out most of our heavy armaments, and included an extra fuel tank. Our job is remote patrol, rather than engagement, so we can usually get a couple of hundred extra out of her. We'll be rolling in on vapor, but that'll do."

Silence fell again. They passed Rome, Cedartown, and Rockmart, traveling well south before swinging back toward Atlanta. Megan nudged Carla. "I'm busting."

Carla winced. "I know how you feel." She leaned forward. "Sergeant Reed, can you tell me if we'll be taking an, umm, comfort stop soon?"

Reed looked back, frowning. He glanced down at a storage crate that held a large bottle. Carla followed his gaze, and her face dropped. "Not in a million years, buddy."

"Do you think you can hold on for another ... hour or two?"

"No," Carla and Megan said in unison.

"Fresh air would be good." Matt squinted as he peered toward Reed. "This insecticide is giving me a headache like I've been on a six-hour vodka binge."

Reed looked at Metzger, who kept his eyes on the road. "What do you think?"

Metzger shrugged. "We just passed Powder Creek. Getting more built up the closer in we get, but still pretty empty out here." He looked at Reed and shrugged again.

Reed nodded, then pointed to a stand of trees just off the road. "Pull in under there." He turned. "We'll take ten."

Metzger bumped up into the field. "Want me to get on the barbecuer?"

Reed looked along the tree line for a moment. "Nah, should be okay, as long as we're quick." He raised his voice. "And we will be quick, ladies and gentlemen." He turned to his driver. "Be good for both of us to stretch our legs as well."

Metzger pushed the ASV farther into the field, bumping across the uneven surface. The independent suspensions and portal-geared hubs lifted the tough machine a good sixteen inches off the ground, clearing the largest holes and bits of debris. The vehicle growled to a halt under some trees, and Metzger let it idle for a few moments before switching it off. Both men sat staring out into the green edges of the field. The long afternoon shadows made the darkness under the low branches deep and secretive.

"I don't like it." Reed's eyes were narrowed. "In and out, and no sightseeing." He punched the release and the rear cabin doors whined open. A rush of fresh air flooded in, and everyone tumbled out, the attraction of leaving the cramped space impossible to resist.

"Not far and not long," Reed called after them.

Joop groaned as he straightened up, putting hands in the center of his back and stretching. "I wonder where Kurt is now."

Matt looked up into a sky darkening toward twilight. "He'll be okay. He's trained to survive."

"I should have gone with him." Joop looked pained, and Matt patted his shoulder.

"Might have been a bad move. For now, it's safer for us to all stick together, and definitely with the soldiers, until we know exactly what we're dealing with."

Joop nodded. "I think so, too."

Matt saw that Carla and Megan were headed toward the trees; he followed. In the warm evening climate, cicadas zummed from the trees and crickets sang in the grass. It took Matt a minute to work out what was missing – there were no birds. This time of year, swallows should be zooming past them, low to the ground, and other birds warbling from within the green branches. He inhaled deeply. Things were different now, the soldiers had said.

"Where do you think you're going?" Megan turned and smiled.

"Just an escort." Matt squared his shoulders and grinned back.

"I don't think so." Megan waved him off.

"I do." Reed had his hands on his hips. He looked squarely at Matt, but his warning was for all of them. "Go with them, and keep a lookout. This is no time or place for shyness." Reed held out a squat handgun, but Matt shook his head.

"It's okay, we'll just be a few feet in." He turned to Megan and Carla. "Won't we?"

"Suuure," Megan threw back over her shoulder as the women ducked behind a couple of large trees.

Metzger had moved into the tree line a few dozen feet farther down, and was urinating in a rapid stream against a trunk, reminding Matt that he needed to go as well.

"Hurry up, I'd like a turn this century too."

"Pass me the roll of paper, will you?" Megan laughed. "Or am I supposed to do the shake?"

"Go the shake ... but just remember, no matter how much you shiver and dance, the last few drops end up in your pants." Matt smiled broadly at the trees.

Carla popped her head around the tree. "Nice one, Matt."

He bowed. "Benefits of a higher education, obviously."

Carla stepped out, zipping up her pants, and – much to Matt's relief – she was soon followed by Megan. Joop had disappeared a few trees farther up. Matt mock-saluted the women. "Changing of the guard?"

Megan pointed to the largest tree. "There's a good one. Need me to stand watch?"

Matt shook his head. "Nope; I suffer from stage fright." Matt jogged into the tree line and looked back. Reed gave him a small wave, keeping a close eye on the spot where he and Joop had entered, and also on the thickets of trees to the north and south of them. *Taking no chances*, Matt thought.

As he relieved himself, he saw that Carla had walked up close to the young soldier and was talking rapidly, while Reed nodded and folded his arms. Matt exhaled slowly at the satisfying release of pressure, and looked up into the trees, noticing that the cicadas' song had silenced. *Bit early for bed-time*, he thought.

"Matt," Megan called, softly but urgently.

"Huh?" He zipped up and stepped out. The group was turned toward him, and he frowned at the scrutiny. As he took a few more steps, he saw that their focus was actually directed beside, or behind him, toward the trees at his rear. He turned his head and froze, feeling a jolt all the way up his spine.

Metzger was being held by the strangest individual he had ever seen. Raggedy, loose clothing, his head completely covered in red-soiled bandages. The creature could have been mistaken for a cheap extra in the next Egyptian mummy movie, but for the fact that, where one hand held the collar of the young soldier, the other held the stubby black pipe of a shortened shotgun, jamming it into Metzger's neck.

Matt eased backward. There was a crackling from the forest as more of the miserable creatures ambled out toward them.

"Keep coming, Professor Kearns ... slowly." It was Reed, but Matt didn't need to be told. He'd keep backing all the way into the truck if he could.

Megan grabbed him and pulled him close. He spoke out of the side of his mouth. "Who ... the hell ... are those guys?"

"Skinner militia – they dose themselves up with a cocktail of steroids, antibacterials, and anything else they can find. They manage to keep functioning, even bandaging their bodies to stop them falling apart." Reed lowered his hand toward his holster.

"We call them militias, but they're more like a cult, or some sort of quasi-religious fundamentalists. They believe that the shedding of their skins is the Lord's punishment – the skin coming off a sign of evil being cast out."

"There's so many of them." Megan sounded nervous.

"Yep, and I'll give you one guess who they blame for their predicament."

"Great." Matt looked over his shoulder toward their vehicle – *running distance*, he thought.

Joop crowded in close. "What do they want?"

Reed licked his lips. "What do they want? They want everything – our food, water, clothing, vehicle ... and us. Back up ... slowly." He started to move.

"Can we talk to them?" Carla stood her ground.

"No, they'll burn us alive, to save us … from ourselves. Now, back up toward the vehicle."

Carla still didn't move, her face becoming furious. "What about Corporal Metzger? We can't leave him – I won't."

"Can't do a thing with a handgun. They'll shoot us all down in a blink. Got to get to the flamethrower – that'll even things up a bit."

Matt saw that the forest was bleeding disembodied spirits wrapped in filthy bandages. The one holding Metzger shook him and marched him forward, leaning in close and whispering something in the corporal's ear. Matt saw that his sidearm had been removed. The soldier's expression was blank, but there was the paleness of fear in his cheeks. He looked like a man who knew he was going to die.

"You folk stop right there now. Believe me, that devil's cannon is not going to be used this day." The voice that came from the bloody slit in the bandages was surprisingly strong and clear. There was intellect and education behind those wrappings.

"Keep going." Reed spoke softly. "When I say run, you damned well run."

Joop, the farthest out, started to creep backward a little faster. The bandaged leader moved the shotgun from Metzger's neck, bringing it around to rest on his shoulder and lining up Joop. He fired, the blast deafeningly loud. Metzger brought a hand up to his ear, gritting his teeth, his eardrum probably ruptured.

Matt looked to Joop, but the scientist was gone. He'd been thrown ten feet farther back; the side of his head was missing just above his right eye.

"Jesus Christ." Matt felt the gorge rise in his throat. Turning back, he saw that the shotgun was now pointed at him. His stomach flipped and he felt himself tingle all over, waiting for the next blast.

Once again the cultured voice rang out. "I'm real sorry you made me do that. I don't want to hurt anyone else, so please stay where you are. Last time I ask ... nicely."

Matt could feel the eyes behind the slit move along each of their faces, weighing, analyzing, before stopping at Carla.

"You ... I know you."

Carla's eyes went wide.

"You are one of those responsible. You made this happen, you brought this to us." His voice rose, strong and sonorous.

"Brothers and sisters, I give you the corrupters, the CDC in all its oppressive and poisonous glory."

"Oh God." Carla edged back.

"Do not move." Reed whispered the words and Matt saw him exhale, his eyes glassy and his face racked with indecision. Metzger still had his hand up beside his head, blood leaking from his ear. His eyes focussed on Reed. The two men stared at each other for several seconds, both becoming calm as an unspoken communication passed between them.

Reed spoke, the words barely audible. "Get ready."

Faster than the bandaged man holding him could react, Metzger slammed his hand down onto the shotgun barrel, gripping it, and whipping his other elbow back – hard.

"Run!"

They all turned and sprinted. Even Carla only hesitated for a split second before dashing toward the armored vehicle.

At the door, Matt glanced back, allowing Megan and Carla to leap in. Metzger was shuddering. His grip was still on the barrel of the gun, but the bandaged attacker had his hand on the hilt of a huge hunting knife buried deep into the soldier's gut. He jerked it upward, slicing deeper into the corporal's belly, and brought his face close to Metzger's, speaking to him – perhaps praying for him.

Matt had seen enough. He grabbed the doorframe just as a shotgun blast roared from behind them.

Reed was in. He yelled over his shoulder, "Door closing … now."

More shotgun blasts, along with other caliber rounds, whacked and pinged off the toughened exterior of the ASV.

Matt leaned forward. "Are you going to use the flamethrower?"

The vehicle roared to life, Reed's face a mask of furious determination.

"They killed them. They just killed them." Carla shook her head in disbelief. Her voice began to rise. "Why would they do that?"

Matt raised his voice over Carla's. "Reed, are you going to use the flamethrower?"

Carla shook her head. "But he knew me. Who are they?" She looked hard at Reed, searching for answers.

"Quiet down. Right now, I'm just going to get the fuck out of here." The ASV started to spin, grass divots flying out from behind it. Reed turned the wheel hard, sending the vehicle into an arc that brought them close to the mob of bandaged horrors.

Now that they were out from under the trees, Matt could see what a putrid group of creatures they were. Most wore bandages on their head and hands, but some were fully wrapped in strips of cloth sodden with fluids that had exuded from their miserable bodies. Some of the creatures weren't completely covered, and between the wrappings he could see the muscles and tendons of exposed flesh, where the dermal layer had been sloughed off.

He felt ill. If it wasn't for Joop and Metzger being so readily dispatched, he might have actually felt sorry for them.

Shots peppered the vehicle, drum-beating against the panels and scarring the windows.

Reed spoke without turning. "Don't worry; this baby can take just about anything these fucking freaks can throw at it."

Matt could see the leader directing his ragged troops, pointing to the wheels. Dozens of weapons fired at the thick rubber tires.

"What about the tires?"

"They're run-flats – they can withstand a lot of punishment. As long as ..." He trailed off, appearing to concentrate on his driving.

Matt looked out again and saw that the mob was keeping pace with the bumping vehicle. Several of them had shotguns, which they pumped and blasted, pumped and blasted, over and over into the tires. Others had handguns or rifles which they used to do the same. The vehicle started to lean toward one side.

"Don't sweat it, we can run on four flats if we have to ..." This time he finished his thought. "Just not very far."

The ASV now had its armored rear facing the skinners. Before the gears could really bite, another of the back tires exploded. Even without his hands on the wheel, Matt could feel the vehicle's performance becoming sluggish.

"Let's go, let's go, let's go." Reed was chanting to himself, his hands white-knuckle tight on the large wheel as he powered toward the road.

Matt turned back to the front windscreen, urging the vehicle on as they approached the end of the grassed area. A line of skinners ran ahead of them and appeared to pull on some ropes. Like something medieval, sharpened logs rose from the ground, six-feet long, pointed ends aimed toward the careening machine. More men arrived, carrying long wooden braces to hold the pikes in place.

Reed's teeth were bared, and Matt could have sworn he heard the man growl. "The hell ... you ... do." He swiveled in his seat. "Get up here now, and get on the flame-thrower."

Matt felt himself go numb. "Huh?"

Reed struggled with the wheel and yelled over his shoulder. "If they stop us, we're all dead. I need you to burn me a path."

Matt started to climb in to the front, but Megan hauled him back. "You have the worst aim of anyone I know." She shoved him aside and climbed in beside the soldier. She copied what she had seen him do before, flipping out the small panel with the control board and miniature screen, then placed a hand on the joystick.

"What do I do now?"

"Toggle the bomb site over what you want to hit, and then press the button down, hard, and keep it down ... now!"

Megan moved the red circle toward a cluster of bandaged bodies. Small-arms fire whacked into the windscreen as she punched down hard on the red button. There was a whoosh, and a jet of jellied fuel shot forty feet toward one of the clustered groups. It coated them, their bodies exploding into greasy flames. Inside the cabin, they couldn't hear the screams.

Megan shot another jet, and this time the skinners dropped their wooden braces and scattered, just a few remaining to dance madly, their clothing ablaze from the super-heated jellied fuel.

Reed accelerated, and without the braces holding them in place, the logs exploded out of the way.

"Yeah, fuck you too." Reed accelerated, and Matt and Carla crowded to the rear window, watching the band of bandaged men and women recede. "We're safe, for now." Reed used a sleeve to wipe his brow.

Matt leaned forward and placed his hand on Megan's shoulder. "Are you okay?"

She shook her head, putting her hands over her face and grinding the heels of her palms into her eyes.

"Who the hell was that guy? The big one in charge – he was no lunatic." Matt asked, rubbing Megan's back between her shoulder blades.

Reed wiped his face again. "I think the big guy was Dillon, their leader. We couldn't have picked a worse place to stop for a piss. Maybe it was just shit luck, but I doubt it. More like they're tracking us somehow. They even managed to set that ambush ... or maybe they've got ambushes everywhere, and they just needed to get to it while we were there."

Megan sat back, her eyes still closed. "They have a leader?"

Reed shrugged. "More like their local messiah; he hangs around the Atlanta outskirts picking off our patrols. We think he knows there's plenty of activity going on inside the CDC, so he continually watches and monitors it."

"How does he know?" Carla had been listening.

Reed's face darkened. "We've found some of our people – they'd been tortured. He wants information ... about us."

"He knew me. He blamed the CDC ... blamed me. His voice, I know it ... from somewhere." Carla frowned.

Reed turned back to the road. "He blames us all ... for everything. You know the type, it was all a government conspiracy, we released it into the poor neighborhoods on purpose, we have a cure but aren't releasing it, etcetera, etcetera." He tilted his head. "But Dillon is different; he's smart, and seems to know what we're doing and when. Gotta be tapped in somehow."

"Do you know who he is?" Carla asked.

Reed shrugged. "Just rumors. Chief suspect is Brock Dillonbeck. He was an evangelist who became a holy-roller senator. Got caught with a hooker and his fly open. He disappeared, but the infestation became a bigger issue than a shamed politician gone missing."

"Dillonbeck ... Senator Brock Dillonbeck. He toured the CDC a year ago. He wanted to cut back our funding, and I was one of the specialists tasked with ... pushing back." Carla seemed to search her memory, trying to make a match with the voice she just heard. "I, I just don't know."

Reed grunted. "Might be him, but we can't ever see him clearly, and the bandages also make a voice match difficult. It's certainly his style of sermonizing, though."

"Nothing like the end of the world to give you a pulpit and an audience," Matt sighed. "So, how far can we travel?"

"We took some serious dents, but we're okay. This is an M1117 Guardian, a highly mobile and lethal Armored Security Vehicle, with armor designed to deal with small-arms fire, mines, IEDs – it can even take an RPG hit. All running on four oversized, high-density, run-flat tires. We can keep going, but it'll be at a reduced speed." He shrugged. "Lucky it was me that picked you up in this tin can, or you'd be …"

"Lucky?" Megan bristled. "Yeah, lucky Joop and lucky Metzger. Just how lucky—"

Reed swung toward her. "He was my cousin." He turned back, his jaws working beneath his cheeks, as though chewing on something tough and unpalatable. The words came through gritted teeth. "So yeah, just be thankful it was him and me that picked you up. If we'd been in an open top, we'd all be dead … or worse. There's talk of cannibalism amongst the militias these days."

Matt saw there were tears on Megan's face. He grasped her shoulder. "Come here, Megs." She nodded and climbed out of the seat then sat down next to him. Carla came and sat on the other side of her.

"Sorry." Her voice was so small, Matt thought he might have imagined the spoken word.

Reed heard it, and shook his head. "No, I'm sorry." He turned briefly. "You saved us back there. Thank you."

She put her head in her hands, all the bravado of a few minutes ago fleeing her body. "I've never killed anyone before."

Matt bet that not many people had ever killed someone like that. Flamethrowers had been dropped from the US military arsenal after the Korean War – way too brutal a way to die, and the effects on the surviving victims were even worse.

"You saved our lives, that's all you need to remember." Matt hugged her.

She snorted wetly, looking up into his face. "For what? The world has gone to shit."

Carla rubbed Megan's neck. "Come on, that's why we're here, remember? To put it all back together."

Megan nodded, but put her face back in her hands.

They roared on, no thought of stopping again. This time the ride wasn't as smooth. Matt noticed Sergeant Reed checking the gas gauge often, and guessed that the shredded tires meant the going was rougher, and therefore fuel consumption had gone up. At least, he thought grimly, with Joop and Metzger gone, they now carried less weight.

"Sorry folks, we need to conserve fuel. I'm only going to turn the air con on for short bursts now." With that, the background whine disappeared. The vehicle started to heat up immediately.

After just twenty minutes, Matt wiped his brow; perspiration ran down his face and made his clothing stick to his chest and back. Carla and Megan were saturated and looked just as uncomfortable. He blinked the sting from his eyes as the repellent washed down from his forehead. He leaned forward.

"This stuff stings like fire."

Reed spoke without turning. "Pretty heavy-duty stuff." He turned to look at them. "We're going to need to reapply soon; it's probably all washed off by now."

Matt tapped the tank; there was only an inch or so left in the bottom. "Looks like there's enough left for one more wash down, but maybe not for all of us."

"Then get in the suits, we're nearly home." Reed turned and grinned. "Gonna be damned hot, but better than ending up a skinner or bloomer, right?"

* * * * *

Dillon dragged Metzger's body to the center of the clearing, ignoring the burning men and women who had been in the flamethrower's path. He dropped Metzger and placed one large foot on his back.

Dillon exhaled slowly through his nose, brown fluid leaking down over the bandages covering his lips and chin. He motioned to the still-burning corpses.

"Oh brothers and sisters, how they treat us." He looked down and shook his head. "Their friend is dead, and they leave him behind like trash. He is dead because they care about nothing but themselves, and yet they turn the flames of hell upon us for simply asking them to join us, asking them to re-examine their own souls."

Slowly, his large, bandaged head came up, his voice growing stronger. Dillon looked around; the field was now filled with bandaged figures, some limping, some bent over or dropping fluid and patches of skin like fleshy leaves from autumn trees. They looked like the damned souls of hell, and he loved them all.

He smiled and raised an arm, pointing to one, and then another. Some whooped with delight, others fell to their knees as his gaze fell upon them. While he watched, a heavily bandaged figure pushed to the front and offered him a military multi-band walkie-talkie. Dillon lifted it slowly to his ear.

"Speak." He listened for several seconds, letting his gaze run across his flock. Behind the bandages his lips slowly began to curl into a smile.

"No, don't touch anything. Bring it to Atlanta; I have an immediate use for it." Dillon tossed the radio device back and nodded to the masses before him.

"Soon, brothers and sisters. Soon they will beg to join us." He pointed after the truck. "And we will find them. We know where they are going, we know where they hide, brewing up more monstrosities to unleash upon us." He opened his arms wide. "We, who are indeed free from pain, know nirvana. But they do not, they are still chained by their fear ... and their pathetic skins."

Dillon closed his eyes and lifted his head, his voice now a stentorian roar. "Without pain, there would be no suffering, without suffering, we would never learn from our mistakes. To make it right, pain and suffering is the key to all windows, without it, there is no way of life. So sayeth the great goddess Angelina Jolie, may her name be forever blessed."

His head dropped again, and his eyes slowly opened. "And we can show them suffering like they have never known."

* * * * *

Matt stood and pulled suits from the rack, then handed one to Megan, and another to Carla. "Ladies' fitting room to the rear." He dropped his suit onto the seat, then unzipped the front of the heavy PVC mesh all-in-one suit and studied the instructions plastered on the inside.

Carla had her legs in the bright orange outfit already, her experience showing. "Air tanks?"

Reed shook his head. "Nope, but it has micro-filters fine enough to keep a good-sized bacterium out, so it'll work on the bugs and their eggs."

Carla grunted her acknowledgment and sat back down with the hood and Perspex face plate hanging down her back. She turned to see if she could assist Megan, while Matt struggled into his own suit.

She looked past Matt to Reed. "Want me to take over while you get into yours?"

"No thanks; I need the extra vision and mobility for driving as we pass into the city proper. I can use some of the spray." Reed continued to drive without turning. Matt suddenly felt very constricted within the large and bulky suit.

In another thirty minutes they passed through Mableton and entered the outskirts of western Atlanta. The streets were still eerily quiet, with mountains of rubbish, and a few open car doors. A miserable-looking German shepherd, with sagging, bloody fur, raked around in an open trash bag. Reed slowed to look hard at it.

"Don't burn it," Megan said sharply.

Matt wondered why she was so suddenly protective of the animal – its days were over anyway. Perhaps she had no stomach for seeing the flamethrower in action again.

"Better for it, and us, if it was dead." Reed watched it a few seconds longer, then pulled away.

"Okay, this is where it gets tricky. I'm going to break radio silence, and try and raise HQ again, now that we're close." Reed pushed a pellet into his ear that looped behind it to hold it in place. He paused, then removed the device and flicked the switch to cabin receive. "Might as well all listen, this concerns us all."

He turned a dial on the dashboard, and spoke in a methodical, clipped manner. "This is Sergeant Reed, in Unit One-Zero-Niner, coming in with special guests. Over."

Matt, Carla, and Megan were transfixed, listening intently. The clear line suddenly began to hiss and crackle, as if it had somehow been altered to a different frequency. A familiar voice floated into the cabin – but not the one they had expected to hear.

"You're not home yet, Sergeant. I'd just like to say that I'm sorry about your friends. It's terrible losing people, isn't it? I've lost hundreds, thousands, hundreds of thousands ... and you know who did this to us, don't you?"

There was more hiss and crackle. "Dillon." Reed spat the name.

The crackle cleared momentarily. "Sergeant, if you bring your special guests to me, I can promise you no harm will come to them. In fact, I can also promise you wealth, power, and ... a cure. Together we can bring the strongholds down. But first they need to shed their corrupt layers and see the beauty of the skinless ..."

"Fuck off." Reed fiddled with the frequency.

"This is Bennings, come back One-Zero-Niner."

"This is Reed, good to hear you, Sir."

"Where'd you go, Sergeant? You dropped out."

"Unwelcome hijack, by you-know-who, sir. We're coming in now."

"Good to hear. We've got a chopper up, that'll keep you under surveillance. You can come in via Houston Mill Road. Do not stop, do not get out – this is heavy skinner and bloomer territory ... and be careful, our hijacker has a lot of friends on the perimeter."

"Copy that. See you all within the hour – God willing."

Reed flicked the switch up, then turned and grinned. "Nearly home, folks."

He turned back to the windscreen and the now lumbering vehicle lurched forward, the tires low and squashy on the debris-covered road.

Matt turned to Megan and shrugged. "Home? I can't even remember what it looks like anymore."

She leaned her head on his shoulder. "Beats a jungle, I guess."

Carla was leaning back against the wall of the cabin, her face turned to the window so she could watch the passing streetscape. Suddenly she jumped forward, startling Matt, and pressed her nose to the armored glass. "Stop!"

"Jesus! What? No way, lady." Reed hunched his shoulders and continued driving.

"I said, stop ... the truck ... *now*!" Carla was yelling, her voice near ear-splitting as she punched out every word. "There's a little kid out there."

Megan and Matt looked, but saw nothing. "Carla, are you sure?"

Her voice didn't lower a single decibel. "I said, stop this fucking truck, or so help me, I'll ..."

Reed jammed on the brakes and swung in his seat. "What part of 'don't stop' did you not understand? Look, you cannot help these people, Dr. Nero. But you can do a hell of a lot more good by being at the—"

Carla hit the door button, and flipped her hood up, sealing it, as the door lifted. She was out before Sergeant Reed could react.

"Wait, Carla, wait!" Matt pulled on his hood and leapt after her, with Megan hot on his heels.

* * * * *

Now free of the vehicle's cabin, they could hear the wails of a little girl drifting from around the corner.

Carla was already running. Matt and Megan did the same, trying not to let her get too far ahead of them. Matt had to hold down the front of his suit to keep the Perspex faceplate centered over his eyes; the hood tended to slip back, obscuring his vision. He breathed in damp air – even though the micro-filters allowed a good flow of air, the transfer was slow, and the heat and humidity of respiration built up in the suits almost immediately. *These things weren't built for running in.*

Rounding the corner, they saw that Carla had stopped about ten feet from a tiny figure. The little girl was holding something that had probably once been white – a rabbit, or an old teddy bear. She was dressed in nothing more than a bedraggled nightdress, her stick-like arms and legs covered in bruises. She had her hands up over her face as she sobbed.

Matt and Megan pulled up behind Carla. The girl was sandwiched between them and a mob of about a dozen people, many holding stones, broomsticks, and, in one man's hand, a long shovel. Around the girl's feet broken debris attested to the mob's actions.

Carla advanced, pointing to the group of people. "Stay where you are. Stay back from her, you ..."

The people stared wide-eyed at the bright orange suit gesturing wildly at them. Matt picked up a broken broomstick and brandished it. A few of the people wandered away, losing interest; several stayed, their faces creased in anger. They pointed at the small girl and said something, but their words were muffled by the masks tied over their chins.

"Piss off." Matt threw his stick with surprisingly good aim, striking one of the men in the chest. The man swore and reached around behind him. When his hand reappeared it held a hunting knife as long as his arm.

"Oh, shit," Matt whispered.

The little girl pulled her hands away from her face. As soon as she saw Carla, she screamed, the bulky suit too much for her already strained nerves. Carla held up her hands and kneeled, keeping her movements slow and calm. She carefully reached up and unzipped her suit, pushing back the hood and exposing her sweat-streaked face. She smiled at the little girl, who stopped crying.

"Carla, that's not a good idea." Matt looked for another weapon. Megan appeared beside him with a trash can lid.

The man with the knife screamed, his voice still muffled through his mask but the volume giving his words form.

"Are you fucking crazy? You wanna die? She's about to pop, man."

He pointed his blade at the girl and took a step toward her just as Reed backed the ASV into the street. The electronic whine coming from the roof-mounted cannon as it swung toward him spoke louder than words.

The knife-man shook his head. "Your funeral, bitch." He motioned to his companions and slowly backed up the deserted street. Carla let fly with a bottle for good measure.

The ASV's door opened, and Reed motioned with his thumb. Carla ignored him and turned back to the girl, holding out her hand. The girl did the same, their fingers touching.

Reed banged on the window with his fist. Matt watched as he shouted to her from behind the armored glass, his motions becoming more determined. He was the only one without a suit, so he was loath to leave the sterilized cabin.

By now Carla had the little girl by the shoulders and was kneeling directly in front of her. Matt and Megan approached, and saw that what they had thought was a teddy bear was in fact a dead cat – or rather, just the remains of its fur, stiffened at one end with something rust-colored.

"Oh God." Megan put her hand to where her mouth would be behind the faceplate.

Carla smiled and brushed hair from the girl's face. "What's your name, sweetheart?" She gently wiped at the girl's grimy brow with her thumb. As the oily dirt came away, they could see the lumps – flesh-colored, and the size of peas under her skin.

"Dr. Nero, please put your suit back on and get away from her." It was too much for Sergeant Reed, who had got out of the vehicle. His sidearm was in his hand, and he kept glancing from Carla to the buildings on either side of the road.

He talked through gritted teeth, perhaps hoping the dental barrier would somehow keep anything nasty from entering his mouth. "I can't be out here. Please, you must get away from her, she's a bloomer, or soon will be. You can't help her."

"What?" Carla's face screwed up into a mix of disbelief and fury. "Well, we're going to goddamn try."

"No ... we are not. Come on people, this is exactly what we were told not to do." Reed spoke while watching the street.

Carla turned back to the girl, ignoring him. "What's your name, sweetie?"

"Maddie; everyone calls me Maddie." She sniffed.

Carla looked like she had received an electric jolt. "Maddie ... Madeleine?" She blinked a few times, then pushed the hair back off Maddie's lumpy face. "My name is Carla. Now, do you remember where your mommy and daddy are?"

Maddie sniffed some more. Her mouth turned down. "Mommy's skin all fell off, and daddy went out to get some food and didn't come back. All I've got left is Baloo." She held up the bedraggled piece of skin and fur.

Carla recoiled slightly – Matt assumed the smell of the dead animal must have been revolting.

Reed edged closer, walking sideways. "Please, please get back from her, she's highly contagious. Those bumps ... they're full of the mite eggs."

Megan grimaced behind the screen of her faceplate. "We've still got enough bug spray on to give an elephant asthma, and we're in suits. We'll be safe."

"No, we won't – we're not safe here, and we're not safe from her." Reed angled himself so he could watch the houses and darker areas of the street. "You know that Dillon has his followers watching for us by now." He glanced at Carla. "And she can't come with us. Sorry."

Reed took a step back toward the ASV, but Carla shook her head.

"We can't, we won't just leave her." Carla stood, gripping the girl's forearm. Maddie winced from the gentle pressure.

Skin sensitive to the touch, Matt noted.

Reed paused, his face imploring. "I'll explain when we're back in the truck. Look, I'll send someone for her, I promise. Okay?"

"No deal. She comes, or I stay." Carla stood firm.

"There must be other options, Sergeant." Megan went and stood with Carla.

Matt motioned to Reed. "Just give us a minute here." He knelt beside the tiny girl and smiled, hoping she could see his face behind the steamed-up faceplate.

"Hi, I'm Matt. How do you feel, angel? Do you hurt, or are you ... itchy anywhere?"

She wiped her nose. "Those men threw rocks at me, but only hit me a few times. They were bad shots."

Matt smiled. "Lucky for you. Umm, and those lumps on you ... when did they come up?"

She looked up and tilted her head, thinking hard for a few seconds. "They started on ..." Her lips moved and she seemed to be counting to herself. "I think it was yesterday, or the day before ... or the day before that. But they were small then. They don't hurt." She shook her head.

Matt nodded. "That's good. Are you thirsty?"

She nodded vigorously. "Yes, and hungry. Have you got any cookies ... the ones with pink icing on them? They're called Pinkies. My mommy always gets them on Saturdays, from ..."

Her face went blank as memories came flooding back.

"It's okay darling." Carla hushed her and started to lead her back to the vehicle.

Reed stepped in front of her, his hand up. "No, Dr. Nero. She cannot enter the vehicle. That is an order." His face was deadly serious.

"Out of our way. You can't order us; we're civilians, remember? Besides, we can dose her in what's left of the repellent. That will cleanse her temporarily."

Reed shook his head violently. There was panic in his eyes now. "No, she's a bloomer. When those blisters pop, she'll cover several square miles in micro larvae. Within an enclosed space, we'll be overwhelmed." Hs eyes were wide. "It's not just skin contact that can be a problem. You haven't seen what a lungful of those parasites will do – they'll eat you from the inside out." He shook his head, frustration creasing his features. "What's the matter with you? You know this better than anyone."

Carla took a step closer to the vehicle's open door. She held up one hand. "Take it easy, Sergeant."

Reed shook his head. "Please." For the first time, Reed's gun hand came into view – the gun not up, but now in sight.

Matt felt torn – he wanted to see the little girl safe, but also knew the danger she posed. He could feel the waves of anguish coming off the soldier – Carla was putting him in an untenable position.

Matt eased a little closer, trying to get in front of Carla. "Uh, maybe we can put her in one of the spare suits. And then get her straight into quarantine once we're back at the CDC."

Maddie had moved behind Carla's leg, and Carla's face was taking on a fierce protective look. This was not just about saving the infested girl. Matt recognized the name – it was about the daughter she couldn't save twenty years ago.

Matt couldn't believe Reed would shoot Carla, but the soldier's eyes kept darting down to the child. Matt didn't like the thought that jumped into his head. *He wouldn't.*

Reed straightened, his face blank. "I'm sorry."

The gunshot was loud in the near-silent street and Reed was punched backward a good six feet. He lay still.

Matt grabbed Megan and pulled her down. He looked back toward where he thought the shot had come from, but all he could see was the inside of his hood. He suddenly remembered: turning his head didn't turn the faceplate. The only window he had on the outside world, and it only offered one-eighty degrees of vision.

Maddie started to cry again and Carla hugged her to her breast. More shots rang out, and chips from the pavement sprayed both of them. Carla turned her face away, offering herself as the only protection.

Matt yelled to Carla. "Okay, we've got no choice now; back to the truck." Megan and Matt sprinted to the fallen soldier. Reed was still motionless on the road, his entire torso blood red. The soldier's gun was beside his hand. Matt grabbed it and spun, holding the faceplate in front of his eyes. The street was deserted.

Great, a sniper, Matt thought. *Fuck you, Dillon.*

"Give me a hand here." He grabbed one of Reed's hands, and Megan took hold of the other one. Together, they started to drag him toward the armored vehicle, leaving a long streak of red on the road, like a garish snail trail of human life.

More shots came, but it was obvious they weren't targeting Megan or Matt, or even Reed, now that he was out of action – the firing concentrated on Carla and Maddie. Carla picked the small girl up, her face pinched as if squinting would offer protection against the flying lead projectiles. She kept the small girl's face pressed into her neck.

A flaming bottle of petrol exploded a few feet from them, a pool of orange flame splashing at Carla and Maddie.

Matt saw the crowd coming back down the street. Some had revolvers, some rifles, and some had bottles with rags already alight, ready to throw. The guy with the knife was at the front. *Here comes payback*, Matt thought.

Most of the men and women had masks over their faces. *At least they're not skinners*, Matt thought crazily, as if the death the non-skinners were about to rain down on them would make them any less dead.

Matt let go of Reed's arm, his body still dozens of feet from the truck. He looked at Carla struggling with the girl, and turned to Megan. "Can you manage?"

She nodded behind her faceplate and started to tug hard on the injured man. His arm would be near wrenched from its socket, but it was life or death now.

Matt zigzagged toward Carla, dragging in deep breaths through the micro-filter and spitting perspiration that ran down into his mouth. He found it hard to see clearly; the steam on the inside of his faceplate made everything swim greasily.

He reached out to Carla and Maddie just as a loud *crack* sounded from close by, and Carla disappeared from his view like magic. She scrambled back up, but blood streaked the front of her suit.

Carla looked down, bewildered, wiping both hands through the red wetness and lifting them to her face. For a second or two she was confused, then she looked down and wailed. Maddie lay small and crumpled at her feet, like a large broken doll. Baloo, or what was left of him, was lying beside her.

Carla sank to her knees. The shooting had stopped, the rabble's bloodthirsty anger perhaps blunted by the death, and satisfied its objective had been achieved.

Matt knelt beside Carla as she rocked back and forth. Even in the heat, the woman shivered, all the death and misfortune seeming to well up from deep in her soul. She threw her head back, screaming to the sky. She'd lost another Maddie, Matt thought, trying to pull her toward the armored vehicle.

Carla shook him off and lifted the tiny body, squeezing it hard to her breast. As Matt watched, some of the small bubbles on Maddie's face and neck seemed to swell, and then burst.

Matt recoiled, remembering what Reed said about the mites devouring you from the inside out. Carla, inches from the tiny face, coughed and gagged, and Matt grabbed her, roughly pulling her back from the lifeless body.

"Let's go, we can't do anything else for her." Carla screamed, but let herself be pulled back, the small body sliding to the ground like a tiny bundle of rags.

The mob came slowly now, keeping their distance, treating them like dangerous creatures to be shooed away, or killed from a distance. Matt saw that one of them had a jerry can in his hand.

"Goddamn, she's bloomed!" There was a roar of disgust from the group. Another flaming bottle exploded nearby.

"Move it." He dragged Carla toward Megan, who was still struggling with Reed. "Grab that arm." He let go of Carla and, almost trancelike, she took hold of the arm that Megan tugged on. Matt grabbed the other.

There was the crash of breaking glass, a thump of ignition, and then a wave of heat erupted from within the open door of the ASV – a dumbass-luck direct hit.

"Oh, no, no, no!"

Matt dropped Reed's arm and sprinted at the flaming vehicle, jumping inside, the heavy suit giving him temporary protection from the flames. He looked around madly, snatching a medical kit, some water, the sample vials, and the last dregs of the insecticide. "Fuck!" The suit started to melt and stick to his skin. The pain was phenomenal, and he gritted his teeth. He still had Reed's gun stuck into the suit's belt at his waist – pointed down at his groin. The bullets had to be getting hot – they'd spontaneously fire soon. That made up his mind. He dove and rolled free.

Matt got to his feet, running as fast as the bulky suit would allow. Megan had taken several paces toward him, leaving the sprawled soldier behind. Matt waved her back as he raced over.

Carla looked up as he arrived, and he jammed the meager supplies he had retrieved into her arms.

Megan grabbed his arm, trying to see the burn on his suit, but he pulled away. "We've got to get to cover ... now!"

He pointed with his chin. "Those buildings. Quick. Let's get out of sight." He and Megan each grabbed one of Reed's arms and started to drag him. They picked up speed, the soldier's boots bouncing along the ground. He groaned – a good sign, Matt thought ... hoped.

The mob ran hard, converging not on Matt and the others, but on the burning ASV. Salvage was obviously on their minds, too. Matt and Megan slowed with the strain of pulling the large man. Megan lifted her head. "Keep up, Carla."

Matt saw that the scientist was slowing, the supplies clutched to her chest. He looked over his shoulder. "Down here." The street was one of few not boiling with running figures. He turned back to the burning armored vehicle. Dozens were swarmed around it when the explosion came. The flamethrower tanks burst in a gigantic ball of superheated jellied fuel, causing a pressure wave that blew Matt, Megan, and Carla off their feet, even though they had managed to get a few hundred feet away.

Matt sat up and looked back. The mob that had been all over the flaming machine was decimated. Bodies, and bits of flaming bodies, were scattered over the road ... few were moving. It was the break they had needed. They got to their feet, grabbed Reed, and scurried around the corner.

"Stop, stop." Megan let go of Reed's arm, dragging in heavy breaths. Her face behind the faceplate was pale. "We need to find shelter, and then work out how to get back to home base."

Matt put his hand on her back and rubbed. "You okay?"

She nodded. He looked at Carla, who had her head down, her hood still hanging limply on her shoulders.

"Carla ... all right?"

Her head bobbed, but she didn't look at him.

"Yeah, shelter. I'm hoping the last traces of the repellent will give Carla and Reed a bit of protection. But we've got to get out of the open spaces – there's too much chance of being infested."

Megan sucked in another deep breath, gathering her strength. "Let's go."

They dragged Reed around the corner, now having to rest every few dozen feet. Matt couldn't believe just how heavy a full-grown man could be. They paused at a plumbing supply store and without a second thought, Matt kicked in the door. He hoped that the owner wasn't home. It seemed to be that kill or be killed was the standard course of action now.

"Hello?" They waited just inside. "Hello?" Matt tilted his head and listened. After a full minute of silence, Carla gently shut the door behind them. They slumped to the floor. Carla leaned against the wall, her eyes shut tight, a look of distress on her face.

Reed groaned again, and Matt crawled across to him and pulled open his shirt, exposing the ugly wound in his upper chest.

"Carla, I need your help."

Megan knelt beside him, dragging the first-aid kit with her, along with a wad of paper towels she had found. The wound still pumped scarlet blood, but it bubbled and popped with escaping gas.

"Punctured lung?" Megan asked as she wiped the blood from around the wound.

"Looks like it." Matt turned. "Carla!" He snapped his fingers to get her attention.

"It's all gone bad." Carla spoke to her hands, folded in her lap.

"No, not all of it, and not yet. Come on Carla, we need your help here." Matt yelled the words, and her head came up slowly, her eyes finally focussing on him. "He's dying ... help us." After a moment she nodded, and wiped her nose on the thick plastic sleeve of her suit.

She went to pull the hood and faceplate back up and then stopped, snorting softly. "What's the point now?" She let the hood hang, and came over to Matt and Megan.

Reed coughed, and blood lifted from his lips. Carla felt around the wound. "Broken ribs, lung punctured and deflated. Might even be bullet fragments in there. We can't fix it here, but we need to keep it clean and drained."

She got to her feet quickly. Matt felt relieved; her business-like professionalism had returned in an instant. Carla busied herself, quickly searching lockers, drawers, and shelves, and came back with some tubing, scissors, and bleach.

She reached into the first-aid kit and grabbed some tape and a small bottle of alcohol, which she opened and splashed onto the wound. "Megan, wipe that down."

Next, she bathed the tubing and scissors with bleach. "Cut me half a dozen six-inch strips of the tape."

Matt and Megan worked quickly. Carla then cut about two inches of the tubing, and carefully inserted it into the bullet wound. She took the tape strips and placed them around the outside, holding the tube in place, then pressed them down, sealing the wound edges at the skin-level. Next, she bandaged him and created a sling, to immobilize his arm and shoulder. "Help me lift him."

They raised Reed into a sitting position. Once seated, he groaned again. Reddish fluid dripped from the tiny tube.

Matt grunted. "Good job. Will that reinflate his lung?"

Carla wiped her hands. "Nope, but it'll give him a fighting chance until we can get him to the medics at the CDC. That's just going to drain him, otherwise he could end up with a pneumothorax – his lung fills with fluid and unescaped gases. He'd be dead in an hour."

She stabbed his leg with a needle from the kit. "Antibiotics and painkillers. He's going to have to be kept upright so he doesn't drown in his own blood. He'll be in a lot of pain, but the sedation will either keep him unconscious or spaced out for another few hours."

Megan tossed damp bandages into the corner. "Lot of blood, not to mention how much he left on the street. Will he …?"

Carla nodded. "He'll need a transfusion, and quickly." She looked over the unconscious man's upper body. She smiled weakly. "Let's take five and then see if the phones are working, or if we can find a radio or something we can use to contact the CDC."

"Roger that." Megan slumped, and Matt picked up the bottle of repellent, a few ounces left sloshing around in the bottom. He swallowed, nervous about bringing up the girl again. "Carla, that poor little thing, Maddie, she was infectious, and you got a blast from the cloud – I saw it." He held the bottle out. "There's enough left in here to dose your head and neck."

Carla stared at the bottle in his hands. Her eyes didn't seem to focus as she spoke. "Bloomers … it's an appropriate name. Like a flower opening, a viral bloom expands outward, via explosive dispersion." She smiled sadly. "This little monster is clever. It knows how to survive … and spread."

"It's managed to exist for hundreds of millions of years." Matt poured the remaining acrid-smelling fluid onto a wad of bandages, soaking them through. He handed them to Carla, who rubbed the repellent over her face and neck, and then through her hair. She dropped the bandages and sat back, breathing hard, as if finishing a long run up a steep hill. She looked up at the ceiling. "I need a holiday." She smiled dreamily, fatigued to the point of collapse.

Megan sat close to her. "Got anywhere in mind – a tropical paradise, perhaps?"

Carla shook her head and rubbed her face hard. "No, had enough of those. Just somewhere with clean sheets and hot water. Now, that would be luxury."

"I hear that." Matt poked around the small office, locating a phone on the wall. He lifted it and listened for a few seconds. There was an emergency broadcast of a recorded message, telling people to stay indoors. It went on to tell citizens to record any crimes they witnessed, but not to get involved, explaining that law enforcement was stretched and may not be able to attend quickly.

Or at all, Matt thought grimly.

He clicked the receiver and listened again – there was a dial tone.

"Got a tone, Carla, over here."

Carla stood and walked slowly toward him. He barely re-cognized the frail and tired-looking person as the same strong, smart woman who had interviewed him not too long ago. She looked about as bad as he felt.

Carla took the phone, listened, and then dialed. She waited, and when she spoke there was relief on her face. She turned on the speakerphone so they could all hear.

"Go ahead, Hew."

"Carla, what happened? You disappeared."

She sighed. "Long story. Bottom line is, Reed's hurt – badly – he's been shot. But we're okay. There was a girl ... a bloomer. The truck is gone – we need help."

Matt could hear Hew's groan over the speaker. "The bloomers are our biggest problem – walking time bombs. Another little gift from these arthropod monsters. If primarily pregnant females infest you, you don't shed skin. Instead, they keep you on your feet so you can bloom. We didn't find out until later – micro-dispersal – it's how they went airborne, and managed to infect everyone and everything so quickly."

"Yeah, we know that ... now. But thanks for the heads up."

"Sorry, probably doesn't make a difference now. Just give them a wide berth – the bloomers are bad news."

Carla snorted. "The bloomers are bad news, the skinners are bad news, the gangs of vigilantes and the militias are bad news. The thin veneer of civilization is getting thinner all the time." She sighed. "We need to get home, Hew ... we're tired."

There was a pause, and then Dr. Francis Hewson spoke again, his voice sounding almost as drained as Carla's. "Yes, yes, that is critical. It's getting dark and we can't land – there are too many mobs in the vicinity now. Are you somewhere safe?"

Carla looked around. "I have no idea. If you mean, are we off the street, the answer is yes."

"Good. I suggest you hole up for the night and make a start first thing."

"*You*, as in 'us' – is that what you mean? I thought *you* would meet *us*."

Carla frowned as she waited for a response. After a moment of silence her head dropped. "So, we have to come to you now?"

There was the sound of a long exhalation over the line. "They're closing in, Carla; ringing us. The militias are picking off our teams, kidnapping our people, and then returning them in states that are abhorrent. Just a week ago we lost a full contingent of military technicians. It's too dangerous right now. We can guide you, but ..."

Carla sniffed and nodded. "Okay, Hew."

"I'm sorry, it's the best we can do."

Carla groaned, and Matt felt his shoulders slump. *So close*, he thought. Megan poured a few drops of alcohol into the repellent bottle, shook it, and then upended the diluted liquid onto the arm of his suit where it had melted through. She wound tape around it as a seal.

Carla leaned her head back against the wall. "Okay, I guess we can stay here tonight. Tomorrow we'll try to find some transportation."

"Good, Carla, stay strong ... nearly home. Okay, same as before, come in via Houston Mill Road. It's been modified to only accept certain visitors – no uninvited walk-ins anymore, I'm afraid. You'll come to a checkpoint. You're expected, so don't stop, don't get out; you'll simply be waved through. When you get to the terminus, you will need to leave the vehicle and proceed to the chemical showers. It'll be unpleasant, but it's the only way for us to be sure you're detoxed and clean."

"Fine with me – a shower is a shower." Megan doused a rag with some water and wiped her faceplate.

"Tomorrow it is, then," Carla said softly.

"Remember, do not stop, and do not get out of the car for any reason ... no matter what you see. Stay safe ... and good luck."

Carla hung up.

Matt sat forward. "I'll board up the door ... in a minute." He lay back down, suddenly feeling dizzy, exhaustion eating away at every atom in his body. He closed his eyes.

CHAPTER 24

Kurt stayed low amongst the shrubbery a few hundred feet from the side of his house. His modest bungalow was on a large plot just off Haul Road in Wayne, New York. It was a little run down, but sat on a few acres of flat, secluded forest, and was as close to being in the country as he could get on the outskirts of one of America's most populated cities.

He had staked it out for an hour. He'd circled twice, and there'd been no movement inside at any time. He kept low and ran to the front door; there was nothing but darkness in the windows. The key was still under the potted plant. In one smooth motion, he unlocked the door, pushed it open, slid inside and closed it behind him as silently as he could manage.

Breathing hard, he stood against the wall in the darkness for another ten minutes, just listening, feeling for movement or a presence. It was his training as a hunter – wait for your prey to move first; see them before they saw you. After several minutes there was still nothing. He exhaled and dropped his heavy bag with a dull metallic clank. His shoulders immediately felt lighter by half.

Kurt had been thinking about his priorities for hours before he had even arrived. Shower all this bug shit off. Seal the windows and doors, and then make a giant meal, followed by ten hours' sack time. Not one part of that sounded like a bad idea.

His clothing came off first and went into a plastic bag, which he sealed. Naked, he went to his linen cupboard, grabbed some towels, wet them, and rolled them up. He placed them under doorframes and along window ledges. Next, he placed cling wrap over air vents, keyholes, and any other entry or exit, no matter how small, that he could find. After another hour, he stood back and nodded. Nothing could get in, no matter how microscopic, unless he wanted it to.

He raced to the shower, luxuriating in the water, bathing away the grease, grime, chemicals, and miles of shitty jungle. Scrubbed pink, he ambled out, still naked, and ran his large hands up through his hair. He stretched and smiled – he felt good.

He opened the fridge; it was just as he had left it. There were a few long-life condiments and some rancid dairy products. Didn't matter, his pantry was stocked with tins and dry food – he always kept bulk supplies in case he got snowed in.

If he ate wisely, he reckoned he could last six months. There'd be nothing to do but listen to the radio and wait. Kurt made himself a huge plate of tinned beans, ham, and tomatoes, and grabbed two warm beers. He would have sat at the table and listened to the radio, but there was one last thing to be taken care of.

He grabbed his satchel and dropped it onto the table. Reaching in carefully, he lifted free a few pieces of the Incan gold. He sat them on the table and brought his smiling face close. Each was polished and gleaming as if it had been cast just yesterday. He smile broke into a grin at the collection.

"Hello, rich man."

He picked up one of the largest pieces – a squat idol that leered madly at him. "Same to you, fatso." He put it down and wiped his hands, taking a big spoonful of beans and ham.

He continued removing the pieces, rummaging through the last items in his pack. He pushed aside the empty insecticide bottle. *Won't need you again*, he thought with satisfaction.

His hand closed on a tiny piece of folded plastic. He lifted it carefully out.

There was something shimmering inside. He frowned. He couldn't remember taking it with him, or picking it up along the way. Kurt opened the small bag and reached in, pulling the iridescent feather free. He turned it in his fingers, confusion suddenly turning to recognition, and then to horror.

"Oh, shit, shit, shit." He dropped the archaeopteryx feather and held his wrist as if his hand had been burnt. He raced for the shower.

CHAPTER 25

If the daytime was mostly devoid of the noises of city life, then the night belonged to the nocturnal denizens – long, noisy, and violent. Groups of people ran in the street – either in pursuit, or being pursued.

Sometimes an individual would creep by, or pause to try their door. That was the worst – it could have been another Maddie, seeking help, or someone looking for an opportunity to loot, maim, or kill. And then there were the infested – those crawling with the parasite, skin drooping or sloughing off in wet blobs, and the others, those who had the mite, but weren't showing symptoms, perhaps believing they were clean, unknowingly being turned into walking egg factories.

Matt blinked eyes that were so gritty it hurt to close them. Tiredness hung on them all like lead weights, but no one could sleep well enough to get any relief. Matt held a small plastic flashlight, but refrained from using it – the light would have acted like a beacon to the rabid hordes outside.

The morning came slowly and breakfast was just like dinner – a few energy bars that they'd found on the counter, and rust-tasting tap water, all gratefully consumed. Matt's initial search of the drawers in the office had yielded little more than tape measures, invoice slips, a set of keys, and some wrenches – not a great haul. Eating was a challenge with the suits. Carla had her suit done up and over her head once again. Reed was still propped up, but this time, his breathing was more like that of a deep sleeper, as opposed to a man fighting for his life. The wound still dripped and needed attention, but for now, he lived.

Reed coughed wetly, and then groaned. Matt poured some water into a coffee mug and held it to the soldier's lips. He groaned again, took a sip, and grimaced.

"Shit, that hurt."

Matt smiled. "Welcome back."

"What happened? Where are we?" His eyes stayed shut, and pain started to crease his features.

"You got shot, the ASV got torched, and we got chased by a mob. Now we're hiding in a plumbing supply store. But that was yesterday." He gave Reed another sip of water. "Today, we're going to head into the CDC ... think you can make it?"

Reed opened his eyes and started to nod. His eyes focussed, then came a look of panic. He grabbed Matt's forearm, sitting forward. "Where the fuck is my suit? Am I covered?"

Matt pushed him down. "Take it easy. You've got residual insecticide, so you should be okay for now. Your biggest issue is that you need a blood transfusion – you've got a punctured lung, and a drip inserted into your chest."

Reed's hand came up slowly, touching the small tube. He winced, and then frowned. "The girl, the bloomer, did she ... where is she?"

Matt kept his voice low, not wanting Carla to hear. "She's gone."

"Did I shoot her?" His face was pained.

"No," Matt responded.

He nodded. "I was going to." He opened his eyes. "If she'd bloomed, we'd have all been fucked."

Too late, Matt thought.

Reed coughed, this time without blood appearing on his lips. He winced again. "You know, the mites prefer the sub-dermal skin layers, but they're happy to munch on the cells of the mouth, throat, lungs – eat you from the inside out."

"Yeah, you said that. Take it easy now – get some rest." Matt pressed the mug of water into his hands and stood.

His stomach sank; he remembered hearing Carla cough in the night. He didn't want her falling to bits in front of them. He looked down at the soldier. "Rest now; we'll be going soon, try-ing to find a car or something we can use to get to the CDC."

Reed nodded. "I'll be fine. I'll make it home, even if I have to crawl."

Matt hoped it wouldn't come to that.

* * * * *

Carla found a small bathroom at the back of the shop and stood in front of a discolored mirror. She leaned forward, try-ing to see herself through her glass faceplate. She swore softly and unzipped the suit, pulling it back down off her shoulders, then dragged her hands up and out of the inbuilt gloves.

She luxuriated in the coolness, her perspiration drying quickly. She snorted – never had bathroom air smelt so sweet. She leaned forward once again and licked her lips. They felt funny – numb and puffy, just like her gums and throat. She grinned, showing her teeth and turning her head from side to side, noticing a slight swelling of her upper lip. She looked like she'd just had a round of collagen injections to give her-self a Sunset Boulevard trout-pout.

She was tired, but felt better knowing they were going to be home soon. A long hot shower, clean sheets, a cooked meal

– any one of those things seemed like such a luxury. There was a knock on the door.

"Carla, you okay in there?"

"Sure Matt, just finishing up." She washed her hands with soap, splashed water on her face, and then ran hands through her hair, scraping at her greasy scalp. She finished by slowly pulling the suit back up and zipping it closed. *One more day*, she thought.

* * * * *

Matt opened the back door a crack and peered out. The morning was silent – no more people about, no birdsong, not even a breeze to stir up some sounds. He went out into the laneway and beheld a streetscape that looked like a third-world war zone. Mountains of debris and rubbish piled high, wrecked cars, bikes, dead bodies, and animal carcasses. The smell was atrocious. Matt knew that only bacteria and insects would worry the dead – even the rats would have succumbed to the mite by now.

There were a few cars parked neatly in the laneway. The owners had probably finished work, gone indoors, and then vanished into some sort of twilight zone, never to return ... or perhaps they were watching him now. Matt looked along the windows, but there was no movement, nor any open or broken panes to suggest anything sinister.

He ventured out farther; there was a single Ford truck, with the same logo on the doors as on the shop they had taken shelter in. Matt tried the door hopefully, then dropped his hand. He turned to Megan and Carla, who were standing in the doorway, holding Reed between them.

"Wait a minute." He charged back past them, and in a few seconds returned with the keys he had found earlier. He opened the truck's door and, on seeing the two-way radio, whispered a soft *thank you*.

"Come on, it's got half a tank." He leapt out and ran around to help with Reed. Together, they pushed him into the cabin, Matt pointed to the radio.

"Carla, see if you can get Dr. Hewson again."

"You bet." She smiled and jumped in.

Matt paled – through the faceplate, he noticed the blood on her teeth. *Eat you from the inside out*, Reed had said.

The soldier slumped, moving in and out of consciousness. The drip at his chest was now leaking a discolored fluid. Without any more antibiotics, the man had days, maybe hours, left.

Megan slammed the door. "Know how to drive this big sucker?"

Matt blew air through his lips dismissively. "It's a Ford F750 with a two-ten horsepower engine."

She laughed. "Okay, that's written on the dash. Can you drive it?" She raised her eyebrows.

"Sure, the F750 is an automatic – that's all I need to know." He fired it up, and the roar was loud in the dead back-street. He jumped it forward, plowing through or pushing over small mountains of rubbish, and other things he didn't want to dwell on. They turned onto the main road and he accelerated, following Carla's directions to CDC headquarters.

Matt moved down streets, turning left or right on Carla's instructions. The morning was as silent as the night had been noisy; the running and screaming denizens of the darkness now home, comatose or dead. But, empty as the streets were, Matt still couldn't shake the feeling that behind the doors and windows, eyes followed their progress.

At the next junction, they had to stop at a wall of trucks, topped with cars. In some places the pile of broken steel, glass, and rubber had been lashed together with cargo netting. It was no random pile-up, but a physical barrier created to keep someone in … or out.

"I don't like it." Matt glanced around quickly, looking out the truck's windows.

Carla folded her arms. "Hew should have told us about this."

"I don't think he knew. Look." Matt pointed to one of the cars, which was leaking oil, the dark fluid running down to the ground where a pool glistened, not yet soaked in. "This has just been erected."

"Last night?" Megan leaned forward.

"Probably. The question is … was it built for us?" Matt turned to her, eyebrows raised.

He wound down the window, and leaned out, raising himself up slightly. From outside the window there was near total silence from a street that used to be crammed with hundreds of cars and pedestrians going about their daily business only weeks before.

Matt turned back to them. "Like a tomb."

Suddenly an explosion of sound hammered the air around them, making them cringe as if from a physical blow. Loudspeakers blared all around them.

Music, screams, a cacophony of jumbled sounds, then a screech of white noise, made them grind their teeth and squeeze their eyes shut. The sounds flattened and organized, becoming a rapper's backbeat. Into it came a voice, deep and stentorian, the perfect vowels incongruous among the thumping, scratching musical beat of the street.

This is the end of days. The end of your life…

Matt wrenched himself back into the car. "What the hell is that? This is a bad joke." He had to shout over the music.

"Move, let's get out of here. Back up, go, go, go!" Megan had her hands over her ears.

Matt put the car in reverse and accelerated.

Say goodbye to your husband … Say goodbye to your wife …

Matt grimaced. Carla kept her head down and her eyes shut.

You caused all this when you took our skins. Now all off to hell, for your terrible sins ...

"Shut up." Carla's voice was loud in the cabin and, as if by magic, the music shut off, leaving a ringing in their ears. It was immediately replaced by the urbane voice of Dillon.

"Carla, Carla Nero. It took me a while, but I knew I recognized you. Come to me, Carla. I have a lot to talk to you about."

"What?" Carla's eyes were wide.

"Not today, asshole." Matt spun the car around and jammed his foot down hard on the accelerator, but evading the voice was impossible. Every corner seemed to have a speaker – on a street pole, hammered into walls, even affixed to abandoned cars.

"Don't make me hurt them, Carla. And I *can* hurt them. You'll see."

Carla pointed, her voice high. "Go left at the next street."

Matt spun the wheel and bounced down the street. The music started again.

This is the end of your world-ddd ...

The words became harsher, louder, and finally they stopped making sense at all and just became an animalistic roar that could have emanated from the bowels of hell itself.

The grotesque song receded as they powered ahead, Matt only just noticing how his heartbeat felt like a hammer behind his ribs.

"Godammit, he's watching us."

"He must be close, or his followers are." Megan's eyes darted as she stared through the windscreen.

"Turn again here, we've got to get back on track. At least this heads us in the right direction." Carla pointed. "And again here. We should be past the barrier now."

Matt turned, and immediately jammed his foot on the brake, skidding the big truck and throwing them all forward. "Shit."

There was a row of upside-down crucifixes. Men and women were tied to them – also upside down. They hung limp and were soaking wet.

Reed moaned and his arm came up slowly, pointing. "Oh God … our people." His head slumped back, his face a mask of anguish.

There was a crackle of static and then came the smooth voice again. "Get out of the truck, Carla."

Matt put the truck in reverse, but before he could stamp on the accelerator a figure dashed out, holding a flaming torch. He ran past the line of crucified people, touching each gently with the flame. One by one, the figures exploded into pillars of orange fire and greasy black smoke. It was obvious now what they were soaked in – gasoline.

Several of the figures thrashed in the flames, tormented souls each in their own personal column of hell. Carla wailed. "God, oh God, they're still alive."

There was a deep sigh over the loudspeakers. "I warned you, Carla. You made me hurt them. Don't make me hurt your friends as well."

"I can't … let … him …" Carla's hand went to the door, and Megan wrapped her arms around her, screaming to Matt. "Get us the fuck out of here."

Matt pulled the truck back, bouncing off a curb and crashing into a parked car. He turned hard, pushing another vehicle out of the way.

"Carla, you need to direct me."

"This is a nightmare. I'm going to be sick."

Matt accelerated. The music exploded at them again, and this time Dillon's calm voice was ripped away, his cultivated and sophisticated mask slipping to reveal a glimpse of the real being that hid beneath the refined exterior.

"Stop! Get out of the car, bitch. I'll fucking kill you all. I'll burn you down. I'll pull you apart and eat your faces. I'll-III..." The words boiled back together, mushing again into the monstrous roar.

Matt gritted his teeth and crushed his eyes shut for a moment, trying to rid his mind of the insane voice and of the images of burning men and women. Carla was right, this was a nightmare – and they were stuck in it.

"Just drive." Carla's voice was devoid of life.

"Just drive, drive, drive." He repeated the words, using them as a mantra to blot everything else from his mind as he pushed the truck to the max down the debris-strewn street.

Megan let go of Carla and sat back. "I used to like REM."

* * * * *

A calm voice came over the radio. "We have you in sight now, Dr. Nero. Keep coming – there are no more roadblocks or militias in view."

"Thank God." Matt slowed a little as he turned into the Houston Mill Road. He could see the military's influence on the facility – the whole block had been barricaded off, and was heavily militarized, with gun turret towers and rotating searchlights. *Martial law, and then some,* he thought.

As they slowly rolled toward the huge walls, guards wearing similar suits to theirs rolled back the ten-foot-high chain-link outer gates. Each of the men had body armor, a semi-automatic weapon over his shoulder, and a sidearm. Just inside the gates, there were more figures with field glasses trained on them.

Houston Mill Road had also been altered – gone were the wide open spaces leading to the large, factory-like building. The road was fenced on each side; a combination of brickwork, metal grating, and chain link forced all approaching vehicles onto a narrow path – one that could be scrutinized and defended, if necessary.

Matt observed that the rolling lawns out the front of the building were covered in row after row of temporary tents – it seemed the staff had taken to spending their nights "in" from now on.

They slowed at the next checkpoint. This one preceded a long, barn-like structure, which they entered. A voice came over the radio, telling them to stay in their vehicle. Another person in a hazmat suit appeared beside them and used a pressure spray to blast the truck with foaming liquid. Once complete, another figure appeared in front of them with two orange aircraft-runway type batons and waved them on, pointing to a large yellow circle in the next section of the building. Matt stopped the truck within it, and a booming voice requested that they step out, hands on their heads.

Matt came first. He waved, indicating that he needed a moment, and then turned to take one of Reed's arms. Megan slid out holding the other. They could barely tell if he was breathing anymore. Last came Carla, wheezing wetly. The men directed them to different stalls – men on one side, women on the other. Matt handed Reed to some suited soldiers who carefully carried him into the stall. Matt was ordered to strip off. He emptied his pockets of anything he wanted to keep – those items would be separately cleansed. The clothing and his suit were sealed into a bag, which was immediately taken away.

The shower was hot, highly chemical, and had enough pressure behind it to scour the skin. Matt was given a tough-bristled brush and instructed to scrub – hard. He was sure he lost eyebrows and some of the hair on his head. Not that it mattered – his long hair was shaved, along with his eyebrows, underarms and pubic area. He ran a hand up over his head. The smooth scalp felt weird, but ... liberating.

He was given a set of paper coveralls and was ordered to pass down a long, plastic-lined walkway to an ultraviolet room for five minutes, and then into another room for a checkup. The room was long and white, like a sterile hospital room, with little more than sheetless cots and steel benches with portable lights overhead. The men and women working here were without hazmat suits, but still wore all-over disposable suits and facemasks. *Guess we're not quite out of the woods yet*, Matt thought.

The door opened and in came Megan and Carla, their heads shaven, and scrubbed pink. Matt smiled and saluted Megan.

"GI Jane, maybe?"

Megan grinned back. "More like Space Oddity ... man, you have one weird-shaped head, Kearns."

Behind her, Carla looked shrunken. Without her mane of hair, her face looked lined, her head way too small. She coughed, the single sound freezing the room.

An attendant backed up. "Don't move. Dr. Nero, have you had your suit off at any time?"

Miserably, Carla nodded. "And I think I've got a rash."

"Goddamn it." The three men and two women seemed frozen in indecision. One – Dr. Jackson, according to his nametag – looked to Matt and Megan and pointed. "What about you two?"

Matt shook his head. Megan did the same.

Jackson seemed to decide. "Okay, don't worry, Dr. Nero. We're going to have to give you some internal treatments, and keep you isolated for a little longer. Please return to the previous sterilization room." He watched her head out, and then turned to Matt and Megan. "You two can proceed to the change rooms."

Megan shook her head. "No, we'd like to stay if that's okay." She went to follow Carla, but she turned to her and held up her hand.

"No ... Megan, Matt, you stay, I'll be fine." She smiled. "Besides, this may take a while." She waved to them. "I'm a tough old thing. I'm not dead yet, and I don't intend to be anytime soon." She looked past them and pointed to the small container that held the two vials of red fluid. "Jackson, get those to Francis Hewson right now, and then have him contact me."

Jackson nodded. "You got it."

Carla stepped back into the corridor. Megan turned to the attendants. "What will happen to her? She'll become a skinner or a bloomer unless you stop it, right?"

The man grunted. "Stop it? We can't stop it. We can slow it down, but for just a while. It's always fatal."

"But if she's a bloomer, they live longer, don't they?"

He shrugged, and Megan literally growled at his indifference. She spoke through gritted teeth.

"Hey! That is Dr. Carla Nero. She just goddamn trekked through the Amazon jungle to find a cure for you ... us ... all of us. The least you could do is answer some goddamn questions!"

There was silence for several seconds.

"Well?" Megan screamed.

Two soldiers appeared. Jackson waved them away. "She's right; they have a right to know."

He looked back to Megan. "She's our friend, too." There was both sadness and resignation on his face. "What you've heard about bloomers is unfortunately all true. When a pregnant alpha female mite infests a body, it sends out a chemical signal that alters the sex of all the other mites – in effect, they all become females. Insects and arthropods have some wonderful adaptive abilities."

He drew in a breath and seemed to sag. "The mites stop their voracious pursuit of the subcutaneous dermal layers and instead start producing egg pouches. They produce millions

and millions of them, swelling the skin and forming an am-
niotic gas that generates the distinctive nursery pockets ...
blisters. When the skin reaches its maximum tension point,
or in response to some unknown prescribed signal, the gas
causes the vesicles to explode, throwing the mite larvae into
the atmosphere. A normal plume can float for days and cover
several miles."

Matt nodded, looking down at his feet. "Yes, we've seen
someone with the lumps ... recently."

Jackson kept his eyes on Megan. "Unfortunately, it doesn't
always end there – the mites continue to lay and burst for
many days. As more eggs are laid, more of the body becomes
infested – inside and out. The human body is a wonderfully
elastic vehicle, but eventually it loses its ability to contain
the billions of larvae. Eventually the body will explode and
collapse. The remains need to be incinerated, as even the exploded host can continue to give off mite clouds for weeks
afterward."

He looked at each of them. "We'll do what we can. But appreciate what we are dealing with here. This is not just about
one doctor, no matter how important. Millions are dead, and
millions more will die."

He turned and continued down the corridor. Matt and
Megan followed in silence.

* * * * *

Dillon lowered the heavy field glasses, his eyes narrowing as
he surveyed the huge, fortified complex.

"We offered them nothing more than our love and the
chance to see how much better they can be."

He turned and handed the heavy binoculars to the
wrapped man beside him. "And in turn they erect the Walls
of Jericho to keep us out. So be it. Then I will be Joshua and

blow them down." He made a fist. "Bring them in. Bring them all in. It is time."

* * * * *

Kurt sneezed, not bothering to wipe the red-brown liquid that ran from his nose. Still naked after his shower, he sat on the floor, propped up against a kitchen cupboard. Empty tins of insect spray rolled around next to him, and his skin glistened with their poisons.

The first lumps had appeared on his wrist a few hours ago, and from then, more had appeared along his arm and then over his chest, making him look like a two-legged alligator. He laughed wetly as he spotted the golden idol on the tabletop. "Should have listened to Kearns." He grinned. "Curse of the Incas, right?"

He ran his fingertips over his cheeks, feeling the pea-sized bumps on his face. "Is it too late to apologize?" He nodded as if listening. "No? Never too late?" He groaned as he pulled himself to his feet. "Okay then."

Kurt shuffled to a drawer and retrieved a box, some plastic padding, and some tape. He lined the box with the plastic and then placed the gold carefully inside, looking at each item, rubbing it once or twice with his thumb. He closed his eyes for a second or two – or so he thought – and then sealed the box. He wrote carefully on the lid with a thick, felt-tipped pen, simply addressing it to the Brazilian Consulate. He left the grinning idol on the tabletop.

"You get to stay with me. I'm adopting you."

He looked at his wristwatch. It had taken him over an hour to perform the simple task. Time was losing all meaning. He reached up to feel his face again and quickly recoiled. His nose was misshapen, and his cheekbones were bloated and threatening to close his eyes.

"There go my boyish good looks."

Kurt went to turn and grunted with the effort. His legs now resembled pipes covered in popcorn and his knees refused to bend. He went to carry the box to the door, and caught sight of his hands. He swallowed the urge to cry out.

Time jumped again, and when he opened his eyes, he found himself back down on the floor. It was dark outside. The idol stared down at him, grinning, always grinning.

"Did you push me?" Kurt nodded, listening again. "You're goddamn right it's funny."

He looked down at his body, wishing he had something to cover himself up with. Worried now about what people would think when they found him. "Disgusting." He shook his head. "Doesn't hurt, though." He lay down, exhausted beyond words. He was thirsty, but doubted he'd be able to get to his feet to drink some water. Kurt Douglas exhaled slowly.

"I had a pretty good life you know," he said, trying to smile, but unsure if his lips could do that anymore. "Gonna rest now." He closed his eyes. "See you in the morning."

* * * * *

The Bell Kiowa scout helicopter looped high over the Atlanta skyline. A military observation chopper with a distinctive mast-mounted sight that resembled a beach ball perched above its single rotor, it had object density scanning and infrared and thermal imaging. With its light, skeletal design, it could scout night and day on very little fuel.

From a distant rooftop there came the flash of a reflection. Corporal Cory Jones, a pilot of four years, would have ignored it, but it came again, this time in a pattern. She opened her mic.

"Atlanta Base, this is Jones in BC447, I've got a pattern flasher signaling me from a rooftop downtown. Request permission to take a look-see."

After a few moments a deep, laconic voice came back. "BC447, permission granted to drop to two hundred feet only." There was a pause. "No passengers or strays today, Jones. We've got work to do."

Jones grinned. "You got it, Pop. Two hundred feet, confirm. Over."

The Kiowa sped like a steel mosquito to the line of buildings, dropping to three hundred feet as it came. As an afterthought, Jones switched to density imaging, and then dropped another hundred feet. A warning sounded from the cockpit console, and she frowned – multiple metallic signatures.

Jones looped around the building and then sucked in a breath. The street behind was filled with people, all streaming in the direction of the Atlanta CDC compound. Most were on foot, but there were some small trucks in amongst the group. Many of the people appeared to be armed. At their center was a huge vehicle with a long, drab, metal crate structure on its back. Jones started the onboard cameras. Photographs were taken and sent home automatically.

What is that? she wondered, as she dropped down another fifty feet. Then the details became clear.

"Holy shit." She pulled up hard.

"Base, emergency, come in, emergency ..."

There was another flash from the rooftop. This one made the cockpit sensors go berserk. Jones' heart pounded hard in her chest as she saw the display – incoming heat signature.

She pulled away, willing the small chopper to outpace the approaching dot of heat. "Please, please, please ..." Cory Jones looked over her shoulder. The flaring dot straightened as it found her and locked on. She recognized it now, a rocket-propelled grenade, and knew it was coming at her at nearly six hundred feet per second.

"Come back, Jones. Say again ..." The voice had lost its laid-back tone.

"Noooo …" The Kiowa jinked and then dove. The RPG followed.

The small helicopter exploded, raining debris and fire down upon the streets.

* * * * *

Major Bennings thrust open the door and strode into the command center.

"Cohen, give me what you've got."

The assembled soldiers at their makeshift communication and surveillance desks looked up briefly, then went back to their multiple screens. An officer raced over, pointing at a large wall display.

"Sir, one of our surveillance birds was just shot out of the sky. They managed to send back some images." He pointed at the screen. "They've got an army, and it's coming in on the western side of the city."

"Organized?"

"Doesn't look like it. But certainly armed – they've got automatic assault rifles and RPGs."

Bennings cursed under his breath. "Where the hell did they get an army, or all their kit?" He shook his head, standing close to the screen. "Probably us. Doesn't matter. Can we get another bird up?"

"We can't risk it – they've got M72 anti-tank RPGs, and after our chopper was hit, we assume they got the heat-seeking upgrade. We need higher altitude, and for that we'd need one of Bragg's birds – it'll take hours to get here. They'll be in our front yard by then."

Bennings looked at the younger officer and nodded. "Show me what we *do* have."

Cohen advanced the images. Several more were displayed, many taken from bad angles as the helicopter dove or banked.

But the picture was clear enough – thousands of troops with weapons held high, the smaller vehicles in amongst all the bandaged bodies, and then, partially obscured, the huge truck.

"Hold it. Enlarge that one." Bennings stepped forward. The image was grainy, but showed an enormous truck with a long mounting on its back, in four distinct sections.

Cohen slumped. "For fuck's sake. Is that what I think it is?"

Bennings exhaled slowly. "Yep. Patriot Launcher – looks to have four in the pipes." He rubbed a hand up over his face, and then through his cropped hair. "The technicians that were taken the other day. Were there any launch specialists in amongst them?"

Cohen sat down. "Yes, sir ... several."

CHAPTER 26

"So, how's your day been?" Francis Hewson came into the room in a bulky suit with a massive lump at the back, indicating it had its own air supply. He smiled at her from behind the Perspex visor.

Carla stood. "Hey, I leave you in charge of the country and you break it – what gives?" Her words were slurred and she grinned, the blood on her teeth causing him to wince. "I'd give you a hug, but well, you know ..."

He nodded. "I've got our best people running tests on your solution – magnificent stuff, and nothing we've ever seen before. From a vine, you say?"

She nodded and coughed, turning away. "From a flowered vine that probably came from the dawn of time – maybe it's representative of the very first vine ... along with everything else in that crazy place." She looked up at him. "I hope it works."

"So do I," he said. "And I hope its toxicity is minimal. We need to get it ... inside you as well."

"Doesn't matter to me – if it's toxic, I mean. I'd rather die from poison in a few minutes than end up slowly turning into ..." She shook her head and sighed. "I can feel them inside

... or rather, I can't anymore. My lips, gums, throat; they're all numb. Now I know what Sergeant Reed meant when he tried to warn us." She looked up and grinned sheepishly. "But I never listen."

"You never have." Hew smiled back sadly.

"How is he?" Carla asked.

"Reed's okay. You did a good job cleaning the wound. He's been given blood and antibiotics. But there are bullet shards embedded in the wall of his heart. He'll need a delicate operation, one we can't do here. For now, he'll get by."

Carla looked anxious. "Is he ...?"

Hew shook his head. "He's clean. From what Matt and Megan told me, you took the full viral blast from the bloomer. You inhaled the larvae, and, well, we need to deal with that."

"I need to get to work."

He held up his hand. "No, you need to—"

"I need to get to work! Put me in a suit, keep me in isolation, but I need to help with the analysis, synthesis, and distribution. This is too important. Use me, while you're still able."

He looked at her, grimacing, but she knew he couldn't disagree with her. "'Look, there's no argument about needing you." He turned away, torn.

"From a toxicological specialization standpoint there's no one better." She reached up to the shoulder of his suit and slowly turned him back toward her.

"Hew, we need to hurry. Indecision is what will kill us all now."

He nodded slowly. "Perhaps we can rig up some sort of suit for you, to allow you to work ... and keep you in your own personal isolation. But it'll have to be from outside. We can't afford to let a bloomer – er, someone infested – into the building."

Carla nodded. "I agree, and fully understand. Set up a remote link and get me a headset, so we can stay in continual contact."

He smiled and shook his head. "Why will I need a headset when I'll be right here beside you?" He shrugged. "Besides, you know as well as I do that if this fails, it'll only be matter of time before we're all dead."

A klaxon horn sounded, making both scientists flinch. Carla gritted her teeth and turned to him. "Contamination – is it a breach?"

Hew shook his head. "I don't think so. Something else."

There was a soft popping sound from outside the laboratory, followed by a deep thump that made the equipment rattle and white dust sprinkle down upon them.

"What the hell? Wait here." Hew raced out of the room.

* * * * *

Bennings watched through high-powered binoculars as the massive mobile launcher was driven to the distant end of Houston Mill Road. It pulled in behind an abandoned bus, and the four-sectioned box was lifted to clear the bus's body.

Bennings groaned. Machine-gun fire rang out, and a few RPGs looped toward their compound, falling well short. They didn't matter – it was the launcher that gave him the cement-like feeling deep in his gut. He knew that each of those four sections housed a deadly surface-to-air missile, twenty feet long and weighing over fifteen hundred pounds apiece. He brought the drab green launcher into focus.

"Shit. Looks like a MIM-104. Proximity fuse and a full bank of high-explosive fragmentation missiles – those bad boys will reach Mach 5 a second after launch, and if it's a PSAC3, then it's got a laser guidance system that can place one between your eyes." He lowered the glasses. "Just one of those will punch a hole right through this building like cheese. Four of them, and we're gonna end up sitting in a crater." He turned to Cohen. "What've we got at our disposal?"

"RPGs, some high-cal sniper rifles, and plenty of M16-A2s. But they're ..."

"Yeah, I know. They're out of our range, but we're not out of theirs. We need to execute a frontal assault, but trying to engage armed hostiles while we're stuck inside hazmat suits will be suicide ... and fighting without them will be even worse. So let's hear your best Plan B."

Cohen looked back at the screen and shook his head. "There's only one ... and it's not a good one."

Bennings nodded. "We've got to go out, but not in force."

"We need a small team."

"The smallest. Maybe one man – perhaps one with nothing to lose." Bennings sighed. "Goddamn, I hate this part." He looked back at the missile launcher. It had swung around toward them. "They'll be talking to us soon – a list of demands. Whatever they want, just keep 'em talking, and buy us some time."

* * * * *

Bennings sat on the edge of Reed's bed. The soldier looked remarkably well, given the trauma he had suffered to his chest. Reed shrugged.

"I feel fine, sir. I'm ready for duty."

Bennings patted his forearm. "You've got a bullet fragment embedded in your ventricle wall." He shook his head, but held the young man's gaze. "It's not good, son. You feel fine because I ordered them to give you enough steroids, adrenalin, and chemical stimulants to take on the entire Russian track team."

"Go Juice." Reed lifted his hands and flexed his fists. He dropped them and looked at his superior officer. "It's not over, is it, sir?"

Bennings stood and straightened his jacket. "No, son, the nightmare keeps coming – right to our front door. You've done a lot for us … more than most. But I need to ask you something – something real hard. Feel free to tell me to go to hell at any time."

"I'll do it."

"You don't know what I'm going to ask you."

Reed smiled without humor. "I heard the gunfire and the larger impacts. The barbarians are at the gate – at our front door, right? Can't let 'em in, can we, sir?"

Reed threw his legs over the side of the bed and winced. "What do you need me to do?"

Bennings reached out and gave Reed his arm, steadying him as he stood.

"I need you to walk into Satan's parlor and blow him back to hell."

Reed gripped the older soldier's arm. "With pleasure."

* * * * *

Dillon sat in the cabin of the mobile launcher behind a busy console, with multiple screens for radar, targeting, guidance, and arming initiators. None were active. He leaned forward to look through the windscreen and down at the three captured soldiers, handcuffed together. They were still in their hazmat suits … for now.

He sighed. "Once more into the breach." He let his fingers walk along the console, flicked on the radio, and sat back. "Hello again, my dear Captain Cohen. I love you dearly, but I do hope you have finished boring me. My request is simple – so simple I'm sure even someone like you can appreciate its clarity. Send out all army personnel holding their weapons over their heads. Those who choose to approach, naked and ready to embrace our flock, will be immediately accepted into our group. The others will be kept safe as our … guests."

He licked his raw lips. "Our warm and tender guests." He laughed softly. "Oh, and if your men decide to come out firing, we will launch a Patriot. Just one. I may decide to launch another. We have plenty, you know."

"I believe you, Mr. Dillon. Can the men and women cover up their genitals for, ah, modesty?"

Dillon shook his head. "Modesty? Did you say 'modesty'?" Dillon let his head fall back for a moment. "Your scientists have polluted our world and turned people into the living dead, and you ask us to accommodate your bashfulness?" He felt his anger rising. "Your entire revolting framework of skin and hair disgusts me. Maybe I should help you overcome your shyness. A demonstration of our power."

Cohen's hurried voice filled the cabin again. "No, no, please, Mr. Dillon, we believe you. But you only asked for the soldiers to come out. What about all the medical, scientific, and administrative personnel we have in here?"

Dillon clenched his fist and squeezed. "You mean those who created this, started this, and now work to develop something even worse? Oh, I have plans for them, my dear man." He closed his eyes and smiled. "They stay right where they are, and await my arrival."

"Okay, Mr. Dillon. That's a lot to action, and may take some time to organize. How about ..."

"*Silence!*" Dillon sat forward. "You want time? How about I give you one hour. Then, in one hour and ten seconds, I'll fire a missile. Maybe two or three, to show you how patient I am. After that I'll have my people walk in and scoop what's left of you all into buckets. How does that sound?"

"I need more time. There are hundreds of men and women. I need ..."

"One hour, and then boom. Your choice." Dillon leaned forward and waved down at the three handcuffed soldiers.

"Got to go now, Captain. I've got some job applicants to interview. Toodle-oo." He flicked off the microphone.

* * * * *

The three men, cuffed wrist to wrist, were led to Dillon. He held up his hands in elaborate disappointment. "Please, uncuff our guests. They must be so uncomfortable. And let's all stand near the fire to keep warm." He looked each man over as he walked along the line. Two were youngish; the third was older, perhaps in his forties. Dillon stopped and lifted the chin of one, peering into the faceplate. "Hmm, not even a whisker yet. Nice." He continued to the older man. He was the only one to meet Dillon's eyes – challenging, full of fight. *Good*, Dillon thought.

Papers were handed to Dillon and he flipped through them, nodding and *hmming* as he paced. He pointed a finger at each man, as though ticking them off a list.

"Excellent, all here." He went back to the youthful soldier and stood before him. The young man stared at the ground. Dillon reached up and began to unwind the bandages from his head, slowly gathering the stained material into a sodden bundle as his face was exposed.

"Look at me."

The young soldier slowly looked up, and sucked in his breath. Dillon was little more than a glistening skull, all exposed muscle and tendon. His eyes were lidless, giving his eyeballs a hellish, popping stare that was now fixed on the young man. Dillon leaned in close.

"Do you think I'm pretty?"

The young man's head went down again. Dillon reached out and lifted his chin.

"I think you already know what I want."

"Tell them nothing." The older soldier strained against the bandaged men holding him.

Dillon crossed to him, glancing briefly down at the papers in his hand. "We already know nearly everything."

He pointed at the older man's chest. "Captain Alfred Rogers. Nice to make your acquaintance." Dillon grinned like a red skull. He pointed at the next young man in line. "First Lieutenant Aaron Goldberg, targeting and logistics. Very pleased to meet you." Then to the last man. "And Second Lieutenant Ben Lin, administration and security." Dillon gave him his best horror-show grin. "Or should I say, administration and *launch codes*. Happy days. You and young Goldberg are very important to me." He turned to Rogers. "But you ... not so much. For now, I'll simply refer to you as 'motivation'."

Dillon's grin fell away. "I want the launch codes to the missiles, and I want the laser targeting unlocked and assigned to my authority. You will do that for me."

"Go to hell." Rogers lunged again, pulling away from the men holding him and then falling at Dillon's feet. Dillon put his boot on the back of Rogers' head.

"My dear Captain, you stopped being in charge the moment you and your men fell into my possession." He lifted his boot and motioned for Rogers to be lifted. Dillon looked into the Captain's faceplate as he rewound the bandages over his face. "Go to hell? You first."

Dillon motioned to the fire, and Captain Rogers was ripped out of his suit. His wrists and ankles were bound with rope. Struggling, he was pulled down flat, and then lifted – onto the flames. His hair burnt away in a flash of sparks, and within a few moments, greasy smoke carried the smell of cooking meat.

"Mmm, anyone else feeling hungry?"

Rogers thrashed and writhed in maddening pain. After another few moments, Dillon motioned for him to be lifted free. The older soldier was held upright, his body in an unconscious slump.

Dillon turned to Goldberg and Lin. "It is not me that tortures or binds you, it is your fears and your pain." He pulled a lighter from his pocket and held the flame under his chin. The skin smoked, crackled, and hissed, but still Dillon didn't flinch. At last he pulled it away. "We are free from pain. We are the enlightened. But you, and even you ..." he motioned to Rogers. "You will all endure untold horrors until you give me what I want."

He waited. "Ready to help?"

The soldiers kept their heads down. Goldberg sobbed quietly.

"Not yet?" Dillon shrugged and then made a twirling motion with one hand. Rogers was spun around to face the fire. Goldberg looked up and cried out at the sight of his captain's back.

"Are you sure you don't want to help? Captain Rogers won't thank you, you know." Dillon spoke to the bandaged figures holding the ropes. "Wake him up." A bucket of water was thrown in Rogers' face. Rogers shook his head, sucked in a long breath, and then screamed for what seemed like ages.

"By the way, Goldberg, you're next."

Rogers was lifted and angled over the flames. Once again he screamed and thrashed. Dillon pulled out a gun and pointed it at the back of the captain's head. "Fast death or slow burn – the money or the gun?" He grinned. "Here we go – 10, 9, 8, 7, 6 ..."

Goldberg wailed, his eyes crushed shut. "Help, please help, help us ..." No one answered, other than some laughter from the swarms of bandaged men and women witnessing their leader's interview techniques.

Dillon shook his head. "Dearest Aaron, there's just us here, no one else. We're all alone this day, dear boy. Now, where was I? Oh yes ... 5, 4, 3 ..."

"Please." Lin kept his eyes on the ground.

"... 2, 1 ..." Dillon turned back to Rogers.

"Stop."

"Pardon me? I didn't catch that." Dillon lowered the gun.

Lin's voice was barely a whisper. "Please stop. I'll help ..."

"Don't – say – a fucking thing – soldier." Rogers' words sounded wet and tortured. Dillon turned back to him and flicked his hand. The captain was dropped facedown onto the flames. His screams seemed endless. Goldberg fainted, and Lin fell to his knees. Dillon quickly knelt before him, the sound of Rogers' hellish torment filling the air.

"End it, please end it. Don't let this happen to young Goldberg as well. I beg you." He placed his hands on Lin's shoulders. The young man nodded, his eyes squeezed closed.

Dillon hugged him. "Good boy." He stroked his head through the hazmat suit. "Good, good boy."

Dillon stood and shot Rogers in the head. His body immediately stopped moving. "Now, unlock those Patriots, enter the launch codes, and assign all targeting authority to me ... right now."

The soldiers nodded. Dillon grunted and looked at the now-still body, grilling on the flames.

"Dinner is served."

* * * * *

Carla sat slumped in the empty laboratory. The sound of explosions had ceased, but Hew was yet to return. Her gaze was directed to a few pea-sized lumps on the back of her hand. She prodded one – there was no pain, no itch or irritation at all. In fact, her skin now felt like it belonged to someone else.

She pressed it again. It was like a blister, but without fluid – just raised skin. But she knew it wasn't empty. It was a brood chamber for hundreds, if not thousands, of young parasites. Her body would produce countless more extrusions like these. They would swell until they burst. She was a walk-ing biological time bomb.

She swallowed, feeling some constriction in her throat – just nerves, she hoped, but she tried hard not to think about what was going on inside her body.

Carla Nero dropped her hands and closed her eyes. "Soon, Maddie. See you soon."

* * * * *

Reed had exited the Atlanta CDC building via one of the service tunnels, coming up a block behind the massive ash-gray edifice. He staggered; the extra weight he carried was heavy, but he still needed to walk several miles. Even though the chemicals he had been given gave him near-superhuman strength and endurance, the effect would be fleeting. He had an hour, max, and then he'd simply collapse. He would need every second.

Reed wore a bulky long-shoreman's coat that finished above knees wrapped in loose sheeting. His hands and head were likewise covered, the cloth stained with brown, red, and ocher colors. He hoped the camouflage would allow him to infiltrate the bedraggled creatures that had gathered to wit-ness the fall of the CDC stronghold.

Rounding one last corner, he saw them. The fires burning, the dancing and gyrating bodies, like a tribe of primitives per-forming a war dance prior to an attack. The Patriot Launcher stood like a colossus at their center. Its bank of four missiles were raised and aimed – and hopefully armed. If they were already primed, then an impact could set them off. That's what Patriots did – proximity detonate. Reed said a silent prayer of hope.

A large fire burned close to the launcher with what looked like a boar or some other large animal being roasted upon it.

People reached over coals to pull bits of cooked meat from its bones. He looked up to the truck's cabin. There were three figures inside – two in army fatigues, with what looked like hazmats pulled down to their waists. Two of the missing technicians, he bet. The third person inside was large and wrapped in bandages. The man's very demeanor spoke of power and dominance – Reed had found his goal. He lifted his pace.

In a few minutes he entered the throng. Even with his nose wrapped, the smell was horrendous – rotting flesh, body odor, and the coppery scent of blood mixed with excrement. It was like the final party of the damned souls of hell, just waiting for the gates to open.

Reed pushed through the crowd, his bandages making him invisible amongst the revelers, who were all similarly covered, or naked, skinless, and gleaming with leaking fluids. He approached the massive truck, stopping just before the fire. He grimaced when he saw what was cooking over the flames, then lowered his head and swallowed, a dry lump of fear in his gut. The body's limbs had been stripped of meat, and now the masses reached in to pull handfuls of charred flesh from its back.

Reed growled in his chest, his disgust and anger peaking. He hated them, all of them. These weren't people anymore. The parasite had taken more than their skin. It had taken every last scrap of their humanity.

He pushed on, covering the final few hundred feet and approaching the last barrier. A ring of large men surrounded the truck. He needed to get through them, to get inside, closer to Dillon. The men were insignificant, but the Patriot Missile launcher had enough shielding to protect Dillon from what he had planned.

Reed paused for only a second or two, a plan forming in his mind. He walked to the vehicle's front and fell to his knees. From his coat pocket he withdrew a jewel-encrusted crucifix. Major Bennings had given it to him, ripped from the CDC chapel. At the time, he thought it was simply intended as a talisman to strengthen his resolve; now he knew different.

Reed held the cross high and yelled up at the truck, his eyes on the heavens. "Father of fathers. You have once again sent your son to us. Praise be to you."

Dillon's head came around, the words obviously resonating with him. He craned forward to peer down at Reed.

"He has sent Dillon to us – the All-Father's son. I have proof that the blessing is upon us."

Dillon waved, nodding.

Reed continued, warming to his role. "Bless me. For you truly are He ... *Jesus Christ!*"

Dillon nodded some more, clapping now. He opened his arms wide. The crowd had stopped and turned. Reed stood and approached the truck's huge door, holding out the crucifix before him. The men went to stop him, but Dillon impatiently waved them aside.

"The son of God is amongst us. I know it." Reed swallowed, easier now, a calm coming over him as the huge door swung open. He climbed up. The atmosphere inside was fetid and warm. Beside Dillon, the soldiers watched with dead eyes, already resigned to their fate. Reed sat down. Dillon was a big man, and swathed in bandages, he seemed even bigger. He dominated the truck's cabin.

"You called me a name – I feel it is right. I have often wondered whether ..." Dillon momentarily closed his eyes and crossed his arms over his bandaged chest. "No, no, I don't wonder, I know. It *is* truly who I am. His son, come to save the world once again."

Reed pulled the truck door closed behind him and quietly locked it. He looked at the console, noting that the launch screens were working, but unable to tell if the codes had been entered, turning it from a dead, multi-ton structure of steel, electronics, and chemicals into four massive bombs. He looked across to the soldiers – their eyes were defeated, their spirits extinguished. He needed them.

Dillon took the crucifix from Reed and held it up before his face. "Once, I died on the cross for you." He looked at Reed, and the bandages around his mouth folding into the semblance of a smile. "I will not make that mistake again. This time, I will live to rule a world changed forever. Now, you said you had proof of who I truly am. Tell me."

Reed leaned around Dillon. "Soldiers, are the MIM-104s armed?"

Both young men swung around at the military authority in his voice. Dillon lowered the crucifix, looking from Reed to the soldiers.

"What?"

Reed raised his voice. "Soldiers, do the Patriots have proximity detonation capability?"

The younger soldier's head came up, his back erect. "Sir, yes sir, we have full detonation capabilities. What are your orders?"

Dillon lowered the cross. "Who are you?" He grabbed at Reed, pulling him forward. Reed's coat tore open and Dillon sucked in a breath. His popping eyes seemed about to leave his skull. Reed's entire torso was strung with M67 grenades. The dull green spherical balls each contained six-and-a-half ounces of composition-B explosive.

Reed now knew that the missiles were armed to detonate if they suffered an impact. The grenades would deliver that impact. Dillon, along with every one of his foul creatures, would be obliterated.

Reed grinned at him. "What would Jesus do?" He pulled on a single wire looping across all the firing mechanisms. It slid free. They had three seconds.

Dillon leapt for the opposite door, but the soldiers blocked his exit, their faces alive and split with grins of triumph.

"Time to go," the younger one said.

Dillon turned back to Reed, his fist flying. Reed grabbed him, held on, and pulled Dillon's eye-popping face close to his own.

"Back to hell, asshole."

* * * * *

The explosion was so powerful it blew in the windows of buildings for several miles. Anything within half a mile was left in ruins. Where Dillon and his corrupt army had gathered, there was nothing left but a huge, smoking crater.

Major Bennings lowered his binoculars. "What we sacrifice today, we earn back tomorrow. God bless you, son."

He turned to Cohen, who stuck out his hand. Bennings gripped it, but shook his head. "We were lucky."

Cohen nodded. "I'll send out a stand-down order, and take some teams out for mop-up."

Bennings brushed the plaster dust off his jacket. "And now, it's all up to the boffins."

CHAPTER 27

Matt sipped his coffee and held Megan's hand. He squeezed it. "You okay?"

She was staring off into the distance, her coffee untouched. She smiled and squeezed back. "Yeah, sure; just thinking."

"Penny for them?"

She looked dazed. "It's like I'm trying to wake up from a nightmare. I went to sleep one day, and when I woke, everyone was dead or dying horribly. Brenner, Steinberg, John, Joop, Jian ... and we have no idea whether Kurt made it." She looked at him. "Do you think he made it home?"

Matt smiled. "I'm sure he did. The one thing I know about that guy is that he's a survivor."

She nodded, not looking convinced.

He let go of her hand. "I bet he's looking at his gold right now – big as hell, and full of life."

* * * * *

The small golden idol sat on the edge of the table, its squat form and leering face seeming to cast judgment over the pile of humanity that lay burst open, like an overripe fruit, on the ground before it.

Human life had long since left the flesh, but the bulb-like protrusions continued to grow and pop, releasing millions and millions of larval spore into the air.

Kurt was dead, but full of life.

* * * * *

"Amazing." Hew scrolled through pages of scientific data. "It acts like a super-inhibiter – the polygodial read is off the chart."

Carla watched as he scrolled to another page, read briefly, and then moved sideways to peer down into a microscope. "I love it – it not only inhibits feeding and growth, but even reproduction. It's no wonder it kept the little bastards under control."

Hew lifted his head from the microscope and grinned. "Our botanists have performed a regression analysis on the DNA and determined that it is, in effect, an ancient form of chrysanthemum – they say they always suspected that the common form started its life as a vine."

He looked back into the small scope again. "Makes sense – chrysanthemums give us most of the truly effective insect control compounds we have today." He scrolled some more. Carla sat beside him, looking at the long chemical compound strings on her screen. She straightened, frowning, confused by the strange chemical composition.

"Nicotine, permethrin, cypermethrin, and deltamethrin ... and a chemical that looks like it could be transfluthrin, but the molecular formula is hybridized – $C15\text{-}H12\text{-}Cl2\text{-}F4\text{-}O2\text{-}'X2'$. The X2 is something unknown – the computer hasn't ever seen it before." She looked perplexed.

Dr. Francis Hewson talked without turning. "It's probably another of the axonic poison class – causes paralysis in the mite by keeping the sodium channels open in the neuronal membranes, effectively creating microscopic perforations in its armor plating. Sodium ions flood in, trigger an action potential, and then our little monster's nerves cannot de-excite; they effectively become paralyzed."

"Hew, is it safe to use?" Carla asked quietly.

"Safe?" He bobbed his head. "Probably. These compounds usually have an extremely low toxicity to mammalian life. Should be okay."

"But long term? We're talking about introducing an unknown chemical into the environment, possibly on an unprecedented scale. I'd like to see some alpha testing done."

Hew folded his arms and looked at a digital clock on the wall – it was five in the afternoon. "Carla, time is against us; it's two minutes to midnight for the world. Indecision is what will kill us all now – they're your words. We'll do testing, but will proceed on the basis that it's going to work." He shrugged, looking resigned. "Do we have a choice?"

Carla stepped closer to him. "Look at me."

He stared hard into her face, struggling to maintain eye contact. She knew her skin was grossly bubbled, and she needed strong steroid shots to maintain energy and keep her airways clear as her body was being converted to a mobile egg case.

"Don't you think I want this to work more than anyone?"

"We'll do tests, I promise," he said slowly. "But I can only meet you halfway – what I can't promise is to do full-scale or long-term testing. I'm sorry."

She searched his face, and then nodded. She knew that at this stage even a fifty percent success rate would be preferable to a hundred percent failure. "Okay." She turned back to her screen. "I think we can combine it with PB, piperonyl butoxide, a known inhibitor of key microsomal oxidase enzymes. PB will prevent the mite's enzymes from flushing the pyrethroid from its body, making the toxin even more lethal."

She made a fist. "These mites are tough, so we need a chemical sledgehammer."

Hew nodded. "We can use the high-volume production labs, and send the formulae out to every facility still operational in the country." He turned away, his eyes focussed inward.

"But ... no one will come out to get it, and we certainly don't have the resources to go door to door. We need to hit the *sarcoptes scabiei primus* hard, and all at once. The country will need to bathe in it, shower with it, be flooded by it." He tapped the heavy polymer suit over his chin. "And that's just the people. What about the environment? Cattle, horses, dogs, cats, birds – the entire mammalian population ... or, what's left of it."

Hew paced. "And we'll need to get bloomers and potential bloomers to ingest the solution as well." He looked pained. "A job of colossal magnitude, and little time ... time you don't have, I'm afraid."

He walked toward her and took hold of her shoulders. "I promise to implement as much testing as time will allow, but we'll need to leap to biological trials ... today ... now."

She could hear what he was asking. "Testing, and doing, all at once, huh?"

He stayed silent. She smiled. "Voluntary clinical trial subjects – guinea pigs?"

He nodded, returning the smile. "After all, from what you've told me, you've already bathed in it several times in the crater basin."

"Hey, what have I got to lose?" She shrugged. "Ready when you are."

"Good ... the question is, how the hell do we get the entire population to shower with it?"

"Easy – you just said it. Shower them with it." She pointed to the roof. "Powderize it and then cloud-seed the entire continent. It'll come down in the rain and cover everything, even end up in the drinking water."

His eyebrows shot up. "See, this is why we needed you here – that might just work … no, it has to work – globally."

"Wait a minute, globally? Shouldn't we wait and make sure our own environment is unharmed?"

Hew shook his head. "Can't chance cleansing one environment only to have another one reinfest it. Besides, if it works, great, we're dancing in the street. If it doesn't, so what? All we'll give them is red snow come winter." He leaned forward. "Carla, it *has* to work … it *will* work."

"It will work, yes …" Carla sat down. "And besides, it's all we've got."

Hew walked over, bent down, and hugged her, then stepped back to pick up the phone. "Bring me down a hundred ccs of the Nero-1 solution, then distribute the formulae on a priority to the labs." He paused for a second. "To all of them. I'll be up to walk the department heads through the logistics of dispersal shortly – we're gonna seed it." He hung up.

"Nero-1 solution?" She raised her eyebrows.

He grinned. "What else were we going to call it? It should be named after the intrepid explorer who discovered it." He sat down next to her. "Your drink is on its way – first round is on me."

They sat in silence for several seconds before he clicked his fingers and spun in his seat toward her.

"Hey, I meant to tell you: the genetic analysis boys did some work on the mite genome, and also on the remnants of DNA they could pull from the charred bones of the archaeopteryx specimen. You know, it was weird; the DNA wasn't what they expected." Hew pulled a face. "Sure, their overall morphology was what was assumed – the creatures were extremely primitive; real primordial remnants from a biological perspective. But here's the thing, the DNA … well, it wasn't a match to the computer extrapolation of what the earliest saurian bird, or *sarcoptes scabiei primus* design, should have looked like. There were traces of modern nucleic acids in the DNA chains, for both creatures." He snorted. "Must have been contaminated."

Carla frowned, and then repeated the word, slowly. "Contamination ... in here ... impossible."

Hew shrugged. "Who knows? Doesn't matter now. It was looking like an analytical dead-end anyway."

"Hew, this is the CDC – one of the most sterile facilities in the world. Just how does something get contaminated in here? What was their theory?" Carla sat forward.

"They had one, but it was ridiculous." He turned to her. "That the bird and the parasite weren't original old forms, they were atavisms – random reappearances of evolutionary throwbacks."

Carla stood and paced. "Atavisms – both of them? A billion to one chance. That bothers me." She walked with her eyes downcast as her mind worked. "Traits reappearing; traits that had disappeared generations before – that had effectively evolved out of the genetic code." She continued to pace as Hew watched her.

"What are you thinking?" he asked.

"I'm thinking that atavism is unbelievably rare. To say it looked to manifest in two specimens that were, species-wise, about as far apart as you can get – that's no coincidence. I've seen human babies born with a vestigial tail, and even heard of whales being sighted with tiny hind legs. It can occur when primitive genes for previously existing phenotypical features are preserved in DNA code. These become expressed through a mutation that either knocks out the overriding genes for the new traits or makes the old traits so dominant that they override the new ones."

She coughed, and waved him away as he approached. "Hew, it's so rare in one species ... for it to spontaneously occur in two is impossible. Something has to trigger it, some damned thing ..."

She spun, staring at him. *Mutagen*, she thought. She felt a shock running through her. "Joop said it was impossible for the creatures to exist. Not just as fantastic individual animals, but all of them together. He didn't think they were from a single point in our history, but vastly different points, stretching for tens of millions of years. One type of animal from the Mesozoic, another from the Jurassic, the Triassic, and so on." She sat down.

She started to breathe faster, each lungful harder to suck in and push out. "I'm scared. What if the vine ..." She went to get to her feet, and then started to gag. Her mouth opened and closed, but nothing came. Her hands flew to her throat, scratching at it.

"Carla!" Hew caught her as she fell. "Oh no." Her throat had ballooned shut from the infestation.

She blinked, unable to speak, and tried to grab at his arm, to make him understand what she feared.

The door hissed open and a suited scientist came in with a beaker of the red fluid. "Get me some adrenalin, *now*!" Hew shouted. The scientist went to turn, but Hew yelled again. "Wait – give me that first."

He took the beaker and held it to her lips. "Carla, please try and swallow this, please ... just a sip."

Carla blinked at him again, knowing that she'd never get the fluid down. Her throat was now so swollen, not an atom of air could pass down it, let alone a drop of the red tincture.

She stared at the red beaker. *Atavism, mutagen, atavism!* her mind screamed, now knowing the secret of the red blooms and the primordial blood jungle. Her vision blurred to blackness.

EPILOGUE

12 MONTHS LATER

The red rains, as they came to be known, proved to be enormously successful. The seeding of clouds continued for several months, and every time it rained, it fell like blood over the land. Lakes, streams, and rivers ran like a biblical curse, and when faucets were turned on, the red would flow out.

When the scientists stopped the seeding and the rains returned to normal, people once again ventured out onto the streets. Birds were seen in trees, badgers, mice, and squirrels reappeared in the fields, and horses and cattle were allowed out of quarantine. It was as if the rain had washed away more than just the infestation.

Over the weeks and months, the country started to function again. The bodies disappeared, mountains of rubbish were removed, and armies of public officials checked everywhere, from the deepest sewer system to behind the smallest skirting board, for traces of the primordial mite. It was the same everywhere – they were still there, but not in the same numbers as before, and only as troublesome as the normal variety of scabies mite. The rains had done their job, and changed them into something more ... benign.

Ten months after the red rains, the first changes started appearing. Children had thickened brow ridges and low, vaulted craniums. Animals were born bigger or smaller than previously – slight abnormalities, nothing more.

The vines started growing soon after. They climbed walls, tree trunks, and even covered fields; everything that rose over a foot in height became a platform for their magnificent red flowered heads. Their poisonous barbs were initially responsible for thousands of deaths, triggering a second nationwide mobilization for eradication. But as fast as they were pulled up, raked under, or burned off, they regrew.

In the end, they just became something else to live with. After all, it seemed a small price to pay. The fire-engine red flowers were a constant reminder of two things – one, to stay clear, and two, that they would never have a problem with the primordial mite again.

It was what came next that the scientists said would take some getting used to.

* * * *

Billy threw the ball for Grumpy, the terrier's long hair bouncing up and down as he charged after it. The tough little animal looked like a couple of mop-heads strung together, and he growled like a little engine in pursuit of his round, bouncing prey.

"Dang." Billy had over-thrown the ball again, and it had rolled under the far hedge, where he wasn't allowed to play.

"Wait – heel, boy." Grumpy halted at the green barrier, sniffing nervously, then charged in, small teeth bared.

"Aw, Grumpy, don't go in there; you'll get into trouble." Billy ran to the edge of the large garden, pumping his six-year-old legs. He stopped at the border, as all kids were trained to do now. He remembered the rhyme they were taught in school: *wear shoes in the yard, coz the thorns stick hard, and beware of the red, or you'll end up dead.*

He grimaced with indecision. Dad and Mom had told him plenty of times not to take any chances … and he had sure told Grumpy as well. It's just that the dang dog didn't ever listen.

"This is your fault," Billy said to the hedge. He got down on his knees. There was a whimper, and something rustled in the deep shadows beneath the thick hedge. "Grumpy? Grumpy, you come out right now."

There was the whimper again. Billy's tone softened. "Are you stuck, boy?" He looked over his shoulder at the house; no one was watching. He bet he could pull the dog out before anyone even noticed.

He reached in.

* * * * *

The eight eyes stared dispassionately from atop the fifty-pound body as it slowly lifted itself from the silken-coated bag it had woven over the small, long-haired animal.

The tall, hairless creature that now leaned in toward it was much larger, but the spider had plenty of venom left. This one would feed it for days. The glossy black, muscular body reared up, opening out like an enormous skeletal hand, finger-sized fangs extended, waiting.

Like the scientists said, things would just take some getting used to.

Gorgon

Alex Hunter has been found – sullen, alone, leaving a path of destruction as he wanders across America. Only the foolish get in the way of the drifter wandering the streets late at night.

Across the world, something has been released by a treasure hunter in a hidden chamber of the Basilica Cisterns in Istanbul. Something hidden there by Emperor Constantine himself, and deemed by him too horrifying and dangerous to ever be set free. It now stalks the land, leaving its victims turned to stone, and is headed on a collision course with a NATO base. The Americans can't let it get there, but can't be seen to intervene. There is only one option – send in the HAWCs.

But Alex and the HAWCs are not the only ones seeking out the strange being – Uli Borshov, Borshov the Beast, who has a score to settle with the Arcadian moves to intercept him, setting up a deadly collision of epic proportions where only one can survive. Join Alex Hunter as he learns to trust his former commander and colleagues again as the HAWCs challenge an age-old being straight from myth and legend.

Gorgon is coming soon in 2014.